PENGUIN CLASSICS

A DEATH IN THE FAMILY

JAMES AGEE was born in Tennessee in 1909 and graduated from Harvard University. His renowned study of Alabama sharecroppers during the Depression, *Let Us Now Praise Famous Men*, appeared in 1941. Agee was known for his movie reviews and screenplays, and published a volume of poetry and a novella, as well. He died in 1955, two years before his major work of fiction, *A Death in the Family*, was published and won the Pulitzer Prize.

BLAKE MORRISON was born in Yorkshire. He has written poetry, memoir and fiction, and his books include *The Ballad of the Yorkshire Ripper*, *And When Did You Last See Your Father?* and *Things My Mother Never Told Me*. He writes for the Guardian and is currently Professor of Creative Writing at Goldsmiths' College, London.

JAMES AGEE

A Death in the Family

with an Introduction by BLAKE MORRISON

PENGUIN BOOKS

PENGUIN BOOKS

Published by the Penguin Group
Penguin Books Ltd, 80 Strand, London wc2r orl, England
Penguin Group (USA) Inc., 375 Hudson Street, New York, New York 10014, USA
Penguin Group (Canada), 90 Eglinton Avenue East, Suite 700, Toronto, Ontario, Canada m4p 2y3
(a division of Pearson Penguin Canada Inc.)
Penguin Ireland, 25 St Stephen's Green, Dublin 2, Ireland, (a division of Penguin Books Ltd)
Penguin Group (Australia), 250 Camberwell Road, Camberwell,
Victoria 3124, Australia (a division of Pearson Australia Group Pty Ltd)
Penguin Books India Pvt Ltd, 11 Community Centre,
Panchsheel Park, New Delhi – 110 017, India
Penguin Group (NZ), cnr Airborne and Rosedale Roads, Albany,
Auckland 1310, New Zealand (a division of Pearson New Zealand Ltd)
Penguin Books (South Africa) (Pty) Ltd, 24 Sturdee Avenue,
Rosebank, Johannesburg 2196, South Africa

Penguin Books Ltd, Registered Offices: 80 Strand, London wc2r orl, England

www.penguin.com

This edition first published in the United States of America by Grosset & Dunlap, Inc., 1967
Published by G. P. Putnam's Sons 1998
This edition first published in Great Britain with an Introduction in Penguin Classics 2006

1

Copyright 1938 © 1956 by The James Agee Trust, Chapter 8 and Part of Chapter 13
Copyright © 1957 by *The New Yorker Magazine*, Inc.
Copyright © 1957 by The James Agee Trust, copyright renewed 1985 by Mia Agee
Introduction copyright © Blake Morrison, 2006
All rights reserved

The moral right of the author has been asserted

Portions of this novel first appeared in *The Partisan Review*, *The Cambridge Review*,
The New Yorker Magazine and *Harper's Bazaar*

Printed in England by Clays Ltd, St Ives plc

isbn-13: 978-0-141-18796-9
isbn-10: 0-141-18796-4

Introduction

OBLIVION IS THE REWARD of writers who work in different genres. Follow a chosen path doggedly through a lifetime and, with luck, you will develop the skills to produce at least one lasting work. Veer about in different directions and the risk is you'll lose your way or be forgotten even if you find it—Jack of all trades, master of none. James Agee, who wrote poetry, fiction, documentary non-fiction, screenplays and film criticism, was a much respected figure in his lifetime. In the US, among the cognoscenti, he still is. But in Britain he remains little-known and scarcely read. Even those who have heard of *Let Us Now Praise Famous Men* (his account of three tenant families in the Deep South during the Depression) or seen films for which he wrote the screenplay (including *The African Queen* and *The Night of the Hunter*) may not realize that he also wrote a classic novel called *A Death in the Family*. Certainly no one recommended it to me when, after the death of my father, I was immersing myself in the literature of bereavement. And even if they had, I wouldn't have found it easy to get hold of: in the UK it has been out of print for nearly two decades.

A possible excuse for this neglect is that Agee died before completing the book, which makes the status of the "final" text—

the one reproduced here—open to question. But he had been working on it for many years, and even the passages in italics, which don't fit the same time-frame as the other twenty chapters, were long pondered and highly polished. His original plan was to write a novel that encompassed several years and three different generations. In the event, he found himself concentrating on the events of just three days. By inclination he was a Modernist, an admirer of Proust, Joyce, Kafka, T. S. Eliot and other writers of disruptive, large-scale texts. But in *A Death in the Family* he reined himself in so as to describe the fallout out from a single, commonplace tragedy—the death in a road accident of thirty-six-year-old Jay Follet, son, husband, brother and father.

From the start the novel reads as though it must be autobiographical, and the bare facts of Agee's life confirm that impression. The setting is Knoxville, Tennessee, where he grew up. The boy in the novel is called Rufus, Agee's middle name and the name he was known by until his teens. His own father, Jay, died exactly as the father in the novel does, when Agee was six. All this lends the book authenticity, not least psychological authenticity. "I find that I value my childhood and my father as they were ... far beyond any transmutation of these matters I have made, or might ever make, into poetry or fiction," Agee noted. But he was reluctant to write mere memoir, and felt it important to distance himself from the material: "I must decide between a completely detached and a deeply subjective treatment. I doubt if in complete detachment there is a story there. Rather, do the subjective, as detachedly as possible." Doing the subjective detachedly meant him writing about his emotions as though they were happening to someone else: a character in a novel, not just the author's inner child.

The accident itself isn't directly observed. It happens off-stage, as in a Greek tragedy, and it's left to an eye-witness to reconstruct the fatal sequence of events—the car being driven too fast, the working loose of a cotter pin, the car leaving the road and

Jay meeting his death in bizarre fashion, by a single sharp blow from the steering wheel against his chin. As with all accidents, there's a haunting sense of avoidability (the crisis which prompted the car journey proves no crisis at all) and an equally strong sense of inevitability: even before his wife Mary is brought the news she suspects the worst. At times the reader becomes a rubbernecker; the details of the crash, and the appearance of Jay's body (the small cut at the point of the chin "as neat and bloodless as if it had been made by a chisel in soft wood") are oddly gripping. But any lingering suspense has gone before the halfway mark; the death is less denouement than prelude.

Rufus sits at the centre of the novel, but he doesn't monopolize it: the death impacts on three generations of the family, not just him. It's this that makes *A Death in the Family* so unusual and compelling: writers telling their own stories—their own real-life death stories—rarely strive to inhabit the minds of the other people involved. Had he written the novel at twenty, Agee might not have done so, either. But having lived with this material for over three decades, he was mature enough to make that leap. It's tempting to think that his talent for inhabiting the consciousness of others was nurtured by the assignment that produced *Let Us Now Praise Famous Men*, when he shared a home with three sharecropper families. Whatever the source of it empathy, *A Death in the Family* is the antithesis of narcissistic trauma-recall. It may be autobiographical but it's not just a memoir, least of all a boo-hoo, pity-me memoir about a ruined childhood.

Agee's capacity for standing back from the circumstances of his own life is integral to the structure of the novel, which adopts multiple narrative points of view. We follow events through the eyes not just of Rufus, but of his father Jay, his mother Mary, Uncle Ralph, Aunt Hannah, Grandpa Joel, Uncle Andrew, and even Catherine, who is still a toddler. There's a bold, democratic spirit to this, as everyone has his or her moment centre-stage and the pain is portioned out. But the shifting perspective never feels forced—we're made to see how many people the tragedy affects, and in what different ways.

Little Catherine's understanding, for instance, is necessarily limited; when first told that her father has "had an accident", she thinks it means the sort of accident she sometimes has, in her knickers. Though she can *physically* register that something bad has happened ("breakfast wasn't like breakfast ... Everything was queer, it was so still and it seemed dark"), and even make sense of the idea that her father has been "put to sleep" by God ("Like the kitties, she thought; she saw a dim, gigantic old man in white take her tiny father by the skin of the neck and put him in a huge slop jar full of water"), she cannot get her head round the idea that he is never coming home again. Mary, her mother, can't quite believe it either, of course, but intellectually she knows it to be true, and can comfort herself "at least I am enduring it. I am aware of what has happened, I am meeting it face to face ... I am carrying a heavier weight than I could have dreamed it possible for a human being to carry, yet I am living through it". Mary's father Joel, who always had his doubts about Jay, is merely surprised by how unsurprised he feels, "as if he had known that this or something like it was bound to happen, sooner or later".

Rufus's reaction to his father's death is different again. He feels "a strange, cold excitement" rising in him, a sense of pride and privilege at being an orphan, or half an orphan, because he knows "that on this day everybody would treat him well, and even look up to him, for something had happened to him today which had not happened to any other boy in school". Making the most of this, he goes into the street in order to tell his exciting news to the older boys who pass his house every morning; normally they tease him, but today, he feels sure, they are "bound to think well of him". The plan backfires; some boys have heard the news already; others are contemptuous, as if "they did not think very well of his father for being killed so easily"; Rufus retreats indoors again, ashamed. The passage is a crucial rite of passage—it's too soon for Rufus to come to terms with his father's death, but he has already embarked on a journey towards maturity and self-knowledge.

A Death in the Family is slow-moving and demands patience from us—a willingness to spend time with people in their sorrow. There's a moment near the end when Uncle Andrew sees the three central characters posed like the Holy Family as if for a painting—"the deceived mother, the false son, the fatally wounded daughter"—and Agee's novel has this kind of stillness: a family portrait not a family saga. The longest scene, spread across several chapters and taking up nearly one-quarter of the novel, is given over to Andrew's breaking of the news to the family, after he has returned from identifying Jay's body. For page after page we watch their faces in agonising close-up and hear their efforts to make sense of the tragedy, but the tone is anything but grim. Just as the family burst out into hysterical laughter in the midst of their grief, so the reader is allowed to see the comic banalities of the situation—the inextricability of the tragic and silly. Rufus's grandmother has to follow the conversation through an ear-trumpet which resembles a pelican's mouth ("Toss in a fish"). Mary, forced to leave the room for a pee, feels "affronted and humbled that one should have to obey such a call at such a time". Andrew bursts out with exasperation after phoning Jay's hapless brother Ralph: "Talking to that fool is like trying to put socks on an octopus". Even the death car creates an occasion for humour, when Jay, leaving the house, attempts to start it, and Agee, with Joycean aplomb, spends two pages attempting to mimic the sound of a misfiring engine:

Uhgh—hy uh yu hy why uhy uh: wheek-uh-wheek-uh:
Ughh—hy why yuh: wheek:
(now the nearly noiseless, desperate adjustments of spark and throttle and choke) . . .

Ughgh—Ughgh—yuhyuh*Ugh* wheek yuh yuh *Ughgh* yuh
wheek wheek yuhyuh: wheek wheek: uh:
(like a hideous, horribly constipated great brute of a beast:
like a lunatic sobbing: like a mouse being tortured)

Agee began life as a poet and his poetry is given freest expression
in the prologue, when he lyrically recaptures the sights and
sounds of a summer evening in Knoxville in 1915—fathers
watering lawns, mothers shushing their children, cars and horses
going by, whole families lying together on quilts, as darkness
falls and the stars come out "wide and alive". It's a beautifully
captured Arcadian moment, "a smile of great sweetness"; the
sprinklers and hoses, especially, create a sense of fruition. (Agee
spends a page trying to capture *their* exact sound, too—and perhaps it was that, Agee's ear for the music of suburban America,
that inspired the composer Samuel Barber to create what is
widely regarded as his greatest work, "Knoxville: Summer of
1915", a 17-minute piece for soprano and orchestra.) Afterwards,
once "the flat of the hand of Death" strikes, the poetry becomes
more sparing, fulfilling Agee's wish "to go plain to the bone and
stay there". But the poetry never entirely disappears. Its rhythms
pulse through the vast, looping sentences that are Agee's trade-
mark. And there are numerous striking metaphors or minutely
observed, heartbreaking details: Mary's face full of lines Rufus
has never seen before, "as small as the lines in her mended best
teacup"; his great-great-grandmother's face, "restoring" itself
from a kiss "like grass that has been lightly stepped on"; Aunt
Hannah's "dry-looking mouth trembli[ing] like the ash of burned
paper in a draft". Agee is attentive to sounds, too: the flickering of
a clock in the small hours, "alien and mysterious as a rat in a
wall". He even does tastes: perhaps the most powerful moment in
the whole book comes when Rufus stands by his father's empty
chair, and puts his finger into the ashtray strapped to the arm, and
then licks it—"his tongue tasted of darkness". Sometimes the

metaphors aspire to the epigrammatic, as when Rufus notes the vigour with which Aunt Hannah shops—"none of the ceremony that held his grandmother's shopping habits in a kind of stiff embroidery; none of the hurrying, sheepish refusal to be judicious in which men shopped". Writing of such quality is itself a kind of stay against death—a pleasure to offset the dark solemnity of the theme.

If the words and rhythms sometimes echo the King James Bible, that's appropriate, since religion is integral to the theme. For the churchy Hannah and Mary, a belief in God is the only way to cope with the tragedy of Jay's death; for their atheistic father, Joel, the tragedy is proof of God's non-existence. Agee plays an even hand as the two sides argue it out: an instinctively spiritual man whose closest lifelong friend was a priest, he lets the women have the better of the debate, while also conveying the bleakness of orthodox belief. The greatest venom in the book is reserved for the priest, Father Jackson, whom the two children suspect of wanting to hurt their mother. As we wait with them outside the room where Father Jackson is talking to her, we're unable to hear what's being said, but catch the rumble of a "voice that loved its own sound". Only later, through Uncle Andrew, do we learn what the conversation was about: the priest's refusal to allow their father a full funeral service, on the grounds that Jay had never been baptised. Andrew, incensed, denounces the priest as "a mealy-mouthed sound of a bitch". But he also describes what he saw during the burial: a butterfly settling on Jay's coffin—a miracle, if ever there was one. For Rufus, at six, the contradictions are confusing. For the reader it makes an oddly satisfying ending—neither too bitter nor too easily affirmative.

Like his father Agee died young, at forty-five. He wasn't around when *A Death in the Family* was published two years later and won a Pulitzer Prize (as surely no unfinished posthumous novel had done before or will ever do again). Nor was he there to see it turned into a Broadway play called *All the Way Home* and then a disappointing film of the same title. Great novels often make bad movies, especially when, as with Agee's, the power lies in the writing and the representation of inner consciousness. Luckily the book itself lives on, untainted. The novels of Mailer, Roth and Bellow may be more celebrated, but in its quiet way *A Death in the Family* packs as big a punch. American writers as diverse as Andre Dubus and Jayne Anne Phillips have acclaimed it as a masterpiece. Now a new generation of readers outside the US can get to know it, too—and discover what an exceptionally stylish and moving writer James Agee could be.

Blake Morrison

⊰ A NOTE ON THIS BOOK ⊱

JAMES AGEE DIED SUDDENLY May 16, 1955. This novel, upon which he had been working for many years, is presented here exactly as he wrote it. There has been no re-writing, and nothing has been eliminated except for a few cases of first-draft material which he later re-worked at greater length, and one section of seven-odd pages which the editors were unable satisfactorily to fit into the body of the novel.

The ending of *A Death in the Family* had been reached sometime before Agee's death, and the only editorial problem involved the placing of several scenes outside the time span of the basic story. It was finally decided to print these in italics and to put them after Parts I and II. It seemed presumptuous to try to guess where he might have inserted them. This arrangement also obviated the necessity of the editors having to compose any transitional material. The short section *Knoxville Summer of 1915,* which serves as a sort of prologue, has been added. It was not a part of the manuscript which

Agee left, but the editors would certainly have urged him to include it in the final draft.

How much polishing or re-writing he might have done is impossible to guess, for he was a tireless and painstaking writer. However, in the opinion of the editors and of the publisher, *A Death in the Family* is a near-perfect work of art. The title, like all the rest of the book, is James Agee's own.

❋ CONTENTS ❋

Knoxville: Summer, 1915

We are talking now of summer evenings in Knoxville, Tennessee, in the time that I lived there so successfully disguised to myself as a child. It was a little bit mixed sort of block, fairly solidly lower middle class, with one or two juts apiece on either side of that. The houses corresponded: middle-sized gracefully fretted wood houses built in the late nineties and early nineteen hundreds, with small front and side and more spacious back yards, and trees in the yards, and porches. These were softwooded trees, populars, tulip trees, cottonwoods. There were fences around one or two of the houses, but mainly the yards ran into each other with only now and then a low hedge that wasn't doing very well. There were few good friends among the grown people, and they were not poor enough for the other sort of intimate acquaintance, but everyone nodded and spoke, and even might talk short times, trivially, and at the two extremes of the general or the particular, and ordinarily nextdoor neighbors talked quite a bit when they happened to run into each other, and never paid calls. The men were mostly small businessmen, one or two very modestly executives, one or two worked with their hands, most of them clerical, and most of them between thirty and forty-five.

But it is of these evenings, I speak.

Supper was at six and was over by half past. There was still daylight, shining softly and with a tarnish, like the lining of a shell; and the carbon lamps lifted at the corners were on in the light, and the locusts were started, and the fire flies were out, and a few frogs were flopping in the dewy grass, by the time the fathers and the children came out. The children ran out first hell bent and yelling those names by which they were known; then the fathers sank out leisurely in crossed suspenders, their collars removed and their necks looking tall and shy. The mothers stayed back in the kitchen washing and drying, putting things away, recrossing their traceless footsteps like the lifetime journeys of bees, measuring out the dry cocoa for breakfast. When they came out they had taken off their aprons and their skirts were dampened and they sat in rockers on their porches quietly.

It is not of the games children play in the evening that I want to speak now, it is of a contemporaneous atmosphere that has little to do with them: that of the fathers of families, each in his space of lawn, his shirt fishlike pale in the unnatural light and his face nearly anonymous, hosing their lawns. The hoses were attached at spiggots that stood out of the brick foundations of the houses. The nozzles were variously set but usually so there was a long sweet stream of spray, the nozzle wet in the hand, the water trickling the right forearm and the peeled-back cuff, and the water whishing out a long loose and low-curved cone, and so gentle a sound. First an insane noise of violence in the nozzle, then the still irregular sound of adjustment, then the smoothing into steadiness and a pitch as accurately tuned to the size and style of stream as any violin. So many qualities of sound out of one hose: so many choral differences out of those several hoses that were in earshot. Out of any one hose, the almost dead silence of the release, and the short still arch of the separate big drops, silent as a held breath, and the only noise the flattering noise on leaves and the slapped grass at the fall of each big drop. That, and the intense hiss with the intense stream; that, and that same intensity not growing less but growing more quiet and delicate with the turn of the nozzle, up to the extreme tender whisper when the water was just a wide bell of film. Chiefly, though, the hoses were set much alike, in a compromise between dis-

tance and tenderness of spray (and quite surely a sense of art behind this compromise, and a quiet deep joy, too real to recognize itself), and the sounds therefore were pitched much alike; pointed by the snorting start of a new hose; decorated by some man playful with the nozzle; left empty, like God by the sparrow's fall, when any single one of them desists: and all, though near alike, of various pitch; and in this unison. These sweet pale streamings in the light lift out their pallors and their voices all together, mothers hushing their children, the hushing unnaturally prolonged, the men gentle and silent and each snail-like withdrawn into the quietude of what he singly is doing, the urination of huge children stood loosely military against an invisible wall, and gentle happy and peaceful, tasting the mean goodness of their living like the last of their suppers in their mouths; while the locusts carry on this noise of hoses on their much higher and sharper key. The noise of the locust is dry, and it seems not to be rasped or vibrated but urged from him as if through a small orifice by a breath that can never give out. Also there is never one locust but an illusion of at least a thousand. The noise of each locust is pitched in some classic locust range out of which none of them varies more than two full tones: and yet you seem to hear each locust discrete from all the rest, and there is a long, slow, pulse in their noise, like the scarcely defined arch of a long and high set bridge. They are all around in every tree, so that the noise seems to come from nowhere and everywhere at once, from the whole shell heaven, shivering in your flesh and teasing your eardrums, the boldest of all the sounds of night. And yet it is habitual to summer nights, and is of the great order of noises, like the noises of the sea and of the blood her precocious grandchild, which you realize you are hearing only when you catch yourself listening. Meantime from low in the dark, just outside the swaying horizons of the hoses, conveying always grass in the damp of dew and its strong green-black smear of smell, the regular yet spaced noises of the crickets, each a sweet cold silver noise three-noted, like the slipping each time of three matched links of a small chain.

But the men by now, one by one, have silenced their hoses and drained and coiled them. Now only two, and now only one, is left, and you see only ghostlike shirt with the sleeve garters, and sober mystery of his mild face like the lifted face of large cattle enquiring of your presence in a pitchdark pool of meadow; and now he too is gone; and it has become that time of evening when people sit on their porches, rocking gently and talking gently and watching the street and the standing up into their sphere of possession of the trees, of birds hung havens, hangars. People go by; things go by. A horse, drawing a buggy, breaking his hollow iron music on the asphalt; a loud auto; a quiet auto; people in pairs, not in a hurry, scuffling, switching their weight of aestival body, talking casually, the taste hovering over them of vanilla, strawberry, pasteboard and starched milk, the image upon them of lovers and horsemen, squared with clowns in hueless amber. A street car raising its iron moan; stopping, belling and starting; stertorous; rousing and raising again its iron increasing moan and swimming its gold windows and straw seats on past and past and past, the bleak spark crackling and cursing above it like a small malignant spirit set to dog its tracks; the iron whine rises on rising speed; still risen, faints; halts, the faint stinging bell; rises again, still fainter, fainting, lifting, lifts, faints forgone: forgotten. Now is the night one blue dew.

Now is the night one blue dew, my father has drained, he has coiled the hose.

Low on the length of lawns, a frailing of fire who breathes.

Content, silver, like peeps of light, each cricket makes his comment over and over in the drowned grass.

A cold toad thumpily flounders.

Within the edges of damp shadows of side yards are hovering children nearly sick with joy of fear, who watch the unguarding of a telephone pole.

Around white carbon corner lamps bugs of all sizes are lifted elliptic, solar systems. Big hardshells bruise themselves, assailant: he is fallen on his back, legs squiggling.

Parents on porches: rock and rock: From damp strings morning glories: hang their ancient faces.

*The dry and exalted noise of the locusts from all the air at once
enchants my eardrums.*

    *On the rough wet grass of the back yard my father and mother
have spread quilts. We all lie there, my mother, my father, my uncle,
my aunt, and I too am lying there. First we were sitting up, then one of
us lay down, and then we all lay down, on our stomachs, or on our
sides, or on our backs, and they have kept on talking. They are not
talking much, and the talk is quiet, of nothing in particular, of nothing
at all in particular, of nothing at all. The stars are wide and alive, they
seem each like a smile of great sweetness, and they seem very near. All
my people are larger bodies than mine, quiet, with voices gentle and
meaningless like the voices of sleeping birds. One is an artist, he is living at home. One is a musician, she is living at home. One is my
mother who is good to me. One is my father who is good to me. By
some chance, here they are, all on this earth; and who shall ever tell the
sorrow of being on this earth, lying, on quilts, on the grass, in a summer evening, among the sounds of night. May god bless my people, my
uncle, my aunt, my mother, my good father, oh, remember them
kindly in their time of trouble; and in the hour of their taking away.*

    *After a little I am taken in and put to bed. Sleep, soft smiling,
draws me unto her: and those receive me, who quietly treat me, as one
familiar and well-beloved in that home: but will not, oh, will not, not
now, not ever; but will not ever tell me who I am.*

❧ PART ONE ❧

Chapter 1

AT SUPPER THAT NIGHT, as many times before, his father said, "Well, spose we go to the picture show."

"Oh, Jay!" his mother said. "That horrid little man!"

"What's wrong with him?" his father asked, not because he didn't know what she would say, but so she would say it.

"He's so *nasty!*" she said, as she always did. "So *vulgar!* With his nasty little cane; hooking up skirts and things, and that nasty little walk!"

His father laughed, as he always did, and Rufus felt that it had become rather an empty joke; but as always the laughter also cheered him; he felt that the laughter enclosed him with his father.

They walked downtown in the light of mother-of-pearl, to the Majestic, and found their way to seats by the light of the screen, in the exhilarating smell of stale tobacco, rank sweat, perfume and dirty drawers, while the piano played fast music and galloping horses raised a grandiose flag of dust. And there was William S. Hart with both guns blazing and his long, horse face and his long, hard lip, and the great country rode away behind him as wide as the world. Then he made a bashful face at a girl and his horse raised its upper lip and everybody laughed, and then the screen was filled with a city and with the sidewalk of a side street of a city, a long line of palms and there was Charlie; everyone laughed the minute they saw him squattily walking with his toes out and his knees wide apart, as if he were chafed; Rufus' father laughed, and Rufus laughed too. This time Charlie stole a whole bag of eggs and when a cop came along he hid them in the seat of his pants. Then he caught sight of a pretty woman and he began to squat and twirl his cane and make silly faces. She tossed her head and walked away with her chin up high and her dark mouth as small as she could make it and he followed her very busily, doing all sorts of things with his cane that made everybody laugh, but she paid no attention. Finally she stopped at a corner to wait for a streetcar, turning her back to him, and pretending he wasn't even there, and after trying to get her attention for a while, and not succeeding, he looked out at the audience, shrugged his shoulders, and acted as if *she* wasn't there. But after tapping his foot for a little, pretending he didn't care, he became interested again, and with a charming smile, tipped his derby; but she only stiffened, and tossed her head again, and everybody laughed. Then he walked back and forth behind her, looking at her and squatting a little while he walked very quietly, and everybody laughed again; then he flicked hold of the straight end of his cane and, with the crooked end, hooked up her skirt to the knee, in exactly the way that disgusted Mama, looking very eagerly at her legs, and everybody laughed loudly; but she pretended she had not noticed. Then he twirled his cane and suddenly squatted, bending the cane and hitching up his pants, and again hooked up her skirt so that you could see the panties she wore, ruffled almost like the edges of curtains, and everybody whooped with laughter, and she suddenly turned in rage and gave him a shove in the chest, and he sat down straight-legged, hard enough to hurt, and everybody whooped again; and she walked haughtily away up the street, forgetting about the streetcar, "mad as a hornet!" as his father exclaimed in delight; and there was Charlie, flat on his bottom on the sidewalk, and the way he looked, kind of sickly and disgusted, you could see that he suddenly remembered those eggs, and suddenly you remembered them too. The way his face looked, with the lip wrinkled off the teeth and the sickly little smile, it made you feel just the way those broken eggs must feel against your seat, as queer and awful as that time in the white pekay suit, when it ran down out of the pants-legs and showed all over your stockings and you had to walk home that way with people looking; and Rufus' father nearly tore his head off laughing and so did everybody else, and Rufus was sorry for Charlie, having been so recently in a similar predicament, but the contagion of laughter was too much for him, and he laughed too. And then it was even funnier when Charlie very carefully got himself up from the sidewalk, with that sickly look even worse on his face, and put his cane under one arm, and began to pick up his pants, front and back, very carefully, with his little fingers crooked, as if it were too dirty to touch, picking the sticky cloth away from his skin. Then he reached behind him and took out the wet bag of broken eggs and opened it and peered in; and took out a broken egg and pulled the shell disgustedly apart, letting the elastic yolk slump from one half shell into the other, and dropped it, shuddering. Then he peered in again and fished out a whole egg, all slimy with broken yolk, and polished it off carefully on his sleeve, and looked at it, and wrapped it in his dirty handkerchief, and put it carefully into the vest pocket of his little coat. Then he whipped out his cane from under his armpit and took command of it again, and with a final look at everybody, still sickly but at the same time cheerful, shrugged his shoulders and turned his back and scraped backward with his big shoes at the broken shells and the slimy bag, just like a dog, and looked back at the mess (everybody laughed again at that) and started to walk away, bending his cane deep with every shuffle, and squatting deeper, with his knees wider apart, than ever before, constantly picking at the seat of his pants with his left hand, and shaking one foot, then the other, and once gouging deep into his seat and then pausing and shaking his whole body, like a wet dog, and then walking on; while the screen shut over his small image a sudden circle of darkness: then the player-piano changed its tune, and the ads came in motionless color. They sat on into the William S. Hart feature to make sure why he had killed the man with the fancy vest—it was as they had expected by her frightened, pleased face after the killing; he had insulted a girl and cheated her father as well—and Rufus' father said, "Well, reckon this is where we came in," but they watched him kill the man all over again; then they walked out.

It was full dark now, but still early; Gay Street was full of absorbed faces; many of the store windows were still alight. Plaster people, in ennobled postures, stiffly wore untouchably new clothes; there was even a little boy, with short, straight pants, bare knees and high socks, obviously a sissy: but he wore a cap, all the same, not a hat like a baby. Rufus' whole insides lifted and sank as he looked at the cap and he looked up at his father; but his father did not notice; his face was wrapped in good humor, the memory of Charlie. Remembering his rebuff of a year ago, even though it had been his mother, Rufus was afraid to speak of it. His father wouldn't mind, but she wouldn't want him to have a cap, yet. If he asked his father now, his father would say no, Charlie Chaplin was enough. He watched the absorbed faces pushing past each other and the great bright letters of the signs: "Sterchi's." "George's." I can read them now, he reflected. I even know how to say "Sturkeys." But he thought it best not to say so; he remembered how his father had said, "Don't you brag," and he had been puzzled and rather stupid in school for several days, because of the stern tone in his voice.

What was bragging? It was bad.

They turned aside into a darker street, where the fewer faces looked more secret, and came into the odd, shaky light of Market Square. It was almost empty at this hour, but here and there, along the pavement streaked with horse urine, a wagon stayed still, and low firelight shone through the white cloth shell stretched tightly on its hickory hoops. A dark-faced man leaned against the white brick wall, gnawing a turnip; he looked at them low, with sad, pale eyes. When Rufus' father raised his hand in silent greeting, he raised his hand, but less, and Rufus, turning, saw how he looked sorrowfully, somehow dangerously, after them. They passed a wagon in which a lantern burned low orange; there lay a whole family, large and small, silent, asleep. In the tail of one wagon a woman sat, her face narrow beneath her flare of sunbonnet, her dark eyes in its shade, like smudges of soot. Rufus' father averted his eyes and touched his straw hat lightly; and Rufus, looking back, saw how her dead eyes kept looking gently ahead of her.

"Well," his father said, "reckon I'll hoist me a couple."

They turned through the swinging doors into a blast of odor and sound. There was no music: only the density of bodies and of the smell of a market bar, of beer, whiskey and country bodies, salt and leather; no clamor, only the thick quietude of crumpled talk. Rufus stood looking at the light on a damp spittoon and he heard his father ask for whiskey, and knew he was looking up and down the bar for men he might know. But they seldom came from so far away as the Powell River Valley; and Rufus soon realized that his father had found, tonight, no one he knew. He looked up his father's length and watched him bend backwards tossing one off in one jolt in a lordly manner, and a moment later heard him say to the man next him, "That's my boy"; and felt a warmth of love. Next moment he felt his father's hands under his armpits, and he was lifted, high, and seated on the bar, looking into a long row of huge bristling and bearded red faces. The eyes of the men nearest him were interested, and kind; some of them smiled; further away, the eyes were impersonal and questioning, but now even some of these began to smile. Somewhat timidly, but feeling assured that his father was proud of him and that he was liked, and liked these men, he smiled back; and suddenly many of the men laughed. He was disconcerted by their laughter and lost his smile a moment; then, realizing it was friendly, smiled again; and again they laughed. His father smiled at him. "That's my boy," he said warmly. "Six years old, and he can already read like I couldn't read when I was twice his age."

Rufus felt a sudden hollowness in his voice, and all along the bar, and in his own heart. But how does he fight, he thought. You don't brag about smartness if your son is brave. He felt the anguish of shame, but his father did not seem to notice, except that as suddenly as he had lifted him up to the bar, he gently lifted him down again. "Reckon I'll have another," he said, and drank it more slowly; then, with a few good nights, they went out.

His father proffered a Life Saver, courteously, man to man; he took it with a special sense of courtesy. It sealed their contract. Only once had his father felt it necessary to say to him, "I wouldn't tell your mama, if I were you"; he had known, from then on, that he could trust Rufus; and Rufus had felt gratitude in this silent trust. They walked away from Market Square, along a dark and nearly empty street, sucking their Life Savers; and Rufus' father reflected, without particular concern, that Life Savers were not quite life saver enough; he had better play very tired tonight, and turn away the minute they got in bed.

The deaf and dumb asylum was deaf and dumb, his father observed very quietly, as if he were careful not to wake it, as he always did on these evenings; its windows showed black in its pale brick, as the nursing woman's eyes, and it stood deep and silent among the light shadows of its trees. Ahead, Asylum Avenue lay bleak beneath its lamps. Latticed in pawnshop iron, an old saber caught the glint of a street lamp, a mandolin's belly glowed. In a closed drug store stood Venus de Milo, her golden body laced in elastic straps. The stained glass of the L&N Depot smoldered like an exhausted butterfly, and at the middle of the viaduct they paused to inhale the burst of smoke from a switch engine which passed under; Rufus, lifted, the cinders stinging his face, was grateful no longer to feel fear at this suspension over the tracks and the powerful locomotives. Far down the yard, a red light flicked to green; a moment later, they heard the thrilling click. It was ten-seven by the depot clock. They went on, more idly than before.

If I could fight, thought Rufus. If I were brave; he would never brag how I could read: Brag. Of course, "Don't you brag." That was it. What it meant. Don't brag you're smart if you're not brave. You've got nothing to brag about. Don't you brag.

The young leaves of Forest Avenue wavered against street lamps and they approached their corner.

It was a vacant lot, part rubbed bare clay, part over-grown with weeds, rising a little from the sidewalk. A few feet in from the sidewalk there was a medium-sized tree and, near enough to be within its shade in daytime, an outcrop of limestone like a great bundle of dirty laundry. If you sat on a certain part of it the trunk of the tree shut off the weak street lamp a block away, and it seemed very dark. Whenever they walked downtown and walked back home, in the evenings, they always began to walk more slowly, from about the middle of the viaduct, and as they came near this corner they walked more slowly still, but with purpose; and paused a moment, at the edge of the sidewalk; then, without speaking, stepped into the dark lot and sat down on the rock, looking out over the steep face of the hill and at the lights of North Knoxville. Deep in the valley an engine coughed and browsed; couplings settled their long chains, and the empty cars sounded like broken drums. A man came up the far side of the street, walking neither slow nor fast, not turning his head, as he paused, and quite surely not noticing them; they watched him until he was out of sight, and Rufus felt, and was sure that his father felt, that though there was no harm in the man and he had as good a right as they did to be there, minding his own business, their journey was interrupted from the moment they first saw him until they saw him out of sight. Once he was out of sight they realized more pleasure in their privacy than before; they really relaxed in it. They looked across the darkness of the lights of North Knoxville. They were aware of the quiet leaves above them, and looked into them and through them. They looked between the leaves into the stars. Usually on these evening waits, or a few minutes before going on home, Rufus' father smoked a cigarette through, and when it was finished, it was time to get up and go on home. But this time he did not smoke. Up to recently he had always said something about Rufus' being tired, when they were still about a block away from the corner; but lately he had not done so, and Rufus realized that his father stopped as much because he wanted to, as on Rufus' account. He was just not in a hurry to get home, Rufus realized; and, far more important, it was clear that he liked to spend these few minutes with Rufus. Rufus had come recently to feel a quiet kind of anticipation of the corner, from the moment they finished crossing the viaduct; and, during the ten to twenty minutes they sat on the rock, a particular kind of contentment, unlike any other that he knew. He did not know what this was, in words or ideas, or what the reason was; it was simply all that he saw and felt. It was, mainly, knowing that his father, too, felt a particular kind of contentment, here, unlike any other, and that their kinds of contentment were much alike, and depended on each other. Rufus seldom had at all sharply the feeling that he and his father were estranged, yet they must have been, and he must have felt it, for always during these quiet moments on the rock a part of his sense of complete contentment lay in the feeling that they were reconciled, that there was really no division, no estrangement, or none so strong, anyhow, that it could mean much, by comparison with the unity that was so firm and assured, here. He felt that although his father loved their home and loved all of them, he was more lonely than the contentment of this family love could help; that it even increased his loneliness, or made it hard for him not to be lonely. He felt that sitting out here, he was not lonely; or if he was, that he felt on good terms with the loneliness; that he was a homesick man, and that here on the rock, though he might be more homesick than ever, he was well. He knew that a very important part of his well-being came of staying a few minutes away from home, very quietly, in the dark, listening to the leaves if they moved, and looking at the stars; and that his own, Rufus' own presence, was fully as indispensable to this well-being. He knew that each of them knew of the other's well-being, and of the reasons for it, and knew how each depended on the other, how each meant more to the other, in this most important of all ways, than anyone or anything else in the world; and that the best of this well-being lay in this mutual knowledge, which was neither concealed nor revealed. He knew these things very distinctly, but not, of course, in any such way as we have of suggesting them in words. There were no words, or even ideas, or formed emotions, of the kind that have been suggested here, no more in the man than in the boy child. These realizations moved clearly through the senses, the memory, the feelings, the mere feeling of the place they paused at, about a quarter of a mile from home, on a rock under a stray tree that had grown in the city, their feet on undomesticated clay, facing north through the night over the Southern Railway tracks and over North Knoxville, towards the deeply folded small mountains and the Powell River Valley, and above them, the trembling lanterns of the universe, seeming so near, so intimate, that when air stirred the leaves and their hair, it seemed to be the breathing, the whispering of the stars. Sometimes on these evenings his father would hum a little and the humming would break open into a word or two, but he never finished even a part of a tune, for silence was even more pleasurable, and sometimes he would say a few words, of very little consequence, but would never seek to say much, or to finish what he was saying, or to listen for a reply; for silence again was even more pleasurable. Sometimes, Rufus had noticed, he would stroke the wrinkled rock and press his hand firmly against it; and sometimes he would put out his cigarette and tear and scatter it before it was half finished. But this time he was much quieter than ordinarily. They slackened their walking a little sooner than usual and walked a little more slowly, without a word, to the corner; and hesitated, before stepping off the sidewalk into the clay, purely for the luxury of hesitation; and took their place on the rock without breaking silence. As always, Rufus' father took off his hat and put it over the front of his bent knee, and as always, Rufus imitated him, but this time his father did not roll a cigarette. They waited while the man came by, intruding on their privacy, and disappeared, as someone nearly always did, and then relaxed sharply into the pleasure of their privacy; but this time Rufus' father did not hum, nor did he say anything, nor even touch the rock with his hand, but sat with his hands hung between his knees and looked out over North Knoxville, hearing the restive assemblage of the train; and after there had been silence for a while, raised his head and looked up into the leaves and between the leaves into the broad stars, not smiling, but with his eyes more calm and grave and his mouth strong and more quiet, than Rufus had ever seen his eyes and his mouth; and as he watched his father's face, Rufus felt his father's hand settle, without groping or clumsiness, on the top of his bare head; it took his forehead and smoothed it, and pushed the hair backward from his forehead, and held the back of his head while Rufus pressed his head backward against the firm hand, and, in reply to that pressure, clasped over his right ear and cheek, over the whole side of the head, and drew Rufus' head quietly and strongly against the sharp cloth that covered his father's body, through which Rufus could feel the breathing ribs; then relinquished him, and Rufus sat upright, while the hand lay strongly on his shoulder, and he saw that his father's eyes had become still more clear and grave and that the deep lines around his mouth were satisfied; and looked up at what his father was so steadily looking at, at the leaves which silently breathed and at the stars which beat like hearts. He heard a long, deep sigh break from his father, and then his father's abrupt voice: *"Well ..."* and the hand lifted from him and they both stood up. The rest of the way home they did not speak, or put on their hats. When he was nearly asleep Rufus heard once more the crumpling of freight cars, and deep in the night he heard the crumpling of subdued voices and words, "Naw: I'll probably be back before they're asleep"; then quick feet creaking quietly downstairs. But by the time he heard the creaking and departure of the Ford, he was already so deeply asleep that it seemed only a part of a dream, and by next morning, when his mother explained to them why his father was not at breakfast, he had so forgotten the words and the noises that years later, when he remembered them, he could never be sure that he was not making them up.

Chapter 2

DEEP IN THE NIGHT they experienced the sensation, in their sleep, of being prodded at, as if by some persistent insect. Their souls turned and flicked out impatient hands, but the tormentor would not be driven off. They both awoke at the same instant. In the dark and empty hall, by itself, the telephone was shrilling fiercely, forlorn as an abandoned baby and even more peremptory to be quieted. They heard it ring once and did not stir, crystallizing their senses into annoyance, defiance and acceptance of defeat. It rang again: at the same moment she exclaimed, "Jay! The children!" and he, grunting, "Lie still," swung his feet thumping to the floor. The phone rang again. He hurried out in the dark, barefooted, tiptoe, cursing under his breath. Hard as he tried to beat it, it rang again just as he got to it. He cut it off in the middle of its cry and listened with savage satisfaction to its death rattle. Then he put the receiver to his hear.

"Yeah?" he said, forbiddingly. "*Hel*lo."

"Is this the residence of, uh . . ."

"Hello, who is it?"

"Is this the residence of Jay Follet?"

Another voice said, "That's him, Central, let me talk to um, that's . . ." It was Ralph.

"Hello," he said. "Ralph?"

"One moment please, your party is not connec . . ."

"Hello, Jay?"

"Ralph? Yeah. Hello. What's trouble?" For there was something wrong with his voice. Drunk, I reckon, he thought.

"Jay? Can you hear me all right? I said, 'Can you hear me all right,' Jay?"

Crying too, sounds like. "Sure, I can hear you. What's the matter?" Paw, he thought suddenly. I bet it's Paw; and he thought of his father and his mother and was filled with cold sad darkness.

"Hit's Paw, Jay," said Ralph, his voice going so rotten with tears that his brother pulled the receiver a little away, his mouth contracting with disgust. "I know I got no business aringin y'up this hour night but I know too you'd never a forgive me if . . ."

"Quit it, Ralph," he said sharply. "Cut that out and tell me about it."

"Hit's only my duty, Jay, God Almighty I . . ."

"All right, Ralph," he said, "I preciate your callin. Now tell me about Paw."

"I just got back fer this, Jay, this minute, hurried home specially to ring you up . . . Course I'm agoan right back, you . . ."

"Listen, Ralph. Listen here. Can you hear me?" Ralph was silent. "Is he dead or alive?"

"Paw?"

Jay started to say, "Yeah, Paw," in tight rage, but he heard Ralph begin again. He can't help it, he thought, and waited.

"Why, naw, he ain't dead," Ralph said, deflated. The darkness lifted considerably from Jay: coldly, he listened to Ralph whickering up his feelings again. Finally, his voice shaking satisfactorily, he said, "But O Lord God, hit looks like the end, Jay!"

"I should come up, huh?" He began to wonder whether Ralph was sober enough to be trusted; Ralph heard, and misunderstood the doubt in his voice.

His voice became dignified. "Course that's entirely up to you,

23

Jay. I know Paw n all of us would feel it was mighty strange if his oldest boy, the one he always thought the most of . . ."

This new voice and this new tack bewildered Jay for a moment. Then he understood what Ralph was driving at, and had misunderstood, and assumed about him, and was glad that he was not where he could hit him. He cut in.

"Hold on, Ralph, you hold on there. If Paw's that bad you know damn well I'm comin so don't give me none of that . . ." But he realized, with self-dislike, how unimportant it was to argue this matter with Ralph and said, "Listen here, Ralph, now don't think I'm jumping on you, just listen. Do you hear me?" His feet and legs were getting chilly. He warmed one foot beneath the other. "Hear me?"

"I can hear you, Jay."

"Ralph, get it straight I'm not trying to jump on you, but sounds to me like you've had a few. Now . . ."

"I . . ."

"Now hold on. I don't give a damn if you're drunk or sober, far's you're concerned: point is this, Ralph. Anyone that's drunk, I know it myself, they're likely to exaggerate . . ."

"You think I'm a lyin to you? You . . ."

"Shut up, Ralph. Course you're not. But if you're drunk you can get an exaggerated idea how serious a thing is. Now you think a minute. Just think it over. And remember nobody's goin to think bad of you if you change your mind, or for calling either. Just how sick is he really, Ralph?"

"Course if you don't want to take my word for . . ."

"Think, Goddamn it!" Ralph was silent. Jay changed his feet around. He suddenly realized how foolish he had been to try to get anything levelheaded out of Ralph. "Listen, Ralph," he said. "I know you wouldn't a phoned if you didn't think it was serious. Is Sally there?"

"Why yeah, she . . ."

"Let me talk to her a minute, will you?"

"Why I just told you she's out home."

"Course Mother's out there."

"Why, Jay, she wouldn't never leave his side. Mother . . ."

"Doctor's been out, of course."

"He's with him still. Was when I left."

"What's he say?"

Ralph hesitated. He did not want to spoil his story. "He says he has a chance, Jay."

By the way Ralph said it, Jay suspected the doctor had said, a good chance.

He was at the edge of asking whether it was a good chance or just a chance when he was suddenly overcome by even more disgust for himself, for haggling about it, than for Ralph. Besides, his feet were so chilly they were beginning to itch.

"Look here, Ralph," he said, in a different voice. "I'm talking too much. I . . ."

"Yeah, reckon our time must be about up, but what's a few . . ."

"Listen here. I'm starting right on up. I ought to be there by—what time is it, do you know?"

"Hit's two-thirty-seven, Jay. I *knowed* you'd . . ."

"I ought to be there by daylight, Ralph, you tell Mother I'm coming right on up just quicks I can get there. Ralph. Is he conscious?"

"Awf an' on, Jay. He's been speakin yore name, Jay, hit like to break muh heart. He'll sure thank his stars that his oldest boy, the one he always thought the most of, that you thought it was worth yer while to . . ."

"Cut it out, Ralph. What the hell you think I am? If he gets conscious just let him know I'm comin'. And Ralph . . ."

"Yeah?"

But now he did not want to say it. He said it anyway. "I know I got no room to talk, but—try not to drink so much that Mother will notice it. Drink some coffee fore you go back. Huh? Drink it black."

"Sure, Jay, and don't think I take offense so easy. I wouldn't

25

add a mite to her troubles, not at this time, not for this world, Jay. You know that. So Jay, I *thank* you. I *thank* you for calling it to my tention. I don't take offense. I *thank* you, Jay. I *thank* you."

"That's all right, Ralph. Don't mention it," he added, feeling hypercritical and a little disgusted again. "Now I'll be right along. So good-bye."

"You tell Mary how it is, Jay. Don't want her thinking bad of me, ringing . . ."

"That's all right. She'll understand. Good-bye, Ralph."

"I wouldn't a ring you up, Jay if . . ."

"That's all right. Thanks for calling. Good-bye."

Ralph's voice was unsatisfied. "Well, good-bye," he said.

Wants babying, Jay realized. Not appreciated enough. He listened. The line was still open. The hell I will, he thought, and hung up. Of all the crybabies, he thought, and went on back to the bedroom.

"Gracious *sake,*"said Mary, under her breath. "I thought he'd talk for*ever!*"

"Oh, well," Jay said, "reckon he can't help it." He sat on the bed and felt for his socks.

"It is your father, Jay?"

"Yup," he said, pulling on one sock.

"Oh, you're going up," she said, suddenly realizing what he was doing. She put her hand on him. "Then it's very grave, Jay," she said very gently.

He fastened his garter and put his hand over hers. "Lord knows," he said. "I can't be sure enough of anything with Ralph, but I can't afford to take the risk."

"Of course not." Her hand moved to pat him; his hand moved on hers. "Has the doctor seen him?" she asked cautiously.

"He says he has a chance, Ralph says."

"That could mean so many things. It might be all right if you waited till morning. You might hear he was better, then. Not that I mean to . . ."

Because, to his shame, he had done the same kinds of wondering himself, he was now exasperated afresh. The thought even flashed across his mind, That's easy for *you* to say. He's not *your* father, and besides you've always looked down at him. But he drove this thought so well away that he thought ill of himself for having believed it, and said, "Sweetheart, I'd rather wait and see what we hear in the morning, just as much as you would. It may all be a false alarm. I know Ralph goes off his trolley easy. But we just can't afford to take that chance."

"Of course not, Jay." There was a loud stirring as she got from bed.

"What *you* up to?"

"Why, your breakfast," she said, switching on the light. "Sakes *alive!*" she said, seeing the clock.

"Oh, Mary. Get on back to bed. I can pick up something downtown."

"Don't be ridiculous," she said, hurrying into her bathrobe.

"Honest, it would be just as easy," he said. He liked night lunchrooms, and had not been in one since Rufus was born. He was very faintly disappointed. But still more, he was warmed by the simplicity with which she got up for him, thoroughly awake.

"Why, Jay, that is out of the question!" she said, knotting the bathrobe girdle. She got into her slippers and shuffled quickly to the door. She looked back and said, in a stage whisper, "Bring your *shoes*—to the *kit*chen."

He watched her disappear, wondering what in hell she meant by that, and was suddenly taken with a snort of silent amusement. She had looked so deadly serious, about the shoes. God, the ten thousand little things every day that a woman kept thinking of, on account of children. Hardly even thinking, he thought to himself, as he pulled on his other sock. Practically automatic. Like breathing.

And most of the time, he thought, as he stripped, they're dead right. Course they're so much in the habit of it (he stepped into his drawers) that sometimes they overdo it. But most of the time if

27

you think even a second before you get annoyed (he buttoned his undershirt), there is good common sense behind it.

He shook out his trousers. His moment of reflection and light-heartedness was overtaken by shadow, and he felt a little foolish, for he couldn't be sure there was anything to worry about yet, much less feel solemn about. That Ralph, he thought, hoisting the trousers and buttoning the top button. And he stood a moment looking at the window, polished with light, a deep blue-black beyond. The hour and the beauty of the night moved in him; he heard the flickering of the clock, and it sounded alien and mysterious as a rat in a wall. He felt a deep sense of solemn adventure, whether or not there was anything to feel solemn about. He sighed, and thought of his father as he could first remember him: beak-nosed, handsome, with a great, proud scowl of black mustache. He had known from away back that his father was sort of useless without ever meaning to be; the amount of burden he left to Jay's mother used to drive him to fury, even when he was a boy. And yet he couldn't get around it: he was so naturally gay and so deeply kindhearted that you couldn't help loving him. And he never meant her any harm. He meant so well. That thought used particularly to enrage Jay, and even now it occurred to him with a certain sourness. But now he reflected also: well, but damn it, he did. He may have traded on it, but he never tried to, never knew it gained him anything. He meant the best in the world. And for a moment as he looked at the window he had no mental image of his father nor any thought of him, nor did he hear the clock. He only saw the window, tenderly alight within, and the infinite dark leaning like water against its outer surface, and even the window was not a window, but only something extraordinarily vivid and senseless which for the moment occupied the universe. A sense of enormous distance stole over him, and changed into a moment of insupportable wonder and sadness.

Well, he thought: we've all got to go sometime.

Then life came back into focus.

Clean shirt, he thought.

He unbuttoned the top buttons of his trousers and spread his knees, squatting slightly, to hold them up. Fool thing to do, he reflected. Do it every time. (He tucked in the deep tails and settled them; the tails of this shirt were particularly long, and this always, for some reason, still made him feel particularly masculine.) If I put on the shirt first, wouldn't have to do that fool squat. (He finished buttoning his fly.) Well (he braced his right shoulder) there's habit for you (he braced his left shoulder and slightly squatted again, readjusting).

He sat on the bed and reached for one shoe.

Oh.

Yup.

He took his shoes, a tie, a collar and collar buttons, and started from the room. He saw the rumpled bed. Well, he thought, I can do *some*thing for her. He put his things on the floor, smoothed the sheets, and punched the pillows. The sheets were still warm on her side. He drew the covers up to keep the warmth, then laid them open a few inches, so it would look inviting to get into. She'll be glad of that, he thought, very well pleased with the looks of it. He gathered up his shoes, collar, tie and buttons, and made for the kitchen, taking special care as he passed the children's door, which was slightly ajar.

She was just turning the eggs. "Ready in a second," he told her, and dodged into the bathroom. Ought to get this upstairs, he reflected for perhaps the five hundredth time.

He thrust his chin at the mirror. Not so bad, he thought, and decided just to wash. Then he reflected: after all, why had he worn a clean shirt? He could hope to God not, all he liked, but the chances were this was going to be a very solemn occasion. I'd do it for a funeral, wouldn't I? he reflected, annoyed at his laziness. He got out his razor and stropped it rapidly.

Mary heard this lavish noise of leather, and with a small spasm of impatience shoved the eggs to the back of the stove.

Ordinarily he took a good deal of time shaving, not because

he enjoyed it (he loathed it) but because if it had to be done he wanted to do it well, and because he hated to cut himself. This time, because he was in a hurry, he gave a special cold glance at the lump of chin before he leaned forward and got to work. But to his surprise, everything worked like a charm; he even had less trouble than usual at the roots of his nostrils, and with his chin, and there were no patches left. He felt so well gratified that he dabbed each cheekbone with lather and took off the little half-moons of fuzz. Still no complaints. He cleaned up the basin and flushed the lathery, hairy bits of toilet paper down the water closet. Do I? he wondered, as the water closet gargled. Nope. He reached for the collar buttons.

When Mary came to the door he was flinging over and noos-ing the four-in-hand, his chin stretched and tilted as it always was during this operation, with the look of an impatient horse.

"Jay," she said softly, a little quelled by this impatient look, "I don't mean to hurry you, but things'll get cold."

"I'll be right out." He set the knot carefully above the button, glaring into his reflected eyes, made an unusually scrupulous part in his hair, and hurried to the kitchen table.

"Aw, *darling!*" There were the bacon and eggs and the coffee, all ready, and she was making pancakes as well.

"Well you got to *eat,* Jay. It'll still be chilly for hours." She spoke as if in a church or library, because of the sleeping children, unconsciously, because of the time of night.

"Sweetheart." He caught her shoulders where she stood at the stove. She turned, her eyes hard with wakefulness, and smiled. He kissed her.

"Eat your eggs," she said. "They're getting cold."

He sat down and started eating. She turned the pancakes. "How many can you eat?" she asked.

"Gee, I don't know," he said, getting the egg down (don't talk with your mouth full) before he answered. He was not yet quite awake enough to be very hungry, but he was touched, and determined to eat a big breakfast. "Better hold it after the first two, three."

She covered the pancake to keep it hot and poured another.

He noticed that she had peppered the eggs more heavily than usual. "Good eggs," he said.

She was pleased. Not more than half consciously, she had done this because within a few hours he would doubtless eat again, at home. For the same reason she had made the coffee unusually strong. And for the same reason she felt pleasure in standing at the stove while he ate, as mountain women did.

"Good *coffee*," he said. "Now that's more *like* it." She turned the pancake. She supposed she really ought to make two pots always, one that she could stand to drink and one the way he liked it, new water and a few fresh grounds put in, without ever throwing out the old ones until the pot was choked full of old grounds. But she couldn't stand it; she would as soon watch him drink so much sulfuric acid.

"Don't you worry," she smiled at him. "You won't get any from me that's *all* the way like it!"

He frowned at her.

"Come on sit down, sweetheart," he said.

"In a minute . . ."

"Come on. I imagine two are gonna be enough."

"You think so?"

"If it won't I'll make the third one." He took her hand and drew her towards her chair. "You'll *sit* here." She sat down. "How about you?"

"I couldn't sleep."

"I know what." He got up and went to the icebox.

"What are you—oh. No, Jay. Well. Thanks."

For before she could prevent him he had poured milk into a saucepan, and now that he put it on the stove she knew she would like it.

"Want some toast?"

"No, thank you, darling. The milk, just by itself, will be just perfect."

He finished off the eggs. She got half out of her chair. He pressed down on her shoulder as he got up. He brought back the pancakes.

"They'll be soggy by now. Let me . . ." She started up again; again he put a hand on her shoulder. "You stay *put*," he said in a mockery of sternness. "They're fine. Couldn't be better."

He plastered on butter, poured on molasses, sliced the pancakes in parallels, gave them a twist with knife and fork and sliced them crosswise.

"There's plenty more butter," she said.

"Got a plenty," he said, spearing four fragments of pancake and putting them in his mouth. "Thanks." He chewed them up, swallowed them, and speared four more. "I bet your milk's warm," he said, putting down his fork.

But this time she was up before he could prevent her. "You eat," she said. She poured the white, softly steaming milk into a thick white cup and sat down with it, warming both hands on the cup, and watching him eat. Because of the strangeness of the hour, and the abrupt destruction of sleep, the necessity for action and its interruptive minutiae, the gravity of his errand, and a kind of weary exhilaration, both of them found it peculiarly hard to talk, though both particularly wanted to. He realized that she was watching him, and watched back, his eyes serious yet smiling, his jaws busy. He was glutted, but he thought to himself, I'll finish up those pancakes if it's the last thing I do.

"Don't stuff, Jay," she said after a silence.

"Hm?"

"Don't eat more than you've appetite for."

He had thought his imitation of good appetite was successful. "Don't worry," he said, spearing some more.

There wasn't much to finish. She looked at him tenderly when he glanced down to see, and said nothing more about it.

"Mnh," he said, leaning back.

Now there was nothing to take their eyes from each other; and still, for some reason, they had nothing to say. They were not disturbed by this, but both felt almost the shyness of courtship. Each continued to look into the other's tired eyes, and their tired eyes sparkled, but not with realizations which reached their hearts very distinctly.

"What would you like to do for your birthday?" he asked.

"Why, Jay." She was taken very much by surprise. "Why you nice thing! Why—why . . ."

"You think it over," he said. "Whatever you'd like best—within reason, of course," he joked. "I'll see we manage it. The children, I mean." They both remembered at the same time. He said, "That is, of course, if everything goes the way we hope it will, up home."

"Of course, Jay." Her eyes lost focus for a moment. "Let's hope it will," she said, in a peculiarly abstracted voice.

He watched her. That occasional loss of focus always mystified him and faintly disturbed him. Women, he guessed.

She came back into this world and again they looked at each other. Of course, in a way, they both reflected, there isn't anything to say, or need for us to say it, anyhow.

He took a slow, deep breath and let it out as slowly.

"Well, Mary," he said in his gentlest voice. He took her hand. They smiled very seriously, thinking of his father and of each other, and both knew in their hearts, as they had known in their minds, that there was no need to say anything.

They got up.

"Now where—*ahh,*" he said in deep annoyance.

"Coat n vest," he said, starting for the stairs.

"You wait," she said, passing him swiftly. "Fraid you'd wake the children," she whispered over her shoulder.

While she was gone he went into the sitting room, turned on one light, and picked up his pipe and tobacco. In the single quiet light in the enormous quietude of the night, all the little objects in the room looked golden brown and curiously gentle. He was touched, without knowing why.

Home.

He snapped off the light.

She was a little slow coming down; seeing if they're covered, he thought. He stood by the stove, idly watching the flexions of the dark and light squares in the linoleum. He was glad he'd gotten it down, at last. And Mary had been right. The plain black and white did look better than colors and fancy patterns.

He heard her on the stairs. Sure enough, first thing she said when she came in was, "You know, I was almost tempted to wake them. I suppose I'm silly but they're so used to—I'm afraid they're going to be very disappointed you didn't tell them goodbye."

"Good night! Really?" He hardly knew whether he was pleased or displeased. Were they getting spoilt maybe?

"I may be mistaken, of course."

"Be silly to wake em up. You might not get to sleep rest of the night."

He buttoned his vest.

"I wouldn't think of it, except: well" (she was reluctant to remind him), "if worst comes to worst, Jay, you might be gone longer than we hope."

"That's perfectly true," he said, gravely. This whole sudden errand was so uncertain, so ambiguous that it was hard for either of them to hold a focused state of mind about it. He thought again of his father.

"You think praps I should?"

"Let me think."

"N-no," he said slowly; "I don't reckon. No. You see, even, well even at the worst I'd be coming back to take you-all up. Funeral I mean. And these heart things, they're generally decided pretty fast. Chances are very good, either way, I'll be back tomorrow night. That's tonight, I mean."

"Yes, I see. Yes."

"Tell you what. Tell them, don't promise them or anything of course, but tell them I'm practicly sure to be back before they're asleep. Tell them I'll do my best." He got into his coat.

"All right, Jay."

"Yes. That's sensible." She reached so suddenly at his heart that by reflex he backed away; the eyes of both were startled and disturbed. With a frowning smile she teased him: "Don't be *frightened,* little Timid Soul; it's only a clean handkerchief and couldn't possibly hurt you."

"I'm sorry," he laughed, "I just didn't know what you were up to." He pulled in his chin, frowning slightly, as he watched her take out the crumpled handkerchief and arrange the fresh one. Being fussed over embarrassed him; he was still more sharply embarrassed by the discreet white corner his wife took care to leave peeping from the pocket. His hand moved instinctively; he caught himself in time and put his hand in his pocket.

"There. You look very nice," she said, studying him earnestly, as if he were her son. He felt rather foolish, tender towards her innocence of this motherliness, and quite flattered. He felt for a moment rather vainly sure that he did indeed look very nice, to her anyhow, and that was all he cared about.

"Well," he said, taking out his watch. "Good Lord a mercy!" He showed her. Three-forty-one. "I didn't think it was hardly three."

"Oh yes. It's very late."

"Well, no more dawdling." He put an arm around her shoulder and they walked to the back door. "All right, Mary. I hate to go, but—can't be avoided."

She opened the door and led him through, to the back porch. "You'll catch cold," he said. She shook her head. "No. It feels milder outside than in."

They walked to the edge of the porch. The moistures of May drowned all save the most ardent stars, and gave back to the earth the sublimated light of the prostrate city. Deep in the end of the back yard, the blossoming peach tree shone like a celestial sentinel. The fecund air lavished upon their faces the tenderness of lovers' adoring hands, the dissolving fragrance of the opened world, which slept against the sky.

"What a heavenly night, Jay," she said in the voice which was dearest to him. "I almost wish I could come with you"—she remembered more clearly "—in whatever happens."

"I wish you could, dear," he said, though his mind had not been on such a possibility; frankly, he had suddenly looked forward to the solitary drive. But now the peculiar quality of her voice reached him and he said, with love, "I wish you could."

They stood bemused by the darkness.

"Well, Jay," she said abruptly, "I mustn't keep you."

He was silent a moment. "Nope," he said, a curious, weary sadness in his voice. "Time to go."

He took her in his arms, leaning back to look at her. It was not really anything of a separation, yet he was surprised to find that it seemed to him a grave one, perhaps because his business was grave, or because of the solemn hour. He saw this in her face as well, and almost wished they had waked the children after all.

"Good-bye, Mary," he said.

"Good-bye, Jay."

They kissed, and her head settled for a moment against him. He stroked her hair. "I'll let you know," he said, "quick as I can, if it's serious."

"I pray it won't be, Jay."

"Well, we can only hope." The moment of full tenderness between them was dissolved in their thought, but he continued gently to stroke the round back of her head.

"Give all my love to your mother. Tell her they're both in my thoughts and wishes—constantly. And your father, of course, if he's—well enough to talk to."

"Sure, dear."

"And take care of yourself."

"Sure."

He patted her back and they parted.

"Then I'll hear from you—see you—very soon."

"That's right."

"All right, Jay." She squeezed his arm. He kissed her, just beneath the eye, and realized her disappointed lips; they smiled, and he kissed her heartily on the mouth. In a glimmer of gaiety, both were on the verge of parting with their customary morning farewell, she singing, "Good-bye John, don't stay long," he singing back, "I'll be back in a week or two," but both thought better of it.

"All right, dear. Good-bye."

"Good-bye, my dear."

He turned abruptly at the bottom of the steps. "Hey," he whispered. "How's your money?"

She thought rapidly. "All right, thank you."

"Tell the children good-bye for me. Tell them I'll see them tonight."

"I better not promise that, had I?"

"No, but probably. And Mary: I hope I can make supper, but don't wait it."

"All right."

"Good night."

"Good night." He walked back towards the barn. In the middle of the yard he turned and whispered loudly, "And you think it over about your birthday."

"Thank you, Jay. All right. Thank you."

She could hear him walking as quietly as possible on the cinders. He silently lifted and set aside the bar of the door, and opened the door, taking care to be quiet. The first leaf squealed; the second, which was usually worse, was perfectly still. Stepping to the left of the car, and assuming the serious position of stealth which the narrowness of the garage made necessary, he disappeared into the absolute darkness.

She knew he would try not to wake the neighbors and the children; and that it was impossible to start the auto quietly. She waited with sympathy and amusement, and with habituated dread of his fury and of the profanity she was sure would ensue, spoken or unspoken.

Uhgh—hy uh yu hy why uhy uh: wheek-uh-wheek-uh:

Ughh—hy wh yuh: wheek:

(now the nearly noiseless, desperate adjustments of spark and throttle and choke)

Ughgh—hyuh yuhyuh wheek yuh yuh wheek wheek wheek yuh yuhyuh: wheek:

(which she never understood and, from where she stayed now, could predict so well):

Ughgh—*Ughgh*—yuhyuh*Ugh* wheek yuh yuh *Ughgh* yuh wheek wheek yuhyuh: wheek wheek: uh:

(like a hideous, horribly constipated great brute of a beast: like a lunatic sobbing: like a mouse being tortured):

Ughgh—*Ughgh*—*Ughgh* (Poor thing, he must be simply furious) *Ughgh*—wheek—*Whughugh*yuh—*Ughwheek*yuh*uughgyugh*-yuhyuhy a a a a a a a h h h h h h R h R h R H R H R H (oh, *stop* it!) R H R H (a window went up) R H R H R H R H R H R yuh-yhhRRHRHRHRHRHRHRHRHRHRH (the door smacked to in rage and triumph) RhRhRh - - - - - - - - (the window went down) RHRHRHRHRH (the machine backed out; crackling on the cinders). RHRH - - - - - (he wrenched it rudely but adroitly in a backward curve, almost to the chicken wire; from between the houses, light from the street caught its black side) rhrh - - - - (and swung as rudely round the corner of the barn and, by opposite turn, into the alley, facing eastward, where it stood) rhrh - - - - - - - - (obedient, conquered, malicious as a mule, while he briefly reappeared, faced towards the house, saw her, waved one hand—she waved, but he did not see her—and drew the gate shut disappearing beyond it) rhrhrhrhrhrhrhRHRHRH-RHRHRHR

                    H
                    R
                    H
                    R
                    H
                    rh
                    rh
                    rh
                    rh
                    rh
                    rh
                    rh
                    rh
                    rh
                   rh
                   rh
                   rh

C utta wawwwwk:
          Craaawwrk?
            Chiquawkwawh.
                Wrrawkuhkuhkuh.
                    Craarrawwk.
                      rwrwk?
                        yrk.
                         rk:

She released a long breath, very slowly, and went into the
house.

There was her milk, untouched, forgotten, barely tepid. She
drank it down, without pleasure; all its whiteness, draining from
the stringing wet whiteness of the empty cup, was singularly
repugnant. She decided to leave things until morning, ran water
over the dishes, and left them in the sink.

If the children had heard so much as a sound, they didn't

show it now. Catherine, as always, was absolutely drowned in sleep, and both of them, as always, were absolutely drowned.

Really, they are too big for that, she thought. Rufus certainly. She carefully readjusted their covers, against catching cold. They scarcely stirred.

I ought to ask a doctor.

She saw the freshened bed. Why, the *dear,* she thought, smiling, and got in. She was never to realize his intention of holding the warmth in for her; for that had sometime since departed from the bed.

Chapter 3

HE IMAGINED THAT BY about now she would about be getting back and finding the bed. He smiled to think of her finding it.

He drove down Forest, across the viaduct, past the smoldering depot, and cut sharply left beneath the asylum and steeply downhill. The L&N yards lay along his left, faint skeins of steel, blocked shadows, little spumes of steam; he saw and heard the flickering shift of a signal, but he could no longer remember what that one meant. Along his right were dark vacant lots, pale billboards, the darker blocks of small sleeping buildings, an occasional light. He would have eaten in one of these places, small, weakly lighted holes-in-the-wall, opaque with the smoke of overheated lard, some for Negroes, some for whites, which served railroad men and the unexplainable nighthawks you found in any fair-sized town. You never saw a woman there, except sometimes behind a counter or sweating over a stove. He never used to talk when he went to them, but he enjoyed the feeling of conspiracy, and the sound of voices. If you went to the right ones, and if you were known, or looked like you could be trusted, you could get a shot or two of liquor, any hour of the night.

He ran his tongue over his teeth, tasting the last of the molasses and coffee and bacon and eggs.

Before long the city thinned out into the darkened evidences of the kind of flea-bitten semi-rurality which always peculiarly depressed him: mean little homes, and other inexplicably new and substantial, set too close together for any satisfying rural privacy or use, too far, too shapelessly apart to have adherence as any kind of community; mean little pieces of ill-cultivated land behind them, and alongside the road, between them, trash and slash and broken sheds and rained-out billboards: he passed a late, late streetcar, no passengers aboard, far out near the end of its run.

Within two more minutes he had seen the last of this sort of thing. The darkness became at once more intimate and more hollow; the engine sounded different, a smooth, easy drone; budding limbs swelled up and swept with sudden speed through the last of the vivid light; the auto bored through the center of the darkness of the universe; its poring shafts of light, like an insect's antennae, feeling into distinctness every relevant small obstacle and ease of passage, and very little else. He unbuttoned his vest and the top button of his trousers and settled back. After a few moments he wondered about taking off his coat; but the rhythm and momentum of night driving were too strongly persuasive to wish to break. He settled still more deeply, his eyes shifting gear constantly between the farthest reach of his lights and the nearest, and gave himself over entirely to the pleasures of the journey, and to its still undetermined but essentially grave significance.

It was just nearing daybreak when he came to the river; he had to rap several times on the window of the little shanty before the ferryman awoke.

"Have to double the charge, mister, cross at night," he said, intent on lighting his lantern.

"That's all right."

At the voice, he looked up, well awake for the first time. "Oh, howdy thur," he said.

"Howdy."

"You generally always come o' Sundays, yer womurn, couple o' young-uns."

"Yeahp."

He walked away, to the edge of the water, and holding his lantern low, examined the fit of his flatboat against the shore. Then he raised the lantern and swung it, as a railroad man would; Jay, who had left his engine running, braked it carefully down the steep, thickly tracked clay, and carefully aboard. He shut off his engine; the sudden silence was magical. He got out and helped the man block the wheels. "All ready here," he said, straightening; but the man said nothing; he was already casting off. They both watched the brown water widen under the lantern light, apparently with equal appreciation. Must be a nice job, Jay reflected, as he nearly always did; except of course winter.

"Run all winter?"

"Eah," said the man, warping his line.

"Tain't so bad," he added after a moment, "only for sleet. I do mislike them sleety nights."

Both were silent. Jay filled his pipe. As he struck a match he felt a difference in motion, a kind of dilation; the ferry was now warped into the bias of the current, which carried it, and the ferryman worked no more; he merely kept one hand on his line. The flat craft rode against the water like a hand on a breast. The water mumbled a little; during this part of the crossing, that was always the only sound. And by now, the surface of the river gave back light which could not as yet be as clearly discerned in the sky, and along both banks the trees which crowded the water like drinking cattle began to take on distinctness one from another. Far back through the country along both sides of the river, roosters screamed. The violet sky shone gray; and now for the first time both men saw, on the opposite shore, a covered wagon, and a little figure motionless beside it.

"I God," said the ferryman. "Reckon how long *they* ben awaitin!" Suddenly he became very busy with his line; he had to build sufficient momentum in crosspower to carry it past the middle of the stream, where the broadside current, at full strength, could lock both line and craft. Jay hurried to help. "Tsch right," the man called him off, too busy for courtesy. Jay quit. After a moment the man's hauling became more casual. He turned, enough to meet Jay's eye. "F'wrn't man enough to hanl that alone, wouldn't be man enough to hanl the job," he explained.

Jay nodded, and watched the expanding light.

"Hope tain't no trouble, brung ya up hyer sich an hour," the ferryman said.

Jay had realized his curiosity, and respected his silence, at the first, and so, although the question slightly altered this respect, he answered, somehow pleased to be able to communicate it to an agent at once so near his sympathies, and so impersonal: "My Paw. Took at the heart. Don't know yet how bad tis."

The man clacked his tongue like an old woman, shaking his head, and looking into the water. "That's a mean way," he said. Suddenly he looked Jay in the eyes: his own were strangely shy. Then he looked again into the brown water, and continued to haul at the line.

"Well, good luck," he said.

"Much obliged," said Jay.

The wagon grew larger and larger, and now the dark, deeply lined faces of the man and woman became distinct: the sad, deeply lined faces of the profound country which seemed ancient even in early maturity and which always gave Jay a sense of peace. The woman sat high above the mule; the flare of her deep bonnet had the shape of the flare of the wagon's canopy. The man stood beside his wagon, one clayed boot cocked on the clayed hub. They gazed gravely into the eyes of the men on the ferry, and neither of them moved, or made any sign of salutation, until the craft was made fast.

"Ben here long?" the ferryman asked.

The woman looked at him; after a moment the man, without moving his eyes, nodded.

"Didn't hear yer holler."

After a moment the man said, "I hollered."

The ferryman put out his lantern. He turned to Jay. "Twarn't rightly a dark crossing, mister. I can't charge ye but the daytime toll."

"All right," Jay said, giving him fifteen cents. "And much obliged to you." He put out his headlights and stooped to crank the car.

"Hold awn, bud," the wagoner called. Jay looked up; the man took two quick strides and took control of the mule's head. The wagoner nodded.

The engine was warm, and started easily; and though with every wrench of the crank a spasm of anguish wrenched the mule, once the engine leveled out the mule stood quietly, merely trembling. Jay put it violently into low to get up the steep mud bank, giving the mule and wagon as wide a berth as possible, nodding his regret of the racket and his friendliness as he passed; their heads turned, the eyes which followed him could not forgive him his noise. At the top he filled his pipe and watched while the mule and wagon descended, the mule held at the head, his hocks sprung uneasily, hoofs prodding and finding base in the treacherous clay, rump bunched high, the wagon tilting, the block-brakes screeching on the broad iron rim.

Poor damn devils, he thought. He was sure they were bound for the Knoxville market. They had probably waited for the ferry as much as a couple of hours. They would be hopelessly late.

He waited out the lovely sight of the water gaping. The ferry took on its peculiar squareness, its look of exquisite silence. He looked at his watch. Not so bad. He lighted his pipe and settled down to drive. He always felt different once he was across the river. This was the real, old, deep country, now. Home country. The cabins looked different to him, a little older and poorer and simpler, a little more homelike; the trees and rocks seemed to come differently out of the ground; the air smelled different. Before long now, he would know the worst; if it was the worst. Quite unconsciously he felt much more deeply at leisure as he watched the flowing, freshly lighted country; and quite unconsciously he drove a little faster than before.

Chapter 4

DURING THE REST OF THE NIGHT, Mary lay in a "white" sleep. She felt as odd, alone in the bed, as if a jaw-tooth had just been pulled, and the whole house seemed larger than it really was, hollow and resonant. The coming of daylight did not bring things back to normal, as she had hoped; the bed and the house, in this silence and pallor, seemed even emptier. She would doze a little, wake and listen to the dry silence, doze, wake again sharply, to the thing that troubled her. She thought of her husband, driving down on one of the most solemn errands of his life, and of his father, lying fatally sick, perhaps dying, perhaps dead at this moment (she crossed herself), and she could not bring herself to feel as deeply about it as she felt that she should, for her husband's sake. She realized that if the situation were reversed, and it was her own father who was dying, Jay would feel much as she felt now, and that she could not blame either him or herself, but that did her no good. For she knew that at the bottom of it the trouble was, simply, that she had never really liked the old man.

She was sure that she didn't look down on him, as many of Jay's relatives all but said to her face and as she feared that Jay himself occasionally believed; certainly not; but she could not like him, as almost everyone else liked him. She knew that if it was

47

Jay's mother who lay dying, there would be no question of her grief, or inadequacy to her husband; and that was a fair measure of how little she really cared for his father. She wondered why she liked him so little (for to say that she actually disliked him, she earnestly assured herself, would be putting it falsely). She realized that it was mainly because everyone forgave him so much, and liked him so well in spite of his shortcomings, and because he accepted their forgiveness and liking so casually, as if this were his natural due or, worse, as if he didn't even realize anything about it. And the worst of this, the thing she resented with enduring anger and distaste, was the burden he had constantly imposed on his wife, and her perfect patience with him, as if she didn't even know it was a burden or that he was taking advantage. It was this unconsciousness in both of them that she could not abide, and if only once Jay's mother had shown one spark of anger, of realization, Mary felt she might have begun to be able to like him. But this brought her into a resentment, almost a dislike, of Jay's mother, which she knew was both unjust and untrue to her actual feelings, and which made her uncomfortable; she was shocked also to realize that she was lying awake in the hour which might well be his last, to think ill of him. *Shame on you,* she said to herself, and thought earnestly of all that she knew was good about him.

He was generous for one thing. Generous to a fault. And she remembered how, time and again, he had given away, "loaned," to the first person who asked him the favor, money or food or things which were desperately needed home to keep body and soul together. Fault, indeed. Yet it was a good fault. It was no wonder people loved him—or pretended to—and took every possible advantage of him. And he was very genuinely kind-hearted. A wonderful virtue. And tolerant. She had never heard him say an unkind or a bitter word of anybody, not even of people who had outrageously abused his generosity—he could not, she realized, bear to believe that they really meant to; and he had never once, of that she was sure, joined with most of the others in their envious, hostile, contemptuous talking about her.

On the other hand she could be equally sure that he had never really stood up for her strongly and bravely, and angrily, against everyone, as his wife had, for he disliked arguments as much as he did unkindness; but she put that out of her mind. He had never, so far as she knew, complained, about his sickness or pain, or his poverty, and chronically, insanely, as he made excuses for others, he had never made excuses for himself. And certainly he had precious little right to complain, or make excuses; but that too she hastened to put out of her mind. She reproached herself by remembering how thoroughly nice and friendly he had always been to her; and if she had to realize that that was not at all for herself but purely because she was "Jay's woman," as he'd probably say, she certainly couldn't hold that against him; her own best feelings towards him came out of her recognition of him as Jay's father. You couldn't like anyone more than you happened to like them; you simply couldn't. And you couldn't feel more about them than that amount of liking made possible to you. There was a special kind of basic weakness about him; that was what she could not like, or respect, or even forgive, or resign herself to accepting, for it was a kind of weakness which took advantage, and heaped disadvantage and burden on others, and it was not even ashamed for itself, not even aware. And worse, at the bottom of it all, maybe, Jay's father was the one barrier between them, the one stubborn, unresolved, avoided thing, in their complete mutual understanding of Jay's people, his "background." Even now she could not really like him much, or feel deep concern. Her thoughts for him were grave and sad, but only as they would be for any old, tired, suffering human being who had lived long and whose end, it appeared, had come. And even while she thought of him her real mind was on his son's grief and her inadequacy to it. She had not even until this moment, she realized with dismay, given Jay's mother a thought; she had been absorbed wholly in

Jay. I must write her, she thought. But of course, perhaps, I'll see her soon.

And yet, clearly as she felt that she realized what the bereavement would mean to Jay's mother, and wrong as she was even to entertain such an idea, she could not help feeling that even more, his death would mean great relief and release. And, it occurred to her, he'll no longer stand between me and Jay.

At this, her soul stopped in utter coldness. God forgive me, she thought, amazed; I almost *wished* for his death!

She clasped her hands and stared at a stain on the ceiling.

O Lord, she prayed; forgive me my unspeakable sinful thought. Lord, cleanse my soul of such abominations. Lord, if it be Thy will, spare him long that I may learn to understand and care for him more, with Thy merciful help. Spare him not for me but for himself, Lord.

She closed her eyes.

Lord, open my heart that I may be worthy in realization of this sorrowful thing, if it must happen, and worthy and of use and comfort to others in their sorrow. Lord God, Lord Jesus, melt away my coldness and apathy of heart, descend and fill my emptiness of heart. And Lord, if it be Thy will, preserve him yet a while, and let me learn to bear my burden more lightly, or to know this burden is a blessing. And if he must be taken, if he is already with Thee now (she crossed herself), may he rest in Thy peace (again she crossed herself).

And Lord, if it be Thy will, that this sorrow must come upon my husband, then I most humbly beseech Thee in Thy mercy that through this tribulation Thou openest my husband's heart, and awake his dear soul, that he may find comfort in Thee that the world cannot give, and see Thee more clearly, and come to Thee. For there, Lord, as Thou knowest, and not in his poor father or my unworthy feelings, is the true, widening gulf between us.

Lord, in Thy mercy, Who can do all things, close this gulf.

Make us one in Thee as we are one in earthly wedlock. For Jesus' sake, Amen.

She lay somewhat comforted, but more profoundly disturbed than comforted. For she had never before so clearly put into words, into visible recognition, their religious difference, or the importance of the difference to her. And how important is it to him, she wondered. And haven't I terribly exaggerated my feeling of it? A "gulf"? And "widening"? Was it really? Certainly he never said anything that justified her in such a feeling; nor did she feel anything of that largeness. It really was only that both of them said so very little, as if both took care to say very little. But that was just it. That a thing which meant so much to her, so much more, all the time, should be a thing that they could not share, or could not be open about. Where her only close, true intimate was Aunt Hannah, and her chief love and hope had to rest in the children. That was it. That was the way it seemed bound to widen (she folded her hands, and shook her head, frowning): it was the children. She felt sure that he felt none of Andrew's anger and contempt, and none of her father's irony, but it was very clear by his special quietness, when instances of it came up, that he was very far away from it and from her, that he did not like it. He kept his distance, that was it. His distance, and some kind of dignity, which she respected in him, much as it hurt her, by this silence and withdrawal. And it would widen, oh, inevitably, because quiet and gentle as she would certainly try to be about it, they were going to be brought up as she knew she must bring them up, as Christian, Catholic children. And this was bound to come into the home, quite as much as in church. It was bound in some ways, unless he changed; it was bound in some important ways, try as hard and be as good about it as she was sure they both would, to set his children apart from him, to set his own wife apart from him. And not by any action or wish of his, but by her own deliberate will. Lord God, she prayed, in anguish. Am I wrong? Show me if I am wrong, I beseech Thee. Show me what I am to do.

But God showed her only what she knew already: that come what might she must, as a Christian woman, as a Catholic, bring up her children thoroughly and devoutly in the Faith, and that it was also her task, more than her husband's, that the family remain one, that the gulf be closed.

But if I do this, nothing else that I can do will close it, she reflected. Nothing, nothing, will avail.

But I must.

I must just: trust in God, she said, almost aloud. Just: do His will, and put all my trust in Him.

A streetcar passed; Catherine cried.

Chapter 5

"DADDY HAD TO GO up to see Grandfather Follet," their mother explained. "He says to kiss both of you for him and he'll probably see you before you're asleep tonight."

"When?" Rufus asked.

"Way, early this morning, before it was light."

"Why?"

"Grampa Follet is very sick. Uncle Ralph phoned up very late last night, when all of us were asleep. Grampa has had one of his attacks."

"What's attack?"

"Eat your cereal, Catherine. Rufus, eat yours. His heart. Like the one he had that time last fall. Only worse, Uncle Ralph says. He wanted very much to see Daddy, just as quick as Daddy could come."

"Why?"

"Because he loves Daddy and if . . . *Eat,* wicker, or it'll all be nasty and cold, and *then* you know how you hate to eat it. Because if Daddy didn't see him soon, Grampa might not get to see Daddy again."

"Why not?"

"Because Grampa is getting old, and when you get old, you

can be sick and not get well again. And if you can't get well again, then God lets you go to sleep and you can't see people any more."

"Don't you ever wake up again?"

"You wake up right away, in heaven, but people on earth can't see you any more, and you can't see them."

"Oh."

"Eat," their mother whispered, making a big, nodding mouth and chewing vigorously on air. They ate.

"Mama," Rufus said, "when Oliver went to sleep did he wake up in heaven too?"

"I don't know. I imagine he woke up in a part of heaven God keeps specially for cats."

"Did the rabbits wake up?"

"I'm sure they did if Oliver did."

"All bloody like they were?"

"No, Rufus, that was only their poor little bodies. God wouldn't let them wake up all hurt and bloody, poor things."

"Why did God let the dogs get in?"

"We don't know, Rufus, but it must be a part of His plan we will understand someday."

"What good would it do *Him?*"

"Children, don't dawdle. It's almost school time."

"What good would it do *Him,* Mama, to let the dogs in?"

"I don't know, but someday we'll understand, Rufus. If we're very patient. We mustn't trouble ourselves with these things we can't understand. We just have to be sure that God knows best."

"I bet they sneaked in when He wasn't looking," Rufus said eagerly. "Cause He sure wouldn't have let them if He'd been there. Didn't they, Mama? Didn't they?"

Their mother hesitated, and then said carefully, "No, Rufus, we believe that God is everywhere and knows everything and nothing can happen without His knowing. But the Devil is everywhere too—everywhere except Heaven, that is—and he is always tempting us. When we do what he tempts us to do, then God lets us do it."

"What's tempt?"

"Tempt is, well, the Devil tempts us when there is something we want to do, but we know it is bad."

"Why does God let us do bad things?"

"Because He wants us to make up our own minds."

"Even to do bad things, right under His nose?"

"He doesn't *want* us to do bad things, but to know good from bad and be good of our own free choice."

"Why?"

"Because He loves us and wants us to love Him, but if He just *made* us be good, we couldn't really love Him enough. You can't love to do what you are *made* to do, and you couldn't love God if He *made* you."

"But if God can do *anything,* why can't He do that?"

"Because He doesn't *want* to," their mother said, rather impatiently.

"Why *doesn't* He want to?" Rufus said. "It would be so much easier for Him."

"*God—doesn't—believe—in—the—easy—way,*" she said, with a certain triumph, spacing the words and giving them full emphasis. "Not for us, not for anything or anybody, not even for Himself. God wants us to *come* to Him, to *find* Him, the best we can."

"Like hide-and-go-seek," said Catherine.

"What was that?" their mother asked rather anxiously.

"Like hide . . ."

"Aw, it isn't a *bit* like hide-and-seek, *is* it, Mama?" Rufus cut in. "Hidenseek's just a *game,* just a *game.* God doesn't fool around playing *games, does* He, Mama! *Does* He! *Does* He!"

"*Shame on* you, Rufus," his mother said warmly, and not without relief. "Why, *shame on* you!" for Catherine's face had swollen and her mouth had bunched tight, and she glared from her brother to her mother and back again with scalding hot eyes.

"Well He *does*n't," Rufus insisted, angry and bewildered at the turn the discussion had taken.

"That's *enough,* Rufus," his mother whipped out sternly, and leaned across and patted Catherine's hand, which made Catherine's chin tremble and her tears overflow. "That's *all right,* little wicker! That's *all right!* He doesn't play games. Rufus is right about that, but it *is,* someways it *is* like hide-and-seek. You're ab-so-lootly *right!*"

But with this, Catherine was dissolved, and Rufus sat aghast, less at her crying, which made him angry and jealous, than at his sudden solitude. But her crying was so miserable that, angry and jealous as he was, he became ashamed, then sorry for her, and was trying, helplessly, to find a way of showing that he was sorry when his mother glanced up at him fiercely and said, "*Now you march* and get ready for school. I ought to tell Daddy, you're a *bad boy!*"

At the door, a few minutes later, when she leaned to kiss him good-bye and saw his face, she mistook the cause of it and said, more gently but very earnestly: "Rufus, I can see you're sorry, but you mustn't be mean to Catherine. She's just a little girl, your *little sister,* and you mustn't ever be unkind to her and hurt her feelings. Do you understand? *Do* you, Rufus?"

He nodded, and felt terribly sorry for his sister and for himself because of the gentleness in his mother's voice.

"Now you come back and tell her how sorry you are, and *hurry,* or you'll be late for school."

He came in shyly with his mother and came up to Catherine; her face was swollen and red and she looked at him bleakly.

"Rufus wants to tell you how sorry he is, Catherine, he hurt your feelings," their mother said.

Catherine looked at him, brutally and doubtfully.

"I *am* sorry, Catherine," he said. "Honest to goodness I am. Because you're a little, *little girl,* and . . ."

But with this Catherine exploded into a roar of angry tears, and brought both fists down into her plate, and Rufus, dumfounded, was hustled brusquely off to school.

Chapter 6

WHEN JAY FOUND how things were at the farm, he was angry at having been so grieved and alarmed; before long, he felt it had all happened very much as he had suspected. Ralph had just lost his head, as usual. Now he was very much ashamed of himself, though still very defensive, and everyone, including Jay, tried to assure him that he had done the right thing. Jay could imagine how much Ralph had needed to feel useful, to take charge. He couldn't think very well of him, but he was sorry for him. He felt he understood very well how it had happened.

Actually, he understood only a little about it, and Ralph understood very little more.

Late in the evening before, their father had suffered a much more severe and painful attack than any up to then. After no more than a few minutes, his wife had realized its terrible gravity, and had woken Thomas Oaks. Thomas had hurried across the hill and roused up Jessie and George Bailey and, without waiting for them, had hurried back, saddled the horse and whipped it as fast as it would go, into LaFollette. The doctor was out on a call; he left a message, and hurried on to Ralph's. Ralph was in a virtual panic of aroused responsibility the instant he heard the news. He asked if the doctor was there yet. Thomas told him; Ralph

57

realized that his mother had told Thomas to rush out the doctor even before he called her son to her side. He put it aside as an ungenerous and mean-spirited thought, yet it stayed, hurting him like a burr. He felt it was no time for resentments, though; not only he, but Sally as well, must come to their help, must be there (Sally'd never forgive me if she wasn't) if Paw was to die (she'd be the only wife there, of the only son; his mother would never forget that). He rushed back and told her what was happening as he hurried into his clothes, hurried two doors away, banged loudly on the Felts's door and apologized for the banging by explaining (his voice was already damp) that his Paw was at death's door if not already passed on, and he wouldn't have roused them only he knew they would be only too willing to help out so Sally could go too. They were very kind to him; Mrs. Felts arrived before Sally had finished fixing her hair. While she was doing so, Ralph sped across the street to his office, unlocked his desk, and took two choking swallows of whiskey in the dark. He rammed the bottle into his pocket and hurried down to start his car. They had been so quick that they overtook Thomas on his horse when he had scarcely passed the edge of town, going, as Ralph said to himself, his eyes low and cold above the steering wheel, "like sixty," anyhow as fast as it was safe to travel on these awful roads, perhaps a little faster, thinking of Barney Oldfield, in the Chalmers he had chosen because it was a better class of auto and a more expensive one than his brother's, a machine people made no smart jokes about. His first impulse, when he saw the horse and rider ahead, was to honk, both in self-advertisement, warning and greeting, but he remembered in time the seriousness of the occasion and did not do so, reflecting, after it was too late, that Thomas might feel he was snubbed, as if he had passed him in the street without speaking, and he was angry with Thomas for possibly having any such feeling about such petty matters, at such a time.

There were nearly two hours of helpless anguish and fright before the doctor arrived. During that time it is possible that

Ralph suffered more acutely than anyone else. For besides suffering, or believing that he suffered, all the pains that his father must be experiencing, and all of his mother's grief and anxiety, and all of the smaller emotions of all the smaller people who were present, he suffered deep humiliation. When he rushed in and swept his mother into his arms he felt that his voice and his whole manner were all that they ought to be; that he showed himself to be a man who, despite his own boundless grief, was capable also of boundless strength to sustain others in their grief, and to take complete charge of all that needed to be done. But even in that first embrace he could see that his mother was only by an effort concealing her desire to draw away from him. He came near her over and over again, hugging her, sobbing over her, fondling her, telling her that she must be brave, telling her she must not try to be brave, to lean on him, and cry her heart out for naturally at such a time she would want to feel her sons close around her; but every time, he felt that same patient stiffening and her voice perplexed him. Everyone in the room, even Ralph in the long run, knew that he was only making things harder for her; only his mother realized that he was beseeching comfort rather than bringing it. She was not in the least angry with him; she was sorry for him and wished that she could be of more help to him, but her mind was not on him, her heart was not with him, and his sobs and the stench of his breath made her a little sick at her stomach. What perplexed him in her voice was its remoteness. He began to realize that he was bringing her no comfort, that she was not leaning on him, that just as he had always feared, she did not really love him. He redoubled his efforts to soothe her and to be strong for her. The harder he tried, the more remote her voice became. At the end of a half hour her face was no less desperate than it had been when he first saw her. And he began to feel that everyone else was watching him, and knew he was no use, and that his mother did not love him. The women watched him one way, the men watched him another. He felt that his wife was thinking ill of him, that she was not even sorry for him; he felt slobbering and fat, the way she looked at him and suddenly with terrible hatred was sure that she would prefer to sleep with flat-bellied men—what man? *Any* man, so long as his belly don't get in the way. As for Jessie, he knew she had always hated him, as much as he hated her. And George Bailey just sitting there look-ing serious and barrel-chested and always being careful to look away when their eyes met: George thought he was twice the man that Ralph was and twice as good right at this time, better with his in-laws than Ralph could be with his own flesh and blood; and they all knew that George was twice the man and were just trying not to say it or think it even, or let Ralph know they thought it. And even Thomas Oaks, an ignorant hand, who couldn't even read or write, just setting there with his ropy hands hung between his knees, staring down at a knot in the floor with those washed-out blue eyes, even Tom was more of a man and more good use too. When Tom got up and said if there wasn't nothing he could do he reckoned he would get on up to the loft, but if there was anything, they would just let him know, Ralph understood it. He knew Tom might be ignorant but he wasn't so ignorant but he knew it was best to leave a family to itself; and when Ralph's mother said, "All right, Tom," Ralph heard more life and kind-ness, and more gratefulness in her voice, than in every word she'd said to him, the whole night; and as he watched Tom climb the ladder, heavily and quietly, rung by rung, he thought: there goes more of a man than I am, he knows how to take himself out of the way, and he thought: he's doing a power more good by going than I can by staying, and he thought: every soul in this room wishes it was me that was going, instead of him, and he called, in a voice which sounded unfriendly, though he had meant to make it sound friendly to everyone except Tom, "That's right, Tom get ye some sleep"; and Tom pulled his head back through the ceiling and looked down at him with those empty blue eyes and said, "That's all right, Mr. Ralph," and suddenly Ralph realized that he had no intention of sleeping and would be there alone, not sleeping a wink, just ready in case he was needed; and that Tom had seen his malice, his desire to belittle him, and had belittled him instead, before his mother and his wife and his dying father. "That's all right, Mr. Ralph." What's all right? What's all right? He wanted to yell it at him, "What's all right, you poor-white-trash son-of-a-bitch?" but he restrained himself.

Every time he felt their eyes on him especially strongly he went over to his mother again and hugged her, and held her head tightly against him, and tried to say things that would make her cry, and every time, her voice was a little bit further away from him and her face looked a little older and dryer, and every time, he was still more acutely aware of their eyes on him and of the thoughts behind their eyes, and every time, he would swing away from his mother as if he could bear to leave her uncomforted for a moment only because there were still more important things to do, matters of life and death, which he and only he, the son, the man of the family, now that poor Paw lay there so near to death, could handle. And every time, there was nothing whatever to do except wait for the doctor. They had already given the medicine the doctor had given them to give, and they had already given him so much of the ginseng tea the doctor had said wouldn't anyhow do any harm, that Ralph's mother decided they shouldn't give any more of it. His head was low; his feet were braced against hot stones wrapped in flannel, and Mother kept everyone except herself at the far, lighted end of the room, except for short visits. There was nothing to do, nothing to take charge of, and every time Ralph swung about from his mother with an air of heroic authority and rediscovered this fact, he felt as if a chair had been pulled out from under him, in front of everybody, and he began to think that he would burn up and die if he didn't have another drink. He said, "Scuse me," once in the choked and modest tone which should signify to the women that he had to empty his bladder, and he got a good, hard swig that time, and found when he came back in that he didn't care whether they were looking at him or not, or guessed what he really went out for; for two cents he'd take out the bottle and wave it at them. Sooner than it was possible to use that excuse again, he became even more thirsty than before. At the same time he first realized that he was drunk. He was bitterly ashamed of himself, drunk at this time, at his father's very deathbed, when his mother needed him so bad as never before, and when he knew, for he had learned by now to take people's word for it, that he was really good for nothing when he was drunk. And then to feel so thirsty on top of that. He braced himself with all the sternness and strength he was capable of. By God, he told himself, you'll pull yourself together. By God, or . . . By God, you will. You will. And he got up abruptly and walked straight through them into the dark, and splashed his face and neck with water. He realized then that he could take another, now. Just a little one. To brace him. He cursed himself and splashed his face again, and dried carefully with his handkerchief before he came back in. He realized that to everyone else in the room, those two silences meant two more drinks. He made a cynical grimace. By God, *he* knew better! He felt as if he had great physical strength, and in his feeling of strength his thirst was merely like the bite under a punch bar, a pleasure to feel and to brace against. But within a short while the thirst returned even more fiercely as irresistible pain. No, by God, he said again to himself. But he began to wonder. If they thought he'd had one anyhow—two in fact—why in a way he owed himself a couple. Three, for that matter: a third, because he knew they mistook that cynical face he had made for a drunken shamelessness. After all, it wasn't *he* who didn't want to be drunk. He was being careful for *their* sake. And by God, if he was going to get blamed for it anyhow, what was the good of that. Besides, when he really took care he knew he could hold his liquor good as the next man. He'd show them. But it wasn't so easy, figuring how to get out. Can't go out to pee so soon. Nor dipper of water. He felt a sudden terrible excess of shame. No, *by God,* he wouldn't sit there scheming himself a shot over his own dying father, and his mother looking on at him, knowing his mind, not saying a word. By *God,* he wouldn't! He set himself to put everything out of his mind except his father, not as he had ever feared him, or wished he approved of him, or wished he was dead, but as he lay there now, old and broken, cast aside near the end of the trail, yes sir, the embers fading; and within a short while he was sobbing, and talking of his father through his sobs, and within a short while more he began to realize that he had found his way out. His struggles against this temptation, his iterations of *"I'm* no good," and, "I'm the son he set least store by, but I'm the one that cares for him the most," and the voices of the women, soothing him, trying to quiet him, only added to his tears, the richness of his emotions, and his verbosity, and before long he had realized that this too was useful, and was using it. Toward the end all genuine emotion left him and he had to scrape, tickle and torture himself into sufficient feeling and sufficient evidence of an impending breakdown he would inflict on nobody, but at length he felt he had achieved the proper moment, and rushed headlong from the room, all but upsetting his wife in her rocking chair. The instant he was outside he felt nothing in the world except the ferocity of his thirst. He leaned against the cabin wall, uncorked the bottle, wrapped his mouth over its mouth as ravenously as a famished baby takes the nipple, and tilted straight up.

NNHhhh; with a sobbing groan he struck his temple against the side of the house so violently that he could scarcely keep his feet, flung the bottle as far from him as he was able. *"Oh, God! God! God! God!"* he moaned, the tears itching on his cheeks. *Fool! Fool! Fool! Why* hadn't he made sure before he left the office? There couldn't have been more than a half a dram left.

He dabbed at his head with his handkerchief and stole leaning into the path of the lamplight. Blood, all right. He felt sick at his stomach. He dabbed again. Not much. He dabbed again;

again. Not running, anyhow. He took a deep breath and went back into the room.

"Stumbled," he said. "Tain't nothin."

But even so, Sally came over, and his mother came over, and they both looked carefully, pretending that it was perfectly natural to stumble in a flat clay dooryard, and when they agreed that it was a mean lump but needed no further attention, he felt, suddenly, sad, and as little as a child, and he wished he were.

His rage and despair and the shock of the blow had so quieted and sobered him that now he was beyond even self-hatred. He felt gentle and clear. The sadness grew and became all but insupportable, and for the first time that evening, one of the few times in his life, he began to see things more or less as they were. Yes, over on the bed beyond the carefully shaded lamp, moaning occasionally, his breathing so shaken and irregular that it was as if sorrow disordered it rather than death, his father, his own father, was indeed coming near his last hour; and his mother, his own mother, sat there as quiet and patient, and so strong. There was not likely anyone in the world enough stronger that she could find comforting him. And he? Yes, he was here, for what little good that was, and he was the only son who was here. But there was no special virtue in that; he was the only son who lived near enough at hand. And he lived so near at hand because he had no courage, no intelligence, no energy, no independence. That was really it: no independence. He always needed to be near. He always needed to feel their support, their company, very near him. He always lived almost from day to day in the hope that by staying near, by always being on hand if he was needed, by always showing how much he loved them, he might at last be sure he had won their approval, their respect. He did not believe, he couldn't remember, one sober breath he had ever drawn, that he had drawn as if in his own right, feeling, I don't care what anybody thinks of me, this is myself and this is how *I* do it. Everything he did, every tone his voice took, was controlled by his idea of what would make the best impression on others. He was worse a slave to that, to his dread for other people's opinion of him, than any nigger had ever been a slave. And his meanness and recklessness when he was drunk enough, he knew that was no good, no good at all. It wasn't even real. It was just the way he wished he was, and it wasn't even that, for what he wished was not to be reckless, but brave, a very different thing, and not to be mean but proud, a different thing too. And what was the worst of it? Why, the worst of it was, that once in a great while he could see himself for what he really was, and almost believe that now that he saw himself so clearly, he could change, all it took was clearness of head, and patience, and courage; and at the same time he had to know that nothing that was in him to do about it could ever be done; that he would never change, except for the worse; that he had no kind of clearness of head, or patience, or courage, that would last beyond the little it took (and even that was enough to make him shiver all over), to just be able, once in ever so long a time, to sit and look at himself for what he really was. He was just weak: he saw that, clear enough. Just no good. He saw that. Just incomplete some way, like a chicken that comes out of the shell with a wry neck and grows on up like that. Like his own poor little Jim-Wilson, that already showed the weakness, with his poor little washed-out eyes, his clinging to Sally, his terror of his father when his father was drunk or even teased him, his readiness to cry. I ought not ever to have fathered children, Ralph thought. I ought not ever to have been born.

And looking at himself now, he neither despised himself nor felt pity for himself, nor blamed others for whatever they might feel about him. He knew that they probably didn't think the incredibly mean, contemptuous things of him that he was apt to imagine they did. He knew that he couldn't ever really know what they thought, that his extreme quickness to think that he knew was just another of his dreams. He was sure, though, that whatever they might think, it couldn't be very good, because there wasn't any very good thing to think of. But he felt that whatever they thought, they were just, as he was almost never just. He knew he was wrong about his mother. He had no doubt whatever, just now, that she really did love him, had never stopped loving him, and never would. He knew even that she was especially gentle to him, that she loved him in a way she loved nobody else. And he knew why he so often felt that she did not really love him. It was because she was so sorry for him, and because she had never had and never possibly could have, any respect for him. And it was respect he needed, infinitely more than love. Just not to have to worry about whether people respect you. Not ever to have to feel that people are being nice to you because they are sorry for you, or afraid of you. He looked at Sally. Poor girl. Afraid of me. That's Sally. And it is all my own fault. Every bit mine. And I hate her for wanting other men, when I know that unfaithfulness never once came into her head, and when I'm the worst tail-chaser in LaFollette and half of the town knows it, and Sally knows it too, and is too gentlehearted and too scared ever to reproach me with it. And sure I ought to be able to do something about that, at least about that. Any *man* could. Only I'm no man. So how can I expect that people can ever look up to me, or at least not look down on me? People are fair to me and more than fair. More than fair, if ever they knew me for what I really am.

And here tonight it comes like a test, like a trial, one of the times in a man's life when he is needed, and can be some good, just by being a man. But I'm not a man. I'm a baby. Ralph is the baby. Ralph is the baby.

Chapter 7

HANNAH LYNCH DECIDED, that day, that she would go shopping and that if Rufus wanted to go, she would like to take him with her. She telephoned Rufus' mother to ask whether she had other plans for Rufus that would interfere, and Mary said no; she asked whether so far as Mary knew, Rufus had planned to do anything else, and Mary, a little surprised, said no, not as far as she knew, and whether he had or not, she was sure he would be glad to go shopping with her. Hannah, in a flicker of anger, was tempted to tell her not to make up children's minds for them, but held onto herself and said, instead, well, we'll see, and that she would be up by the time he came back from school. Mary urgently replied that she mustn't come up—much as she would like to see her, of course—but that Rufus would make the trip instead. Hannah, deciding not to make an issue of it, said very well, she would be waiting, but he wasn't to come unless he really wanted to. Mary said warmly that of course he would want to and Hannah again replied, more coolly, "We'll see; it's no matter"; and, getting off the subject, asked, "Have you had any message from Jay?"

For Mary had telephoned her father, that morning, to explain why Jay could not be at the office. "No," Mary said, with slight

67

defensiveness, for she felt somehow that criticism might be involved; and hadn't expected to unless, of course . . .

"Of course," Hannah replied quickly (for she had intended no criticism), "so no doubt we needn't worry."

"No, I'm sure he would have called if his father had—even if there was any grave *danger,"* Mary said.

"Of course he would," Hannah replied. Was there anything she could bring Mary? Let's see, Mary said a little vaguely; why; aah; and she realized that Catherine could well use a new underwaist and that—and—but suddenly recalled, also, that it was sometimes difficult to persuade her aunt to accept money, or even to render account, for things she bought this way; and lied, with some embarrassment, why, no, thank you so much, it's very stupid of me but I just can't think of a thing. All right, Hannah said, honoring her embarrassment, and resolved to take care to embarrass her less often (but after all, *little gifts* should be possible from time to time without this silly pride); all right; I'll be waiting, till three, and if Rufus has other things to do, just let me know. All right, Aunt Hannah, and it's so nice of you to think of him. Not a bit of it, I *like* to take him shopping. Well that's very nice and I'm sure *he* likes it. Perhaps so. Why *certainly* so, Aunt Hannah. All right. All right; *good*-bye. You'll let us know if you *do* hear from Jay? Of course. Right away. But by now I don't really expect to. He'll very likely be back by supper time, or a little after. He was sure he could—if—everything was, well, relatively all right. All right. All right; *good*-bye. Good-bye. Good-bye, Mary's voice trailed, gently.

"Jay?" Andrew called over the banisters.

"No, just talking to Mary," Hannah said. "I guess it can't be so very serious, after all."

"Let's hope not," said Andrew, and went back to his painting.

Hannah made herself ready for town. When Rufus arrived, all out of breath, he found her on a hard little couch in the living room, sitting carefully, not to rumple her long white-speckled black dress, and poring gravely through an issue of *The Nation* which she held a finger length before her thick glasses.

"Well," she smiled, putting the magazine immediately aside. "You're very prompt" (he was not; his mother had required him to wash and change his clothes) "and" (peering at him closely as he hurried up) "you look very nice. But you're all out of breath. Would you really like to come?"

"Oh, yes," he said, with a trace of falseness, for he had been warned to convince her; "I'm *very glad* to come, Aunt Hannah, and thank you very much for thinking of me."

"Huh . . ." she said, for she knew direct quotation when she heard it, but she was also convinced that in spite of the false words, he really meant it. "That's very nice," she said. "Very well; let's be on our way." She took her hard, plain black straw hat from its place on the sofa beside her and Rufus followed her to the mirror in the dark hallway and watched her careful planting of the hat pin. "Dark as the inside of a cow," she muttered, almost nosing the somber mirror, "as your grandfather would say." Rufus tried to imagine what it would be like, inside a cow. It would certainly be dark, but then it would be dark inside anybody or anything, so why a cow? Grandma came prowling dim-sightedly up the hallway from the dining room, smiling fixedly, even though she fancied she was alone, and the little boy and his great-aunt drew quickly aside, but even so, she collided, and gasped.

"Hello, Grandma, it's me," Rufus shrilled, and his aunt Hannah leaned close across her to her good ear at the same moment and said loudly, "Catherine, hello; it's only Rufus and I"; and as they spoke each laid a reassuring hand on her; and upstairs Rufus heard Andrew bite out, "Oh, *G-godd*"; but his grandmother, used to such frights, quickly recovered, laughed her tinkling ladylike laugh (which was beginning faintly to crack) very sportingly, and cried, "Goodness gracious, how you startled me!" and laughed again. "And there's little *Rufus!*" she smiled, leaning deeply towards him with damaged, merry eyes and playfully patting his cheek.

"So you're ready to go!" she said brightly to Hannah.

Hannah nodded conspicuously and leaning again close across her to get at her good ear, cried, "Yes; all ready!"

"Have a nice time," Grandma said, "and give Grandma a good hug," and she hugged him close, saying, "Mum-*mum;* nice little boy," and vigorously slapping his back.

"Good-bye," they shouted.

"*Good*-bye," she beamed, following them to the door.

They took the streetcar and got out at Gay Street. There was no flurry and no dawdling as there would have been with any other woman Rufus knew; none of the ceremony that held his grandmother's shopping habits in a kind of stiff embroidery; none of the hurrying, sheepish refusal to be judicious in which men shopped. Hannah steered her way through the vigorous sidewalk traffic and along the dense, numerous aisles of the stores with quiet exhilaration. Shopping had never lost its charm for her. She prepared her mind and her disposition for it as carefully as she dressed for it, and Rufus had seldom seen her forced to consult a shopping list, even if she were doing intricate errands for others. Her personal tastes were almost as frugal as her needs; hooks and eyes, lengths of black tape and white tape, snappers so tiny it was difficult to handle them, narrow lace, a few yards, sometimes, of black or white cotton cloth, and now and then two pairs of black cotton stockings. But she loved to do more luxurious errands for others, and even when there were no such errands, she would examine a rich variety of merchandise she had no intention of buying, always skillful, in these examinations, never to disturb a clerk, and never to leave disturbed anything that she touched, imposing her weak eyes as intently as a jeweler with his glass and emitting little expletives of irony or admiration. Whenever she did have a purchase to make, she got hold of a clerk and conducted the whole transaction with a graceful efficiency which had already inspired in Rufus a certain contempt for every other woman he had seen shopping. Rufus, meanwhile, paid relatively little attention to what she was saying or buying; words passed above him, merely decorating the world he stared at with as much fascination as his aunt's; and best of all were the clashing, banging wire baskets which hastened along on little trolleys, high over them all, bearing to and fro wrapped and unwrapped merchandise, and hard leather cylinders full of money. Taken shopping with anyone else, Rufus suffered extreme boredom, but Hannah shopped much as a real lover of painting visits a gallery; and her pleasure clarified Rufus' eyes and held the whole merchant world in a clean focus of delight. If his mother or his grandmother was shopping, the tape which hung around the saleswoman's neck and the carbon pad in which she recorded purchases seemed twitchy and clumsy to Rufus; but in his great-aunt's company, the tape and pad were instruments of fascination and skill, and the housewives who ordinarily made the air of the stores heavy with fret and foolishness were like a challenging sea, instead, which his aunt navigated most deftly. She did not talk to him too much, nor did she worry over him, nor was Rufus disposed to wander beyond the range of her weak sight, for he enjoyed her company, and of all grown people she was the most considerate. She would remember, every ten minutes or so, to inquire courteously whether he was tired, but he was seldom tired in her company; with her, he never felt embarrassment in saying he had to go to the bathroom, for she never seemed annoyed, but in consequence he seldom found it necessary to go when they came together on these downtown trips. Today Hannah bought a few of the simplest things for herself and several more elaborate things for her sister-in-law and a beautifully transparent, flowered scarf for Mary's birthday, taking Rufus into this surprise; then, in the art store, she inquired whether the *Grammar of Ornament* had arrived. But when they showed her the enormous and magnificently colored volume, she exclaimed with laughter, "Mercy, that is no grammar; it's a whole encyclopedia," and the clerk laughed politely, and she said she was afraid it was larger than she could carry; she would like to have it delivered. She must be sure, though, that it was delivered personally to her, no later than May twenty-first, that's three days, can I be sure of that? No, she interrupted herself, in one of her rare confusions or changes of decision, that won't do. She explained to Rufus, parenthetically, "Suppose there was an accident, and your Uncle Andrew saw it too soon!" She paused. "Do you think you can help me with a few more of these bundles?" she asked him. He replied proudly that of course he could. "Then we'll take it now," his aunt told the clerk, and after careful testing and distribution of the various bundles, they came back into the street. And there his Aunt Hannah made a proposal which astounded Rufus with gratitude. She turned to him and said, "And now if you'd like it, I'd like to give you a cap."

He was tongue-tied; he felt himself blush. His aunt could not quite see the blush but his silence disconcerted her, for she had believed that this would make him really happy. Annoyed with herself, she nevertheless could not help feeling a little hurt.

"Or is there something else you'd rather have?" she asked, her voice a little too gentle.

He felt a great dilation in his chest. *"Oh, no!"* he exclaimed with passion. *"Oh, no!"*

"Very well then, let's see what we can do about it," she said, more than reassured; and suddenly she suspected in something like its full magnitude the long, careless denial, and the importance of the cap to the child. She wondered whether he would speak of it—would try, in any cowardly or goody-goody way, to be "truthful" about his mother's distaste for the idea (though she supposed he *ought* to be—truthful, that is); or, better, whether he could imagine, and try to warn her that in buying it for him, she risked displeasing his mother; and realized, then, that she must take care not to set him against his mother. She waited with some curiosity for what he might say, and when he found no words, said, "Don't worry about Mar—about your mother. I'm sure if she knew you *really* wanted it, you would have had it long ago."

He just made a polite, embarrassed little noise and she realized, with regret, that she did not know how to manage it properly. But she was certainly not going, on that account, to deny what she had offered; she compressed her lips and, by unaccountable brilliance of intuition went straight past Miller's, a profoundly matronly store in which Rufus' mother always bought the best clothes which were always, at best, his own second choice, and steered round to Market Street and into Harbison's, which sold clothing exclusively for men and boys, and was regarded by his mother, Rufus had overhead, as "tough" and "sporty" and "vulgar." And it was indeed a world most alien to women; not very pleasant men turned to stare at this spinster with the radiant, appalled little boy in tow; but she was too blind to understand their glances and, sailing up to the nearest man who seemed to be a clerk (he wore no hat) asked briskly, without embarrassment, "Where do I go, please, to find a cap for my nephew?" And the man, abashed into courtesy, found a clerk for her, and the clerk conducted them to the dark rear of the store. "Well, just see what you like," said Aunt Hannah; and still again, the child was astonished. He submitted so painfully conservative a choice, the first time, that she smelled the fear and hypocrisy behind it, and said carefully, "That is very nice, but suppose we look at some more, first." She saw the genteel dark serge, with the all but invisible visor, which she was sure would please Mary most, but she doubted whether she would speak of it; and once Rufus felt that she really meant not to interfere, his tastes surprised her. He tried still to be careful, more out of courtesy, she felt, than meeching, but it was clear to her that his heart was set on a thunderous fleecy check in jade green, canary yellow, black and white, which stuck out inches to either side above his ears and had a great scoop of visor beneath which his face was all but lost. It was a cap, she reflected, which even a colored sport might think a little loud, and she was painfully tempted to interfere. Mary would have conniption fits; Jay wouldn't mind, but she was afraid for Rufus' sake that he would laugh; even the boys in the block, she was afraid,

73

might easily sneer at it rather than admire it—all the more, she realized sourly, if they *did* admire it. It was going to cause no end of trouble, and the poor child might soon be sorry about it himself. But she was switched if she was going to boss him! "That's very nice," she said as little drily as she could manage. "But think about it, Rufus. You'll be wearing it a long time, you know, with all sorts of clothes." But it was impossible for him to think about anything except the cap; he could even imagine how tough it was going to look after it had been kicked around a little. "You're very sure you like it," Aunt Hannah said.

"Oh, yes," said Rufus.

"Better than this one?" Hannah indicated the discreet serge.

"Oh, yes," said Rufus, scarcely hearing her.

"Or this one?" she said, holding up a sharp little checkerboard.

"I think I like it best of all," Rufus said.

"Very well, you shall have it," said Aunt Hannah, turning to the cool clerk.

Walking in darkness, he saw the window. Curtains, a tall, cloven wave, towered almost to the floor. Transparent, manifold, scalloped along their inward edges like the valves of a sea creature, they moved delectably on the air of the open window.

Where they were touched by the carbon light of the street lamp, they were as white as sugar. The extravagant foliage which had been wrought into them by machinery showed even more sharply white where the light touched, and elsewhere was black in the limp cloth.

The light put the shadows of moving leaves against the curtains, which moved with the moving curtains and upon the bare glass between the curtains.

Where the light touched the leaves they seemed to burn, a bitter green. Elsewhere they were darkest gray and darker. Beneath each of these thousands of closely assembled leaves dwelt either no natural light or richest darkness. Without touching each other these leaves were stirred as, silently, the whole tree moved in its sleep.

Directly opposite his window was another. Behind this open window, too, were curtains which moved and against them moved the scattered shadows of other leaves. Beyond these curtains and beyond the bare glass between, the room was as dark as his own.

He heard the summer night.

All the air vibrated like a fading bell with the latest exhausted screaming of locusts. Couplings clashed and conjoined; a switch engine breathed heavily. An auto engine bore behind the edge of audibility the furious expletives of its incompetence. Hooves broached, along the hollow street, the lackadaisical rhythms of the weariest of clog dancers, and endless in circles, narrow iron tires grinced continuously after. Along the sidewalks, with incisive heels and leathery shuffle, young men and women advanced, retreated.

A rocking chair betrayed reiterate strain, as of a defective lung; like a single note from a stupendous jew's-harp, the chain of a porch swing twanged.

Somewhere very near, intimate to some damp inch of the grass between these homes, a cricket peeped, and was answered as if by his echo.

Humbled beneath the triumphant cries of children, which tore the whole darkness like streams of fire, the voices of men and women on their porches rubbed cheerfully against each other, and in the room next his own, like the laboring upward of laden windlasses and the mildest pouring out of fresh water, he heard the voices of men and women who were familiar to him. They groaned, rewarded; lifted, and spilled out: and watching the windows, listening at the heart of the proud bell of darkness, he lay in perfect peace.

Gentle, gentle dark.

My darkness. Do you listen? Oh, are you hollowed, all one taking ear?

My darkness. Do you watch me? Oh, are you rounded, all one guardian eye?

Oh gentlest dark. Gentlest, gentlest night. My darkness. My dear darkness.

Under your shelter all things come and go.

Children are violent and valiant, they run and they shout like the winners of impossible victories, but before long now, even like me, they will be brought into their sleep.

Those who are grown great talk with confidence and are at all times skillful to serve and to protect, but before long now they too, before long, even like me, will be taken in and put to bed.

Soon came those hours when no one wakes. Even the locusts, even the crickets, silent shall be, as frozen brooks

In your great sheltering.

I hear my father; I need never fear.

I hear my mother; I shall never be lonely, or want for love.

When I am hungry it is they who provide for me; when I am in dismay, it is they who fill me with comfort.

When I am astonished or bewildered, it is they who make the weak ground firm beneath my soul: it is in them that I put my trust.

When I am sick it is they who send for the doctor; when I am well and happy, it is in their eyes that I know best that I am loved; and it is towards the shining of their smiles that I lift up my heart and in their laughter that I know my best delight.

I hear my father and my mother and they are my giants, my king and my queen, beside whom there are no others so wise or worthy or honorable or brave or beautiful in this world.

I need never fear: nor ever shall I lack for loving-kindness.

And those also who talk with them in that room beneath whose door and light lies like a guardian slave, a bar of gold, my witty uncle, and my girlish aunt: I have yet to know them well, but they and my father and my mother are all fond of each other, and I like them, and I know that they like me.

I hear the easy chiming of their talk and their laughter.

But before long now they too will leave and the house will become almost silent and before long the darkness, for all its leniency, will take my father and my mother and will bring them, even as I have been brought, to bed and to sleep.

You come to us once each day and never a day rises into brightness but you stand behind it; you are upon us, you overwhelm us, all of each night. It is you who release from work, who bring parted families and friends together, and people for a little while are calm and free, and all at ease together; but before long, before long, all are brought down silent and motionless.

Under your sheltering, your great sheltering, darkness.

And all through that silence you walk as if none but you had ever breathed, had ever dreamed, had ever been.

My darkness, are you lonely?

Only listen, and I will listen to you.

Only watch me, and I will watch into your eyes.

Only know that I am awake and aware of you, only be my friend, and I will be your friend.

You need not ever fear; or ever be lonely; or want for love.

Tell me your secrets; you can trust me.

Come near. Come very near.

Darkness indeed came near. It buried its eye against the eye of the child's own soul, saying:

Had ever breathed, had ever dreamed, had ever been.

And somewhat as in blind night, on a mild sea, a sailor may be made aware of an iceberg, fanged and mortal, bearing invisibly near, by the unwarned charm of its breath, nothingness now revealed itself: that permanent night upon which the stars in their expiring

generations are less than the glinting of gnats, and nebulae, more triv-
ial than winter breath; that darkness in which eternity lies bent and
pale, a dead snake in a jar, and infinity is the sparkling of a wren
blown out to sea; that inconceivable chasm of invulnerable silence in
which cataclysms of galaxies rave mute as amber.

Darkness said:

When is the meeting, child, where are we, who are you, child,
who are you, do you know who you are, do you know who you are,
child; are you?

He knew that he would never know, though memory, almost captured, unrecapturable, unbearably tormented him. That this little boy
whom he inhabited was only the cruelest of deceits. That he was but
the nothingness of nothingness, condemned by some betrayal, condemned to be aware of nothingness. That yet in that desolation, he was
not without companions. For featureless on the abyss, invincible,
moved monstrous intuitions. And from the depth and wide throat of
eternity burned the cold, delirious chuckle of rare monsters beyond
rare monsters, cruelty beyond cruelty.

Darkness said:

Under my sheltering: in my great sheltering.

In the corner, not quite possible to detach from the darkness, a
creature increased, which watched him.

Darkness said:

You hear the man you call your father: how can you ever fear?

Under the washstand, carefully, something moved.

You hear the woman who thinks you are her child.

Beneath his prostrate head, eternity opened.

Hear how he laughs at you; in what amusement she agrees.

The curtain sighed as powers unspeakable passed through it.

Darkness purred with delight and said:

What is this change your eye betrays?

Only a moment ago, I was your friend, or so you claimed; why
this sudden loss of love?

Only a moment ago you were all eagerness to know my secrets;
where is your hunger now?

Only be steadfast: for now, my dear, my darling, the moment comes when hunger and love will be forever satisfied.

And darkness, smiling, leaned ever more intimately inward upon him, laid open the huge, ragged mouth—

Ahhhhh . . . !

Child, child, why do you betray me so?
Come near. Come very near.

Ohhhhhh . . . !

Must *you be naughty? It would grieve me terribly to have to force you.*

You know that you can never get away: you don't even want to get away.

But with that, the child was torn into two creatures, of whom one cried out for his father.

The shadows lay where they belonged, and he lay shaken in his tears. He saw the window; waited.

Still the cricket struck his chisel; the voices persisted, placid as bran.

But behind his head, in that tall shadow which his eyes could never reach, who could dare dream what abode its moment?

The voices chafed, untroubled: grumble and babble.

He cried out again more fiercely for his father.

There seemed a hollowing in the voices, as if they crossed a high trestle.

Serenely the curtain dilated, serenely failed.

The shadows lay where they belonged, but strain as he might, he could not descry what lay in the darkest of them.

The voices relaxed into their original heartlessness.

He swiftly turned his head and stared through the bars at the head of the crib. He could not see what stood there. He swiftly turned again.

Whatever it might be had dodged, yet more swiftly: stood once more, still, forever, beyond and behind his hope of seeing.

He saw the basin and that was only itself; but its eye was wicked ice.

Even the sugar curtains were evil, a senselessly fumbling mouth; and the leaves, wavering, stifled their tree like an infestation.

Near the window, a stain on the wallpaper, pale brown, a serpent shape.

Deadly, the opposite window returned his staring.

The cricket cherished what avaricious secret: patiently sculptured what effigy of dread?

The voices buzzed, pleased and oblivious as locusts. They cared nothing for him.

He screamed for his father.

And now the voices changed. He heard his father draw a deep breath and lock it against his palate, then let it out harshly against the bones of his nose in a long snort of annoyance. He heard the Morris chair creak as his father stood up and he heard sounds from his mother which meant that she was disturbed by his annoyance and that she would see to him, Jay; his uncle and his aunt made quick, small, attendant noises and took no further part in the discussion and his father's voice, somewhat less unkind than the snort and the way he had gotten from his chair but still annoyed, saying, "No, he hollered for me, I'll see to him"; and heard his mastering, tired approach. He was afraid, for he was no longer deeply frightened; he was grateful for the evidence of tears.

The room opened full of gold, his father stooped through the door and closed it quietly; came quietly to the crib. His face was kind.

"Wuzza matter?" he asked, teasing gently, his voice at its deepest.

"Daddy," the child said thinly. He sucked the phlegm from his nose and swallowed it.

His voice raised a little. "Why, what's the trouble with my little boy," he said and fumbled and got out his handkerchief. "What's the trouble! What's *he* crine *about!*" *The harsh cloth smelt of tobacco; with his fingertips, his father removed crumbs of tobacco from the child's damp face.*

"*Blow,*" *he said.* "*You know your mamma don't like you to swallah that stuff.*" *He felt the hand strong beneath his head and a sob overtook him as he blew.*

"*Why, what's wrong?*" *his father exclaimed; and now his voice was entirely kind. He lifted the child's head a little more, knelt and looked carefully into his eyes; the child felt the strength of the other hand, covering his chest, patting gently. He endeavored to make a little more of his sobbing than came out, but the moment had departed.*

"*Bad dream?*"

He shook his head, no.

"*Then what's the trouble?*"

He looked at his father.

"*Feared a—fraid of the dark?*"

He nodded; he felt tears on his eyes.

"*Noooooooo,*" *his father said, pronouncing it like* do. "*You're a* big *boy now. Big* boys don't get skeered of a little dark. *Big* boys don't *cry. Where's the dark that skeered you? Is it over here?*" *With his head he indicated the darkest corner. The child nodded. He strode over, struck a match on the seat of his pants.*

Nothing there.

"*Nothing there that oughtn't to be. . . . Under here?*" *He indicated the bureau. The child nodded, and began to suck at his lower lip. He struck another match, and held it under the bureau, then under the washstand.*

Nothing there. There either.

"*Nothing there but an old piece of baby-soap. See?*" *He held the soap close where the child could smell it; it made him feel much younger. He nodded.* "*Any place else?*"

The child turned and looked through the head of the crib; his father struck a match. "*Why, there's poor ole Jackie,*" *he said. And sure enough, there he was, deep in the corner.*

He blew dust from the cloth dog and offered it to the child. "You want Jackie?"

He shook his head.

"You don't want poor little ole Jackie? So lonesome? Alayin back there in the corner all this time?"

He shook his head.

"Gettin too big for Jackie?"

He nodded, uncertain that his father would believe him.

"Then you're gettin too big to cry."

Poor ole Jackie.

"Pore ole Jackie."

"Pore little ole Jackie, so lonesome."

He reached up for him and took him, and faintly recalled, as he gave him comfort, a multitude of fire-tipped candles (and bristling needles) and a strong green smell, a dog more gaily colored and much larger, over which he puzzled, and his father's huge face, smiling, saying, "It's a dog." His father too remembered how he had picked out the dog with great pleasure and had given it too soon, and here it was now too late. Comforting gave him comfort and a deep yawn, taking him by surprise, was half out of him before he could try to hide it. He glanced anxiously at his father.

"Gettin sleepy, uh?" his father said; it was hardly even a question.

He shook his head.

"Time you did. Time we all got to sleep."

He shook his head.

"You're not skeered any more are you?"

He considered lying, and shook his head.

"Boogee man, all gone, scared away, huh?"

He nodded.

"Now go on to sleep then, son," his father said. He saw that the child very badly did not want him to go away, and realized suddenly that he might have lied about being scared, and he was touched, and put his hand on his son's forehead. "You just don't want to be lonesome," he said tenderly, "just like little ole Jackie. You just don't want to be left alone." The child lay still.

"*Tell you what I'll do,*" *his father said,* "*I'll sing you one song, and then you be a good boy and go on to sleep. Will you do that?*" *The child pressed his forehead upward against the strong warm hand and nodded.*

"*What'll we sing?*" *his father asked.*

"*Froggy would a wooin go,*" *said the child; it was the longest.*

"*At's a long one,*" *his father said,* "*at's a long old song. You won't ever be awake that long, will you?*"

He nodded.

"*Ah* right," *said his father; and the child took a fresh hold on Jackie and settled back looking up at him. He sang very low and very quietly:* Frog he would a wooin' go uh-hooooo!, Frog he would go wooin' go uh-*hooooo, uh-hooooooo, and all about the courting-clothes the frog wore, and about the difficulties and ultimate success of the courtship and what several of the neighbors said and who the preacher would be and what he said about the match, uhhoooo, and finally, what will the weddin supper be uhooooo, catfish balls and sassafras tea uh-hoooo, while he gazed at the wall and the child gazed up into his eyes which did not look at him and into the singing face in the dark. Every couple of verses or so the father glanced down, but the child's eyes were as darkly and steadfastly open at the end of the long song as at the beginning, though it was beginning to be an effort for him.*

He was amused and pleased. Once he got started singing, he always loved to sing. There were ever so many of the old songs that he knew, which he liked best, and also some of the popular songs; and although he would have been embarrassed if he had been made conscious of it, he also enjoyed the sound of his own voice. "*Ain't you asleep yet?*" *he said, but even the child felt there was no danger of his leaving, and shook his head quite frankly.*

"*Sing gallon,*" *he said, for he liked the amusement he knew would come into his father's face, though he did not understand it. It came, and he struck up the song, still more quietly because it was a fast, sassy tune that would be likely to wake you up. He was amused because his son had always mistaken the word* "gal and" *for* "gallon," *and because his wife and to a less extent her relatives were not entirely amused by*

83

*his amusement. They felt, he knew, that he was not a man to take the
word "gallon" so purely as a joke; not that the drinking had been any
sort of problem, for a long time now. He sang:*

I got a gallon an a sugarbabe too, my honey, my baby,
I got a gallon an a sugarbabe too, my honey, my sweet thing.
I got a gallon an a sugarbabe too,
Gal don't love me but my sugarbabe do
        This mornin,
        This evenin,
          So soon.

When they kill a chicken, she saves me the wing, my honey,
    my baby,
When they kill a chicken, she saves me the wing, my honey,
    my sweet thing,
When they kill a chicken, she saves me the wing, my honey
Think I'm aworkin ain't adoin a thing
        This mornin,
        This evenin,
          So soon.

Every night about a half past eight, my honey, my baby,
Every night about a half past eight, my honey, my sweet
    thing
Every night about a half past eight, my honey
Ya find me awaitin at the white folks' gate
        This mornin,
        This evenin,
          So soon.

*The child still stared up at him; because there was so little light or
perhaps because he was so sleepy, his eyes seemed very dark, although
the father knew they were nearly as light as his own. He took his hand*

away and blew the moisture dry on the child's forehead, smoothed his hair away, and put his hand back:

What in the world you doin, Google Eyes? he sang, very slowly, while he and the child looked at each other,

> *What in the world you doin, Google Eyes?*
> *What in the world you doin, Google Eyes?*
> *What in the world you doin, Google Eyes?*

His eyes slowly closed, sprang open, almost in alarm, closed again.

> *Where did you get them great big Google Eyes?*
> *Where did you get them great big Google Eyes?*
> *You're the best there is and I need you in my biz,*
> *Where in the world did you get them Google Eyes?*

He waited. He took his hand away. The child's eyes opened and he felt as if he had been caught at something. He touched the forehead again, more lightly. "Go to sleep, honey," he said. "Go on to sleep now." The child continued to look up at him and a tune came unexpectedly into his head, and lifting his voice almost to tenor he sang, almost inaudibly:

> *Oh, I hear them train car wheels arumblin,*
> *Ann, they're mighty near at hand,*
> *I hear that train come arumblin,*
> *Come arumblin through the land.*
>> *Git on board, little children,*
>> *Git on board, little children,*
>> *Git on board, little children,*
>> *There's room for many and more.*

To the child it looked as if his father were gazing off into a great distance and, looking up into these eyes which looked so far away, he too looked far away:

> Oh, I look a way down yonder,
> Ann, uh what dyou reckon I see,
> A band of shinin angels,
> A comin' after me.
> > Git on board, little children,
> > Git on board, little children,
> > Git on board, little children,
> > There's room for many and more.

He did not look down but looked straight on into the wall in silence for a good while, and sang:

> Oh, every time the sun goes down,
> There's a dollar saved for Betsy Brown,
> > Sugar Babe.

He looked down. He was almost certain now that the child was asleep. So much more quietly that he could scarcely hear himself, and that the sound stole upon the child's near sleep like a band of shining angels, he went on:

> There's a good old sayin, as you all know,
> That you can't track a rabbit when there ain't no snow
> > Sugar Babe.

Here again he waited, his hand listening against the child, for he was so fond of the last verse that he always hated to have to come to it and end it; but it came into his mind and became so desirable to sing that he could resist it no longer:

Oh, tain't agoin to rain on, tain't agoin to snow:

He felt a strange coldness on his spine, and saw the glistening as a great cedar moved and tears came into his eyes:

But the sun's agoin to shine, and the wind's agoin to blow
Sugar Babe.

A great cedar, and the colors of limestone and of clay; the smell of wood smoke and, in the deep orange light of the lamp, the silent logs of the walls, his mother's face, her ridged hand mild on his forehead: Don't you fret, Jay, don't you fret. And before his time, before even he was dreamed of in this world, she must have lain under the hand of her mother or her father and they in their childhood under other hands, away on back through the mountains, away on back through the years, it took you right on back as far as you could ever imagine, right on back to Adam, only no one did it for him; or maybe did God?

How far we all come. How far we all come away from ourselves. So far, so much between, you can never go home again. You can go home, it's good to go home, but you never really get all the way home again in your life. And what's it all for? All I tried to be, all I ever wanted and went away for, what's it all for?

Just one way, you do get back home. You have a boy or a girl of your own and now and then you remember, and you know how they feel, and it's almost the same as if you were your own self again, as young as you could remember.

And God knows he was lucky, so many ways, and God knows he was thankful. Everything was good and better than he could have hoped for, better than he ever deserved; only, whatever it was and however good it was, it wasn't what you once had been, and had lost, and could never have again, and once in a while, once in a long time, you remembered, and knew how far you were away, and it hit you hard enough, that little while it lasted, to break your heart.

He felt thirsty, and images of stealthiness and deceit, of openness, anger and pride, immediately possessed him, and immediately he fought them off. If ever I get drunk again, he told himself proudly, I'll

*kill myself. And there are plenty good reasons why I won't kill myself.
So I won't even get drunk again.*

He felt consciously strong, competent both for himself and against
himself, and this pleasurable sense of firmness contended against the
perfect and limpid remembrance he had for a moment experienced,
and he tried sadly, vainly, to recapture it. But now all that he remembered, clear as it was to him, and dear to him, no longer moved his
heart, and he was in this sadness, almost without thought, staring at
the wall when the door opened softly behind him and he was caught by
a spasm of rage and alarm, then of shame for these emotions.

"Jay," his wife called softly. "Isn't he asleep yet?"

"Yeah, he's asleep," he said, getting up and dusting his knees.
"Reckon it's later than I knew."

"Andrew and Amelia had to go," she whispered, coming over. She
leaned past him and straightened the sheet. "They said tell you good
night." She lifted the child's head with one hand, while her husband,
frowning, vigorously shook his head; "It's all right, Jay, he's sound
asleep"; she smoothed the pillow, and drew away: "They were afraid if
they disturbed you they might wake Rufus."

"Gee. I'm sorry not to see them. Is it so late?"

"You must have been in here nearly an hour! What was the matter with him?"

"Bad dream, I reckon; fraid of the dark."

"He's all right? Before he went to sleep, I mean?"

"Sure he's all right." He pointed at the dog. "Look what I found."

"Goodness sake, where was it?"

"Back in the corner, under the crib."

"Well shame on me! But Jay, it must be awfully dirty!"

"Naww; I dusted it off."

She said, shyly, "I'll be glad when I can stoop again."

He put his hand on her shoulder. "So will I."

"Jay," she drew away, really offended.

"Honey!" he said, amused and flabbergasted. He put his arm
around her. "I only meant the baby! I'll be glad when the baby's here!"

She looked at him intently (she did not yet realize that she was near-sighted), understood him, and smiled and then laughed softly in her embarrassment. He put his finger to her lips, jerking his head towards the crib. They turned and looked down at their son.

"So will I, Jay darling," she whispered. "So will I."

His mother sang to him too. Her voice was soft and shining gray like her dear gray eyes. She sang, "Sleep baby sleep, Thy father watches the sheep," and he could see his father sitting on a hillside looking at a lot of white sheep in the darkness but why; "thy mother shakes the dream-land tree and down fall little dreams on thee," and he could see the little dreams floating down easily like huge flakes of snow at night and covering him in the darkness like babes in the wood with wide quiet leaves of softly shining light. She sang, "Go tell Aunt Rhoda," three times over, and then, "The old gray goose is dead," and then "She's worth the saving," three times over, and then "To make a featherbed," and then again. Three times over. Go tell Aunt Rhoda; and then again the old gray goose is dead. He did not know what "she's worth the saving" meant, and it was one of the things he always took care not to ask, because although it sounded so gentle he was also sure that somewhere inside it there was something terrible to be afraid of exactly because it sounded so gentle, and he would become very much afraid instead of only a little afraid if he asked and learned what it meant. All the more, because when his mother sang this song he could always see Aunt Rhoda, and she wasn't at all like anybody else, she was like her name, mysterious and gray. She was very tall, as tall even as his father. She stood near a well on a big flat open place of hard bare ground, quite a way from where he saw her from, and even so he could see how very tall she was. Far back behind her there were dark trees without any leaves. She just stood there very quiet and straight as if she were waiting to be gone and told that the old gray goose is dead. She wore a long gray dress with a skirt that touched the ground and her hands were *hidden in the great falling folds of the skirt. He could never see her face because it was too darkly within the shadow of the sunbonnet she wore, but from within that shadow he could always just discern the shining of her eyes, and they were looking straight at him, not angrily, and not kindly either, just looking and waiting. She is worth the saving.*

She sang, "Swing low, sweet cherryut," and that was the best song of all. "Comin for to care me home." So glad and willing and peaceful. A cherryut was a sort of a beautiful wagon because home was too far to walk, a long, long way, but of course it was like a cherry, too, only he could not understand how a beautiful wagon and a cherry could be like each other, but they were. Home was a long, long way. Much too far to walk and you can only come home when God sends the cherryut for you. And it would care him home. He did not even try to imagine what home was like except of course it was even nicer than home where he lived, but he always knew it was home. He always especially knew how happy he was in his own home when he heard about the other home because then he always felt he knew exactly where he was and that made it good to be exactly there. His father loved to sing this song too and sometimes in the dark, on the porch, or lying out all together on a quilt in the back yard, they would sing it together. They would not be talking, just listening to the little sounds, and looking up at the stars, and feeling ever so quiet and happy and sad at the same time, and all of a sudden in a very quiet voice his father sang out, almost as if he were singing to himself, "Swing low," and by the time he got to "cherryut" his mother was singing too, just as softly, and then their voices went up higher, singing "comin for to carry me home," and looking up between their heads from where he lay he looked right into the stars, so near and friendly, with a great drift of dust like flour across the top of the sky. His father sang it differently from his mother. When he sang the second "Swing" she just sang "swing low," on two notes, in a simple, clear voice, but he sang "swing" on two notes, sliding from the note above to the one she sang, and blurring his voice and making it more forceful on the first note, and springing it, dark and blurry, off the "l" in "low," with a rhythm that made his son's body stir. And when he came to "Tell all my friends I'm comin too," *he started four full notes above her, and slowed up a little, and sort of dreamed his way down among several extra notes she didn't sing, and some of these notes were a kind of blur, like hitting a black note and the next white one at the same time on Grandma's piano, and he didn't sing* "I'm comin'" *but* "I'm uh-comin," *and there too, and all through his singing, there was that excitement of rhythm that often made him close his eyes and move his head in contentment. But his mother sang the same thing clear and true in a sweet, calm voice, fewer and simpler notes. Sometimes she would try to sing it his way and he would try to sing it hers, but they always went back pretty soon to their own way, though he always felt they each liked the other's way very much. He liked both ways very much and best of all when they sang together and he was there with them, touching them on both sides, and even better, from when they sang* "I look over Jordan what do I see," *for then it was good to look up into the stars, and then they sang* "A band of angels comin after me" *and it seemed as if all the stars came at him like a great shining brass band so far away you weren't quite sure you could even hear the music but so near he could almost see their faces and they all but leaned down deep enough to pick him up in their arms.* Come for to care me home.

They sang it a little slower towards the end as if they hated to come to the finish of it and then they didn't talk at all, and after a minute their hands took each other across their child, and things were even quieter, so that all the little noises of the city night raised up again in the quietness, locusts, crickets, footsteps, hoofs, faint voices, the shufflings of a switch engine, and after awhile, while they all looked into the sky, his father, in a strange and distant, sighing voice said "Well..." *and after a little his mother answered, with a quiet and strange happy sadness,* "Yes..." *and they waited a good little bit longer, not saying anything, and then his father took him up into his arms and his mother rolled up the quilt and they went in and he was put to bed.*

He came right up to her hip bone; not so high on his father.

She wore dresses, his father wore pants. Pants were what he wore too, but they were short and soft. His father's were hard and rough and went right down to his shoes. The cloths of his mother's clothes were soft like his.

His father wore hard coats too and a hard celluloid collar and sometimes a vest with hard buttons. Mostly his clothes were scratchy except the striped shirts and the shirts with little dots or diamonds on them. But not as scratchy as his cheeks.

His cheeks were warm and cool at the same time and they scratched a little even when he had just shaved. It always tickled, on his cheek or still more on his neck, and sometimes hurt a little, too, but it was always fun because he was so strong.

He smelled like dry grass, leather and tobacco, and sometimes a different smell, full of great energy and a fierce kind of fun, but also a feeling that things might go wrong. He knew what that was because he overheard them arguing. Whiskey.

For awhile he had a big mustache and then he took it off and his mother said, "Oh Jay, you look just worlds nicer, you have such a nice mouth, it's a shame to hide it." After awhile he grew the mustache again. It made him look much older, taller and stronger, and when he frowned the mustache frowned too and it was very frightening. Then he took it off again and she was pleased all over again and after that he kept it off.

She called it mustásh. He called it must'ash and sometimes mush'tash but then he was joking, talkin like a darky. He liked to talk darky talk and the way he sang was like a darky too, only when he sang he wasn't joking.

His neck was dark tan and there were deep crisscross cracks all over the back of it.

His hands were so big he could cover him from the chin to his bath-thing. There were big blue strings under the skin on the backs of them. Veins, those were. Black hair even on the backs of the fingers and ever so much hair on the wrists; big veins in his arms, like ropes.

For some time now his mother had seemed different. Almost always when she spoke to him it was as if she had something else very much on her mind, and so was making a special effort to be gentle and attentive to him. And it was as if whatever it was that was on her mind was very momentous. Sometimes she looked at him in such a way that he felt that she was very much amused about something. He did not know how to ask her what she was amused by and as he watched her, wondering what it was, and she watched his puzzlement, she sometimes looked more amused than ever, and once when she looked particularly amused, and he looked particularly bewildered, her smile became shaky and turned into laugher and, quickly taking his face between her hands, she exclaimed, "I'm not laughing at you, darling!" and for the first time he felt that perhaps she was.

There were other times when she seemed to have almost no interest in him, but only to be doing things for him because they had to be done. He felt subtly lonely and watched her carefully. He saw that his father's manner had changed towards her ever so little; he treated her as if she were very valuable and he seemed to be conscious of the tones of his voice. Sometimes in the mornings Grandma would come in and if he was around he was told to go away for a little while. Grandma did not hear well and carried a black ear trumpet which was sticky and sour on the end that she put in her ear; but try as he would they talked so quietly that he could hear very little, and none of it enlightened him. There were special words which were said with a special kind of hesitancy or shyness, such as "pregnancy" and "kicking" and "discharge," but others, which seemed fully as strange, such as "layette" and "bassinette" and "belly-band," seemed to inspire no such fear. Grandma also treated him as if something strange was going on, but whatever it was, it was evidently not dangerous, for she was always quite merry with him. His father and his Uncle Andrew and Grandma seemed to treat him as they always had, though there seemed to be some hidden kind of strain in Uncle Andrew's feeling for his mother. And Aunt Hannah was the same as ever with him, except that she paid more attention to his mother, now. Aunt Amelia looked at his *mother a good deal when she thought nobody else was watching, and once when she saw him watching her she looked quickly away and turned red.*

Everyone seemed either to look at his mother with ill-concealed curiosity or to be taking special pains not to look anywhere except, rather fixedly and cheerfully, into her eyes. For now she was swollen up like a vase, and there was a peculiar lethargic lightness in her face and in her voice. He had a distinct feeling that he should not ask what was happening to her. At last he asked Uncle Andrew, "Uncle Andrew, why is Mama so fat?" and his uncle replied, with such apparent anger or alarm that he was frightened, "Why, don't you know?" and abruptly walked out of the room.

Next day his mother told him that soon he was going to have a very wonderful surprise. When he asked what a surprise was she said it was like being given things for Christmas only ever so much nicer. When he asked what he was going to be given she said that she did not mean it was a present, specially for him, or for him to have, or keep, but something for everybody, and especially for them. When he asked what it was, she said that if she told him it wouldn't be a surprise any more, would it? When he said that he wanted to know anyway, she said that she would tell him, only it would be so hard for him to imagine what it was before it came that she thought it was better for him to see it first. When he asked when it was coming she said that she didn't know exactly but very soon now, in only a week or two, perhaps sooner, and she promised him that he would know right away when it did come.

He was aflame with curiosity. He had been too young, the Christmas before, to think of looking for hidden presents, but now he looked everywhere that he could imagine to look until his mother understood what he was doing and told him there was no use looking for it because the surprise wouldn't be here until exactly when it came. He asked where was it, then, and heard his father's sudden laugh; his mother looked panicky and cried, "Jay!" all at once, and quickly informed him, "In heaven; still up in heaven."

He looked quickly to his father for corroboration and his father, who appeared to be embarrassed, did not look at him. He knew about heaven because that was where Our Father was, but that was all he knew about it, and he was not satisfied. Again, however, he had a feeling that he would be unwise to ask more.

"Why don't you tell him, Mary?" his father said.

"Oh, Jay," she said in alarm; then said, by moving her lips, "Don't talk of it in front of him!"

"Oh, I'm sorry," and he, too, said with his lips—only a whisper leaked around the silence, "but what's the good? Why not get it over with?"

She decided that it was best to speak openly. "As you know, Jay, I've told Rufus about our surprise that's coming. I told him I'd be glad to tell him what it was, except that it would be so very hard for him to imagine it and such a lovely surprise when he first sees it. Besides, I just have a feeling he might m-make see-oh-en-en-ee-see-tee-eye-oh-en-ess, between—between one thing and another."

"Going to make them, going to make em anyhow," his father said.

"But Jay, there's no use simply forcing it on his att-eigh-ten-ten, his attention, now, is there? Is there, Jay?"

She seemed really quite agitated, he could not understand why.

"You're right, Mary, and don't you get excited about it. I was all wrong about it. Of course I was." And he got up and came over to her and took her in his arms, and patted her on the back.

"I'm probably just silly about it," she said.

"No, you're not one bit silly. Besides, if you're silly about that, so am I, some way. That just sort of caught me off my guard, that about heaven, that's all."

"Well, what can you say?"

"I'm Godd—I can't imagine, sweetheart, and I better just keep my mouth shut."

She frowned, smiled, laughed through her nose and urgently shook her head at him, all at once.

And then one day without warning the biggest woman he had

ever seen, shining deep black and all in magnificent white with bright gold spectacles and a strong smile like that of his Aunt Hannah, entered the house and embraced his mother and swept down on him crying with delight, "Lawd, chile, how mah baby has growed!", and for a moment he thought that this must be the surprise and looked inquiringly at his mother past the onslaught of embraces, and his mother said, "Victoria; Victoria, Rufus!"; and Victoria cried, "Now bless his little heart, how would he remembuh," and all of a sudden as he looked into the vast shining planes of her smiling face and at the gold spectacles which perched there as gaily as a dragonfly, there was something that he did remember, a glisten of gold and a warm movement of affection, and before he knew it he had flung his arms around her neck and she whooped with astonished joy. "Why God bless him, why chile, chile," and she held him away from her and her face was the happiest thing he had ever seen, "ah believe you do remembuh! Ah sweah ah believe you do! Do you?" She shook him in her happiness. "Do you remembuh y'old Victoria?" She shook him again. "Do you, honey?" And realizing at last that he was specifically being asked, he nodded shyly, and again she embraced him. She smelled so good that he could almost have leaned his head against her and gone to sleep then and there.

"Mama," he said later, when she was out shopping, "Victoria smells awful good."

"Hush, Rufus," his mother said. "Now you listen very carefully to me, do you hear? Say yes if you hear."

"Yes."

"Now you be very careful that you never say anything about how she smells where Victoria can hear you. Will you? Say yes if you will."

"Yes."

"Because even though you like the way she smells, you might hurt her feelings terribly if you said any such thing, and you wouldn't want to hurt dear old Victoria's feelings, I know. Would you, would you, Rufus?"

"No."

"Because Victoria is—is *colored*, Rufus. That's why her skin is so dark, and colored people are very sensitive about the way they smell. Do you know what *sensitive* means?"

He nodded cautiously.

"It means there are things that hurt your feelings so badly, things you can't help, that you feel like crying, and nice colored people feel that way about the way they smell. So you be very careful. Will you? Say yes if you will?"

"Yes."

"Now tell me what I've asked you to be careful about, Rufus."

"Don't tell Victoria she smells."

"Or say anything about it where she can hear."

"Or say anything about it where she can hear."

"Why not?"

"Because she might cry."

"That's right. And Rufus, Victoria is *very very* clean. *Absolutely spic and span.*"

Spic and span.

Victoria would not allow his mother to get dinner and after they had eaten she also took entire charge of packing some of his clothes into a box, asking advice, however, on each thing that she took out of the drawer. Then Victoria bathed him and dressed him in clean clothes from the skin out, much to his mystification, and once he was ready, his mother called him to her and told him that Victoria was going to take him on a little visit to stay a few days with Granpa and Granma and Uncle Andrew and Aunt Amelia, and he must be a very good boy and do his very best not to wet the bed because when he came back, very soon now, in only a few more days, the surprise would be there and he would know what it was. He said that if the surprise was coming so soon he wanted to stay and see it, and she replied that that was just why he was going away to Granma's, so the surprise could come all by itself. He asked why it couldn't come if he was there and she said because he might frighten it away because it would still be very tiny *and very much afraid, so if he really wanted the surprise to come, he could help more than anything else by being a good boy and going right along to Granma's. Victoria would come and bring him home again just as soon as the surprise was ready for him; "Won't you, Victoria?" And Victoria, who throughout this conversation had appeared to be tremendously amused about something, giving tight little cackles of swallowed laughter and murmuring, "Bless his heart," whenever he spoke, said that indeed she most certainly would.*

"And say your prayers," his mother said, looking at him suddenly with so much love that he was bewildered. "You're a big boy now, and you can say them by yourself; can't you?" He nodded. She took him by the shoulders and looked at him almost as if she were threading a needle. As she looked at him, some kind of astonishment and some kind of fear grew in her face. Her face began to shine; she smiled; her mouth twitched and trembled. She took him close to her and her cheek was wet. "God bless my dear little boy," she whispered, "for ever and ever! Amen," and again she held him away; her face looked as if she were moving through space at extraordinary speed. "Good-bye, my darling; oh, good-bye!"

"Now you keep aholt a my hand," Victoria told him, the sun flashing her lenses as she looked both ways from the curb. Arching his neck and his forelegs, a bright brown horse drew a buggy crisply but sedately past; in the washed black spokes, sunlight twittered. Far down the sunlight, like a bumblebee, a yellow streetcar buzzed. The trees moved. They did not wait.

"Victoria," he said.

"Wait, chile," said Victoria, breathing hard. "You wait till we're safe across."

"Now what is it, honey?" she asked, once they had attained the other curb.

"Why is your skin so dark?"

He saw her bright little eyes thrust into him through the little lenses and he felt a strong current of pain or danger. He knew that something was wrong. She did not answer him immediately but peered down at him sharply. Then the current passed and she looked away from him, readjusting her fingers so that she took his hand. Her face looked very far away, and resolute. "Just because, chile," she said in a stern and gentle voice. "Just because that was the way God made me."

"Is that why you're colored, Victoria?"

He felt a change in her hand when he said the word "colored." Again she did not answer immediately, nor would she look at him. "Yes," she said at length, "that's why I'm colored."

He felt deeply sad as they walked along, but he did not know why. She seemed to have no more to say, and he had a feeling that it was not proper for him to say anything either. He watched her great, sad face beneath its brilliant cap, but she did not seem to know that he was watching her or even that he was there. But then he felt the pressure of her hand, and squeezed her hand, and he felt that whatever had been wrong was all right again.

After quite a little while Victoria said, "Chile, I want to tell you sumpn." He waited: they walked. "Victoria don't pay it no mind, because she knows you. She knows you wouldn't say a mean thing to nobody, not for this world. But dey is lots of other colored folks dat don't know you, honey. And if you say that, you know, about their skins, about their coloh, they goan think you're tryin to be mean to em. They goan to feel awful bad and maybe they be mad at you too, when Victoria knows you doan mean nuthin by it, cause they don't know you like Victoria do. Do you understand me, chile?" He looked earnestly up at her. "Don't say nuthin bout skins, or coloh, wheah colored people can heah you. Cause they goana think you're mean to em. So you be careful." And again she squeezed his hand.

He thought about Victoria while they walked and he wished that she was happy, and he felt that it was because of him that she was not happy. "Victoria," he said.

"What is it, honey?"

"I didn't want to be mean to you."

She stopped abruptly and with creaking and difficulty squatted down in the middle of the sidewalk so that a man who was passing stepped suddenly aside and looked coldly down as he went by. She put both hands on his shoulders and her large, kind face and her kind smell were close to him. "Lord bless you, baby, Victoria knows you didn't! Victoria knows you is de goodest little boy in all dis world! She just had to tell you, you see. Cause colored folks has a hard time in dis world and she knows you wouldn't want to make em feel bad, not even if you didn't mean to."

"I didn't want to make you feel bad."

"Bless your little heart. I don't feel bad, not one bit. You make me feel happy, and your mama makes me feel happy, and there's not one thing in the world I wouldn't do for de bofe of you, honey, and dat you know. Dat you know," she said again, rocking her head and smiling and patting both his shoulders. "I missed you terrible, honey," she said, but somehow he felt that she was not talking exactly to him. "I couldn't hardly love you more if you was my own baby." A silence opened around them in which he felt at once great space, the space almost of darkness itself, and great peace and comfort; and the whole of this immensity was pervaded by her vague face and by the waving light of leaves. "Now let's git along," she said, creaking upright and smoothing her starched garments. "We don't want to keep your gran-maw waitin."

And there was the dusty ivy on the wall, the small glass-house in front, and on the porch, Aunt Amelia and his grandma. Even when they were still across the street he saw his Aunt Amelia wave and Victoria waved gaily back, chuckling and croaking, "Hello," and he waved too; and Amelia leaned towards his grandmother who sought out and tilted her little trumpet and Amelia leaned close to it and then they both turned to look and Grandma got up and he could hear her high, "Hello," and they were at the front steps, and Grandma came cautiously down the steps from the porch, and they all met on the brick walk in the shade of the magnolia, while Aunt Amelia came up smiling from behind her mother. And soon Victoria left; she disappeared around a corner, a few blocks up the street, handsomely and gradually as a sailboat.

❧ PART TWO ❧

Chapter 8

A FEW MINUTES BEFORE TEN, the phone rang. Mary hurried to quiet it. "Hello?"

The voice was a man's, wiry and faint, a country voice. It was asking a question, but she could not hear it clearly.

"Hello!" she asked again. "Will you please talk a little louder? I can't hear. . . . I said I can't hear you! Will you talk a little louder please? Thank you."

Now, straining and impatient, she could hear, though the voice seemed still to come from a great distance.

"Is this Miz Jay Follet?"

"Yes; what is it?" (for there was a silence); "yes, this is she."

After further silence the voice said, "There's been a slight— your husband has been in a accident."

His head! she told herself.

"Yes," she said, in a caved-in voice. At the same moment the voice said, "A serious accident."

"Yes," Mary said more clearly.

"What I wanted to ask, is there a man in his family, some kin, could come out? We'd appreciate if you could send a man out here, right away."

"Yes; yes, there's my brother. Where should he come to?"

103

"I'm out at Powell Station, at Brannick's Blacksmith Shop, bout twelve miles out the Ball Camp Pike."

"Brannick's bl—"

"B-r-a-n-n-i-c-k. It's right on the left of the Pike comin out just a little way this side, Knoxvul side of Bell's Bridge." She heard muttering, and another muttering voice. "Tell him he can't miss it. We'll keep the light on and a lantern out in front."

"Do you have a doctor?"

"How's that again, ma'am?"

"A doctor, do you have one? Should I send a doctor?"

"That's all right, ma'am. Just some man that's kin."

"He'll come right out just as fast as he can." Walter's auto, she thought. "Thank you very much for calling."

"That's all right, ma'am. I sure do hate to give you bad news."

"Good night."

"Good-bye, ma'am."

She found she was scarcely standing, she was all but hanging from the telephone. She stiffened her knees, leaned against the wall, and rang.

"Andrew?"

"Mary?"

She drew a deep breath.

"Mary."

She drew another deep breath; she felt as if her lungs were not large enough.

"Mary?"

Dizzy, seeing gray, trying to control her shaking voice, she said, "Andrew, there's been an—a man just phoned, from Powell's Station, about twelve miles out towards LaFollette, and he says—he says Jay—has met with a very serious accident. He wants . . ."

"Oh, my God, Mary!"

"He said they want some man of his family to come out just as soon as possible and, help bring him in, I guess."

"I'll call Walter, he'll take me out."

"Yes do, will you, Andrew?"

"Of course I will. Just a minute."

"What?"

"Aunt Hannah."

"May I speak to her when you're through?"

"Certainly. Where is he hurt, Mary?"

"He didn't say."

"Well, didn't you—no matter."

"No I didn't," she said, now realizing with surprise that she had not, "I guess because I was so sure. Sure it's his head, that is."

"Do they—shall I get Dr. Dekalb?"

"He says no; just you."

"I guess there's already a doctor there."

"I guess."

"I'll call Wa—wait, here's Aunt Hannah."

"Mary."

"Aunt Hannah, Jay is in a serious accident, Andrew has to go out. Would you come up and wait with me and get things ready just in case? Just in case he's well enough to be brought home and not the hospital?"

"Certainly, Mary. Of course I will."

"And will you tell Mama and Papa not to worry, not to come out, give them my love. We might as well just be calm as we can, till we know."

"Of course we must. I'll be right up."

"Thank you, Aunt Hannah."

She went into the kitchen and built a quick fire and put on a large kettle of water and a small kettle, for tea. The phone rang.

"Mary! Where do I go?"

"Why, Powell's Station, out the Pike towards . . ."

"I know, but exactly where? Didn't he say?"

"He said Brannick's blacksmith shop. B-r-a-n-n-i-c-k. Do you hear?"

"Yes. Brannick."

"He said they'll keep the lights on and you can't miss it. It's just to the left of the Pike just this side of Bell's Bridge. Just a little way this side."

"All right, Mary, Walter will come by here and we'll bring Aunt Hannah on our way."

"All right. Thank you, Andrew."

She put on more kindling and hurried into the downstairs bedroom. How do I know, she thought; he didn't even say; I didn't even ask. By the way he talks he may be—she whipped off the coverlet, folded it, and smoothed the pad. I'm just simply not going to think about it until I know more, she told herself. She hurried to the linen closet and brought clean sheets and pillow-cases. He didn't say whether there was a doctor there or not. She spread a sheet, folded it under the foot of the mattress, pulled it smooth, and folded it under all around. Then she spread her palms along it; it was cold and smooth beneath her hands and it brought her great hope. Oh God, let him be well enough to come home where I can take care of him, where I can take *good* care of him. How good to rest! That's all right, ma'am. Just some man that's kin. She spread the top sheet. That's all right, ma'am. That can mean anything. It can mean there's a doctor there and although it's serious he has it in hand, under control, it isn't so dreadfully bad, although he did say it's serious or it can . . . A light blanket, this weather. Two, case it turns cool. She hurried and got them, unaware whether she was making such noise as might wake the children and unaware that even in this swiftness she was moving, by force of habit, almost silently. Just some man that's kin. That means it's bad, or he'd ask for me. No, I'd have to stay with the children. But *he* doesn't know there are children. My place'd be home anyhow, getting things ready, he knows that. He didn't suggest getting anything ready. He knew I'd know. He is a man, wouldn't occur to him. She took the end of a pillow between her teeth and pulled the slip on and plumped it and put it in place. She took the end of the second pillow between her teeth and bit it so hard the roots of her teeth ached, and pulled the slip on and plumped it. Then she set the first pillow up on edge and set the second pillow on edge against it and plumped them both and smoothed them and stood away and looked at them with her head on one side, and for a moment she saw him sitting up in bed with a tray on his knees as he had sat when he strained his back, and he looked at her, almost but not quite smiling, and she could hear his voice, grouchy, pretending to be for the fun of it. If it's his head, she remembered, perhaps he'll have to lie very flat.

How do I know? How do I know?

She left the pillows as they were, and turned down the bed on that side, next to the window, and smoothed it. She carefully refolded the second blanket and laid it on the lower foot of the bed, no, it would bother his poor feet. She hung it over the foot-board. She stood looking at the carefully made bed, and, for a few seconds, she was not sure where she was or why she was doing this. Then she remembered and said, "oh," in a small, stupefied, soft voice. She opened the window, top and bottom, and when the curtains billowed she tied them back more tightly. She went to the hall closet and brought out the bedpan and rinsed and dried it and put it under the bed. She went to the medicine chest and took out the thermometer, shook it, washed it in cool water, dried it, and put it beside the bed in a tumbler of water. She saw that the hand towel which covered this table was dusty, and threw it into the dirty-clothes hamper, and replaced it with a fresh one, and replaced that with a dainty linen guest towel upon the border of which pansies and violets were embroidered. She saw that the front pillow had sagged a little, and set it right. She pulled down the shade. She turned out the light and dropped to her knees, facing the bed, and closed her eyes. She touched her forehead, her breastbone, her left shoulder and her right shoulder, and clasped her hands.

"O God, if it be Thy will," she whispered. She could not think of anything more. She made the sign of the Cross again, slowly, deeply, and widely upon herself, and she felt something of the shape of the Cross; strength and quiet.

Thy will be done. And again she could think of nothing more. She got from her knees and without turning on the light or glancing towards the bed, went into the kitchen. The water for tea had almost boiled away. The water in the large kettle was scarcely tepid. The fire was almost out. While she was putting in more kindling, she heard them on the porch.

Hannah came in with her hands stretched out and Mary extended her own hands and took them and kissed her cheek while at the same instant they said, "Mary" and, "my dear"; then Hannah hurried to put her hat on the rack. Andrew stayed at the open door and did not speak but merely kept looking into her eyes; his own eyes were as hard and bright as those of a bird and they spoke to her of a cold and bitter incredulity, as if he were accusing something or someone (even perhaps his sister) which it was useless beyond words to accuse. She felt that he was saying, "And you can still believe in the idiotic God of yours?" Walter Starr stayed back in the darkness; Mary could just see the large lenses of the glasses, and the darkness of his mustache and of his heavy shoulders.

"Come in, Walter," she said, and her voice was as overwarm as if she were coaxing a child.

"We can't stop," Andrew said sharply.

Walter came forward and took her hand, and gently touched her wrist with his other hand. "We shan't be long," he said.

"Bless you," Mary murmured, and so pressed his hand that her arm trembled.

He patted her trembling wrist four times rapidly, turned away saying, "Better be off, Andrew," and went towards his automobile. She could hear that he had left the engine running, and now she realized all the more clearly how grave matters were.

"Everything's ready here in case—you know—he's—well enough to be brought home," Mary told Andrew.

"Good. I'll phone, the minute I know. Anything."

"Yes, dear."

His eyes changed and abruptly his hand reached out and caught her shoulder. "Mary, I'm so sorry," he said, almost crying.

"Yes, dear," she said again, and felt that it was a vacuous reply; but by the time this occurred to her, Andrew was getting into the automobile. She stood and watched until it had vanished and, turning to go in, found that Hannah was at her elbow.

"Let's have some tea," she said. "I've hot water all ready," she said over her shoulder as she hurried down the hall.

Let her, Hannah thought, following. By all means.

"Goodness no, it's boiled away! Sit down, Aunt Hannah, it'll be ready in a jiff." She hustled to the sink.

"Let me . . ." Hannah began; then knew better, and hoped that Mary had not heard.

"What?" She was drawing the water.

"Just let me know, if there's anything I can help with."

"Not a thing, thank you." She put the water on the stove. "Goodness, sit down." Hannah took a chair by the table. "Everything is ready that I can think of," Mary said. "That we can know about, yet." She sat at the opposite side of the table. "I've made up the downstairs bedroom" (she waved vaguely towards it), "where he stayed when his poor back was sprained, you remember." (Of course I do, Hannah thought; let her talk.) "It's better than upstairs. Near the kitchen and bathroom both and no stairs to climb and of course if need be, that is, if he needs a nurse, night nursing, we can put her in the dining room and eat in the kitchen, or even set up a cot right in the room with him; put up a screen; or if she minds that, why she can just sleep on the living-room davenport and keep the door open between. Don't you think?"

"Certainly," Hannah said.

"I think I'll see if I can possibly get Celia, Celia Gunn, if she's available, or if she's on a case she can possibly leave, it'll be so much nicer for everyone to have someone around who is an old friend, really one of the family, rather than just a complete stranger, don't you think?"

Hannah nodded.

"Even though of course Jay doesn't specially, of course she's really an old friend of mine, rather than Jay's, still, I think it would be more, well, harmonious, don't you think?"

"Yes indeed."

"But I guess it's just as well to wait till we hear from Andrew, not—create any needless disturbance, I guess. After all, it's very possible he'll have to be taken straight to a hospital. The man *did* say it was serious, after all."

"I think you're wise to wait," Hannah said.

"How's that water?" Mary twisted in her chair to see. "Sakes alive, the watched pot." She got up and stuffed in more kindling, and brought down the box of tea. "I don't know's I really want any tea, anyway, but I think it's a good idea to drink something warm while we're waiting, don't you?"

"I'd like some," said Hannah, who wanted nothing.

"Good, then we'll have some. Just as soon as the water's ready." She sat down again. "I thought one light blanket would be enough on a night like this but I've another over the foot of the bed in case it should turn cool."

"That should be sufficient."

"Goodness knows," Mary said, vaguely, and became silent. She looked at her hands, which lay loosely clasped on the table. Hannah found that she was watching Mary closely. In shame, she focused her sad eyes a little away from her. She wondered. It was probably better for her not to face it if she could help until it had to be faced. If it had to be. Just quiet, she said to herself. Just be quiet.

"You know," Mary said slowly, "the queerest thing." She began slowly to turn and rub her clasped fingers among each other. Hannah waited. "When the man phoned," she said, gazing quietly upon her moving fingers, "and said Jay had been in a—serious accident"; and now Hannah realized that Mary was looking at her, and met her brilliant gray eyes; "I felt it just as certainly as I'm sitting here now, 'It's his head.' What do you think of that?" she asked, almost proudly.

Hannah looked away. What's one to say, she wondered. Yet Mary had spoken with such conviction that she herself was half convinced. She looked into an image of still water, clear and very deep, and even though it was dark, and she had not seen so clearly since her girlhood, she could see sand and twigs and dead leaves at the bottom of the water. She drew a deep breath and let it out in a long slow sigh and clucked her tongue once. "We never know," she murmured.

"Of course we just have to wait," Mary said, after a long silence.

"Hyesss," Hannah said softly, sharply inhaling the first of the word, and trailing the sibilant to a hair.

Through their deep silence, at length, they began to be aware of the stumbling crackle of the water. When Mary got up for it, it had boiled half away.

"There's still plenty for two cups," she said, and prepared the strainer and poured them, and put on more water. She lifted the lid of the large kettle. Its sides, below the water line, were rich beaded; from the bottom sprang a leisured spiral of bubbles so small they resembled white sand; the surface of the water slowly circled upon itself. She wondered what the water might possibly be good for.

"Just in case," she murmured.

Hannah decided not to ask her what she had said.

"There's ZuZus," Mary said, and got them from the cupboard. "Or would you like bread and butter? Or toast. I could toast some."

"Just tea, thank you."

"Help yourself to sugar and milk. Or lemon? Let's see, do I have le ..."

"Milk, thank you."

"Me too." Mary sat down again. "My, it's frightfully *hot* in here!" She got up and opened the door to the porch, and sat down again.

"I wonder what ti ..." She glanced over her shoulder at the kitchen clock. "What time did they leave, do you know?"

"Walter came for us at quarter after ten. About twenty-five after, I should think."

"Let's see, Walter drives pretty fast, though not so fast as Jay, but he'd be driving faster than usual tonight, and it's just over twelve miles. That would be, supposing he goes thirty miles an hour, that's twelve miles in, let's see, six times four is twenty-four, six times five's thirty, twice twelve is twenty-four, sakes alive. I was always dreadful at arithmetic ..."

"Say about half an hour, allowing for darkness, and Walter isn't familiar with those roads."

"Then we ought to be hearing pretty soon. Ten minutes. Fifteen at the outside."

"Yes, I should think."

"Maybe twenty, allowing for the roads, but that is a good road out that far as roads go."

"Maybe."

"Why didn't he *tell* me!" Mary burst out.

"What is it?"

"Why didn't I *ask*?" She looked at her aunt in furious bewilderment. "I didn't even *ask*! *How* serious! *Where* is he hurt? Is he living or *dead.*"

There it is, Hannah said to herself. She looked back steadily into Mary's eyes.

"That we simply have to wait to find out," she said.

"Of *course* we have," Mary cried angrily. "That's what's so *unbearable!*" She drank half her tea at a gulp; it burned her painfully but she scarcely noticed. She continued to glare at her aunt.

Hannah could think of nothing to say.

"I'm sorry," Mary said. "You're perfectly right. I've just got to hold myself together, that's all."

"Never mind," Hannah said, and they fell silent.

Hannah knew that silence must itself be virtually unbearable for Mary, and that it would bring her face to face with likelihoods still harder to endure. But she has to, she told herself; and the sooner the better. But she found that she herself could not bear to be present, and say nothing which might in some degree protect, and postpone. She was about to speak when Mary burst out: "In heaven's *name,* why didn't I ask him! *Why* didn't I? Didn't I *care?*"

"It was so sudden," Hannah said. "It was such a shock."

"You *would* think I'd *ask,* though! Wouldn't you?"

"You thought you knew. You told me you were sure it was his—in the head."

"But how *bad? What!*"

We both know, Hannah said to herself. But it's better if you bring yourself to say it. "It certainly wasn't because you didn't care, anyway," she said.

"No. No it certainly wasn't that, but I think I do know what it was. I think, I think I must have been too afraid of what he would have to say."

Hannah looked into her eyes. Nod, she told herself. Say yes I imagine so. Just say nothing and it'll be just as terrible for her. She heard herself saying what she had intended to venture a while before, when Mary had interrupted her: "Do you understand why J—your father stayed home, and your mother?"

"Because I asked them not to come."

"Why did you?"

"Because if all of you came, up here in a troop like that, it would be like assuming that—like assuming the very worst before we even know."

"That's why they stayed home. Your father said he knew you'd understand."

"Of course I do."

"We just must try to keep from making any assumptions—*good* or bad."

"I know. I know we must. It's just, this waiting in the dark like this, it's just more than I can stand."

"We ought to hear very soon."

Mary glanced at the clock. "Almost any minute," she said.

She took a little tea.

"I just can't help wondering," she said, "why he didn't say *more*. 'A serious accident,' he said. Not a 'very' serious one. Just 'serious.' Though, goodness knows, that's serious enough. But why couldn't he *say?*"

"As your father says, it's ten to one he's just a plain damned fool," Hannah said.

"But it's such an *important* thing to say, and so *simple* to say, at least to give some general idea about. At least whether he could come home, or go to a hospital, or . . . He didn't say anything about an ambulance. An ambulance would mean hospital, almost for sure. And surely if he meant the—the *very* worst, he'd have just said so straight out and not leave us all on tenterhooks. I know it's just what we have no earthly business guessing about, good *or* bad, but really it does seem to me there's every good reason for hope, Aunt Hannah. It seems to me that if . . ."

The telephone rang; its sound frightened each of them as deeply as either had experienced in her lifetime. They looked at each other and got up and turned towards the hall. "I . . ." Mary said, waving her hand right at Hannah as if she would wave her out of existence.

Hannah stopped where she stood, bowed her head, closed her eyes, and made the sign of the Cross.

Mary lifted the receiver from its hook before the second ring, but for a moment she could neither put it to her ear, nor speak. God *help me, help me,* she whispered. "Andrew?"

"Poll?"

"Papa!" Relief and fear were equal in her. "Have you heard anything?"

"You've heard?"

"No. I said. *'Have you heard from Andrew?'* "

"No. Thought you might have by now."

"No. Not yet. Not yet."

"I must have frightened you."

"Never mind, Papa. It's all right."

"Sorry as hell, Poll, I shouldn't have phoned."

"Never mind."

"Let us know, quick's you hear anything."

"Of course I will, Papa. I promise. Of course I will."

"Shall we come up?"

"No, bless you, Papa, it's better not, yet. No use getting all worked up till we *know,* is there?"

"That's my girl!"

"My love to Mama."

"Hers to you. Mine, too, needless to say. You let us know."

"Certainly. Good-bye."

"Poll."

"Yes?"

"You know how I feel about this."

"I do, Papa, and thank you. There's no need to say it."

"Couldn't if I tried. Ever. And for Jay as much as you, and your mother too. You understand."

"I do understand, Papa. Good-bye."

"It's only Papa," she said, and sat down, heavily.

"Thought Andrew had phoned."

"Yes . . ." She drank tea. "He scared me half out of my wits."

"He had no business phoning. He was a perfect fool to phone."

"I don't blame him. I think it's even worse for them, sitting down there, than for us here."

"I've no doubt it is hard."

"Papa feels things a lot more than he shows."

"I know. I'm glad you realize it."

"I realize how very much he really does think of Jay."

"Great—heavens, I should hope you do!"

"Well, for a long time there was no reason to be sure," Mary retorted with spirit. "Or Mama either." She waited a moment. "You and her, Aunt Hannah," she said. "You know that. You tried not to show it, but I knew and you knew I did. It's all right, it has been for a long time, but you do know that."

Hannah continued to meet her eyes. "Yes, it's true, Mary. There were all kinds of—terrible misgivings; and not without good reason, as you both came to know."

"Plenty of good reasons," Mary said. "But that didn't make it any easier for us."

"Not for any of us," Hannah said. "Particularly you and Jay, but your mother and father too, you know. Anyone who loved you."

"I know. I *do* know, Aunt Hannah. I don't know how I got onto this tack. There's nothing there to resent any more, or worry over, or be grieved by, for any of us, and hasn't been for a long time, thank God. Why on earth did I get *off* on such a tangent! Let's not say another word about it!"

"Just one word more, because I'm not sure you've ever quite known it. Have you ever realized how very highly your father *always* thought of Jay, right from the very beginning?"

Mary looked at her, sensitively and suspiciously. She thought carefully before she spoke. "I know he's *told* me so. But every time he told me he was warning me, too. I know that, as time passed, he came to think a great deal of Jay."

"He thinks the world of him," Hannah rapped out.

"But, no, I never quite believed he really liked him, or respected him from the first and I never will. I think it was just some kind of soft soap."

"Is Jay a man for soft soap?"

"No," she smiled a little, "he certainly isn't, ordinarily. But what *am* I to make of it? Here he was praising Jay to the skies on the one hand and on the other, why practically in the same breath, telling me one reason after another why it would be plain foolhardiness to marry him. What would *you* think!"

"Can't you see that both things might be so—or that he might very sincerely have felt that both things were so, rather?"

Mary thought a moment. "I don't know, Aunt Hannah. No, I don't see quite how."

"You learned how yourself, Mary."

"Did I!"

"You learned there was a lot in what your father—in all our misgivings, but learning it never changed your essential opinion of him, did it? You found you could realize both things at once."

"That's true. Yes. I did."

"We had to learn more and more that was good. You had to learn more and more that wasn't so good."

Mary looked at her with smiling defiance. "All the same, blind as I began it," she said, "I was more right than Papa, wasn't I? It wasn't a *mistake*. Papa was right there'd be trouble—more than he'll ever know or any of you—but it *wasn't* a mistake. Was it?"

Don't *ask* me, child, *tell* me, Hannah thought. "Obviously not," she said.

Mary was quiet a few moments. Then she said, shyly and proudly, "In these past few months, Aunt Hannah, we've come to a—kind of harmoniousness that—that," she began to shake her head. "I've no business talking about it." Her voice trembled. "Least of all right now!" She bit her lips together, shook her head again, and swallowed some tea, noisily. "The way we've been talking," she blurted, her voice full of tea, "it's just like a post-mortem!" She struck her face into her hands and was shaken by tearless sobbing. Hannah subdued an impulse to go to her side. God help her, she whispered. God keep her. After a little while

Mary looked up at her; her eyes were quiet and amazed. "If he dies," she said, "if he's dead, Aunt Hannah, I don't know what I'll do. I just don't know what I'll do."

"God help you," Hannah said; she reached across and took her hand. "God keep you." Mary's face was working. "You'll do well. Whatever it is, you'll do well. Don't you doubt it. Don't you fear." Mary subdued her crying. "It's well to be ready for the worst," Hannah continued. "But we mustn't forget, we don't know yet."

At the same instant, both looked at the clock.

"Certainly by very soon now, he should phone," Mary said. "Unless *he's* had an accident!" she laughed sharply.

"Oh soon, I'm sure," Hannah said. Long before now, she said to herself, if it were anything but the worst. She squeezed Mary's clasped hands, patted them, and withdrew her own hand, feeling, there's no little comfort anyone can give, it'd better be saved for when it's needed most.

Mary did not speak, and Hannah could not think of a word to say. It was absurd, she realized, but along with everything else, she felt almost a kind of social embarrassment about her speechlessness.

But after all, she thought, what *is* there to say! What earthly help am I, or anyone else?

She felt so heavy, all of a sudden, and so deeply tired, that she wished she might lean her forehead against the edge of the table.

"We've simply got to wait," Mary said.

"Yes," Hannah sighed.

I'd better drink some tea, she thought, and did so. Lukewarm and rather bitter, somehow it made her feel even more tired.

They sat without speaking for fully two minutes.

"At least we're given the mercy of a little time," Mary said slowly, "awful as it is to have to wait. To try to prepare ourselves for whatever it may be." She was gazing studiously into her empty cup.

Hannah felt unable to say anything.

"Whatever is," Mary went on, "it's already over and done with." She was speaking virtually without emotion; she was absorbed beyond feeling, Hannah became sure, in what she was beginning to find out and to face. Now she looked up at Hannah and they looked steadily into each other's eyes.

"One of three things," Mary said slowly. "Either he's badly hurt but he'll live, and at best even get thoroughly well, and at worst be a helpless cripple or an invalid or his mind impaired." Hannah wished that she might look away, but she knew that she must not. "Or he is so terribly hurt that he will die of it, maybe quite soon, maybe after a long, terrible struggle, maybe breathing his last at this very minute and wondering where I am, why I'm not beside him." She set her teeth for a moment and tightened her lips, and spoke again, evenly: "Or he was gone already when the man called and he couldn't bear to be the one to tell me, poor thing.

"One, or the other, or the other. And no matter what, there's not one thing in this world *or* the next that we can do or hope or guess at or wish or pray that can change it or help it one iota. Because whatever is, is. That's all. And all there is now is to be ready for it, strong enough for it, whatever it may be. That's all. That's all that matters. It's all that matters because it's all that's possible. Isn't that so?"

While she was speaking, she was with her voice, her eyes and with each word opening in Hannah those all but forgotten hours, almost thirty years past, during which the cross of living had first nakedly borne in upon her being, and she had made the first beginnings of learning how to endure and accept it. *Your turn now, poor child,* she thought; she felt as if a prodigious page were being silently turned, and the breath of its turning touched her heart with cold and tender awe. Her soul is beginning to come of age, she thought; and within those moments she herself became much older, much nearer her own death, and was content to be.

Her heart lifted up in a kind of pride in Mary, in every sorrow she could remember, her own or that of others (and the remembrances rushed upon her); in all existence and endurance. She wanted to cry out *Yes! Exactly! Yes. Yes. Begin to see. Your turn now.* She wanted to hold her niece at arms' length and to turn and admire this blossoming. She wanted to take her in her arms and groan unto God for what it meant to be alive. But chiefly she wanted to keep stillness and to hear the young woman's voice and to watch her eyes and her round forehead while she spoke, and to accept and experience this repetition of her younger experience, which bore her high and pierced like music.

"Isn't that so?" Mary repeated.

"That and much more," she said.

"You mean God's mercy?" Mary said softly.

"Nothing of the kind," Hannah replied sharply. "What I mean, I'd best not try to say." (I've begun, though, she reflected; and I startled her, I hurt her, almost as if I'd spoken against God.) "Only because it's better if you learn it for yourself. *By* yourself."

"What do you mean?"

"Whatever we hear, learn, Mary, it's almost certain to be hard. Tragically hard. You're beginning to know that and to face it: very bravely. What I mean is that this is only the beginning. You'll learn much more. Beginning very soon now."

"Whatever it is, I want so much to be *worthy* of it," Mary said, her eyes shining.

"Don't try too hard to be worthy of it, Mary. Don't think of it that way. Just do your best to endure it and let any question of worthiness take care of itself. That's more than enough."

"I feel so utterly unprepared. So little time to prepare *in.*"

"I don't think it's a kind of thing that can be prepared for; it just has to be lived through."

There was a kind of ambition there, Hannah felt, a kind of pride or poetry, which was very mistaken and very dangerous. But she was not yet quite sure what she meant; and of all the times to become beguiled by such a matter, to try to argue it, or warn about it! She's so young, she told herself. She'll learn; poor soul, she'll learn.

Even while Hannah watched her, Mary's face became diffuse and humble. *Oh, not yet,* Hannah whispered desperately to herself. *Not yet.* But Mary said, shyly, "Aunt Hannah, can we kneel down for a minute?"

Not yet, she wanted to say. For the first time in her life she suspected how mistakenly prayer can be used, but she was unsure why. *What can I say,* she thought, almost in panic. *How can I judge?* She was waiting too long; Mary smiled at her, timidly, and in a beginning of bewilderment; and in compassion and self-doubt Hannah came around the table and they knelt side by side. We can be seen, Hannah realized; for the shades were up. *Let us,* she told herself angrily.

"In the name of the Father and of the Son and of the Holy Ghost, Amen," Mary said in a low voice.

"Amen," Hannah trailed.

They were silent and they could hear the ticking of the clock, the shuffling of fire, and the yammering of the big kettle.

God is not here, Hannah said to herself; and made a small cross upon her breastbone, against her blasphemy.

"O God," Mary whispered, "strengthen me to accept Thy will, whatever it may be." Then she stayed silent.

God hear her, Hannah said to herself. God forgive me. God forgive me.

What can I know of the proper time for her, she said to herself. God forgive me.

Yet she could not rid herself: something mistaken, unbearably piteous, infinitely malign was at large within that faithfulness; she was helpless to forfend it or even to know its nature.

Suddenly there opened within her a chasm of infinite depth and from it flowed the paralyzing breath of eternal darkness.

I believe nothing. Nothing whatever.

"Our Father," she heard herself say, in a strange voice; and Mary, innocent of her terror, joined in the prayer. And as they continued, and Hannah heard more and more clearly than her own the young, warm, earnest, faithful, heartsick voice, her moment of terrifying unbelief became a remembrance, a temptation successfully resisted through God's grace.

Deliver us from evil, she repeated silently, several times after their prayer was finished. But the malign was still there, as well as the mercifulness.

They got to their feet.

As it became with every minute and then with every flickering of the clock more and more clear that Andrew had had far more than enough time to get out there, and to telephone, Mary and her aunt talked less and less. For a little while after their prayer, in relief, Mary had talked quite volubly of matters largely irrelevant to the event; she had even made little jokes and had even laughed at them, without more than a small undertone of hysteria; and in all this, Hannah had thought it best (and, for that matter, the only thing possible), to follow suit; but that soon faded away; nor was it to return; now they merely sat in quietness, each on her side of the kitchen table, their eyes cast away from each other, drinking tea for which they had no desire. Mary made a full fresh pot of tea, and they conversed a little about that, and the heated water with which to dilute it, they discussed that briefly; but such little exchanges wore quickly down into silence. Mary, whispering, "Excuse me," retired to the bathroom, affronted and humbled that one should have to obey such a call at such a time; she felt for a few moments as stupid and enslaved as a baby on its potty, and far more ungainly and vulgar; then, with her wet hands planted in the basin of cold water she stared incredulously into her numb, reflected face, which seemed hardly real to her until, with shame, she realized that at this of all moments she was mirror gazing. Hannah, left alone, was grateful that we are ani-

mals; it was this silly, strenuous, good, humble cluttering of animal needs which saw us through sane, fully as much as prayer;
and towards the end of these moments of solitude, with her mind
free from the subtle deceptions of concern, she indulged herself in
whispering, aloud, "He's dead. There's no longer the slightest
doubt of it"; and began to sign herself with the Cross in prayer for
the dead, but sharply remembering *we do not know,* and feeling as
if she had been on the verge of exercising malign power against
him, deflected the intention of the gesture towards God's mercy
upon him, in whatsoever condition he might now be. When Mary
returned, she put more wood on the fire, looked into the big kettle, saw that a third of the water had boiled away, and refilled it.
Neither of them said anything about this, but each knew what the
other was thinking, and after they had sat again in silence for well
over ten minutes, Mary looked at her aunt who, feeling the eyes
upon her, looked into them; then Mary said, very quietly, "I only
wish we'd hear now, because I am ready."

Hannah nodded, and felt: you really are. How good it is that
you don't even want to touch my hand. And she felt something
shining and majestic stand up within her darkness as if to say
before God: Here she is and she is adequate to the worst and she
has done it for herself, not through my help or even, particularly,
through Yours. See to it that You appreciate her.

Mary went on: "It's just barely conceivable that the news is so
much less bad than we'd expected, that Andrew is simply too
overjoyed with relief to bother to phone, and is bringing him
straight home instead, for a wonderful surprise. That would be
like him. If things were that way. And like Jay, if they were, if he
were, conscious enough, to go right along with the surprise and
enjoy it, and just *laugh* at how scared we've been." By her shining
eyes, and her almost smiling face, she seemed almost to be believing this while she said it; almost to be sure that within another
few minutes it would happen in just that way. But now she went
on, "That's just barely conceivable, just about one chance in a

million, and so long as there *is* that chance, so long as we don't absolutely know to the contrary, I'm not going to dismiss the possibility entirely from my mind. I'm not going to say he's dead, Aunt Hannah, till I know he is," she said as if defiantly.

"Certainly *not!*"

"But I'm all but certain he is, all the same," Mary said; and saying so, and meeting Hannah's eyes, she could not for a few moments remember what more she had intended to say. Then she remembered, and it seemed too paltry to speak of, and she waited until all that she saw in her mind was again clear and full of its own weight; then again she spoke, "I think what's very much more likely is, that he was already dead when the man just phoned, and that he couldn't bear to tell me, and I don't blame him, I'm grateful he didn't. It ought to come from a man in the family, somebody—close to Jay, and to me. I think Andrew was pretty sure—what was up—when he went out, and had every intention not to leave us in mid-air this way. He meant to phone. But all the time he was hoping against hope, as we all were, and when—when he *saw* Jay—it was more than he could do to phone, and he knew it was more than I could stand to *hear* over a phone, even from him, and so he didn't, and I'm infinitely grateful he didn't. He must have known that as time kept—wearing on in this terrible way, we'd draw our own conclusions and have time to—time. And that's best. He wanted to be with me when I heard. And that's right. So do it. Straight from his lips. I think what he did—what he's doing, it's . . ."

Hannah saw that she was now nearer to breaking than at any time before, and she could scarcely resist her impulse to reach for her hand; she managed, with anguish, to forbid herself. After a moment Mary continued, quietly and in control, "What he's doing is to come in with Jay's poor body to the undertaker's and soon now he'll come home to us and tell us."

Hannah continued to look into her gentle and ever more incredulous and shining eyes; she found that she could not speak and that she was nodding, as curtly, and rapidly, almost as if she were palsied. She made herself stop nodding.

"That's what I think," Mary said, "and that's what I'm ready for. But I'm not going to say it, or accept it, or do my husband any such dishonor or danger—not until I know beyond recall that it's so."

They continued to gaze into the other's eyes; Hannah's eyes were burning because she felt she must not blink; and after some moments a long, crying groan broke from the younger woman and in a low and shaken voice she said, "Oh I do beseech my God that it not be so," and Hannah whispered, "So do I"; and again they became still, knowing little and seeing nothing except each other's suffering eyes; and it was thus that they were when they heard footsteps on the front porch. Hannah looked aside and downward; a long, breaking breath came from May; they drew back their chairs and started for the door.

Chapter 9

SHE WAS WATCHING for him anxiously as he came back into the living room; he bent to her ear and said, "Nothing."

"No word yet?"

"No." He sat down. He leaned towards her. "Probably too soon to expect to hear," he said.

"Perhaps." She did not resume her mending.

Joel tried again to read *The New Republic*.

"Does she seem well?"

Good God, Joel said to himself. He leaned towards her, "Well's can be expected."

She nodded.

He went back to *The New Republic*.

"Shouldn't we go up?"

That's about all it would need, Joel thought, to have to bellow at us. He leaned towards her and put his hand on her arm. "Better not," he said, "till we know what's what. Too much to-do."

"To much what?"

"*To-do.* Fuss. Too many people."

"Oh. Perhaps. It does seem our place to, Joel."

Rot! he said to himself. "Our place," he said rather more loudly, "is to stay where she prefers us to be." He began to realize that she had not meant *our place* in mere propriety. Goddamn it all, he thought, why *can't* she be there! He touched her shoulder. "Try not to mind it, Catherine," he said. "I asked Poll, and she said, better not. She said, there's no use our getting all wrought up until we know."

"Very sensible," she said, dubiously.

"*Damned* sensible," he said, with conviction. "She's just trying her best to hold herself together," he explained.

Catherine turned her head in courteous inquiry.

"Trying—to hold—herself—together!"

She winced. "Don't—shout at me, Joel. Just speak distinctly and I can hear you."

"I'm sorry," he said; he knew she had not heard. He leaned close to her ear. "I'm sorry," he said again, carefully and not too loudly. "Jumpy, that's all."

"No matter," she said in that level of her voice which was already old.

He watched her a moment, and sighed with sorrow for her, and said, "We'll know before long."

"Yes," she said. "I presume." She relaxed her hands in her sewing and gazed out across the shadowy room.

It became mere useless torment to watch her; he went back to *The New Republic*.

"I wonder how it happened," she said, after a while.

He leaned towards her: "So do I."

"There must have been others injured, as well."

Again he leaned towards her. "Maybe. We don't know."

"Even killed, perhaps."

"We don't—know, Catherine."

"No."

Jay drives like hell broken loose, Joel thought to himself; he decided not to say it. Whatever's happened, he thought, one thing he doesn't need is that kind of talk about him. Or even thinking.

He began to realize, with a kind of sardonic amusement, that he was being superstitious as well as merely courteous. Why I don't want to go up till we hear, too, he said to himself. Hands off. Lap of the gods. Don't rock the boat.

Particularly not a wrecked boat.

"Of course, it does seem to me, Jay drives rather recklessly," Catherine said, carefully.

"*Everybody* does," he told her. *Rather,* indeed!

"I remember I was *most uneasy* when they decided to purchase it."

Well, you're vindicated.

"Progress," he told her.

"Beg pardon?"

"*Progress.* We mustn't—stand—in the way—of Progress."

"No," she said uneasily, "I suppose not."

Good—God, woman!

"That's a joke, Catherine, a very—poor—joke."

Oh.

"I don't think it's a time for levity, Joel."

"Nor do I."

She tilted her head courteously. Taking care not to yell, he said, "You're right. Neither—do—I."

She nodded.

Working his way through another editorial as through barbed wire, Joel thought: I had no business calling her. Why couldn't I trust her to let me know, quick's she heard. Hannah, anyhow.

He pushed ahead with his reading.

A heaviness had begun in him from the moment he had heard of the accident; he had said to himself, *uh-huh,* and without expecting to, had nodded sharply. It had been as if he had known that this or something like it was bound to happen, sooner or later; and he was hardly more moved than surprised. This heaviness had steadily increased while he sat and waited and by now the air felt like iron and it was almost as if he could taste in his mouth the sour and cold, taciturn taste of iron. Well what else are we to expect, he said to himself. What life is. He braced against it quietly to accept, endure it, relishing not only his exertion but the sullen, obdurate cruelty of the iron, for it was the cruelty which proved and measured his courage. Funny I feel so little about it, he thought. He thought of his son-in-law. He felt respect, affection, deep general sadness. No personal grief whatever. After all that struggle, he thought, all that courage and ambition, he was getting nowhere. Jude the Obscure, he suddenly thought; and then of the steady thirty-years' destruction of all of his own hopes. If it has to be a choice between crippling, invalidism, death, he thought, let's hope he's out of it. Even just a choice between that and living on another thirty or forty years; he's well out of it. In my opinion, damn it; not his. He thought of his daughter: all her spirit, which had resisted them so admirably to marry him, then only to be broken and dissolved on her damned piety; all her intelligence, hardly even born, came to nothing in the marriage, making ends meet and again above all, the Goddamned piety; all her innocent eagerness, which it looked as if nothing could ever kill, still sticking its chin out for more. And again, he could feel very little personal involvement. She made her bed, he thought, and she's done a damned creditable job of lying in it; not one whine. And if he's—if that's—finished now, there's hell to pay for her, and little if anything I can do. Now he remembered vividly, with enthusiasm and with sadness, the few years in which they had been such good friends, and for a moment he thought *perhaps again,* and caught himself up in a snort of self-contempt. Bargaining on his death, he thought, as if I were the rejected suitor, primping up for one more try: *once more unto the breach.* Besides, that had never been the real estrangement; it was the whole stinking morass of churchiness that really separated them, and now that was apt to get worse rather than better. Apt? Dead certain to.

And his wife, while she mended, was thinking: such a tragedy. Such a burden for her. Poor dear Mary. How on earth is she to manage. Of course it's still entirely possible that he isn't—passed away. But that could make matters even more—tragic, for both of them. Such an active man, unable to support his family. How dreadful, in any event. Of course, we can help. But not with the hardest of the burden. Poor dear child. And the poor children. And beneath such unspoken words, while with her weak eyes she bent deeply to her mending, her generous and unreflective spirit was more deeply grieved than she could find thought for, and more resolute than any thought for resoluteness could have made it. How very swiftly life goes! she thought. It seems only yesterday that she was my little Mary, or that Jay first came to call. She looked up from her mending into the silent light and shadow, and the kind of long and profound sighing of the heart flowed out of her which, excepting music, was her only way of yielding to sadness.

"We must be very good to them, Joel," she said.

He was startled, almost frightened, by her sudden voice, and he wanted, in some vengeful reflex of exasperation, to ask her what she had said. But he knew he had heard her and, leaning towards her, replied, "Of course we must."

"Whatever has happened."

"Certainly."

He began to realize the emotion, and the loneliness, behind the banality of what she had said; he was ashamed of himself to have answered as if it were merely banal. He wished he could think what to say that would make up for it, but he could not think of what to say. He knew of his wife, with tender amusement, that she almost certainly had not realized his unkindness, and that she would be hopelessly puzzled if he tried to explain and apologize. Let it be, he thought.

He feels much more than he says, she comforted herself; but she wished that he might ever say what he felt. She felt his hand on her wrist and his head close to hers. She leaned towards him.

"I understand, Catherine," he said.

What does he mean that he understands, Catherine wondered. Something I failed to hear, no doubt, she thought, though their words had been so few that she could not imagine what. But she quickly decided not to exasperate him by a question; she was sure of his kind intention, and deeply touched by it.

"Thank you, Joel," she said, and putting her other hand over his, patted it rapidly, several times. Such endearments, except in their proper place, embarrassed her and, she had always feared, were still more embarrassing to him; and now, though she had been unable to resist caressing him, and take even greater solace from his gentle pressing of her wrist, she took care soon to remove her hand, and soon after, he took his own away. She felt a moment of solemn and angry gratitude to have spent so many years, in such harmony, with a man so good, but that was beyond utterance; and then once more she thought of her daughter and of what she was facing.

Joel, meanwhile, was thinking: she needs that (pressing her wrist), and, as she shyly took her hand away, I wish I could do more; and suddenly, not for her sake but by an impulse of his own, he wanted to take her in his arms. Out of the question. Instead, he watched her dim-sighted, enduring face as she gazed out once more across the room, and felt a moment of incredulous and amused pride in her immense and unbreakable courage, and of proud gratitude, regardless of and including all regret, to have had so many years with such a woman; but that was beyond utterance: and then once more he thought of his daughter and of what she had been through and now must face.

"Sometimes life seems more—cruel—than can be borne," she said. "Theirs, I'm thinking of. Poor Jay's, and poor dear Mary's."

She felt his hand and waited, but he did not speak. She looked toward him, apprehensively polite, her beg-pardon smile, by habit, on her face; and saw his bearded head, unexpectedly close and huge in the light, nodding deeply and slowly, five times.

Chapter 10

ANDREW DID NOT BOTHER TO KNOCK, but opened the door and closed it quietly behind him and, seeing their moving shadows near the kitchen threshold, walked quickly down the hall. They could not see his face in the dark hallway but by his tight, set way of walking, they were virtually sure. They were all but blocking his way. Instead of going into the hall to meet him, they drew aside to let him into the kitchen. He did not hesitate with their own moment's hesitation but came straight on, his mouth a straight line and his eyes like splintered glass, and without saying a word he put his arms around his aunt so tightly that she gasped, and lifted her from the floor. "Mary," Hannah whispered, close to his ear; he looked; there she stood waiting, her eyes, her face, like that of an astounded child which might be pleading. Oh, don't hit me; and before he could speak he heard her say, thinly and gently, "He's dead, Andrew, isn't he?" and he could not speak, but nodded, and he became aware that he was holding his aunt's feet off the floor and virtually breaking her bones, and his sister said, in the same small and unearthly voice, "He was dead when you got there"; and again he nodded; and then he set Hannah down carefully on her feet and, turning to his sister, took her by her shoulders and said, more loudly than he had expected, "He was instantly killed," and he kissed her upon the mouth and they embraced, and without tears but with great violence he sobbed twice, his cheek against hers, while he stared downwards through her loose hair at her humbled back and at the changeful blinking of the linoleum; then, feeling her become heavy against him, said, "Here, Mary," catching her across the shoulders and helping her to a chair, just as she, losing strength in her knees, gasped, "I've got to sit down," and looked timidly towards her aunt, who at the same moment saying, in a broken voice, "Sit down, Mary," was at her other side, her arm around her waist and her face as bleached and shocking as a skull. She put an arm tightly around each of them and felt gratitude and pleasure, in the firmness and warmth of their moving bodies, and they walked three abreast (like bosom friends, it occurred to her, the three Musketeers) to the nearest chair; and she could see Andrew twist it towards her with his outstretched left hand, and between them, slowly, they let her down into it, and then she could see only her aunt's face, leaning deep above her, very large and very close, the eyes at once intense and tearful behind their heavy lenses, the strong mouth loose and soft, the whole face terrible in love and grief, naked and undisciplined as she had never seen it before.

"Let Papa know and Mama," she whispered. "I promised."

"I will," Hannah said, starting for the hall.

"Walter's bringing them straight up," Andrew said. "They know by now." He brought another chair. "Sit down, Aunt Hannah." She sat and took both Mary's hands in her own, on Mary's knees, and realized that Mary was squeezing her hands with all her strength, and as strongly as she was able. She replied in kind to this constantly shifting, almost writhing pressure.

"Sit with us, Andrew," Mary said, a little more loudly; he was already bringing a third chair and now he sat, and put his hands upon theirs, and, feeling the convulsing of her hands, thought, Christ, it's as if she were in labor. *And she is.* Thus they sat in silence a few moments while he thought: now I've got to tell them how it happened. In God's name, how can I begin!

"I want whiskey," Mary said, in a small, cold voice, and tried to get up.

"I'll get it," Andrew said, standing.

"You don't know where it is," she said, continuing to put aside their hands even after they were withdrawn. She got up and they stood as if respectfully aside and she walked between them and went into the hall; they heard her rummaging in the closet, and looked at each other. "She needs it," Hannah said.

He nodded. He had been surprised, because of Jay, that there was whiskey in the house; and he was sick with self-disgust to have thought of it. "We all do," he said.

Without looking at them Mary went to the kitchen closet and brought a thick tumbler to the table. The bottle was almost full. She poured the tumbler full while they watched her, feeling they must not interfere, and took a deep gulp and choked on it, and swallowed most of it.

"Dilute it," Hannah said, slapping her hard between the shoulders and drying her lips and her chin with a dish towel. "It's much too strong, that way."

"I will," Mary croaked, and cleared her throat, "I will," she said more clearly.

"Just sit down, Mary," Andrew and Hannah said at the same moment, and Andrew brought her a glass of water and Hannah helped her to her chair.

"I'm going to have some, too," Andrew said,

"Goodness, do!" said Mary.

"Let me fix us a good strong toddy," Hannah said. "It'll help you to sleep."

"I don't want to sleep," Mary said; she sipped at her whiskey and took plenty of the water. "I've got to learn how it happened."

"Aunt Hannah," Andrew asked quietly, motioning towards the bottle.

"Please."

While he broke ice and brought glasses and a pitcher of water, none of them spoke; Mary sat in a distorted kind of helplessness at once meek and curiously sullen, waiting. Months later, seeing a horse which had fallen in the street, Andrew was to remember her; and he was to remember it wasn't drunkenness, either. It was just the flat of the hand of Death.

"Let me pour my own," Mary said. "Because," she added with deliberation while she poured, "I want it just as strong as I can stand it." She tasted the dark drink, added a little more whiskey, tasted again, and put the bottle aside. Hannah watched her with acute concern, thinking, if she gets drunk tonight, and if her mother sees her drunk, she'll half die of shame, and thinking, nonsense. It's the most sensible thing she could do.

"Drink it very slowly, Mary," Andrew said gently. "You aren't used to it."

"I'll take care," Mary said.

"It's just the thing for shock," Hannah said.

Andrew poured two small straight drinks and gave one to his aunt; they drank them off quickly and took water, and he prepared two pale highballs.

"Now, Andrew, I want to hear all about it," Mary said.

He looked at Hannah.

"Mary," he said. "Mama and Papa'll be here any minute. You'd just have to hear it all over again. I'll tell you, of course, if you prefer, right away but—could you wait?"

But even as he was speaking she was nodding, and Hannah was saying. "Yes, child," as all three thought of the confusions and repetitions which were, at best, inevitable. Now after a moment Mary said, "Anyway, you say he didn't have to suffer. *Instantly,* you said."

He nodded, and said, "Mary, I saw him—at Roberts'. There was just one mark on his body."

She looked at him. "His head."

"Right at the exact point of the chin, a small bruise. A cut so small—they can close it with one stitch. And a little blue bruise on his lower lip. It wasn't even swollen."

"That's all," she said.

"All," Hannah said.

"That's all," Andrew said. "The doctor said it was concussion of the brain. It was instantaneous."

She was silent; he felt that she must be doubting it. Christ, he thought furiously, at least she could be spared *that!*

"He can't have suffered, Mary, not even for a fraction of a second. Mary, I saw his face. There wasn't a glimmer of pain in it. Only—a kind of surprise. Startled."

Still she said nothing. I've got to make her sure of it, he thought. How in heaven's name can I make it clearer? If necessary, I'll get hold of the doctor and make him tell her hims . . .

"He never knew he was dying," she said. "Not a minute, not one moment, to know, 'my life is ending.'"

Hannah put a quick hand to her shoulder; Andrew dropped to his knees before her; took her hands and said, most earnestly, "Mary, in God's name be thankful he didn't! That's a hideous thing for a man in the prime of life to have to know. He wasn't a *Christian,* you know," he blurted it fiercely. "He didn't have to make his peace with God. He was a man, with a wife and two children, and I'd say that sparing him *that* horrible knowledge was the one thing we can thank God for!" And he added, in a desperate voice, "I'm so terribly sorry I said that, Mary!"

But Hannah, who had been gently saying, "He's right, Mary, he's right, be thankful for that," now told him quietly, "It's all right, Andrew"; and Mary, whose eyes fixed upon his, had shown increasing shock and terror, now said tenderly, "Don't mind, dear. Don't be sorry. I understand. You're right."

"That venomous thing I said about Christians," Andrew said after a moment. "I can never forgive myself, Mary."

"Don't grieve over it, Andrew. Don't. Please. Look at me, please." He looked at her. "It's true I was thinking as I was bound to as a Christian, but I was forgetting we're human, and you set me right and I'm thankful. You're right. Jay wasn't—a religious man, in that sense, and to realize could have only been—as you said for him. Probably as much so, even if he were religious." She looked at him quietly. "So just please know I'm not hurt or angry. I needed to realize what you told me and I thank God for it."

There was a noise on the porch; Andrew got from his knees and kissed his sister on the forehead. "Don't be sorry," she said. He looked at her, tightened his lips, and hurried to the door.

"Papa," he said, and stood aside to let him past. His mother fumbled for his arm, and gripped it hard. He put his hand gently across her shoulders and said, next her ear, "They're back in the kitchen"; she followed her husband. "Come in, Walter."

"Oh no. Thank you," Walter Starr said. "These are family matters. But if there's . . ."

Andrew took him by the arm. "Come in a minute, anyway," he said. "I know Mary'll want to thank you."

"Well now . . ." Andrew led him in.

"Papa," Mary said, and got up and kissed him. He turned with her towards her mother. "Mama?" she said in a pinched, almost crying voice, and they embraced. "There, there, there," her mother said in a somewhat cracked voice, clapping her loudly on the back. "Mary, dear. There, there, there!"

She saw Walter Starr, looking as if he were sure he was unwelcome. "Why, Walter!" she whispered, and hurried to meet him. He put out his hand, looking frightened, and said, "Mrs. Follet, I just couldn't ever . . ."

She threw her arms around him and kissed him on the cheek. "Bless you," she whispered, crying softly.

"There now," he said, blushing deeply and trying to embrace and to sustain her without touching her too closely. "There now," he said again.

"I must stop this," she said, drawing away from him and looking about wildly for something.

"Here," said Andrew and her father and Walter Starr, each

offering a handkerchief. She took her brother's, blew her nose, dried her eyes, and sat down. "Sit down, Walter."

"Oh thank you, no. I don't think," Walter said. "Only dropped in a moment; really must be off."

"Why Walter, what nonsense, you're one of the family," Mary said, and those who could hear nodded and murmured "Of course," although they knew this was embarrassing for him, and hoped he would go home.

"Now that's ever so kind," Walter said. "But I can't stay. Really must be off. Now if . . ."

"Walter, I want to thank you," she said; for now she too had reconsidered.

"So do we all," Andrew said.

"More than I can say," Mary finished.

He shook his head. "Nothing. Nothing," he said. "Now I just want you to know, if there's anything in the world I can do, be of help in any way, let me please, don't hesitate to tell me."

"Thank you, Walter. And if there is, we certainly will. Gratefully."

"Good night then."

Andrew walked with him to the front door. "Just let me know, Andrew. *Anything,*" Walter said.

"I will and thank you," Andrew replied. Their eyes met, and for a moment both were caught in astonishment. *He wishes it was me!* Andrew thought. *He wishes it was himself!* Walter thought. *Perhaps I do, too,* Andrew thought, and once again, as he had felt when he first saw the dead body, he felt absurd, ashamed, guilty almost of cheating, even of murder, in being alive.

"Why, Jay, of all people?" Andrew said, in a low voice.

Still watching his splintered eyes, Walter heavily shook his head.

"Good night, Andrew."

"Good night, Walter."

He shut the door.

Mary's father caught her eye; with his chin he beckoned her

to a corner of the kitchen. "I want to talk to you alone a minute," he said in a low voice.

She looked at him thoughtfully, then took her glass from the table, said, "Excuse us a minute," over her shoulder, and ushered him into the room she had prepared for her husband. She turned on the bedside lamp, quietly closed both doors, and stood looking at him, waiting.

"Sit down, Poll," he said.

She looked about. One of them would have to sit on the bed. It was neatly laid open, cool and pleasant below the plumped pillows.

"I had it all ready," she said, "but he never came back."

"What's that?"

"Nothing, Papa."

"Don't stay on your feet," he said. "Let's sit down."

"I don't care to."

He came over to her and took her hand and looked at her searchingly. Why he's just my height, she realized again. She saw how much his eyes, in sympathy and pain, were like his sister's, tired, tender and resolute beneath the tired, frail eyelids. He could not speak at first.

You're a *good* man, she said to herself, and her lips moved. A good, good man. My father. In an instant she experienced afresh the whole of their friendship and estrangement. Her eyes filled with tears and her mouth began to tremble. "Papa," she said. He took her close to him and she cried quietly.

"It's hell, Poll," she heard him say. "Just hell. It's just plain hell." For a few moments she sobbed so deeply that he said nothing more, but only stroked the edge of her back, over and over, from her shoulder to her waist, and cried out within himself in fury and disgust. God*damn* it! God *damn* such a life! She's too young for this. And thinking of that, it occurred to him that it was at just her age that his own life had had its throat twisted, and not by death, but by her own birth and her brother's.

"But you gotta go through with it," he said.

Against his shoulder he could feel her vigorous nodding. You will, he thought; you've got spunk.

"No way out of it," he said.

"I think I *will* sit down." She broke from him and with an almost vindictive sense of violation sat heavily at the edge of the bed, just where it was turned down, next the plumped pillows. He turned the chair and sat with her knee to knee.

"Something I've got to tell you," he said.

She looked at him and waited.

"You remember what Cousin Patty was like? When she lost George?"

"Not very well. I wasn't more than five or six."

"Well, I do. She ran around like a chicken with its head off. 'Oh, why does it have to be *me*? What did *I* ever do that it happened to *me*?' Banging her head against the furniture, trying to stab herself with her scissors, yelling like a stuck pig: you could hear her in the next block."

Her eyes became cold. "You needn't worry," she said.

"I don't, because you're not a fool. But *you'd* better, and that's what I want to warn you about."

She kept looking at him.

"See here, Poll," he said. "It's bad enough right now, but it's going to take a while to sink in. When it really sinks in it's going to be any amount worse. It'll be so much worse you'll think it's more than you can bear. Or any other human being. And worse than that, you'll have to go through it alone, because there isn't a thing on earth any of us can do to help, beyond blind animal sympathy."

She was gazing slantwise towards the floor in some kind of coldly patient irony, he felt sick to death of himself.

"Look at me, Poll," he said. She looked at him. "That's when you're going to need every ounce of common sense you've got," he said. "Just spunk won't be enough; you've got to have gumption. You've got to bear it in mind that nobody that ever lived is specially privileged; the axe can fall at any moment, on any neck, without any warning or any regard for justice. You've got to keep your mind off pitying your own rotten luck and setting up any kind of a howl about it. You've got to remember that things as bad as this and a hell of a lot worse have happened to millions of people before and that they've come through it and that you will too. You'll bear it because there isn't any choice—except to go to pieces. You've got two children to take care of. And regardless of that you owe it to yourself and you owe it to him. You understand me."

"Of course."

"I know it's just unmitigated tommyrot to try to say a word about it. To say nothing of brass. All I want is to warn you that a lot worse is yet to come than you can imagine yet, so for God's sake brace yourself for it and try to hold yourself together." He said, with sudden eagerness, "It's a kind of test, Mary, and it's the only kind that amounts to anything. When something rotten like this happens. Then you have your choice. You start to really be alive, or you start to die. That's all." Watching her eyes, he felt fear for her and said, "I imagine you're thinking about your religion."

"I am," she said, with a certain cool pride.

"Well, more power to you," he said. "I know you've got a kind of help I could never have. Only one thing: take the greatest kind of care you don't just—crawl into it like a hole and hide in it."

"I'll take care," she said.

She means there is nothing I can tell her about that, he thought; and she is right.

"Talk to Hannah about it," he said.

"I will, Papa."

"One other thing."

"Yes?"

"There are going to be financial difficulties. We'll see just what, and just how to settle them, course of time. I just want to *take* that worry off your hands. Don't worry. We'll work that out."

"Bless you, Papa."

"Rats. Drink your drink."

She drank deeply and shuddered.

"Take all you can without getting drunk," he said. "I wouldn't give a whoop if you got blind drunk, best thing you could do. But you've got tomorrow to reckon with." And tomorrow and tomorrow.

"It doesn't' seem to have any effect," she said, her voice still liquid. "The only times I drank before I had a terribly weak head, just one drink was enough to make me absolutely squiffy. But now it doesn't seem to have any effect in the slightest." She drank some more.

"Good," he said. "That can happen. Shock, or strain. I know once when your mother was very sick I . . ." They both remembered her sickness. "No matter. Take all you want and I've more if you want it, but keep an eye on yourself. It can hit you like a ton of bricks."

"I'll be careful."

"Time we went back to the others." He helped her to her feet, and put a hand on her shoulder. "Just bear in mind what I said. It's just a test, and it's one that good people come through."

"I will, Papa, and thank you."

"I've got absolute confidence in you," he said, wishing that this was entirely true, and that she could entirely care.

"Thank you, Papa," she said. "That's going to be a great help to know."

Her hand on the doorknob, she turned off the light and preceded him into the kitchen.

Chapter 11

"WHY WHERE . . ." Mary began, for there was nobody in the kitchen.

"Must be in the living room," her father said, and took her arm.

"There's more room here," Andrew told her, as they came in. Although the night was warm, he was nursing a small fire. All the shades, Mary noticed, were drawn to the window sills.

"Mary," her mother said loudly, patting a place beside her on the sofa. Mary sat beside her and took her hand. Her mother took Mary's left hand in both of her hands, drew it into her lap, and pressed it against her thin thighs with all her strength.

Her aunt sat to one side of the fireplace and now her father took a chair at the other side. The Morris chair just stood empty beside its reading lamp. Even after the fire was going nicely, Andrew squatted before it, making small adjustments. Nobody spoke, and nobody looked at the Morris chair or at another person. The footsteps of a man, walking slowly, became gradually louder along the sidewalk, and passed the house, and diminished into silence; and in the silence of the universe they listened to their little fire.

Finally Andrew stood up straight from the fire and they all

looked at his despairing face, and tried not to demand too much of him with their eyes. He looked at each of them in turn, and went over and bent deeply towards his mother.

"Let me tell you, Mama," he said. "That way, we can all hear. I'm sorry, Mary."

"Dear," his mother said gratefully, and fumbled for his hand and patted it. "Of course," Mary said, and gave him her place beside the "good" ear. They shifted to make room, and she sat at her mother's deaf side. Again her mother caught her hand into her lap; with the other, she tilted her ear trumpet. Joel leaned toward them, his hand behind his ear; Hannah stared into the wavering hearth.

"He was all alone," Andrew said, not very loudly but with the most scrupulous distinctness. "Nobody else was hurt, or even in the accident."

"That's a mercy," his mother said. It was, they all realized; yet each of them was shocked. Andrew nodded sharply to silence her.

"So we'll never know exactly how it happened," he went on. "But we know *enough,*" he said, speaking the last word with a terrible and brutal bitterness.

"Mmh," his father grunted, nodding sharply; Hannah drew in and let out a long breath.

"I talked with the man who found him. He was the man who phoned you, Mary. He waited there for me all that time because he thought it would help if—if the man who first saw Jay was there to tell one of us all he could. He told me all he knew of course," he said, remembering, with the feeling that he would never forget it, the awed, calm, kind, rural face and the slow, careful, half-literate voice. "He was just as fine as a human being can be." He felt a kind of angry gratitude that such a man had been there, and had been there first. Jay couldn't have asked for anyone better, he said to himself. Nobody could.

"He said he was on his way home, about nine o'clock, coming in towards town, and he heard an auto coming up from behind, terrifically fast, and coming nearer and nearer, and he thought, There's somebody that's sure got to get some place in a bad hurry" ("He was hurrying home," Mary said) "or else he's crazy" (he had said "crazy drunk").

"He wasn't crazy," Mary said. "He was just trying to get home (bless his heart), he was so much later than he'd said."

Andrew looked at her with dry, brilliant eyes and nodded.

"He'd told me not to wait supper," she said, "but he wanted to get home before the children were asleep."

"What is it?" her mother asked, with nervous politeness.

"Nothing important, Mama," Andrew said gently. "I'll explain later." He drew a deep breath in very sharply, and felt less close to tears.

"All of a sudden, he said, he heard a perfectly terrifying noise, just a second or two, and then dead silence. He knew it must be whoever was in that auto and that they must be in bad trouble, so he turned around and drove back, about a quarter of a mile, he thinks, just the other side of Bell's Bridge. He told me he almost missed it altogether because there was nothing on the road and even though he'd kind of been expecting that and driving pretty slowly, looking off both sides of the road, he almost missed it because just next the bridge on that side, the side of the road is quite a steep bank."

"I know," Mary whispered.

"But just as he came off the far end of the bridge—you come down at a sort of angle, you know . . ."

"I know," Mary whispered.

"Something caught in his lights and it was one of the wheels of the automobile." He looked across his mother and said, "Mary, it was still turning."

"Beg pardon?" his mother said.

"It was still turning," he told her. "The wheel he saw."

"Mercy, Andrew," she whispered.

"*Hahh!*" her husband exclaimed, almost inaudibly.

"He got out right away and hurried down there. The auto was upside down and Jay . . ."

Although he did not feel that he was near weeping he found that for a moment he could not speak. Finally he said, "He was just lying there on the ground beside it, on his back, about a foot away from it. His clothes were hardly even rumpled."

Again he found that he could not speak. After a moment he managed to force himself to.

"The man said somehow he was sure he was—dead—the minute he saw him. He doesn't know how. Just some special kind of stillness. He lighted matches though, of course, to try and make sure. Listened for his heartbeat and tried to feel for his pulse. He moved his auto around so he could see by the head-lights. He couldn't find anything wrong except a little cut, exactly on the point of his chin. The windshield of Jay's car was broken and he even took a piece of it and used it like a mirror, to see if there was any breath. After that he just waited a few minutes until he heard an auto coming and stopped them and told them to get help as soon as possible."

"Did they get a doctor?" Mary asked.

"Mary said, 'Did they get a doctor,'" Andrew said to his mother. "Yes, he told them to and they did. And other people. Including—Brannick, Papa," he said; "that blacksmith you know. It turns out he lives quite near there."

"*Huh!*" said Joel.

"The doctor said the man was right," Andrew said. "He said he must have been killed instantly. They found who he was, by papers in his pocket, and that was when he phoned you, Mary.

"He asked me if I'd please tell you how dreadful he felt to give you such a message, leaving you uncertain all this time. He just couldn't stand to be the one to tell you the whole thing—least of all just bang like that, over a phone. He thought it ought to be somebody in the family."

"That's what I imagined," Mary said.

"He was right," Hannah said; and Joel and Mary nodded and said, "Yes."

"By the time Walter and I got there, they'd moved him," Andrew said. "He was at the blacksmith shop. They'd even brought in the auto. You know, they say it ran perfectly. Except for the top, and the windshield, it was hardly even damaged."

Joel asked, "Do they have any idea what happened?"

Andrew said to his mother, "Papa says, 'Do they have any idea how it happened?'" She nodded, and smiled her thanks, and tilted her trumpet nearer his mouth.

"Yes, some idea," Andrew said. "They showed me. They found that a cotter pin had worked loose—that is, it had fallen all the way out—this cotter pin had fallen out, that held the steering mechanism together."

"*Hahh?*"

"Like this, Mama—*look,*" he said sharply, thrusting his hands under her nose.

"Oh *excuse* me," she said.

"See here," he said; he had locked a bent knuckle between two bent knuckles of the other hand. "As if it were to hold these knuckles together—see?"

"Yes."

"There would be a hole right through the knuckles and that's where the cotter pin goes. It's sort of like a very heavy hairpin. When you have it all the way through, you open the two ends flat—spread them—like this . . ." he showed her his thumb and forefinger, together, then spread them as wide and flat as he could. "You understand?"

"No matter."

"Let it go, son," his father said.

"It's all right, Mama," Andrew said. "It's just something that holds two parts together—in this case, his steering gear—what he guided the auto with. Th . . ."

"*I understand,*" she said impatiently.

"*Good,* Mama. Well this cotter pin, that held the steering mechanism together down underneath the auto, where there was no chance of seeing it, had fallen out. They couldn't find it anywhere, though they looked all over the place where it happened and went over the road for a couple of hundred yards with a fine-tooth comb. So they think it may have worked loose and fallen out quite a distance back—it could be, even miles, though probably not so far. Because they showed me," again he put his knuckles where she could see, "even without the pin, those two parts might hang together," he twisted them, "you might even steer with them, and not have the slightest suspicion there was anything wrong, if you were on fairly smooth road, or didn't have to wrench the wheel, but if you hit a sharp bump or a rut or a loose rock, or had to twist the wheel very hard very suddenly, they'd come apart, and you'd have no control over anything."

Mary put her hands over her face.

"What they think is that he must have hit a loose rock with one of the front wheels, and that gave everything a jolt and a terrific wrench at the same time. Because they found a rock, oh, half the size of my head, down in the ditch, very badly scraped and with tire marks on it. They showed me. They think it must have wrenched the wheel right out of his hands and thrown him forward very hard so that he struck his chin, just one sharp blow against the steering wheel. And that must have killed him on the spot. Because he was thrown absolutely clear of the car as it ran off the road—they showed me. I never saw anything to equal it. Do you know what happened? That auto threw him out on the ground as it careened down into that sort of flat, wide ditch, about five feet down from the road; then it went straight on up an eight-foot embankment. They showed me the marks where it went, almost to the top, and then toppled backward and fell bottom side up right beside him, without even grazing him!"

"Gracious," Mary whispered. "*Tst,*" Hannah clucked.

"How are they so sure it was—instant, Andrew?" Hannah asked.

"Because if he'd been conscious they're sure he wouldn't have been thrown out of the auto, for one thing. He'd have grabbed the wheel, or the emergency brake, still trying to control it. There wasn't time for that. There wasn't any time at all. At the most there must have been just the tiniest fraction of a second when he felt the jolt and the wheel was twisted out of his hand, and he was thrown forward. The doctor says he probably never even knew what hit him—hardly even felt the impact, it was so hard and quick."

"He may have just been unconscious," Mary groaned through her hands. "Or conscious and—paralyzed; unable to speak or even seem to breathe. If only there'd been a doctor, right there, mayb . . ."

Andrew reached across his mother and touched her knees. "No, Mary," he said. "I have the doctor's word for that. He says the only thing that could have caused death was concussion of the brain. He says that when that—happens to kill, it—does so instantly, or else takes days or weeks. I asked him about it very particularly because—I knew you'd want to be sure just how it was. Of course I wondered the same thing. He said it couldn't have been even a few seconds of unconsciousness, and then death, because nothing more happened, after that one blow, that could have added to what it did. He said it's even more sudden than electrocution. Just an enormous shock to the brain. The quickest death there is." He returned to his mother. "I'm sorry, Mama," he said. "Mary was saying, perhaps he was only unconscious. That maybe if the doctor had been there right on the spot, he could have been saved. I was telling her, no. Because I asked the doctor everything I could think to, about that. And he said no. He says that when a concussion of the brain—is fatal—it's the quickest death there is."

He looked at each of them in turn. In a light, vindictive voice he told them, "He says it was just a chance in a million."

"Good God, Andrew," his father said.

"Just that one tiny area, at just a certain angle, and just a certain sharpness of impact. If it had been even a half an inch to one side, he'd be alive this minute."

"Shut up, Andrew," his father said harshly; for with the last few words that Andrew spoke, a sort of dilation had seized Mary, so that she had almost risen from her place, seeming larger than herself, and then had collapsed into a shattering of tears.

"Oh Mary," Andrew groaned, and hurried to her, while her mother took her head against her breast. "I'm so sorry. God, what possessed me! I must be out of my mind!" And Hannah and Joel had gotten from their chairs and stood nearby, unable to speak.

"Just—have a little *mercy,*" she sobbed. "A little *mercy.*"

Andrew could say only, "I'm so sorry. I'm *so* sorry, Mary," and then he could say nothing.

"Let her cry," Joel said quietly to his sister, and she nodded. As if anything on earth could stop her, he said to himself.

"O God, *forgive* me," Mary moaned. "*Forgive* me! *Forgive* me! It's just more than I can bear! Just more than I can bear! *Forgive* me!" And Joel, with his mouth fallen open, wheeled upon his sister and stared at her; and she avoided his eyes, saying to herself, *No, No,* and *protect her, O God, protect Thy poor child and give her strength;* and Andrew, his face locked in a murderer's grimace, continued the furious and annihilating words which were bursting within him to be spoken, groaned within himself, *God, if You exist, come here and let me spit in Your face. Forgive her, indeed!*

Then Hannah moved him aside and stooped before Mary, taking her wrists and talking earnestly into her streaming hands: "Mary, listen to me. Mary. There's nothing to ask forgiveness for. There's nothing to ask forgiveness for, Mary. Do you hear me? Do you hear me, Mary?" Mary nodded within her hands. "God would never ask of you not to grieve, not to cry. Do you hear? What you're doing is absolutely natural, absolutely right. Do you hear! You wouldn't be human if you did otherwise. Do you hear me, Mary? You're not human to ask His forgiveness. You're wrong. You're terribly mistaken. Do you hear me, my dear? Do you hear me?"

While she was speaking, Mary, within her hands, now nodded and now shook her head, always in contradiction of what her aunt was saying, and now she said, "It isn't what you think. I spoke to Him as if He had no mercy!"

"Andrew? Andrew was ju . . ."

"No: to God. As if He were trying to rub it in. Torment me. That's what I asked forgiveness for."

"There, Mary," her mother said; she could hear virtually nothing of what was said, but she could feel that the extremity of the crying had passed.

"Listen, Mary," Hannah said, and she bent so close to her that she could have whispered. "Our Lord on the Cross," she said, in a voice so low that only Mary and Andrew could hear, "do you remember?"

"My God, my God, why hast Thou forsaken me?"

"Yes. And then did He ask forgiveness?"

"He was God. He didn't have to."

"He was human, too. And He didn't ask it. Nor was it asked of Him to ask it, no more are you. And no more *should* you. What was it He said, instead? The very next thing He said."

"Father, into Thy hands I commend my spirit," she said, taking her hands from her face and looking meekly at her aunt.

"Into Thy hands I commend my spirit," her aunt said.

"There, dear," her mother said, and Mary sat upright and looked straight ahead.

"Please don't feel sorry, Andrew," she said. "You're right to tell me every last bit you know. I want to know—all of it. It was just—it just overwhelmed me for a minute."

"I shouldn't tell you so much all in a heap."

"No, that's better. Than to keep hearing—horrible little new things, just when you think you've heard the worst and are beginning to get used to it."

"That's right, Poll," her father said.

"Now just go straight on telling me. Everything there is to tell. And if I do break down, why don't reproach yourself. Remember I *asked* you. But I'll try to not. I think I'll be all right."

"All right, Mary."

"Good, Poll," her father said. They all sat down again.

"And Andrew, if you'll get it for me, I think I'd like some more whiskey."

"Of course I will." He had brought the bottle in; he took her glass to the table.

"Not quite so strong as last time, please. Pretty strong, but not so strong as that."

"This all right?"

"A little more whiskey, please."

"Certainly."

"That looks all right."

"You all right, Poll?" her father asked. "Isn't going to your head too much?"

"It isn't going anywhere so far as I can tell."

"Good enough."

"I think perhaps it would be best if we didn't—prolong the discussion any further tonight," Catherine said, in her most genteel manner; and she patted Mary's knee.

They looked at her with astonishment and suddenly Mary and then Andrew began to laugh, and then Hannah began to laugh, and Joel said, "What's up? What's all the hee-hawing about?"

"It's Mama," Andrew shouted joyfully, and he and Hannah explained how she had suggested, in her most ladylike way, that they adjourn the discussion for the evening when all they were discussing was how much whiskey Mary could stand, and it was as if she meant that Mary was much too thirsty to wait out any more of it; and Joel gave a snort of amusement and then was caught into the contagion of this somewhat hysterical laughter, and they all roared, laughing their heads off, while Catherine sat there watching them, disapproving such levity at such a time, and unhappily suspecting that for some reason they were laughing at her; but in courtesy and reproof, and an expectation of hearing the joke, smiling and lifting her trumpet. But they paid no attention to her; they scarcely seemed to know she was there. They would quiet down now and then and moan and breathe deeply, and dry their eyes; then Mary would remember, and mimic, precisely the way her mother had patted her knee with her ringed hand, or Andrew would mimic her precise intonation as she said *"prolong,"* or any of the four of them would roll over silently upon the tongue of the mind some particularly ticklish blend of the absurdity and horror and cruelty and relief, or would merely glance at Catherine with her smile and her trumpet, and would suddenly begin to bubble and then to spout with laughter, and another would be caught into the machinery, and then they would start all over again. Some of the time they deliberately strained for more laughter, or to prolong it, or to revive it if it had died, some of the time they tried just as hard to stop laughing or, having stopped, not to laugh any more. They found that on the whole they laughed even harder if they tried hard not to, so they came to favor that technique. They laughed until they were weak and their bellies ached. Then they were able to realize a little more clearly what a poor joke they had all been laughing at, and the very feebleness of the material and outrageous disproportion of their laughter started them whooping again; but finally they quieted down, because they had no strength for any more, and into this nervous and somewhat aborted silence Catherine spoke, "Well, I have never in my life been so thoroughly shocked and astonished," and it began all over again.

But by now they were really worn out with laughter; moreover, images of the dead body beside the capsized automobile began to dart in their minds, and then to become cold, immense, and immovable; and they began fully to realize, as well, how shamefully they had treated the deaf woman.

"Oh, *Mama,*" Andrew and Mary cried out together, and Mary embraced her and Andrew kissed her on the forehead and on the mouth. "It was awful of us," he said. "You've just got to try to forgive us. We're all just a little bit hysterical, that's all."

"Better tell her, Andrew," his father said.

"Yes, poor thing," Hannah said; and he tried as gently as he could to explain it to her, and that they weren't really laughing at her expense, or even really at the joke, such as it was, because it wasn't really very funny, he must admit, but it had simply been a Godsend to have something to laugh about.

"I see," she said ("I see, said the blindman," Andrew said), and gave her polite, tinkling, baffled little laugh. "But of course it wasn't the—question of spirits that I meant. I just felt that perhaps for poor dear Mary's sake we'd better . . ."

"Of course," Andrew shouted. "We understand, Mama. But Mary'd rather hear now. She'd already said so."

"Yes, Mama," Mary screamed, leaning across towards her "good" ear.

"Well in that case," Catherine said primly, "I think it would have been kind so to inform me."

"I'm awfully sorry, Mama," Andrew said. "We should have. We really would have. In about another minute."

"Well," Catherine said; "no matter."

"Really we would, Mama," Mary said.

"Very well," Catherine said. "It was just a misfortune, that's all. I know I make it—very difficult, I try not to."

"Oh, Mama, no."

"No. I'm not hurt. I just suggest that you ignore me now, for everybody's convenience. Joel will tell me, later."

"She means it," Joel said. "She's not hurt any more."

"I know she does," Andrew said. "That's why I'm *God-*

damned if I'll leave her out. Honestly, Mama," he told her, "just let me tell you. Then we can all hear. Don't you see?"

"Well, if you're sure; of course I'd be most grateful. Thank you." She bowed, smiled, and tilted her trumpet.

It required immediate speech. That trumpet's like a pelican's mouth, he thought. Toss in a fish. "I'm sorry, Mama," he said. "I've got to try to collect my wits."

"That's perfectly all right," his mother said.

What was I—oh. Doctor. Yes.

"I was telling you what the doctor said."

Mary drank.

"Yes," Catherine replied in her clear voice. "You were saying that it was only by merest chance, where the blow was struck, a chance in a million, that . . ."

"Yes, Mama. It's just unbelievable. But there it is."

"Hyesss," Hannah sighed.

Mary drank.

"It does—beat—all—hell," Joel said. He thought of Thomas Hardy. There's a man, he thought, who knows what it's about. (And *she* asks God to forgive *her!*) He snorted.

"What is it, Papa?" Mary asked quietly.

"Nothing," he said, "just the way things go. As flies to wanton boys. That's all."

"What do you mean?"

"As flies to wanton boys are we to the gods; they kill us for their sport."

"No," Mary said; she shook her head. "No, Papa. It's not that way."

He felt within him a surge of boiling acid; he contained himself. If she tries to tell me it's God's inscrutable mercy, he said to himself, I'll have to leave the room. "Ignore it, Poll," he said. "None of us knows one damned thing about it. Myself least of all. So I'll keep my trap shut."

"But I can't bear to have you even *think* such things, Papa."

Andrew tightened his lips and looked away.

"Mary," Hannah said.

"I'm afraid that's something none of us can ask—or change," her father said.

"Yes, Mary," Hannah said.

"But I can assure you of this, Poll. I have very few thoughts indeed and none of 'em are worth your minding about."

"Is there something perhaps I should be hearing?" Catherine asked.

They were silent a moment. "Nothing, Mama," Andrew said. "Just a digression. I'd tell you if it was important."

"You were about to continue, with what the doctor told you."

"Yes I was. I will. He told me a number of other things and I can—assure—everybody—that such as they are, at least they're some kind of cold comfort."

Mary met his eyes.

"He said that if there had to be such an accident, this was pretty certainly the best way. That with such a thing, a concussion, he might quite possibly have been left a hopeless imbecile."

"Oh, Andrew," Mary burst out.

"The rest of his life, and that could have been another forty years as easily as not. Or maybe only a semi-invalid, laid up just now and then, with terrific recurrent headaches, or spells of amnesia, of feeblemindedness. Those are the things that *didn't* happen, Mary," he told her desperately. "I think I'd just better get them over and done with right now."

"Yes," she said through her hands. "Yes, you had. Go on, Andrew. Get it over."

"He pointed out what would have happened if he'd stayed conscious, if he hadn't been thrown clear of the auto. Going fast, hopelessly out of control, up that eight-foot embankment and then down. He'd have been crushed, Mary. Horribly mangled. If he'd died it would have been slowly and agonizingly. If he'd lived, he'd have probably been a hopeless cripple."

"Dreadful," Catherine cried loudly.

"An idiot, or a cripple, or a paralytic," Andrew said. "Because another thing a concussion can do, Mary, is paralyze. Incurably. Those aren't fates you can prefer for anyone to dying. Least of all a man like Jay, with all his vigor, of body and mind too, his independence, his loathing for being laid up even one day. You remember how impossible it was to keep him quiet enough when his back was strained."

"Yes," she said. "Yes, I do." Her hands were still to her face and she was pressing her fingers tightly against her eyeballs.

"Instead . . ." Andrew began; and he remembered his face in death and he remembered him as he lay on the table under the glare. "Instead of that, Mary, he died the quickest and most painless death there is. One instant he was fully alive. Maybe more alive than ever before for that matter, for something had suddenly gone wrong and everything in him was roused up and mad at it and ready to beat it—because you know that of Jay, Mary, probably better than anyone else on earth. He didn't know what fear was. Danger only made him furious—and tremendously alert. It made him every inch of the man he was. And the next instant it was all over. Not even time to know it was hopeless, Mary. Not even one instant of pain, because that kind of blow is much too violent to give pain. Immediate pain. Just an instant of surprise and every faculty at its absolute height, and then just a tremendous blinding shock, and then nothing. You see, Mary?"

She nodded.

"I saw his face, Mary. It just looked startled, and resolute, and mad as hell. Not one trace of fear or pain."

"There wouldn't have been any fear, anyway," she said.

"I saw him—stripped—at the undertaker's," Andrew said. "Mary, there wasn't a mark on his body. Just that little cut on the chin. One little bruise on his lower lip. Not another mark on his body. He had the most magnificent physique I've ever seen in a human being."

Nobody spoke for a long while; then Andrew said, "All I can say is, when my time comes, I only hope I die half as well."

His father nodded; Hannah closed her eyes and bowed her head. Catherine waited, patiently.

"In his strength," Mary said; and took her hands from her face. Her eyes were still closed. "That's how he was taken," she said very tenderly; "in his strength. Singing, probably"—her voice broke on the word—"happy, all alone, racing home because he loved so to go fast and couldn't except when he was alone, and because he didn't want to disappoint his children. And then just as you said, Andrew. Just one moment of trouble, of something that might be danger—and was; it was death itself—and everything in his nature springing to its full height to fight it, to get it under control, not in fear. Just in bravery and nobility and anger and perfect confidence he could. It's how he'd look Death itself in the face. It's how he did! In his strength. Those are the words that are going to be on his gravestone, Andrew."

That's what they're for, epitaphs, Joel suddenly realized. So you can feel you've got some control over the death, you *own* it, you choose a name for it. The same with wanting to know all you can about how it happened. And trying to imagine it as Mary was. Andrew, too. Any poor subterfuge'll do; and welcome to 'em.

"Don't you think?" Mary asked shyly; for Andrew had not replied.

"Yes I do," he said, and Hannah said, "Yes, Mary," and Joel nodded.

Hannah: I want to *know* when I die, and not just for religious reasons.

"Mama," Mary called, drawing at her arm. Her mother turned eagerly, thankfully, with her trumpet. "I was telling Andrew," Mary told her, "I think I know the words, the epitaph, that ought to go on Jay's—on the headstone." Her mother tilted her head politely. "In his strength," Mary said. Her mother looked still more polite. "In—his—*strength,*" Mary said, more loudly. Christ, I don't think I can stand this, Andrew thought.

"Because that was the way it happened, Mama. Just so suddenly, without any warning, or suffering, or weakness, or illness. Just—instantly. In the very prime of his life. Do you see?"

Her mother patted her knee and took her hand. "Very appropriate, dear," she said.

"*I* think so," Mary said; she wished she had not spoken of it.

"It is, Mary," Andrew assured her.

"Why didn't you answer when I asked you?"

"I was just thinking about him."

There was a silence; Catherine who had still held her trumpet hopefully extended, turned away.

"He was thirty-six," Mary said. "Just exactly a month and a day ago."

Nobody spoke.

"And last night—great *goodness* it was only last night! Just think of that. Less than twenty-four hours ago, that awful phone ringing and we sat in the kitchen together—thinking of *his father*! We both thought it was his father who was at death's door. That's why he went up there. That's why it happened! And that miserable Ralph was so drunk he couldn't even be sure of the need. He just had to go *in case*. Oh, it's just beyond words!"

She finished her drink and stood up to get more.

"I'll get it," Andrew said quickly, and took her glass.

"Not quite so strong," she said. "Thank you."

"It's like a checkerboard," her father said.

"*What* is?"

"What you were saying. You think everything bears on one person's dying, and b'God it's another who does. One instant you see the black squares against the red and the next you see the red against the black."

"Yes," Mary said, somewhat in her mother's uncertain tone.

"None of us know what we're doing, any given moment."

How you manage not to have religious faith, Hannah wanted to tell him, is beyond me. She held her tongue.

"A tale told by an idiot . . . signifying nothing."

"Signifying something," Andrew said, "but we don't know what."

"Just as likely. Choice between rattlesnake and skunk."

"Jay knows what; now," Mary said.

"I certainly won't swear he doesn't," her father said.

"He does, Mary," her aunt said.

"Of course he does," Mary said.

Child, you'd better believe it, her aunt thought, disturbed by the "of course."

"I wonder," Catherine said; everyone turned towards her. "Mary's suggestion—for—an epitaph—is very lovely and appropriate, but I *wonder,* whether people will quite—*understand* it."

"Agh," Joel growled.

"What if they don't?" Andrew said.

Mary leaned across her. "Yes, Mama! What if they *don't! We* understand it. *Jay* understands it. What do *we* care if they *don't*!"

She was surprised and somewhat hurt by the violence of this attack. "It was merely something to be considered," she said with dignity. "After all, it will be in a *public place.* Many people will see it besides ourselves. I've always supposed, it was the business of *words*—to *communicate*—*clearly.*"

"Oh Mama, don't be mad," Mary cried. "I understand. I appreciate the suggestion. I just can't see that in a—that in this particular case, it's anything to be seriously concerned about. It's Jay we're thinking of. Not other people."

"I see; perhaps you're right. Praps I shouldn't have me . . ."

"We're very glad you mentioned it, Mama. We appreciate you mentioning it. It hadn't even occurred to me and it ought to. Only now that it does, now that you've told me, why, well, I just still think it's all right as it is. That's all."

"Let it go, Catherine, for God's sake let it go!" Joel was saying in a low voice; but now she nodded and became quiet.

"I hate to hurt Mama's feelings," Mary said, "but *really!*"

"It's all right, Mary," Andrew said.

"Let it go, Poll," her father said.

"I am," Mary said; she took a drink.

"We've got to let them know," she said. "His mother. We'll have to phone Ralph. Andrew, will you do that?"

"Of course I will." He got up.

"Just tell them I'm sorry, I couldn't come to the phone. Will you, Andrew? I'm sure they'll understand."

"Of course they will."

"Just tell them—how it happened. Tell Ralph I send his mother all my love." He nodded. "And Andrew. Be sure and ask how Jay's father is." He nodded. "And let them know when— why; why we don't even *know*, do we? When the—what day he'll—be—the *funeral*, Andrew!"

"Not for sure. I told them I'd see them in the morning about all that."

"Well you'll just have to tell them we'll let them know as soon as we do. In plenty of time. To get here I mean."

"What's the number, Mary?"

"Number?"

"What is Ralph's telephone number?"

"I—can't remember. I guess I don't know for sure. You'll have to ask Central. It's always Jay who called."

"All right."

"It's LaFollette," she called, as he went into the hall.

"All right, Mary." He went out.

"And, Andrew."

"Yes, Mary?" He put his head in.

"Talk as quietly as you can. We don't want to wake the children."

"Yes, Mary."

"It's queer I don't know," she told the others. "But it was always Jay who called."

"Tell your mother what's up," her father advised, for she was looking inquiring. Mary leaned across her.

"Bathroom?" her mother whispered discreetly.

"No, Mama. He's gone to telephone Jay's brother."

Her mother nodded, and still extended her trumpet, but Mary had nothing to say.

"I hope he will extend all our most—heartfelt—sympathies," her mother said.

Mary nodded conspicuously. "I specially asked him to," she lied.

After a few moments Catherine gave up, and relaxed her trumpet between her withered hands into her lap.

Chapter 12

ANDREW HAD SHUT THE DOOR but they could hear him, trying to talk quietly. He was talking, indeed, very quietly, close to the mouthpiece with his hand around it; even so, Mary and Hannah could hear most of what he said. They did not want to listen, but they couldn't help it.

He said, "I want to make a long-distance call, please," and the quietness of his voice made them listen the more carefully. It was full of covered danger.

"Hello? Hello, is this long distance? Long distance I want to call Ralph Follet, Ralph, Follet, F, O, L, L, E, T, no, Central, F, as in father—F, O,—have you got that?—L, L, ET. FOLLET. At LaFollette, Tennessee. No, I haven't. Thank you. I said, thank you."

"I don't see how his mother's going to bear it," Mary said, in a subdued voice. "I said I just don't see how Jay's mother is going to bear it," she told her mother.

"Her own husband right at death's door," she said to Hannah, "and now this. He was just the apple of her eye, that's all."

"Hello?"

"She has a world of grit," Hannah said.

"Ralph? Is this Ralph Follet?"

163

"If she hadn't she wouldn't be alive today," Mary said.

"Ralph, this is Andrew Lynch." They sat very still and made no pretense of not listening.

"Yes. Andrew. Ralph, I have to tell you about Jay." Hannah and Mary looked at each other. With everything that Andrew said, from then on, they realized in a sense which they had failed to before, that it had really happened and that it was final.

"Jay died tonight, Ralph.

"He's dead.

"He died in an auto accident, on the way home, out near Powell's Station. He was instantly killed."

Mary looked down into the whiskey and began to tremble.

"Instantly. I have a doctor's word for it. He couldn't even have known what hit him.

"It was concussion of the brain, Ralph. Concussion—of the brain. Just so hard a shock to the brain that it killed him instantly."

"They mustn't tell his father," Mary said suddenly. "It'll just kill his father."

"I don't see how they can avoid it," Hannah said. "Mary says they mustn't tell his, Jay's, father," Hannah told her brother. "In his condition the news might kill him. I told her I simply don't see how they can avoid it. They'll have to account for coming away to the funeral, after all."

"Just tell him he's hurt," Joel said.

Mary hurried into the hall. "Andrew," she whispered loudly. With a contortion of the face which terrified her he slapped his hand through the air at her as if she had been a mosquito. "Just that one place, on the point of the chin," he was saying. He turned to Mary, but the voice held him and he turned away. "He may have driven for miles that way. They don't know. They looked all around and quite a distance up the road—yes, of course with flashlights—and they couldn't find it." Again she heard the voice, squirming like a wire. "No, they haven't any idea. Except that there are some very rough stretches in those roads and Jay was driving very fast. Just a minute, Ralph." He covered the mouth-piece. "What is it, Mary?"

She could hear the distraught and squirming voice. Like a worm on a hook, she thought. Poor nasty fat thing! "Tell Ralph not to tell his father," she whispered. "In his condition it might kill him. If they have to say anything, about—coming down—tell him he's hurt." Andrew nodded.

"Ralph," he said. "Go away," he whispered, for she was lingering. "We just want to remind you, it might be very dangerous to your father" (by now Mary heard him through the door; she took her seat) "if he heard this now. Of course you and your mother'll know best but in case you have to explain, when you come away to the funeral, it might be better just to say that Jay's been hurt; not in danger. Don't you think?

"What did you say?

"Why no, we . . .

"He's at Roberts'. I came in with him tonight.

"Why I'd suppose that . . ."

"Oh *heavens!*" Mary said, loudly enough that her father jumped. "Ralph's an undertaker!"

"Of course, I see your point, Ralph.

"No. Not yet.

"Well the saving of money is not a question in this . . .

"Look here, Ralph, will you just . . .

"Will you just hold the phone a minute, please? I really think we should leave this up to Mary, don't you?

"Of course she does. You too. I . . .

"I don't doubt it at all.

"No, I appreciate it very deeply, Ralph, and I know Mary will, but just let me consult her wishes on it, please. Just wait."

They heard his rapid walk and he thrust his infuriated face into the room.

"Ralph," he announced, "is an undertaker. I imagine you know what he wants. I told him it was up to you to decide."

"Good—God!" Joel exclaimed.

"Andrew, you'll have to tell him—I—just simply can't."

"He's blaming himself for Jay's . . . He wants to try to make up for it."

"How on earth can he blame himself!"

"For phoning Jay in the first place."

"What nonsense," Hannah said.

"But Jay's already at Ro . . ."

"Ralph says that's easily arranged. He can come down first thing tomorrow."

"Well, then we just can't. We just won't, no matter what. Tell him how very *very* much I appreciate it and thank him, but I just can't. Tell him I'm prostrated. I don't care what you tell him, you handle it, Andrew."

"I'll handle it." He went back to the phone.

"Seems downright incestuous," Joel said.

His sister laughed harshly.

"Nothing important, Mama," Mary said. "Just—arrangements about the funeral."

Nothing important! Joel thought. People can only get through these things by being blind at least half the time. No: she was just cutting a corner for Catherine.

"When will the ceremony be held?"

Hannah stifled a laugh and Joel did not. Mary's face worked curiously with a smile as she told her mother, "We don't know yet. This was a question of where. Here or LaFollette?"

"I would have supposed that his home was Knoxville."

"We think so, too. That's how it's settled."

"That seems as it should be."

Andrew came in. "Well," he said, "it was either Ralph or you and I chose you."

"Oh, Andrew, you must have hurt him."

"There wasn't any way out. He just wouldn't take no for an answer."

"He's going to make an awful case of it to his mother."

"Well he'll just have to, then."

"She's got sense, Mary," Hannah said.

"I'm going to have a drink," Andrew said. *"God!"* he groaned. "Talking to that fool is like trying to put socks on an octopus!"

"Why, Andrew," Mary laughed; she had never heard the expression. "I'm very grateful to you, dear," she said. "You must be worn to a frazzle."

"We all are," Hannah said. "You most of all, Mary. We better think about getting some sleep."

"I suppose we must, but I really don't feel as if I *could* sleep. *You*-all better though."

"We're all right," Andrew said. "Except maybe Mama. And Papa, you'd b . . ."

"Never sleep before two in the morning," Joel said. "You know that."

"Let me fix you a good stiff hot toddy," Hannah said. "It'll help you sleep."

"It all just seems to wake me up."

"Hot."

"Maybe just some hot milk. *No I won't, either,*" she cried out, with sudden tears; they looked at her and looked away; she soon had control of herself.

"One of the last things Jay did for me," she explained, "way early in the morning before he—went away. He fixed me some hot milk to help me sleep." She began to cry again. "Bless his heart," she said. "Bless his dear heart."

"You know almost the last thing he said to me?

"He asked me to think what I wanted for my birthday.

" 'Within reason,' he said. He was just joking.

"And he said not to wait supper, but he'd—he'd try to be back before the children were asleep, for sure."

She'd feel better later on if she'd kept a few of these things to herself, Joel thought.

Or would she. I would. But I'm not Poll.

"Rufus just—*wouldn't* give up. He just *wouldn't* go to sleep. He was so proud of that cap, Aunt Hannah. He wanted *so much* to show it to his father."

Hannah came over to her and leaned to her, an arm around her shoulder.

"Talk if you want to, Mary," she said. "If you think it does you good. But try not to harp on these things."

"And I was so mad at him, only a few hours ago, for not phoning all day, and because of Rufus. I had such a good supper ready, and I *did* wait it, and . . ."

"It wasn't *his* fault it was good," Hannah said.

"Of *course* it isn't his fault and I had no *business* waiting it but I *did,* and I was so angry with him—why I even—I even . . ."

But this she found she would not tell them. I even thought he was drunk, she said to herself. And if he was, why what in the world of it. Let's hope if he was he really loved being, God bless him always. *Always.*

And then a terrifying thought occurred to her, and she looked at Andrew. No, she thought, he wouldn't lie to me if it were so. No, I won't even ask it. I won't even imagine it. I just don't see how I could bear to live if that were so.

But there he was, all that day, with Ralph. He *must* have. Well he probably did. That was no part of the promise. But not really *drunk.* Not so he couldn't—navigate. Drive well.

No.

Oh, no.

No I won't even dishonor his dear memory by asking. Not even Andrew in secret. No, I won't.

And she thought with such exactness and with such love of her husband's face, and of his voice, and of his hands, and of his way of smiling so warmly even though his eyes almost never lost their sadness, that she succeeded in driving the other thought from her mind.

"Hark!" Hannah whispered.

"What *is* it?"

"*Ssh!* Listen."

"What's up?" Joel asked.

"Be quiet, Joel, *please.* There's something."

They listened most intently.

"I can't hear anything," Andrew whispered.

"Well *I* do," Hannah said, in a low voice. "Hear it or feel it. There's *something.*"

And again in silence they listened.

It began to seem to Mary, as to Hannah, that there was someone in the house other than themselves. She thought of the children; they might have waked up. Yet listening as intently as she could, she was not at all sure that there was any sound; and whoever or whatever it might be, she became sure that it was no child, for she felt in it a terrible forcefulness, and concern, and restiveness, which were no part of any child.

"There *is* something," Andrew whispered.

Whatever it might be, it was never for an instant at rest in one place. It was in the next room; it was in the kitchen; it was in the dining room.

"I'm going out to see," Andrew said; he got up.

"Wait, Andrew, don't, not yet," Mary whispered. "No; no"; now it's going upstairs, she thought; it's along the—it's in the children's room. It's in *our* room.

"Has somebody come into the house?" Catherine inquired in her clear voice.

Andrew felt the flesh go cold along his spine. He bent near her. "What made you think so, Mama?" he asked quietly.

"It's right here in the room with us," Mary said in a cold voice.

"Why, how very stupid of me, I *thought* I *heard.* Footsteps." She gave her short, tinkling laugh. "I must be getting old and dippy." She laughed again.

"*Sshh!*"

"It's Jay," Mary whispered. "I know it now. I was so wrapped up in wondering *what* on earth . . . Jay. Darling. Dear heart, can you hear me?

"Can you tell me if you hear me, dearest?

"Can you?

"Can't you?

"Oh try your best, my dear. Try your *very* hardest to let me know.

"You can't, can you? You can't, no matter *how* hard.

"But O, do hear me, Jay. I do pray God with all my heart you can hear me, I want so to assure you.

"Don't be troubled, dear one. Don't you worry. Stay near us if you can. *All* you can. But let not your heart be troubled. They're all right, my sweetheart, my husband. I'm going to be all right. Don't you worry. We'll make out. Rest, my dear. Just rest. Just rest, my heart. Don't ever be troubled again. Never again, darling. Never, never again."

"May the souls of the faithful through the mercy of God rest in peace," Hannah whispered. "Blessed are the dead."

"Mary!" her brother whispered. He was crying.

"He's not here any more now," she said. "We can talk."

"Mary, in God's name what was it?"

"It was Jay, Andrew."

"It was *something*. I haven't any doubt of that, but—good God, Mary."

"It was Jay, all right. I *know!* Who else would be coming here tonight, so terribly worried, so terribly concerned for us, and restless! Besides, Andrew, it—it simply *felt* like Jay."

"You mean . . ."

"I just mean it felt like his *presence*."

"To me, too," Hannah said.

"I don't like to interrupt," Joel said, "but would you mind telling me, please, what's going on here?"

"You felt it too, Papa?" Mary asked eagerly.

"Felt what?"

"You remember when Aunt Hannah said there was something around, someone or something in the house?"

"Yes, and she told me to shut up, so I did."

"I simply asked you please to be quiet, Joel, because we were trying to hear."

"Well, what did you hear?"

"I don't know's I *heard* anything, Joel. I'm not a bit sure. I don't think I did. But I *felt* something, very distinctly. So did Andrew."

"Yes I did, Papa."

"And Mary."

"Oh, very much so."

"What do you mean you *felt* something?"

"Then you didn't, Papa?"

"I got a feeling there was some kind of a strain in the room, something or other was up among you; Mary looking as if she'd seen a ghost; *all* of you . . ."

"She did," Andrew said. "That is, she didn't actually see anything, but she felt it. She knew something was there. She says it was Jay."

"*Hahh?*"

"Jay. Aunt Hannah thinks so too."

"Hannah?"

"Yes I do, Joel. I'm not as sure as Mary, but it did seem like him."

"What's 'it'?"

"The thing, Papa, whatever it was. The thing we all felt."

"What did it feel like?"

"Just a . . ."

"You think it was Jay?"

"No, I had no idea *what* it was. But I know it was *something*. Mama felt it too."

"Catherine?"

"Yes. And it couldn't have been through us because she didn't even know what we were doing. All of a sudden she said, 'Has somebody come into the house?' and when I asked her why she thought so she said she thought she'd heard footsteps."

"Could be thought transference."

"None of the rest of us thought we heard footsteps."

"All the same. It can't be what you think."

"I don't know what it was, Papa, but there are four of us here independently who are sure there was something."

"Joel, I know that God in a wheelbarrow wouldn't convince you," his sister said. "We aren't even trying to convince you. But while you're being so rational, why at least please be rational enough to realize that we experienced what we experienced."

"The least I can do is accept the fact that three people had a hallucination, and honor their belief in it. That I can do, too, I guess. I believe you, for yourself, Hannah. All of you. I'd have to have the same hallucination myself to be convinced. And even then I'd have my doubts."

"What on earth do you mean, *doubts,* Papa, if you had it yourself?"

"I'd suspect it was just a hallucination."

"Oh, good Lord! You've got it going and coming, haven't you!"

"Is this a dagger that I see before me? Wasn't, you know. But you could never convince Macbeth it wasn't."

"Andrew," Mary broke in, "tell Mama. She's just dying to know what we're . . ." she trailed off. I must be out of my mind, she said to herself. *Dying!* And she began to think with astonishment and disgust of the way they had all been talking—herself most of all. How can we bear to chatter along in normal tones of voice! she thought; how can we even use ordinary words, or say words at all! And now, picking his poor troubled soul to pieces, like so many hens squabbling over—she thought of a worm, and covered her face in sickness. She heard her mother say, "Why, Andrew, how perfectly *extraordinary!*" and then she heard Andrew question her, had she had any special *feeling* about what *kind* of a person or thing it was, that is, was it quiet or active, or young or old, or disturbed or calm, or was it anything: and her mother answered that she had had no particular impression except that there was someone in the house besides themselves, not the children either, somebody mature, some sort of intruder; but that when nobody had troubled to investigate, she had decided that it must be a hallucination—all the more so because, as she'd said, she thought she'd actually *heard* someone, whereas with her poor old ears (she laughed gracefully) that was simply out of the question, of course. Oh, I do wish they'd leave him in peace, she said to herself. A thing so wonderful. Such a *proof!* Why can't we just keep a reverent silence! But Andrew was asking his mother, had she, a little later than that, still felt even so that there was somebody? or not. And she said that indeed she had had such an *impression.* Where? Why she couldn't say where, except that the *impression* was even stronger than before, but, of course, by then she realized it was a hallucination. But they felt it too! Why how perfectly uncanny!

"Mary thinks it was Jay," Andrew told her.

"Why, I . . ."

"So does Aunt Hannah."

"Why how—how perfectly extraordinary, Andrew!"

"She thinks he was worried about . . ."

"Oh, Andrew!" Mary cried. "Andrew! *Please* let's don't *talk* about it any more! Do you mind?"

He looked at her as if he had been slapped. "Why, Mary, of course not!" He explained to his mother: "Mary'd rather we didn't discuss it any more."

"Oh, it's not that, Andrew. It just—means so much more than anything we can *say* about it or even think about it. I'd give anything just to sit quiet and think about it a little while! Don't you see? It's as if we were driving him away when he wants so much to be here among us, with us, and can't."

"I'm *awfully* sorry, Mary. Just *awfully* sorry. Yes, of *course* I *do* see. It's a kind of sacrilege."

So they sat quietly and in the silence they began to listen again. At first there was nothing, but after a few minutes Hannah whispered, "He's there," and Andrew whispered, "Where?" and Mary said quietly, "With the children," and quietly and quickly left the room.

When she came through the door of the children's room she could feel his presence as strongly throughout the room as if she had opened a furnace door: the presence of his strength, of virility, of helplessness, and of pure calm. She fell down on her knees in the middle of the floor and whispered, "Jay. My dear. My dear one. You're all right now, darling. You're not troubled any more, are you, my darling? Not any more. Not ever any more, dearest. I can feel how it is with you. I know, my dearest. It's terrible to go. You don't want to. Of *course* you don't. But you've got to. And you know they're going to be all right. Everything is going to be all right, my darling. God take you. God keep you, my own beloved. God make His light shine upon you." And even while she whispered, his presence became faint, and in a moment of terrible dread she cried out "Jay!" and hurried to her daughter's crib. "Stay with me one minute," she whispered, "just one minute, my dearest"; and in some force he did return; she felt him with her, watching his child. Catherine was sleeping with all her might and her thumb was deep in her mouth; she was scowling fiercely. "Mercy, child," Mary whispered, smiling, and touched her hot forehead to smooth it, and she growled. "God bless you, God keep you," her mother whispered, and came silently to her son's bed. There was the cap in its tissue paper, beside him on the floor; he slept less deeply than his sister, with his chin lifted, and his forehead flung back; he looked grave, serene and expectant.

"Be with us all you can," she whispered. "This is good-bye."

And again she went to her knees. Good-bye, she said again, within herself; but she was unable to feel much of anything. "God help me to *realize* it," she whispered, and clasped her hands before her face: but she could realize only that he was fading, and that it was indeed good-bye, and that she was at that moment unable to be particularly sensitive to the fact.

And now he was gone entirely from the room, from the house, and from this world.

"Soon, Jay. Soon, dear," she whispered; but she knew that it would not be soon. She knew that a long life lay ahead of her, for the children were to be brought up, and God alone could know what change and chance might work upon them all, before they met once more. She felt at once calm and annihilating emptiness, and a cold and overwhelming fullness.

"God help us all," she whispered. "May God in His loving mercy keep us all."

She signed herself with the Cross and left the room.

She looks as she does when she has just received, Hannah thought as she came in and took her old place on the sofa; for Mary was trying, successfully, to hide her desolation; and as she sat among them in their quietness it was somewhat diminished. After all, she told herself, he *was there*. More strongly even than when he was here in the room with me. Anyhow. And she was grateful for their silence.

Finally Andrew said, "Aunt Hannah has an idea about it, Mary."

"Maybe you'd prefer not to talk about it," Hannah said.

"No; it's all right; I guess I'd rather." And with mild surprise she found that this was true.

"Well, it's simply that I thought of all the old tales and beliefs about the souls of people who die sudden deaths, or violent deaths. Or as Joel would prefer it, not souls. Just their life force. Their consciousness. Their life itself."

"Can't get around that," Joel said. "Hannah was saying that everything of any importance leaves the body then. I certainly have to agree with that."

"And then even whether you believe or not in life after death," Mary said, "in the soul, as a living, immortal thing, creature, why it's certainly very believable that for a little while afterwards, this force, this life, stays on. Hovers around."

"Sounds highly unlikely to me, but I suppose it's conceivable."

"Like looking at a light and then shutting your eyes. No, not like that but—but it does stay on. Specially when it's someone very strong, very vital, who hasn't been worn down by old age, or a long illness or something."

"That's exactly it," Andrew said. "Something that comes out whole, because it's so quick."

"Why they're as old as the hills, those old beliefs."

"I should imagine they're as old as life and death," Andrew said.

"The thing I mean is, they aren't taken straight to God," Hannah said. "They've had such violence done them, such a shock, it takes a while to get their wits together."

"That's why it took him so long to come," Mary said. "As if his very *soul* had been struck unconscious."

"I should think maybe."

"And above all with someone like Jay, young, and with children and a wife, and not even dreaming of such a thing coming on him, no time to adjust his mind and feelings, or prepare for it."

"That's just it," Andrew said; Hannah nodded.

"Why he'd feel, 'I'm worried. This came too fast without warning. There are all kinds of things I've got to tend to. I can't just leave them like this.' *Wouldn't* he! And that's just how he was, how we felt he was. So *an*xious. So awfully concerned, and disturbed. Why yes, it's just exactly the way it was!

"And only when they feel convinced you know they care, and

everything's going to be taken good care of, just the very best possible, it's only then they can stop being anxious and begin to rest."

They nodded and for a minute they were all quiet.

Then Mary said tenderly, "How awful, pitiful, beyond words it must be, to be so terribly anxious for others, for others' good, and not be able to do anything, even to say so. Not even to help. Poor things.

"Oh, they *do* need reassuring. They *do* need rest. I'm *so grateful* I could assure him. It's so good he can rest at last. I'm *so glad*." And her heart was restored from its desolation, into warmth and love and almost into wholeness.

Again they were all thoughtfully silent, and into this silence Joel spoke quietly and slowly, "I *don't—know*. I *just—don't—know*. Every bit of gumption I've got tells me it's impossible, but if this kind of thing is so, it isn't with gumption that you see it is. I *just —don't—know*.

"If you're right, and I'm wrong, then chances are you're right about the whole business, God, and the whole crew. And in that case I'm just a plain damned fool.

"But if I can't trust my common sense—I know it's nothing much, Poll, but it's all I've got. If I can't trust that, what in hell *can* I trust!

"God, you'n Hannah'd say. Far's I'm concerned, it's out of the question."

"Why, Joel?"

"It doesn't seem to embarrass your idea of common sense, or Poll's, and for that matter I'm making no reflections. You're got plenty of gumption. But how you can reconcile the two, I can't see."

"It takes faith, Papa," Mary said gently.

"That's the word. That's the one makes a mess of everything, far's I'm concerned. Bounces up like a jack-in-the-box. Solves everything.

"Well it doesn't solve anything for me, for I haven't got any.

"Wouldn't hurt it if I had. Don't believe in it.

"Not for me.

"For you, for anyone that can manage it, all right. More power to you. Might be glad if I could myself. But I can't.

"I'm not exactly an atheist, you know. Least I don't suppose I am. Seems as unfounded to me to say there isn't a God as to say there is. You can't prove it either way. But that's it: I've got to have proof. And on anything can't be proved, be damned if I'll jump either way. All I can say is, I hope you're wrong but I just don't know."

"I don't, either," Andrew said. "But I hope it's so."

He saw Mary and Hannah look at him hopefully.

"I don't mean the whole business," he said. "I don't know anything about that. I just mean tonight."

Can't eat your cake and have it, his father thought.

Like slapping a child in the face, Andrew thought; he had been rougher than he had intended.

"But, Andrew dear," Mary was about to say, but she caught herself. What a thing to argue about, she thought; and what a time to be wrangling about it!

Each of them realized that the others felt something of this; for a little while none of them had anything to say. Finally Andrew said, "I'm sorry."

"Never mind," his sister said. "It's all right, Andrew."

"We just each believe what we're able," Hannah said, after a moment.

"Even you, Joel. You have faith in your mind. Your reason."

"Not very much: all I've got, that's all. All I can be sure of."

"That's all I mean."

"Let's not talk about it any more," Mary said. "Tonight," she added, trying to make her request seem less peremptory.

The word was a reproach upon them all, much more grave, they were sure, than Mary had intended, so that to spare her regret they all hastened to say, kindly and as if somewhat callously, "No, let's not."

In the embarrassment of having spoken all at once they sat helpless and sad, sure only that silence, however painful to them all and to Mary, was less mistaken than trying to speak. Mary wished that she might ease them; her continued silence, she was sure, intensified their self-reproach; but she felt, as they did, that an attempt to speak would be worse than quietness.

In this quietness their mother sat, and smiled nervously and politely, and tilted her trumpet in a generalized way towards all of them. She realized that nobody was speaking and it was at such times, ordinarily, that she felt sure that she could speak without interrupting anyone, but she feared that anything that she might say might brutally or even absurdly disrupt a weaving of thought and feeling whose motions within the room she could most faintly apprehend.

After a little while it occurred to her that even to hold out her trumpet might seem to require something of them; she held it in her lap. But lest any of them should feel that this was in any sense a reproach, or should in the least feel sorry for her, she kept her little smile, thinking, how foolish, how very foolish, to smile.

Smiling at grief, Joel thought. He wondered whether his sister and his son and his daughter, if they were thinking of it at all, understood the smile as he was sure he did. He wished that he could pat her hand. By God, they'd better, he thought.

Andrew could not get out of his mind the image of his brother-in-law as he had first seen him that night. By the mere shy, inactive way the men stood who, as he and Walter first came up, stood between them and Jay, he had realized, instantly, before anyone spoke, "He's dead." Somebody had murmured something embarrassed about identification and he had answered sharply that they'd managed to phone the family, hadn't they?, and again they had murmured embarrassedly, and ashamed of his sharpness he had assented, and there in the light of the one bulb one of the men had gently turned down the sheet (for he gathered a little later that the blacksmith's wife, finding him covered with a reeking horse blanket, had hurried to bring this sheet); and there he was; and Andrew nodded, and made himself say, "Yes," and he heard Walter's deep, quiet breathing at his shoulder and heard him say, "Yes," and he stood a little aside in order that Walter might have room, and together they stood silent and looked at the uncovered head. The strong frown was still in the forehead but, even as they watched, it seemed to be fading very slowly; already the flesh had settled somewhat along the bones of the prostrate skull; the temples, the forehead and the sockets of the eyes were more subtly molded than they had been in life and the nose was more finely arched; the chin was thrust upward as if proudly and impatiently, and the small cut at its point was as neat and bloodless as if it had been made by a chisel in soft wood. They watched him with the wonder which is felt in the presence of anything which is great and new, and, for a little while, in any place where violence has recently occurred; they were aware, as they gazed at the still head, of a prodigious kind of energy in the air. Without turning his head, Andrew became aware that tears were running down Walter's cheeks; he himself was cold, awed, embittered beyond tears. After perhaps a half minute he said coldly, "Yes, that's he," and covered the face himself and turned quickly away; Walter was drying his face and his glasses; aware of some obstacle, Andrew glanced quickly down upon a horned, bruised anvil; and laid his hand flat against the cold, wheemed iron; and it was as if its forehead gave his hand the stunning shadow of every blow it had ever received.

Now these images manifolded upon each other with great rapidity, at their constant center, the proud, cut chin, and could be driven from his mind's eye only by two others, Jay as he felt he had seen him, the contact after the accident, lying, they had told him, so straight and unblemished beside the car, the dead eyes shining with starlight and the hand still as if ready to seize and wrestle; and as he had last actually seen him, naked on the naked table, a block beneath his nape.

Somebody sighed, from the heart; he looked up; it was Hannah. They were all looking downward and sidelong. His sister's face had altered strangely among this silence; it had become thin, shy and somehow almost bridal. He remembered her wedding in Panama; yes, it was much the same face. He looked away.

"Aunt Hannah, will you please stay with me here tonight?" Mary asked.

Mama, Andrew thought, and his heart went out to her as he looked at her deaf, set smile.

"Why certainly, Mary."

Joel decided not to look at his watch. Andrew covertly glanced at the mantel clock. It was . . .

"I hope Mama won't mind too much. I hope she'll understand. Poor thing. Mama," she suddenly called, and put her hand on her mother's hand and on the trumpet. Her mother eagerly tilted it. "I think it's about time we all tried to get some sleep." Her mother nodded, and seemed to be about to speak; Mary pressed her hand for silence and continued, "Mama, I've asked Aunt Hannah if she'll stay here tonight with me." Her mother nodded and again seemed to be about to speak. Again Mary pressed her hand: "I'd love it if you could, but I know how it would disrupt things at eleven-fifteen,"—*"Hahh,"* her father exclaimed— "and I just . . ."

"Tell her, Poll!"

"Also, Mama. Also it's just—I hope you'll understand and not mind, Mama dear—it's just it would be so very hard for us to *talk, quietly,* and with the children and all, why I just sort of think . . ."

"Why certainly, Mary," her mother interrupted, in her somewhat ringing voice. "I absolutely agree with you. I think it's so nice that Hannah can stay!" she added, almost as if Mary and Hannah were little girls.

"I hope you know, Mama, how *very much!*—I hope you don't mind. I just appreciate it so much, I . . ."

Her mother patted her hand rapidly. "It's perfectly all right, Mary. It's very *sensible,*" she smiled.

Mary put an arm around her and hugged her; she turned her aging face and smiled very brightly and Mary could see the tears in her eyes. She was speechless and her head was shaking in her effort to convey her love and the entirety of her feeling. "*Anything I can do, dear child,*" she said after a few moments. "*Anything!*"

"Bless you, Mama!"

"Beg pardon?"

"I said *bless* you, dear!"

Catherine patted her hand on the back and smiled even more tightly.

I love you so much! Mary exclaimed within herself.

"Praps the children," Catherine said. "I could take care, if—it would be more, *convenient . . .*"

"Oh, I don't think we should wake them up!" Mary said.

"She doesn't mean . . ." Andrew began.

"Tomorrow," her mother said. "Just, perhaps, during the— interim . . ."

"That's wonderful, Mama, that may turn out to be just the thing and if it is I most certainly will. *Most gratefully.* It's just, I'm in such a spin it's just too soon to quite know yet, make any plans. Anything. Tomorrow."

"Tomorrow then."

"Thank you, Mama."

"Not at all."

"Thank you all the same."

Her mother smiled and shook her head.

Joel and his sister stood up.

"Mary before we go," Andrew said.

"?"

"It's much too late, Mary, you're much too tired."

"Not if it's important, Andrew."

"Let's let it go till morning."

"What is it, Andrew?"

"Just—various things we'll have to discuss pretty soon." He took a deep breath and said in a loud voice, "Getting a plot, making arrangements about the funeral; seeing about a headstone. Let's wait till morning."

Earth, stone, a coffin. The ugly craft of undertakers became real and tangible to her, but as if she touched them with frozen hands. She looked at him with glazed eyes.

"That'll be plenty of time, Mary," she heard her aunt say.

"Of course it will," Andrew said. "It was foolish of me to even speak of it tonight."

"Well if there's time," she said vaguely. "Yes *if* there's time, Andrew," she said more distinctly. "Yes, then I'd rather, if you don't mind. Tomorrow in the morning." She glanced at the clock. "Goodness *this* morning," she exclaimed.

"Of course not," Andrew said. He turned to his aunt and said in a low voice, as one speaks before an invalid, "Let her sleep if she can. You phone me."

Hannah nodded.

"Must've . . ." Joel said, and went into the hall.

"What's . . ." Hannah began.

"Hat I guess. Mine too." Andrew left the room; in the hall he met his father, carrying his own hat, his wife's, and Andrew's.

"Left them in the kitchen," his father said.

"Thank you, Papa," Andrew took his hat.

Catherine was standing uneasily in the middle of the room, holding her trumpet and her purse and looking towards the hall door. "Thank you, Joel," she said. She settled and pinned her hat by touch, a little crooked, and looked at Hannah inquiringly.

"It's all right, Catherine," her husband said.

Andrew was watching his sister. It seemed to him that these preparations for departure put her into some kind of silent panic.

Maybe we should stay, he thought. All night. I could. But Mary was chiefly watching her mother's difficulties with the hat. No, it's the slowness, he corrected himself. Sooner the better.

"Well, Mary," he said, and stepped to her and put his arms around her. He saw that her eyes were speckled; it was as if the irises had been crushed into many small fragments; and in her eyes and her presence he felt something of the shock and energy which had radiated so strongly from the dead body. She was new; changed. Nothing I can do, he thought.

"Thank you for everything," she said. "I'm so sorry you had it to do."

He could not answer or continue to look into her eyes; he embraced her more closely. "Mary," he said finally.

"I'm all right, Andrew," she said quietly. "I've got to be."

He nodded sharply.

"You come up in the morning. We'll—make our plans."

"Sleep if you can."

"Just come up first thing because I know there's an awful lot to do and not much time."

"All right."

"Good night, Andrew."

"Good night, Mary."

"Bless you," her mother exploded, almost as if she were cursing; deaf, near-sighted, she caught her daughter in her arms with all her strength and patted her back with both hands, thinking: how young and good she smells!

She wants so to help, Mary realized. To stay! Under her caress she felt the hard, round shoulders, sharp backbone, already hunching with age. Leaning back in her mother's embrace, she straightened the hat, looked into the trembling face, and kissed her hard on the mouth. Her mother twice returned the kiss, then stood aside, gathering her long skirt for the porch steps.

"Poll," her father said; she felt the beard against her cheek and heard his whisper: "Good girl. Keep it up."

She nodded.

"Good night," Hannah said.

"Good night, Aunt Hannah," Andrew replied.

"Night, Hannah," her brother said. He steered Catherine by one elbow, Andrew by the other; they went onto the porch.

"Light!" Mary exclaimed.

"What?" Andrew and Hannah asked, startled.

Mary switched on the porch light. "Tsall right," her father said in mild annoyance. "Thank you," her mother chimed, politely. Mary and Hannah stood at the door while they carefully descended the porch steps, and they watched them until they reached the corner and then until they had safely crossed the street. Under the corner lamp, Andrew turned his head and lifted and let fall his hand in something less than a wave. The others did not turn; and now Andrew also had turned away, and they went carefully away along the sidewalk, and Mary switched off the light, and still watched. Hannah could no longer see them now, and after a few moments, gave up pretending to watch them and watched Mary as she looked after them, as intently, Hannah felt, as if it were of more importance than anything else, to see them until the last possible instant. And still Mary could see them, somewhat darker against the darkness and of uneven heights, growing smaller, so that it was not finally the darkness which made them impossible to see, but the corner of the Biddles' house.

When they were gone she continued to look up and down the street as far as she could see. There was the strong carbon light at the corner, and there was the glow of an unseen light at a more distant corner to the west; and of another, still more distant, to the east. There was no sound, and there were no lights on in any of the houses. The air moved mildly on her forehead. She turned, and saw that her aunt was watching her, and looked into her eyes.

"Time to sleep," she said.

She closed the door; they continued to look at each other.

"It was just about this time last night," she said.

Hannah sighed, very low; after a moment she touched Mary's hand. Still they stood and looked at each other.

"Yes, just about," Mary whispered strangely.

Through the silence they began to hear the kitchen clock.

"Let's not even *try* to talk now," Mary said. "We're both worn out."

"Let me fix you a good hot toddy," Hannah said, as they turned towards the living room. "Help you sleep."

"I honestly don't think I'll *need* it, Aunt Hannah."

I'll make one and you take it or not as you like, Hannah wanted to say; suddenly she realized: I'm only trying to think I'm useful. She said nothing.

There was an odd kind of shyness or constraint between them, which neither could understand. They stood still again, just inside the living room; the silence was somewhat painful for both of them, each on the other's account. Does she really *want* me to stay, Hannah wondered; what earthly use am I! Does she think I don't *want* her to stay, Mary wondered, just because I can't talk? No, she's no talker.

"I just can't talk just now," she said.

"Of course you can't, child."

Hannah felt that she probably ought to take charge of everything, but she felt still more acutely that she should be at the service of Mary's wishes, or lack of them for that matter, she told herself.

I can't stand to *send* her to bed, Mary thought.

"It's all ready," she said abruptly and, she feared, rather ruthlessly, and walked quickly across to the downstairs bedroom door and opened it. "See?" She walked in and turned on the light and faced her aunt. "I got it ready in case Jay," she said, and absently smoothed the pillow. "Just as well I did."

"You go straight to bed, Mary," Hannah said. "Let me help if I . . ."

Mary went into the kitchen; then Hannah could hear her in the hall; after a moment she came back. "Here's a clean night-gown," she said, "and a wrapper," putting them across her aunt's embarrassed hands. "It'll be big, I'm afraid, the wrapper, it's— was—it's Jay's, but if you'll turn up the sleeves it'll do in a pinch, I guess." She went past Hannah into the living room.

"I'll see to that, Mary," Hannah hurried after her; she was already gathering tumblers towards the tray.

"Great—goodness!" Mary exclaimed. She lifted the bottle. "Do you mean to say *I* drank all *that*?" It was three-quarters empty.

"No. Andrew had some, so did I, so did J—your father."

"But—just one apiece, Aunt Hannah. I *must* have. Nearly all of it."

"It hasn't had any effect."

"How on earth!" She held the low whiskey close to her eyes and looked at it as if she were threading a needle. "Well I most *certainly* don't need a *hot toddy*," she said.

"I never *heard* of such a thing!" she exclaimed quietly.

"Aspirin, perhaps."

"Aspirin?"

"You might wake up with a headache."

"It must just, Papa, Papa says, he said it sometimes doesn't, in a state of shock or things ... Aunt Hannah?" She called more loudly. "Aunt Hannah?" Mustn't wake them, she remembered. She waited. Her aunt came in from the hall with a glass of water and two aspirins.

"Here," she said, "you take these."

"But I ..."

"Just swallow them. You don't want to wake up with a headache and they'll help you sleep, too."

She took them docilely; Hannah loaded and lifted the tray.

Chapter 13

ALONG LAUREL, it was much darker; heavy leaves obscured the one near street lamp. Andrew could hear only their footsteps; his father and mother, he realized, could hear nothing even of that. How still we see thee lie. Yes, and between the treetops; the pale scrolls and porches and dark windows of the homes drifting past their slow walking, and not a light in any home, and so for miles, in every street of home and of business; above thy deep and dreamless sleep, the silent stars go by.

He helped his mother from the curb; this slow and irregular rattling of their little feet.

The stars are tired by now. Night's nearly over.

He helped her to the opposite curb.

Upon their faces the air was so marvelously pure, aloof and tender; and the silence of the late night in the city, and the stars, were secret and majestic beyond the wonder of the deepest country. Little houses, bigger ones, scrolled and capacious porches, dark windows, leaves of trees already rich with May, homes of rooms which chambered sleep as honey is cherished, drifted past their slow walking and were left behind, and not a light in any home. Along Laurel Avenue it was still darker. The lamp behind them no longer cast their shadows; in the light of the lamp ahead, a small and distant bit of pavement looked scalded with emptiness, a few leaves were touched to acid flame, the spindles and turned posts of one porch were rigidly white. Helping his mother along through the darkness, Andrew was walking much more slowly than he was used to walking, and all these things entered him calmly and thoroughly. Full as his heart was, he found that he was involved at least as deeply in the loveliness and unconcern of the spring night, as in the death. It's as if I didn't even care, he reflected, but he didn't mind. He knew he cared; he felt gratitude towards the night and towards the city he ordinarily cared little for. *How still we see thee lie,* he heard his mind say. He said the words over, drily within himself, and heard the melody; a child's voice, his own, sang it in his mind.

Hm.

He tried to remember when he had last walked in the open night at such an hour. He wasn't sure he even . . . God, years. Seven—about sixteen, when he still thought he was Shelley, watching the river. Leaning on the bridge rail and literally praying with gratitude for being alive.

Instinctively, he turned his head so that his parents could not see his face.

I don't want to see it, either, he thought.

By that time, Jay was trying to teach himself law.

Above thy deep and dreamless sleep, the silent stars go by.

The words had always touched him; every year they still brought back Christmas to him, for some reason, as nothing else could. Now they seemed to him as beautiful as any poetry he had ever known.

He said them over to himself very slowly and calmly: just a statement.

They do indeed, he thought, looking up. They do indeed. And God, how tired they look!

It's the time of night.

The silent stars go by, he said aloud, not whispering, but so quietly he was sure they would not hear.

His eyes sprang full of tears; his throat, his chest knotted into a deep sob which he subdued, and the tears itched on his cheeks.

Yet in thy dark streets shineth, he sang loudly, almost in fury, within himself: *the everlasting light!* and upon these words a sob leapt up through him which he could not subdue but could only hope to conceal.

They did not notice.

This is crazy, he told himself incredulously. *No sense in this at all!*

Everlasting light!

The hopes and fears, a calm and implacable voice continued within him; he spoke quietly: *Of all the years.*

Are met in thee tonight, he whispered: and in the middle of a wide plain, the middle of the dark and silent city, slabbed beneath shadowless light, he saw the dead man, and struck his thigh with his fists with all his strength.

All he could hear in this world was only their footsteps; his father and mother, he realized, could hear nothing even of that.

He helped her from the curb; this slow and irregular rattling of their little feet; and across the space of bitter light.

He helped her to the opposite curb; they followed their absurd shadows until all was once more one shadow.

None of the three of them spoke, throughout their walk; when they came to the corner at which they would turn for home, it was as if all three spoke, accepting the fact: for each man tightened his hand gently at the woman's elbows and, bowing her head, she pressed their hands against her sides. They turned down the steep hill, walking still more slowly and tightening their knees, and saw the one light which had been left burning, and entered their home, quietly as burglars, by the back way.

They stopped at the foot of the stairs.

"Mary," Hannah asked, "is there anything I can do?"

You want to come up with me, Mary realized. "I think I just better be alone," she said. "But thank you. Thank you, Aunt Hannah."

"Just call if you want me. You know how lightly I sleep."

"I'll be all right, I really will."

"You rest in the morning. I'll take care of the children."

Mary looked at her with brightened eyes, and said, "Aunt Hannah, I'll have to tell them."

Hannah nodded, and sighed: "Yesss. Good night then," she said, and kissed her niece. "God bless you," she said, in a broken voice.

Mary looked at her carefully and said, "God help us all."

She turned and went up the stairs, and leaned, smiling, just before she disappeared, and whispered, "Good night."

"Good night, Mary," Hannah whispered.

She turned off the hall light and the light in the living room and went into the lighted bedroom and pulled down the shade and shut the doors to the kitchen and the living room. She took off her dress and laid it over the back of a chair and sat on the edge of the bed to unlace her shoes, and hesitated, until she was certain that she remembered, clearly, putting out the lights in the kitchen and bathroom. She put on the nightgown except for the sleeves and finished undressing under the nightgown; it was rather large for her and she gathered and lifted it about her. She knelt beside the bed and said an Our Father and a Hail Mary, and found that her heart and mind were empty of further prayer or even of feeling. May the souls of the faithful, she tried; she clamped her teeth and, after a moment, prayed angrily: May the souls of everyone who has ever had to live and die, in the Faith or outside it, rest in peace. And especially his!

Strike me down, she thought. Visit upon me Thy lightnings. I don't care. I can't care.

Forgive me if I'm wrong, she thought. If You can. If You will. But that's how I feel, and that's all there is to it.

Again her heart and mind were empty; even now, feeling the breath of the abyss, she could not feel otherwise, or even care or fear.

Lord, I believe. Help Thou mine unbelief.

But I don't really know's I do.

I can't pray, God. Not now. Try to forgive me. I'm just too tired and too appalled.

Thirty-six years old.

Thirty-six.

Well, why not? Why one time worse than another? God knows it's no picnic or ever was intended as such.

Into Thy hands I commend my spirit.

She made the sign of the Cross, raised the shade, opened the window, and got into bed. As her bare feet slid along the cold, clean linen and she felt its cold, clean blandness beneath her and above her, she was taken briefly by trembling and by loneliness, and remembered touching her dead mother's cheek.

Oh, why am I alive!

She took off her glasses and laid them carefully in reach at the foot of the lamp, and turned out the light. She straightened formally on her back, folded her hands upon her breast, and shut her eyes.

I can't worry any more about anything tonight, she said to herself. He'll just have to take care of it.

Till morning.

Mary did not bother to turn on the light; she could see well enough by the windows. She put on her nightgown and undressed beneath it, and saw to it that the door was left ajar for the children, and climbed into bed before she realized that these were the same sheets and before it occurred to her that she had not said her prayers; and for such a while now she had felt that if only she could be alone, only for that!

It's all right, she whispered to herself; it's all right, she whispered aloud. She had meant that she was sure that God would understand and forgive her inability to pray, but she found that she meant too that it really was all right, everything, the whole thing, really all right. Thy will be done. All right. Truly all right. She lay straight on her back with her hands open, upward at her sides and could just make out, in the subtly diminished darkness, a familiar stain which at various times had seemed to resemble a crag, a galleon, a fish, a brooding head. Tonight it was just itself, with one meaningless eye. It seemed to her that she was falling backward and downward, prostrate, through eternity; she felt no concern. Without concern she heard a voice speak within her: Out of the deep have I called unto Thee, O Lord; Lord, hear my voice, she joined in. O let Thine ears consider well the voice of my complaint. And now the first voice said no more and, aware of its silent presence, Mary continued, whispering aloud: If Thou, Lord, wilt be extreme to mark what is done amiss O Lord, who may abide it? And with these last words she began to cry freely and quietly, her hands turned downward and moved wide on the bed.

Oh, Jay! Jay!

Under the lid of the large kettle the low water was lukewarm; one by one, along the curved firmament, the last of the bubbles broke and vanished.

Hannah lay straight on her back with her hands folded: in their deep sockets, beneath lids as frail as membranes, her eyeballs were true spheres. No lines were left in her face; she might have been a young woman. Her lips were parted, and each breath was a light sigh.

Mary lay watching the ceiling: Who may abide it, she whispered.

Silently.

One by one, million by million, in the prescience of dawn, every leaf in that part of the world was moved.

Rufus' house was on the way to school for a considerable neighborhood, and within a few minutes after his father had waved for the last time and disappeared, the walks were filled with another exciting thing to look at as the boys and girls who were old enough for school came by. At first he was content to watch them through the front window; they were creatures of an all but unimaginable world; he personally knew nobody who was big enough even for kindergarten. Later he felt more kinship with them, more curiosity, great envy, and considerable awe. It did not yet occur to him that he could ever grow up to be one of them, but he began to feel that in any case they were somehow of the same race. He wandered out into the yard, even to the sidewalk, even, at length, to the corner, where he could see them coming from three ways at once. He was fascinated by the way they looked, the boys so powerfully dressed and the girls almost as prettily as if they were going to a party. Nearly all of them walked in two's and three's, and members of these groups often called to others of the groups. You could see how well they all knew each other; any number of people; a whole world. And they all carried books of different colors and thicknesses, and lunches done up in packages or boxes, and pencils in still other boxes; or carried all these things together in a satchel. He loved the way they carried these things, it seemed to give them wonderful dignity and purpose, to be the mark that set them apart in their privileged world. He particularly admired and envied the way the boys who carried their books in brown canvas straps could swing them, except when they swung them at his head. Then he was at the same time frightened and very much surprised, and the boy who had pretended he meant to hit him, and anyone else who saw, would laugh to see that look of fear and surprise on his face, and he felt puzzled and unhappy because they laughed.

But that did not happen often enough to discourage him, and going to the corner at the time they went to school, and at the time they could be expected back again, became quite a habit with him, almost as happy and exciting, in its way, as watching for the first glimpse of his father, late in the afternoon. Sometimes when he caught an eye he would even say, "Hello," as much out of embarrassment as eagerness to communicate. Of course he was very seldom answered; the boys would merely stare at him for a second or so, with the stare turning hot or more often cold, and the girls, depending on age or disposition, either giggled in a way that made him look quickly away, or pretended that they had not even seen or heard him. But since he did not, after all, expect any answer, it was wonderfully pleasant when, occasionally, a much older boy would smile and say, "Hello there"; a few times they even reached out and mussed up his hair. Once, too, when he had said hello to some much older girls, one of them cried out in the strange, sticky voice he had heard grown women use, "Ooh, just look at the darlin little boy!"

He had felt embarrassed but pleasantly flattered for a moment; then he heard several boys squealing the same words, but insincerely, in fact with a hatred and scorn which appalled him, and he had wished that he could not be seen.

He never learned the names of more than two or three of these boys, for most of them lived several blocks away; but quite a few of them, in time, knew him very well. They would come up, nearly always, with the same question: "What's your name?" It seemed strange to him that they could not remember his name from one day to the next, for he always told it to them perfectly clearly, but he felt that if they forgot, and asked again, he ought to tell them again, and when he told them, politely, they all laughed. After a while he began to real- ize that they only asked him, day after day, not because they had really forgotten, but only to tease him. So he became more careful. When they asked, "What's your name?" he would feel embarrassed and say, "Oh, you know my name, you're only trying to tease me."

And some of them would snicker, but invariably the boy who had asked it this time would say very seriously and politely, "No, I don't *know your name, you never told me your name," and he would begin to wonder; had he or hadn't he.*

"Yes I did, too," he would say, "I remember. It was only day before yesterday."

And again there would be snickering, but the questioner looked even more serious and kind, and one or two of the boys next to him looked equally serious, and he would say, "No, honest. Honest, it couldn't have been me. I don't know your name."

And one of the other boys would say, very reasonably, "Gee, he wouldn't ast you if he knowed it already, would he?"

And Rufus would say, "Aw, you're just trying to tease me. You all know my name."

And one of the other boys would say, "I've forgot it. I knew it but I've plumb forgot it. I'd tell him if I could but I just can't remember it."

And he too would look very sincere. And the first questioner would say, almost pleading, and very kind-looking, "Come on, tell us your name. Maybe you told it to him but he don't remember. If he could remember he'd tell me, now wouldn't he? Wouldn't you tell me?"

"Sure I'd tell you if I could remember it. Wisht you'd tell it to me again."

And two or three other boys, in similar tones of kindness, respect and concern, would chime in, "Aw come on, tell us your name."

And he was taken aback by all this kindness and concern, for they did not seem to act in that way towards him at any other time, and yet it did seem real. And after thinking a moment he would say, looking cautiously and earnestly, at the boy who had forgotten, "Do you promise you really honestly forgot?"

And looking back just as earnestly the boy said, "Cross my heart and body," and did so.

Then there was a snicker again from somebody, and Rufus realized that some of them were undoubtedly teasing; but he felt that he did not much mind, if these central boys were not. So he paid no atten-

tion to the snickering and said to every one of the kind-looking serious boys, "You promise you honestly aren't teasing this time?" and they promised. Then he said, "If I tell you this time will you promise to do your very best to remember, and not ask me again?" and they said that they sure would, they crossed their hearts and bodies. At the last moment, just as he was beginning to tell them, he always felt such sudden, profound doubt of their sincerity that he did not want to go ahead, but he always felt, too, Maybe they mean it. If they do, it would be mean not to tell them. So he always told them. "Well," he always said rather doubtfully, and brought out his name in a peculiarly muffled and shy way (he had come almost to feel that the name itself was being physically hurt, and he did not want it to be hurt again) "Well, it's Rufus."

And the instant it was out of his mouth he knew that he had been mistaken once again, that not a single soul of them had meant one thing that he had said, for with that instant every one of them screamed as loudly as he could with a ferocious kind of joy, and it was as if the whole knot exploded and sent its fragments tearing all over the neighborhood, screaming his name with amusement and apparently with some kind of contempt; and many of them screamed, as well, a verse which they seemed to think very funny, though Rufus could not understand why.

> Uh-Rufus, Uh-Rastus, Uh-Johnson, Uh-Brown,
> uh-What ya gonna do when the rent comes roun?

and others yelled, "Nigger's name, nigger's name," and chanted a verse that he had often heard them yell after the backs of colored children and even grown-up colored people,

> Nigger, nigger, black as tar,
> Tried to ride a lectric car,
> Car broke down and broke his back
> Poor nigger wanted his nickel back.

Three or four, instead of running, stood screaming his name and these verses at him, and the word, "nigger," jumping up and down and shoving their fingers at his chest and stomach and face while he stood in abashment, and followed by these, he would walk unhappily home.

It puzzled him very deeply. If they knew his name all the time, as apparently they did, then why did they keep on asking as if they had never heard it, or as if they couldn't remember it? It was just to tease. But why did they want to tease? Why did they get such fun out of it? Why was it so much fun, to pretend to be so nice and so really interested, to pretend it so well that somebody else believed you in spite of himself, just so that he would show that he was deceived once again, because if you honestly did mean it, this time, he didn't want to not tell you when you honestly seemed to want so much to know. Why was it that when some of them were asking him, and others were backing them up or just looking on, there was some kind of a strange, tight force in the air all around them that made them all seem very much together and that made him feel very much alone and very eager to be liked by them, together with them? Why did he keep on believing them? It happened over and over and he could not think of a single time that they had looked so interested, and friendly, and kind, but what it had turned out that they didn't really mean one bit of it. The ones who were really nice, the ones who never deceived him or teased him, were a few of the much bigger boys, who were never so attentive or kind as this, but just said, "Hello, there," and smiled as they went by, or maybe mussed up his hair or gave him a little punch, not to hurt or scare him, but only in play. They were very different from these, they never paid him such close attention or looked so affectionate, but they were the nice ones and these were mean to him, every time. But every time, it was the same. When they started he was always absolutely sure that this time, he would not give in to them; but every time, as they kept talking, he became less sure. At the same time that he became less sure, he became more sure, but that confused and troubled him, and the more sure he was that all this apparent kindness was merely deception and meanness, the more eagerly he studied their faces in the hope that this time they really meant it. The less he believed them, the more he was led to believe them, and the easier it was for him to believe them. The more alone he felt, the more he wanted to feel that he was not alone, but one of them. And every time he finally gave in, he became a little more sure, just before he gave in, that he would not take this chance again. And every time he finally spoke his name, he spoke it a little more shyly, a little more in shame, until he began to feel some kind of shame about the name itself. The way they all screamed it at him, and screamed that rhyme they all laughed at, the more he came to feel that there must be something wrong with the name itself, so that even at home sometimes, even when Mama said it, if he heard it without expecting it, he felt some kind of obscure, wincing shock and shame. But when he asked her if Rufus was really a nigger's name, and why that made everybody laugh at it, she turned to him sharply and said to him in a sharp voice, as if she were accusing him of something, "Who told you that?", and he had answered, in fear, that he did not know who, and she had said, "Don't you just pay any attention to them. It's a very fine old name. Some colored people take it too, but that is perfectly all right and nothing for them to be ashamed of or for white people to be ashamed of who take it. You were given that name because it was your great-grandfather Lynch's name, and it's a name to be proud of. And Rufus: don't ever speak that word 'nigger'."

But he had felt that although maybe she was proud of the name, he was not. How could you be proud of a name that everybody laughed at? Once when they were less noisy, and one of them said to him, quietly, "That's a nigger's name," he had tried to feel proud and had said, "It is not either, it's a very fine old name and I got it from my Great-granpa Lynch," they yelled, "Then your granpa's a nigger too," and ran off down the street yelling, "Rufus is a nigger, Rufus' granpa's a nigger, he's a ning-ger, he's a nin-ger," and he had yelled after them, "He is not, either, it's my great-granpa *and he is* not!*"; but after that they sometimes opened a conversation by asking, "How's your nigger granpaw?" and he had to try to explain all over again that it was his great-grandpa and he was* not *colored, but they never seemed to pay any attention.*

He could not understand what amused them so much about this game, or why they should pretend to be all kindness and interest for the sake of deceiving him into doing something still again that he knew they knew better than to do, but it gradually became clear to him that no matter how much they pretended good, they always meant mean-ness, and that the only way to guard against this was never to believe them, and never to do what they asked him to. And so in time he found that no matter how nice they asked, he was not deceived by them and would not tell them his name, and this made him feel much better, except that now they seemed to have much less interest in him. He did not want them to go by without even looking at him, or just saying something mean or sneering as they passed, pretending so successfully that they meant to hit him with their books, that he had to duck; he only wanted them not to tease and fool him; he only wanted them to be nice to him and like him. And so he remained very ready to do what-ever seemed necessary to be liked, except that one thing, telling his name, which was clearly not ever a good thing to do. And so, as long as they didn't ask him his name (and they soon knew that this joke was no good any more), he continued to hope against hope that in every other way, they were not trying to tease or fool him. Now they would come up to him looking quite serious, the older boys, and say, as if it were a very serious question,

> *Rufus Rastus Johnson Brown*
> *What you gonna do when the* rent *comes roun?*

He always felt that they were still teasing him about his name, when they said that; there was something about the word "Rastus" that they said in such a tone that he knew they disliked both names and held both in contempt, and he could not understand why they gave him so many names when only one was really his and his last name was really Follet. But at least they knew what his name was now, even if most of them pronounced it "Roofeass"; at least they weren't pre-tending they didn't know; it wasn't as bad as that. Besides, what they were really doing was asking him a question, "What you gonna do when the rent comes roun?" Though they asked it every time and it seemed a nonsensical question. They seemed to really want to know, and if he could answer them, then he could really tell them something they really didn't know and then maybe they would really like him and not tease him. Yet he realized that this too must be teasing. They did not really want to know. How could they, when the question had no meaning? What was the rent? What did it look like when it came roun? It probably looked very mean or maybe it looked nice but was mean when you got to know it. And what would you do when it came roun? What could you do if you didn't even know what it was? Or if it was just something they made up, that wasn't really alive, just a story? He wanted to ask what the rent was, but he suspected that that was exactly what they wanted him to ask, and that if or when he asked it, it would turn out that the whole thing was a trap of some kind, a joke, and that he had done something shameful or ridiculous in asking. So that was one thing he was now wise enough never to do: he never asked what the rent was, and this was one of the things he felt sure that somehow he had better not ask his mother or his father, either. So when they came up to him now, he always knew they were going to ask this foolish question, and when they asked it he felt stubborn and shy, determined not to ask what the rent was; and once they had asked it, and stood looking at him with a curious, cold look as if they were hungry, he looked back at them until he felt too embarrassed, and saw them start to smile in a way that might be mean or might possibly be friendly, and on the possibility that they were friendly, smiled unsurely too, and looked down at the pavement, and muttered, "I don't know"; which seemed to amuse them almost as much as when he had told what his name was, though not so loudly; and then sometimes he would walk away from them, and after a while he learned that he should not answer this question any more than he should answer the question about his name.

When he walked away, or when he refused to answer, he always realized that in some way he had defeated them, but he also always felt disconsolate and lonely, and sometimes because of this he would turn around after he had gone a little way, and look and they would come up and go round him again, and other times, when he kept on walking away, he felt even more lonely and unhappy, so much so that he went down between the houses into the back yard and stayed for a while because he felt uneasy about being seen, yet, by his mother. He began to anticipate going out to the corner with as much unhappiness as hope, and sometimes he did not go at all; but when he went again, after not going at all, he was asked where he had been and why he had not been there the day before, and he had not known what to answer, and had been much encouraged because they spoke in such a way that they really seemed to care where he had been. And within the next days things did seem to change. The older and more perceptive of the boys realized that the shape of the game had shifted and that if they were to count on him to be there, and to be such a fool as always before, they had to act much more friendly; and the more stupid boys, seeing how well this worked, imitated them as well as they could. Rufus quickly came to suspect the more flagrant exaggerations of friendliness, but the subtler boys found, to their intense delight, that if only they varied the surface, the bait, from time to time, they would almost always deceive him. He was ever so ready to oblige. How it got started none of them remembered or cared, but they all knew that if they kept at him enough he would sing them his song, and be fool enough to think they actually liked it. They would say, "Sing us a song, Roofeass," and he would look as if he knew they were teasing him and say, "Oh, you don't want to hear it."

And they would say that they sure did want to hear it, it was a real pretty song, better than they *could sing, and they liked the way he danced when he sang it, too. And since they had very early learned to take pains to listen to the song with apparent respect and friendliness, he was very soon and easily persuaded. And so, feeling odd and foolish not because he felt they were really deceiving him or laughing at him, but only because with each public repetition of it he felt more silly, and less sure that it was really as pretty and enjoyable as he liked to think it was, he would give them one last anxious look, which always particularly tickled them, and would then raise his arms and turn round and round, singing,*

> *I'm a little busy bee, busy bee, busy bee,*
> *I'm a little busy bee, singing in the clover.*

As he sang and danced he could hear through his own verses a few obscure, incredulous cackles, but nearly all of the faces which whirled past him, those of the older boys, were restrained, attentive and smiling, and this made up for the contempt he saw on the faces of the middle-sized boys; and when he had finished, and was catching his breath, these older boys would clap their hands in real approval, and say, "That's an awful pretty song, Rufus, where did you learn that song?"

And again he would suspect some meanness behind it and so would refuse to say until they had coaxed him sufficiently and then out it came, "My mama"; and at that point some of the smaller boys were liable to spoil everything by yelling and laughing, but often even if they did, the older boys could save it all by sternly crying, "You shut up! Don't you know a pretty song when you hear it?" and by turning to him, with faces which shut out those boys and included him among the big boys, and saying, "Don't you care about them, Rufus, they're just ignorant and don't know nothing. You sing your song." And another would chime in, "Yeah, Rufus, sing it again. Gee, that's a pretty song"; and a third would say, "And don't forget to dance"; and for this reduced but select audience he would do the whole thing over again.

At that point someone usually said, abruptly, "Come on, we got to go," and as suddenly as if a chair had been pulled from under him, he would be left by himself; they hardly even clapped their hands before they walked away. But some of the boys with the nicest faces always took care, before they left, to tell him, "Gee, thanks, Rufus, that was mighty pretty," and to say, "Don't you forget, you be here tomorrow";

and this more than made up for the thing which never failed to perplex him. Why did they walk off, so suddenly as all that? Why did they all keep looking back and laughing in that queer way; subdued talk, their heads close together, and then those sudden whoops of laughter? It almost seemed as if they were laughing at him. And once when one of the bigger boys suddenly flung up his arms and whirled into the street, piping in a high, squeaky voice, "I'm a little busy bee," he was quite sure that they had not really liked the song, or him for singing it. But if they didn't, then why did they ask him to sing it? And then once he heard one of them, far down the block, squeak, "My mama," and he felt as if something went straight through his stomach, and they all laughed, and he was practically certain that to those boys at least, the whole thing was just some kind of mean joke. But then he remembered how nice the boys he liked best and trusted most had been, and he knew that anyway the boys he liked best were not in any way trying to tease him.

After a while, however, he began to wonder even about them. Maybe their being so extra nice was just their way of getting him to do things he would never do if they were only nice part of the time and then laughed at him. Yet if they were nice all the time, it must be because they honestly meant it. And yet the way some of the others laughed, what he was doing must be wrong or silly somehow. He would be much more careful. He would be careful not to do anything or say anything anybody asked him to, unless he was sure they were really nice and really meant it. He now watched even the boys he liked best with very particular caution, and they saw that unless they were much more shrewd the game was likely to be spoiled again. They began to promise him rewards, a stick of chewing gum, the stub of a pencil, chalk, a piece of candy, and this seemed to convince him. The less shrewd of the boys often did not give him the promised reward, and this of course was more fun, but the smarter ones were always consistent, so that he never refused them. It was all so easy, in fact, that it began to bore them. They began to appreciate the tricks the more stupid boys played, one getting down behind him while he danced and another pushing him over backwards, but they were intelligent enough never to take part in this, always to pretend thorough disapproval, always to help him to his feet and brush him off and console him if he had struck his head hard and was crying, and always to conceal their astonished delight at his utter bewilderment and gullibility and their astonished contempt at his complete lack of spirit to strike out against his tormentors, his lack of ability, even, for real solid anger. And because they were always there, and always seemed to be on his side, they could always keep him sufficiently deceived to come back for more than anyone in his right senses would come back for.

The oldest of them began to be obscurely ashamed, as well as bored. They were all much older and smarter than he was; even the youngest of the boys who went to school were enough older than he was that it seemed no wonder that he was continually fooled, and that he never fought back. They felt that this little song, for instance, was too sissy to be fun for much longer. They felt that more violent things should be done. But they themselves could not do such things. If they showed him they were not on his side, the fun would all be over. And even if it were not, they knew that it would be unfair of them to do the really violent things, which absolutely required violence in return, to anyone so much younger and smaller, no matter how big a fool he was. Besides, they had received more than enough hints that even if he were driven to fight, he would not have the nerve to, probably wouldn't even know he had to. They were curious to see what would happen. They left the game wider and wider open to the smaller, crueler and more simple boys. But it was no good. He would just look at them with surprise, pain and reproach, and get up and walk away; and if any of these older, normally friendly boys consoled him too closely, he would burst into sobs which disgusted as well as delighted them.

At length they found the right formula. They would put some boys as small as he was, up to some trick which nobody bigger would have any right to do.

———

After dinner the babies and all the children except Rufus were laid out on the beds to take their naps, and his mother thought he ought to lie down too, but his father said no, why did he need to, so he was allowed to stay up. He stayed out on the porch with the men. They were so full up and sleepy they hardly even tried to talk, and he was so full up and sleepy that he could hardly see or hear, but half dozing between his father's knees in the thin shade, trying to keep his eyes open, he could just hear the mild, lazy rumbling of their voices, and the more talkative voices of the women back in the kitchen, talking more easily, but keeping their voices low, not to wake the children, and the rattling of the dishes they were doing, and now and then their walking here or there along the floor; and mused with half-closed eyes which went in and out of focus with sleepiness, upon the slow twinkling of the millions of heavy leaves on the trees and the slow flashing of the blades of the corn, and nearer at hand, the hens dabbing in the pocked dirt yard and the ragged edge of the porch floor, and everything hung dreaming in a shining silver haze, and a long, low hill of blue silver shut off everything against a blue-white sky, and he leaned back against his father's chest and he could hear his heart pumping and his stomach growling and he could feel the hard knees against his sides, and the next thing he knew his eyes opened and he was looking up into his mother's face and he was lying on a bed and she was saying it was time to wake up because they were going on a call and see his great-great-grandmother and she would most specially want to see him because he was her oldest great-great-grandchild. And he and his father and mother and Catherine got in the front seat and his Granpa Follet and Aunt Jessie and her baby and Jim-Wilson and Ettie Lou and Aunt Sadie and her baby got in the back seat and Uncle Ralph stood on the running board because he was sure he could remember the way and that was all there was room for, and they started off very carefully down the lane, so nobody would be jolted, and even before they got out to the road his mother asked his father to stop a minute, and she insisted on taking Ettie Lou with them in front, to make a little more room in back, and after she insisted for a while, they gave in, and then

they all got started again, and his father guided the auto so very care-
fully across the deep ruts into the road, the other way from LaFollette
as Ralph told him to ("Yeah, I know," his father said, "I remember
that much anyhow."), that they were hardly joggled at all, and his
mother commented on how very nicely and carefully his father always
drove when he didn't just forget and go too fast, and his father blushed,
and after a few minutes his mother began to look uneasy, as if she had
to go to the bathroom but didn't want to say anything about it, and
after a few minutes more she said, "Jay, I'm awfully sorry but now I
really think you are forgetting."

"Forgetting what?" he said.

"I mean a little too fast, dear," she said.

"Good road along here," he said. "Got to make time while the
road's good." He slowed down a little. "Way I remember it," he said,
"there's some stretches you can't hardly ever get a mule through, we're
coming to, ain't they Ralph?"

"Oh mercy," his mother said.

"We are just raggin you," he said. "They're not all that bad. But
all the same we better make time while we can." And he sped up a
little.

After another two or three miles Uncle Ralph said, "Now around
this bend you run through a branch and you turn up sharp to the
right," and they ran through the branch and turned into a sandy woods
road and his father went a little slower and a cool breeze flowed
through them and his mother said how lovely this shade was after that
terrible hot sun, wasn't it, and all the older people murmured that it
sure was, and almost immediately they broke out of the woods and ran
through two miles of burned country with stumps and sometimes
whole tree trunks sticking up out of it sharp and cruel, and blackberry
and honeysuckle all over the place, and a hill and its shadow ahead.
And when they came within the shadow of the hill, Uncle Ralph said
in a low voice, "Now you get to the hill, start along the base of it to
your left till you see your second right and then you take that," but
when they got there, there was only the road to the left and none to the

right and his father took it and nobody said anything, and after a minute Uncle Ralph said, "Reckon they wasn't much to choose from there, was they?" and laughed unhappily.

"That's right," his father said, and smiled.

"Reckon my memory ain't so sharp as I bragged," Ralph said.

"You're doin fine," his father said, and his mother said so too.

"I could a swore they was a road both ways there," Ralph said, "but it was nigh on twenty years since I was out here." Why for goodness sake, his mother said, then she certainly *thought he had a wonderful memory.*

"How long since you were here, Jay?" He did not say anything. "Jay?"

"I'm a-studyin it," he said.

"There's your turn," Ralph said suddenly, and they had to back the auto to turn into it.

They began a long, slow, winding climb, and Rufus half heard and scarcely understood their disjointed talking. His father had not been there in nearly thirteen years; the last time was just before he came to Knoxville. He was always her favorite, Ralph said. Yes, his grandfather said, he reckoned that was a fact, she always seemed to take a shine to Jay. His father said quietly that he always did take a shine to her. It turned out he was the last of those in the auto who had seen her. They asked how she was, as if it had been within a month or two. He said she was failing lots of ways, specially getting around, her rheumatism was pretty bad, but in the mind she was bright as a dollar, course that wasn't saying how they might find her by now, poor old soul; no use saying. Nope, Uncle Ralph said, that was a fact; time sure did fly, didn't it; seemed like before you knew it, this year was last year. She had never yet seen Jay's children, or Ralph's, or Jessie's or Sadie's, it was sure going to be a treat for her. A treat and a surprise. Yes it sure would be that, his father said, always supposing she could still recognize them. Mightn't she even have died? his mother wanted to know. Oh no, all the Follets said, they'd have heard for sure if she'd died. Matter of fact they had *heard she had failed a good bit. Some-*

times her memory slipped up and she got confused, poor old soul. His mother said well she should think so, poor old lady. She asked, carefully, if she was taken good care of. Oh, yes, they said. That she was. Sadie's practically giving her life to her. That was Grandpa Follet's oldest sister and young Sadie was named for her. Lived right with her tending to her wants, day and night. Well, isn't that just wonderful, his mother said. Wasn't anybody else could do it, they agreed with each other. All married and gone, and she wouldn't come live with any of them, they all offered, over and over, but she wouldn't leave her home. I raised my family here, she said, I lived here all my life from fourteen years on and I aim to die here, that must be a good thirty-five, most, a good near forty year ago, Grampaw died. Goodness sake, his mother said, and she was an old old woman then! His father said soberly, "She's a hundred and three years old. Hundred and three or hundred and four. She never could remember for sure which. But she knows she wasn't born later than eighteen-twelve. And she always reckoned it might of been eighteen-eleven."

"Great heavens, Jay! Do you mean that?" He just nodded, and kept his eyes on the road. "Just imagine that, Rufus," she said. "Just think of that!"

"She's an old, old lady," his father said gravely; and Ralph gravely and proudly concurred.

"The things she must have seen!" Mary said, quietly. "Indians. Wild animals." Jay laughed. "I mean man-eaters, Jay. Bears, and wildcats—terrible things."

"There were cats back in these mountains, Mary—we called em painters, that's the same as a panther—they were around here still when I was a boy. And there is still bear, they claim."

"Gracious Jay, did you ever see one? A panther?"

"Saw one'd been shot."

"Goodness," Mary said.

"A mean-lookin varmint."

"I know," she said. "I mean, I bet he was. I just can't get over— why she's almost as old as the country, Jay."

"Oh, *no*," he laughed. "Aint' nobody that *old*. Why I read some-where, that just these mountains here are the oldest . . ."

"Dear, I meant the nation," she said. "The United States, I mean. Why let me see, why it was hardly as old as I am when she was born." They all calculated for a moment. "Not *even* as old," she said triumphantly.

"By golly," his father said. "I never thought of it like that." He shook his head. "By golly," he said, "that's a fact."

"Abraham Lincoln was just two years old," she murmured. "Maybe three," she said grudgingly. "Just try to imagine *that*, Rufus," she said after a moment. "Over a hundred years." But she could see that he couldn't comprehend it. "You know what she is?" she said, "she's Granpa Follet's grandmother!"

"That's a fact, Rufus," his grandfather said from the back seat, and Rufus looked around, able to believe it but not to imagine it, and the old man smiled and winked. "Woulda never believed you'd hear me *call nobody* 'Granmaw,' now would you?"

"No sir," Rufus said.

"Well, yer gonna," his grandfather said, "quick's I see her."

Ralph was beginning to mutter and to look worried and finally his brother said, "What's eaten ye, Ralph? Lost the way?" And Ralph said he didn't know for sure as he had lost it exactly, no, he wouldn't swear to that yet, but by golly he was damned if he was sure this was hit *anymore*, all the same.

"Oh dear, *Ralph*, how too bad," Mary said, "but don't you mind. Maybe we'll find it. I mean maybe soon you'll recognize landmarks and set us all straight again."

But his father, looking dark and painfully patient, just slowed the auto down and then came to a stop in a shady place. "Maybe we better figure it out right now," he said.

"Nothin round hyer I know," Ralph said, miserably. "What I mean, maybe we ought to start back while we still know the way back. Try it another Sunday."

"Oh, Jay."

"*I hate to but we got to get back in town tonight, don't forget. We could try it another Sunday. Make an early start.*" But the upshot of it was that they decided to keep on ahead awhile, anyway. They descended into a long, narrow valley through the woods of which they could only occasionally see the dark ridges and the road kept bearing in a direction Ralph was almost sure was wrong, and they found a cabin, barely even cut out of the woods, they commented later, hardly even a corn patch, big as an ordinary barnyard; but the people there, very glum and watchful, said they had never even heard of her; and after a long while the valley opened out a little and Ralph began to think that perhaps he recognized it, only it sure didn't look like itself if it was it, and all of a sudden a curve opened into half-forested meadow and there were glimpses of a gray house through swinging vistas of saplings and Ralph said, "By golly," and again, "By golly, *that is* hit. *That's* hit all right. Only we come on it from behind!" And his father began to be sure too, and the house grew larger, and they swung around where they could see the front of it, and his father and his Uncle Ralph and his Grandfather all said, "Why sure enough," and sure enough it was: and, "There she is," and there she was: it was a great, square-logged gray cabin closed by a breezeway, with a frame second floor, and an enormous oak plunging from the packed dirt in front of it, and a great iron ring, the rim of a wagon wheel, hung by a chain from a branch of the oak which had drunk the chains into itself, and in the shade of the oak, which was as big as the whole corn patch they had seen, an old woman was standing up from a kitchen chair as they swung slowly in onto the dirt and under the edge of the shade, and another old woman continued to sit very still in her chair.

The younger of the two old women was Great Aunt Sadie, and she knew them the minute she laid eyes on them and came right on up to the side of the auto before they could even get out. "Lord God," she said in a low, hard voice, and she put her hands on the edge of the auto and just looked from one to the other of them. Her hands were long and narrow and as big as a man's and every knuckle was swollen and split. She had hard black eyes, and there was a dim purple splash all *over the left side of her face. She looked at them so sharply and silently from one to another that Rufus thought she must be mad at them, and then she began to shake her head back and forth.* "Lord God," *she said again.* "Howdy, John Henry," *she said.*

"Howdy, Sadie," *his grandfather said.*

"Howdy, Aunt Sadie," *his father and his Aunt Sadie said.*

"Howdy, Jay," *she said, looking sternly at his father,* "howdy, Ralph," *and she looked sternly at Ralph.* "Reckon you must be Jess, and yore Sadie. Howdy, Sadie."

"This is Mary, Aunt Sadie," *his father said.* "Mary, this is Aunt Sadie."

"I'm proud to know you," *the old woman said, looking very hard at his mother.* "I figured it must be you," *she said, just as his mother said,* "I'm awfully glad to know you too." "And this is Rufus and Catherine and Ralph's Jim-Wilson and Ettie Lou and Jessie's Charlie after his daddy and Sadie's Jessie after her Granma and her Aunt Jessie," *his father said.*

"Well, Lord God," *the old woman said.* "Well, file on out."

"How's Granmaw?" *his father asked, in a low voice, without moving yet to get out.*

"Good as we got any right to expect," *she said,* "but don't feel put out if she don't know none-a-yews. She mought and she mought not. Half the time she don't even know me."

Ralph shook his head and clucked his tongue. "Pore old soul," *he said, looking at the ground. His father let out a slow breath, puffing his cheeks.*

"So if I was you-all I'd come up on her kind of easy," *the old woman said.* "Bin a coon's age since she seen so many folks at onct. Me either. Mought skeer her if ye all come a whoopin up at her in a flock."

"Sure," *his father said.*

"Ayy," *his mother whispered.*

His father turned and looked back. "Whyn't you go see her the first, Paw?" *he said very low.* "Yore the eldest."

"Tain't me she wants to see," *Grandfather Follet said.* "Hit's the younguns ud tickle her most."

"*Reckon that's the truth, if she can take notice,*" *the old woman said. "She shore like to cracked her heels when she heared* yore *boy was born," she said to Jay, "Mary or no Mary. Proud as Lucifer. Cause that was the first," she told Mary.*

"*Yes, I know," Mary said. "Fifth generation, that made."*

"*Did you get her postcard, Jay?"*

"*What postcard?"*

"*Why no," Mary said.*

"*She tole me what to write on one a them postcards and put hit in the mail to both a yews so I done it. Didn't ye never get it?"*

Jay shook his head. "First I ever heard tell of it," he said.

"*Well I shore done give hit to the mail. Ought to remember. Cause I went all the way into Polly to buy it and all the way in again to put it in the mail."*

"*We never did get it," Jay said.*

"*What street did you send it, Aunt Sadie?" Mary asked. "Because we moved not long be . . ."*

"*Never sent it to no street," the old woman said. "Never knowed I needed to, Jay working for the post office."*

"*Why, I quit working for the post office a long time back, Aunt Sadie. Even before that."*

"*Well I reckon that's how come then. Cause I just sent hit to 'Post Office, Cristobal, Canal Zone, Panama,' and I spelt hit right, too. C-r-i . . ."*

"*Oh," Mary said.*

"*Aw," Jay said. "Why, Aunt Sadie, I thought you'd a known. We been living in Knoxvul since pert near two years before Rufus was born."*

She looked at him keenly and angrily, raising her hands slowly from the edge of the auto, and brought them down so hard that Rufus jumped. Then she nodded, several times, and still she did not say anything. At last she spoke, coldly, "Well, they might as well just put me out to grass," she said. "Lay me down and give me both barls threw the head."

"*Why, Aunt Sadie," Mary said gently, but nobody paid any attention.*

After a moment the old woman went on solemnly, staring hard into Jay's eyes: "I knowed that like I know my own name and it plumb slipped my mind."

"Oh what a shame," Mary said sympathetically.

"Hit ain't shame I feel," the old woman said, "hit's sick in the stummick."

"Oh I didn't m . . ."

"Right hyer!" and she slapped her hand hard against her stomach and laid her hand back on the edge of the auto. "If I git like that too," she said to Jay, "then who's agonna look out fer her?"

"Aw, tain't so bad, Aunt Sadie," Jay said. "Everybody slips up nown then. Do it myself an I ain't half yer age. And you just ought see Mary."

"Gracious, yes," Mary said. "I'm just a perfect scatterbrain."

The old woman looked briefly at Mary and then looked back at Jay. "Hit ain't the only time," she said, "not by a long chalk. Twarn't three days ago I . . ." she stopped. "Takin on about yer troubles ain't never holp nobody," she said. "You just set hyer a minute."

She turned and walked over to the older woman and leaned deep over against her ear and said quite loudly, but not quite shouting, "Granmaw, ye got company." And they watched the old woman's pale eyes, which had been on them all this time in the light shadow of the sunbonnet, not changing, rarely ever blinking, to see whether they would change now, and they did not change at all, she didn't even move her head or her mouth. "Ye hear me, Granmaw?" The old woman opened and shut her sunken mouth, but not as if she were saying anything. "Hit's Jay and his wife and younguns, come up from Knoxvul to see you," she called, and they saw the hands crawl in her lap and the face turned towards the younger woman and they could hear a thin, dry crackling, no words.

"She can't talk any more," Jay said, almost in a whisper.

"Oh no," Mary said.

But Sadie turned to them and her hard eyes were bright. "She knows ye," she said quietly. "Come on over." And they climbed slowly *and shyly out onto the swept ground. "I'll tell her about the rest a yuns in a minute," Sadie said.*

"Don't want to mix her up," Ralph explained, and they all nodded.

It seemed to Rufus like a long walk over to the old woman because they were all moving so carefully and shyly; it was almost like church. "Don't holler," Aunt Sadie was advising his parents, "hit only skeers her. Just talk loud and plain right up next her ear."

"I know," his mother said. "My mother is very deaf, too."

"Yeah," his father said. And he bent down close against her ear. "Granmaw?" he called, and he drew a little away, where she could see him, while his wife and his children looked on, each holding one of the mother's hands. She looked straight into his eyes and her eyes and her face never changed, a look as if she were gazing at some small point at a great distance, with complete but idle intensity, as if what she was watching was no concern of hers. His father leaned forward again and gently kissed her on the mouth, and drew back again where she could see him well, and smiled a little, anxiously. Her face restored itself from his kiss like grass that has been lightly stepped on; her eyes did not alter. Her skin looked like brown-marbled stone over which water has worked for so long that it is as smooth and blind as soap. He leaned to her ear again. "I'm Jay," he said. "John Henry's boy." Her hands crawled in her skirts: every white bone and black vein showed through the brown-splotched skin; the wrinkled knuckles were like pouches; she wore a red rubber guard ahead of her wedding ring. Her mouth opened and shut and they heard her low, dry croaking, but her eyes did not change. They were bright in their thin shadow, but they were as impersonally bright as two perfectly shaped eyes of glass.

"I figure she know you," Sadie said quietly.

"She can't talk, can she?" Jay said, and now that he was not looking at her, it was as if they were talking over a stump.

"Times she can," Sadie said. "Times she can't. Ain't only so seldom call for talk, reckon she loses the hang of it. But I figger she knows ye and I am tickled she does."

His father looked all around him in the shade and he looked sad, and unsure, and then he looked at him. "Come here, Rufus," he said.

"Go to him," his mother whispered for some reason, and she pushed his hand gently as she let it go.

"Just call her Granmaw," his father said quietly. "Get right up by her ear like you do to Granmaw Lynch and say, 'Granmaw, I'm Rufus.'"

He walked over to her as quietly as if she were asleep, feeling strange to be by himself, and stood on tiptoe beside her and looked down into her sunbonnet towards her ear. Her temple was deeply sunken as if a hammer had struck it and frail as a fledgling's belly. Her skin was crosshatched with the razor-fine slashes of innumerable square wrinkles and yet every slash was like smooth stone; her ear was just a fallen intricate flap with a small gold ring in it; her smell was faint yet very powerful, and she smelled like new mushrooms and old spices and sweat, like his fingernail when it was coming off. "Granmaw, I'm Rufus," he said carefully, and yellow-white hair stirred beside her ear. He could feel coldness breathing from her cheek.

"Come out where she can see you," his father said, and he drew back and stood still further on tiptoe and leaned across her, where she could see. "I'm Rufus," he said, smiling, and suddenly her eyes darted a little and looked straight into his, but they did not in any way change their expression. They were just colors: seen close as this, there was color through a dot at the middle, dim as blue-black oil, and then a circle of blue so pale it was almost white, that looked like glass, smashed into a thousand dimly sparkling pieces, smashed and infinitely old and patient, and then a ring of dark blue, so fine and sharp no needle could have drawn it, and then a clotted yellow full of tiny squiggles of blood, and then a wrong-side furl of red-bronze, and little black lashes. Vague light sparkled in the crackled blue of the eye like some kind of remote ancestor's anger, and the sadness of time dwelt in the blue-breathing, oily center, lost and alone and far away, deeper than the deepest well. His father was saying something, but he did not hear and now he spoke again, careful to be patient, and Rufus heard, "Tell her 'I'm Jay's boy.' Say, 'I'm Jay's boy Rufus.'"

And again he leaned into the old fragrant cavern next her ear and said, "I'm Jay's boy Rufus," and he could feel her face turn towards him.

"Now kiss her," his father said, and he drew out of the shadow of her bonnet and leaned far over and again entered the shadow and kissed her paper mouth, and the mouth opened, and the cold sweet breath of rotting and of spice broke from her with the dry croaking, and he felt the hands take him by the shoulders like knives and forks of ice through his clothes. She drew him closer and looked at him almost glaring, she was so filled with grave intensity. She seemed to be sucking on her lower lip and her eyes filled with light, and then, as abruptly as if the two different faces had been joined without transition in a strip of moving-picture film, she was not serious any more but smiling so hard that her chin and her nose almost touched and her deep little eyes giggled for joy. And again the croaking gurgle came, making shapes which were surely words but incomprehensible words, and she held him even more tightly by the shoulders, and looked at him even more keenly and incredulously with her giggling, all but hidden eyes, and smiled and smiled, and cocked her head to one side, and with sudden love he kissed her again. And he could hear his mother's voice say, "Jay," almost whispering, and his father say, "Let her be," in a quick, soft, angry voice, and when at length they gently disengaged her hands, and he was at a little distance, he could see that there was water crawling along the dust from under her chair, and his father and his Aunt Sadie looked gentle and sad and dignified, and his mother was trying not to show that she was crying, and the old lady sat there aware only that something had been taken from her, but growing quickly calm, and nobody said anything about it.

Late one afternoon Uncle Ted and Aunt Kate came, all the way from Michigan. Aunt Kate had red hair. Uncle Ted had glasses and he could make faces. They brought him a book and what he liked best was a picture of a fat man with a cloth around his head, sitting on a tasseled cushion with a long snakey tube in his mouth, and it said:

> There was a fat man of Bombay
> Who was smoking his pipe one fine day
> When a bird called a snipe
> Flew away with his pipe,
> Which vexed that fat man of Bombay.

But there wasn't any bird in the picture. His father said he reckoned it was still out snipe-hunting.

They weren't really his uncle and aunt, it was like Aunt Celia. Just a friend. But Aunt Kate was a kind of cousin. She was Aunt Carrie's daughter and Aunt Carrie was Granma's half-sister. You were a half-sister if you had the same father or mother but not the same other one, and they had the same mother.

They slept on the brand-new davenport in the sitting room.

Next morning before daylight they all got up and went to the L&N depot. A man came for them in an auto because there was no streetcar to the L&N. They had so much to carry that even he was given a box to carry. They sat in the big room and it was full of people. His mother told his Uncle Ted she liked it better than the Southern depot because there were so many country folks and his father said he did too. It smelled like chewing tobacco and pee, and like a barn. Some of the ladies wore sunbonnets and lots of the men wore old straw hats, not the flat kind. One lady was nursing her baby. They had a long time to wait for their train; his father said, "Count on Mary and you won't never miss a train, but you may get the one the day before you aimed to," and his mother said, "Jay," and Uncle Ted laughed; so he heard the man call several trains in his fine, echoing voice, and finally he started calling out a string of stations and his father got up saying. "That's us," and they got everything together and as soon as the man called the track they hurried fast, so they got two seats and turned them to face each other, and afterwhile the train pulled out and it was already *broad daylight. The older people were all kind of sleepy and didn't talk much, though they pretended to, and afterwhile Aunt Kate dropped off to sleep and leaned her head against his mother's shoulder and the men laughed and his mother smiled and said, "Let* her, *the dear."*

The news butcher came through and in spite of his mother, Uncle Ted bought him a glass locomotive with little bright-colored pieces of candy inside and Catherine a glass telephone with the same kind of candy inside, which his father had never done. His father and Uncle Ted spent a good deal of time in the smoking car, to smoke, and to make more room. It got hot and dull. But after quite a while his father came hurrying back down the aisle and told his mother to look out the window and she did and said, "Well what?" *and he said, "No—up ahead," and they all three looked up ahead and there on the sky above the scrubby hill, there was a grand great lift of grayish blue that looked as if you could see the light through it, and then the train took a long curve and these liftings of gray blue opened out like a fan and filled the whole country ahead, shouldering above each other high and calm and full of shadowy light, so that he heard his mother say, "Ohhh! How perfectly glorious!", and his father say shyly, a little as if he owned them and was giving them to her, "That's them. That's the Smokies all right," and sure enough they did look smoky, and as they came nearer, smoke and great shadows seemed to be sailing around on them, but he knew that must be clouds. After a while he could begin to see the shapes of them clearly, great bronzy bulges that looked as if they were blown up tight like balloons, and solemn deep scoops of shady blue that ran from the tops on down below the tops of the near hills, deeper than he could see. "They're just like huge waves, Jay," his mother said with awe. "That's right," he said; "you remember?" "Sure I do," she said; "just like seeing sunlight striking through waves, just before they topple."*

"Yeah," his father said.

"Kate mustn't miss this," his mother said; "Kate!" and she took Aunt Kate by the shoulder.

"Sssh!" his father hissed, and he frowned. "Let her alone!" But

Aunt Kate was already waked up, though she was still very sleepy, wondering what it was all about.

"Just look, *Kate," his mother said. "Out* there!" *Aunt Kate looked. "See?" his mother said.*

"Yes," Aunt Kate said.

"That's where we're going," his mother said.

"Yes," Aunt Kate said.

"Aren't they grand?" *his mother said.*

"Yes," Aunt Kate said.

"Well I think *they're absolutely* breathtaking," *his mother said.*

"So do I," Aunt Kate said, and went back to sleep.

His mother made one of the funniest faces he had ever seen, looking at his father all bewildered and surprised and holding in her laughter, and his father laughed out loud but Aunt Kate didn't wake up. "Just like Catherine," his mother whispered, laughing, and they all looked at Catherine, who was staring out at the mountains and looking very heavy and earnest; and they laughed and Catherine looked at them and began to realize they were laughing at her, and that made her face get red and that made them laugh some more, and even Rufus joined in, and they only stopped when Catherine began to stick out her lower lip and her mother said, "Mercy, child, you've got to learn to take a joke."

But her father said, "Doesn't anybody like to be laughed at," and took her on his lap, and she pulled her lip in and looked out the window again. Now they could even see the separate trees all over the sides of the mountains like rice, all shades of green and some almost black, and before much longer they were climbing more slowly past the feathery tops of trees and the high shoulders of the mountains and the great deep scoops were turning past them and beneath them as if they were very slowly and seriously dancing in sunlight and in cloud and in shadows almost of night, and now and then they could see a tiny cabin and a corn patch far off on the side of a mountain, and twice they even saw a tinier mule and a man with it, one of the men waved; and high above them in the changing sunlight, slowest of all, the tops of the mountains twisted and changed places. And after quite a while his father said he reckoned they better start getting their stuff together, and before much longer they got off.

That night at supper when Rufus asked for more cheese Uncle Ted said, "Whistle to it and it'll jump off the table into your lap."

"Ted!" his mother said.

But Rufus was delighted. He did not know very well how to whistle yet, but he did his best, watching the cheese very carefully: it didn't jump off the table into his lap; it didn't even move.

"Try some more," Uncle Ted said. "Try harder."

"Ted!" his mother said.

He tried his very best and several times he managed to make a real whistle, but the cheese didn't even move, and he began to realize that Uncle Ted and Aunt Kate were shaking with laughter they were trying to hold in, though he couldn't see what there was to laugh about in a cheese that wouldn't even move when you whistled even when Uncle Ted said it would and he was really whistling, not just trying to whistle.

"Why won't it jump to me, Daddy?" he asked, almost crying with embarrassment and impatience, and at that Uncle Ted and Aunt Kate burst out laughing out loud, but his father didn't laugh, he looked all mixed up, and mad, and embarrassed, and his mother was very mad and she said, "That's just about enough of that, Ted. I think it's just a perfect shame, deceiving a little child like that who's been brought up to trust people, and laughing right in his face!"

"Mary," his father said, and Uncle Ted looked very much surprised and Aunt Kate looked worried, though they were still laughing a little, as if they couldn't stop yet.

"Now, Mary," his father said again, and she turned on him and said angrily, "I don't care, Jay! I just don't care a hoot, and if you won't stand up for him, I will, I can promise you that!"

"Ted didn't mean any harm," his father said.

"Course I didn't, Mary," Uncle Ted said.

"Of course not," Aunt Kate said.

"It was just a joke," his father said.

"That's all it was, Mary," Uncle Ted said.

"He just meant it for a joke," his father and Aunt Kate said together.

"Well, it's a pretty poor kind of a joke, if you ask me," his mother said, "violating a little boy's trust."

"Why, Mary, he's got to learn what to believe and what not to," Uncle Ted said, and Aunt Kate nodded and put her hand on Uncle Ted's knee. "Gotta learn common sense."

"He's got plenty of *common sense*," his mother flashed. "He's a very bright child indeed, if you *must* know. But he's been brought up to trust older people when they tell him something. Not be suspicious of everybody. And so he trusted *you*. Because he likes you, Ted. Doesn't that make you ashamed?"

"Come on, Mary, cut it out," his father said.

"But Mary, you wouldn't *think* anybody'd *believe* what I said about the cheese," Uncle Ted said.

"Well you certainly expected *him* to believe it," she said, with fury, "otherwise why'd you ever *say* it?"

Uncle Ted looked puzzled, and his father said, trying to laugh, "Reckon she cornered you there, Ted," and Uncle Ted smiled uncomfortably and said, "I guess that's so."

"Of course it's so," his mother blazed, though his father frowned at her and said "Ssh!"

❧ PART THREE ❧

Chapter 14

WHEN HE WOKE it was already clear daylight and the sparrows were making a great racket and his first disappointed thought was that he was too late, though he could not yet think what it was he was too late for. But something special was on his mind which made him eager and happy almost as if this were Christmas morning and within a second after waking he remembered what it was and, sitting up, his lungs stretching full with anticipation and pride, he put his hand into the crisp tissue paper with a small smashing noise and took out the cap. There was plenty of light to see the colors well; he quickly turned it around and over, and smelled of the new cloth and of the new leather band. He put it on and yanked the bill down firmly and pelted down the hallway calling *"Daddy! Daddy!"*, and burst through the open door into their bedroom; then brought up short in dismay, for his father was not there. But his mother lay there, propped up on two pillows as if she were sick. She looked sick, or very tired, and in her eyes she seemed to be afraid of him. Her face was full of little lines he had never seen before; they were as small as the lines in her mended best teacup. She put out her arms towards him and made an odd, kind noise. "Where's Daddy?" he shouted imperiously ignoring her arms. "Daddy—isn't here yet," she told him, in a voice like hot ashes, and her arms sank down along the sheet.

"Where *is* he, then!" he demanded, in angry disappointment, but she thrust through these words with her own: "Go wake— little Catherine and bring her straight here," she said in a voice which puzzled him; "there's something I must tell you both together."

He was darting his eyes everywhere for clues of his father. Clothes? watch? tobacco? nightshirt? *"Right away,"* she said, in a desperate voice.

Startled by its mysterious rebuke, and uneasy in his stomach because she had said "little Catherine," he hurried out—and all but collided with his Aunt Hannah. Her mouth was strong and tightly pressed together beneath her glittering spectacles as she stooped, peering forward.

"Hello, Aunt Hannah," he called with astonishment, as he sped around and past her; he saw her go into the bedroom, her hair sticking out from her thin neck in two twiggy braids; he hurried to Catherine's crib.

"Wake *up*, Catherine!" he yelled, "Mama says wake *up*! Right *away!*"

"*Stob*bit," she bawled, her round, red face glaring.

"Well Mama *said* so, Mama *said* so, wake *up!*"

And a few moments later he hurried back ahead of her and hollered breathlessly, "She's coming!" and she trailed in, two-thirds asleep, snuffling with anger, her lower lip stuck out.

"Take off that cap!" his Aunt Hannah snapped with frightening sternness, and his hands only just caught it against her snatching. He was appalled by this inexplicable betrayal, and the hardness of her mouth as she struggled with self-astonishment and repentance was even more ominous.

"Oh, Hannah, no, let him," his mother said in her strange voice, "he was so crazy for Jay to see it," and even as she said it he was surprised all over again for his aunt, whispering something inaudible, touched his cheek very gently. And now as she had done before, his mother lifted forward her hands and her kind arms. "Children, come close," she said.

Aunt Hannah went silently out of the room.

"Come close"; and she touched each of them. "I want to tell you about Daddy." But upon his name her voice shook and her whole dry-looking mouth trembled like the ash of burned paper in a draft. "Can you hear me, Catherine?" she asked, when she had recovered her voice. Catherine peered at her earnestly as if through a thick fog. "Are you waked up enough yet, my darling?" And because of her voice, in sympathy and for her protection, they both came now much nearer, and she put her arms around both of them, and they could smell her breath, a little like sauerkraut but more like a dried-up mouse. And now even more small lines like cracked china branched all over her face. "Daddy," she said, "your father, children": and this time she caught control of her mouth more quickly, and a single tear spilled out of her left eye and slid jaggedly down all the jagged lines: "Daddy didn't come home. He isn't going to come home ever any more. He's—gone away to heaven and he isn't ever coming home again. Do you hear me, Catherine? Are you awake?" Catherine stared at her mother. "Do *you* understand, Rufus?"

He stared at his mother. "Why not?" he asked.

She looked at him with extraordinary closeness and despair, and said, "Because God wanted him." They continued to stare at her severely and she went on: "Daddy was on his way home last night—and he was—he—got hurt and—so God let him go to sleep and took him straight away with Him to heaven." She sank her fingers in Catherine's springy hair and looked intently from one to the other. "Do you see, children? Do you understand?" They stared at her, and now Catherine was sharply awake.

"Is Daddy *dead?*" Rufus asked. Her glance at him was as startled as if he had slapped her, and again her mouth and then her whole face began to work, uncontrollably this time, and she did not speak, but only nodded her head once, and then again, and then several times rapidly, while one small squeaky *"yes"* came out of her as if it had been sneezed out; then suddenly sweeping both of them close against her breasts, she tucked her chin down tightly between the crowns of their heads and they felt her whole body shaken as if by a wind, but she did not cry. Catherine began to sniffle quietly because everything seemed very serious and very sad. Rufus listened to his mother's shattered breathing and gazed sidelong past her fair shoulder at the sheet, rumpled, and at a rubbed place in the rose-patterned carpet and then at something queer, that he had never seen before, on the bedside table, a tangle of brown beads and a little cross; through her breathing he began once more to hear the quarreling sparrows; he said to himself: *dead, dead,* but all he could do was see and hear; the streetcar raised and quieted its grim, iron cry; he became aware that his cap was pushed crooked against her and he felt that he ought to take it off but that he ought not to move just now to take it off, and he knew why his Aunt Hannah had been so mad at him. He could no longer hear even a rumor of the streetcar, and his mother's breathing had become quiet again. With one hand she held Catherine still more closely against her, and Catherine sniffled a little more comfortably; with the other hand she put Rufus quietly away, so that she could look clearly into his eyes; tenderly she took off his cap and laid it beside her, and pushed the hair back from his forehead. "Neither of you will quite understand for a while," she said. "It's—very hard to understand. But you will," she said (I do, he said to himself; he's dead. That's what.) and she repeated rather dreamily, as if to herself, though she continued to look into his eyes, "You will"; then she was silent, and some kind of energy intensified in her eyes and she said: "When you want to know more—*about it*" (and her eyes became still more vibrant) "just, just ask me and I'll tell you because you ought to know." *How did he get hurt,* Rufus wanted to ask, but he knew by her eyes that she did not mean at all what she said, not now anyway, not this minute, he must not ask; and now he did not want to ask

because he too was afraid; he nodded to let her know he understood her. "Just ask," she said again, and he nodded again; a
strange, cold excitement was rising in him; and in a cold intuition
that it would be kind, and gratefully received, he kissed her. "God
bless you," she groaned, and held them passionately against herself; "*both* of you!" She loosened her arms. "And now you be a
good boy," she said in almost her ordinary voice, wiping Catherine's nose. "Get little Catherine dressed, can you do that?" He
nodded proudly; "and wash and dress yourself, and by then Aunt
Hannah will have breakfast ready."

"Aren't you getting up, Mama?" he asked, much impressed
that he had been deputized to dress his sister.

"Not for a while," she said, and by her way of saying it, he
knew that she wanted them to go out of the room right away.

"Come on, Catherine," he said, and found, with surprise, that
he had taken her hand. Catherine looked up at him, equally surprised, and shook her head.

"Go with Rufus, dear," her mother said, "he's going to help
you get dressed, and eat your breakfast. Mother will see you
soon."

And Catherine, feeling that for some reason to do with her
father, who was not where he ought to be, and her mother too, she
must try to be a very good girl, came away with him without further protest. As they turned through the door to go down, Rufus
saw that his mother had taken the beads and cross from the bedside table (they were like a regular necklace) and the beads ran
among her fingers and twined and drooped from her hands and
one wrist while she looked so intently at the upright cross that she
did not realize that she had been seen. *She'd be mad if she knew,* he
was sure.

Before he did anything about Catherine he put his cap back
in the tissue paper. Then he got her clothes. "Take off your
nightie," he said. "Sopping wet," he added, as nearly like his
mother as possible.

"You're sopping wet too," she retorted.

"No, I didn't either," he said, "not last night."

He found that she could do a certain amount of dressing herself; she got on the panties and she nearly got her underwaist on right too, except that it was backwards. "That's all right," he told her, as much like his mother as he was able, "you do it fine. Just a *little bit* crooked"; and he fixed it right.

He buttoned her panties to her underwaist. It was much less easy, he found, than buttoning his own clothes. "Stand still," he said, because to tell her so seemed only a proper part of carrying out his duty.

"I am," Catherine replied, with such firmness that he said no more.

That was all that either of them said before they went down to breakfast.

Chapter 15

CATHERINE DID NOT like being buttoned up by Rufus or bossed around by him, and breakfast wasn't like breakfast either. Aunt Hannah didn't say anything and neither did Rufus and neither did she, and she felt that even if she wanted to say anything she oughtn't. Everything was queer, it was so still and it seemed dark. Aunt Hannah sliced the banana so thin on the Post Toasties it looked cold and wet and slimy. She gave each of them a little bit of coffee in their milk and she made Rufus' a little bit darker than hers. She didn't say, "Eat"; "Eat your breakfast, Catherine"; "Don't dawdle," like Catherine's mother; she didn't say anything. Catherine did not feel hungry, but she felt mildly curious because things tasted so different, and she ate slowly ahead, tasting each mouthful. Everything was so still that it made Catherine feel uneasy and sad. There were little noises when a fork or spoon touched a dish; the only other noise was the very thin dry toast Aunt Hannah kept slowly crunching and the fluttering sipping of the steamy coffee with which she wet each mouthful of dry crumbs enough to swallow it. When Catherine tried to make a similar noise sipping her milk, her Aunt Hannah glanced at her sharply as if she wondered if Catherine was trying to be a smart aleck but she did not say anything. Catherine was not trying to be a smart aleck but she felt she had better not make that noise again. The fried eggs had hardly any pepper and they were so soft the yellow ran out over the white and the white plate and looked so nasty she didn't want to eat it but she ate it because she didn't want to be told to and because she felt there was some special reason, still, why she ought to be a good girl. She felt very uneasy, but there was nothing to do but eat, so she always took care to get a good hold on her tumbler and did not take too much on her spoon, and hardly spilled at all, and when she became aware of how little she was spilling it made her feel like a big girl and yet she did not feel any less uneasy, because she knew there was something wrong. She was not as much interested in eating as she was in the way things were, and listening carefully, looking mostly at her plate, every sound she heard and the whole quietness which was so much stronger than the sounds, meant that things were not good. What it was was that he wasn't here. Her mother wasn't either, but she was upstairs. He wasn't even upstairs. He was coming home last night but he didn't come home and he wasn't coming home now either, and her mother felt so awful she cried, and Aunt Hannah wasn't saying anything, just making all that noise with the toast and big loud sips with the coffee and swallowing, *grrmm*p, and then the same thing over again and over again, and every time she made the noise with the toast it was almost scary, as if she was talking about some awful thing, and every time she sipped it was like crying or like when Granma sucked in air between her teeth when she hurt herself, and every time she swallowed, *crrmmp,* it meant it was all over and there was nothing to do about it or say or even ask, and then she would take another bite of toast as hard and shivery as gritting your teeth, and start the whole thing all over again. Her mother said he wasn't coming home ever any more. That was what she said, but why wasn't he home eating breakfast right this minute? Because he was not with them eating breakfast it wasn't fun and everything was so queer. Now maybe in just a minute he would walk right in and grin at her and say, "Good morning, merry sunshine," because her lip was sticking out, and even bend down and rub her cheek with his whiskers and then sit down and eat a big breakfast and then it would be all fun again and she would watch from the window when he went to work and just before he went out of sight he would turn around and she would wave but why wasn't he right here now where she wanted him to be and why didn't he come home? Ever any more. He won't come home again ever any more. Won't come home again ever. But he will, though, because it's home. But why's he not here? He's up seeing Grampa Follet. Grampa Follet is very, very sick. But Mama didn't feel awful then, she feels awful now. But why didn't he come back when she said he would? He went to heaven and now Catherine could remember about heaven, that's where God lives, way up in the sky. Why'd he do that? God took him there. But why'd he go there and not come home like Mama said? Last night Mama said he was coming home last night. We could even wait up a while and when he didn't and we had to go to bed she *promised* he would come if we went to sleep and she promised he'd be here at breakfast time and now it's breakfast time and she says he won't come home ever any more. Now her Aunt Hannah folded her napkin, and folded it again more narrowly, and again still more narrowly, and pressed the butt end of it against her mouth, and laid it beside her plate, where it slowly and slightly unfolded, and, looking first at Rufus and then at Catherine and then back to Rufus, said quietly, "I think you ought to know about your father. Whatever I can tell you. Because your mother's not feeling well."

Now I'll know when he *is* coming home, Catherine thought.

All through breakfast, Rufus had wanted to ask questions, but now he felt so shy and uneasy that he could hardly speak. "Who hurt him?" he finally asked.

"Why nobody hurt him, Rufus," she said, and she looked shocked. "What on earth made you think so?"

Mama said so, Catherine thought.

"Mama said he got hurt so bad God put him to sleep," Rufus said.

Like the kitties, Catherine thought; she saw a dim, gigantic old man in white take her tiny father by the skin of the neck and put him in a huge slop jar full of water and sit on the lid, and she heard the tiny scratching and the stifled mewing.

"That's true he was hurt, but nobody hurt him," her Aunt Hannah was saying. How could that be, Catherine wondered. "He was driving home by himself. That's all, all by himself, in the auto last night, and he had an accident."

Rufus felt his face get warm and he looked warningly at his sister. He knew it could not be that, not with his father, a grown man, besides, God wouldn't put you to sleep for *that,* and it didn't hurt, anyhow. But Catherine might think so. Sure enough, she was looking at her aunt with astonishment and disbelief that she could say such a thing about her father. Not in his *pants,* you dern fool, Rufus wanted to tell her, but his Aunt Hannah continued: "A *fatal* accident"; and by her voice, as she spoke the strange word, "fatal," they knew she meant something very bad. "That means that, just as your mother told you, that he was hurt so badly that God put him to sleep right away."

Like the rabbits, Rufus remembered, all torn white bloody fur and red insides. He could not imagine his father like that. Poor little things, he remembered his mother's voice comforting his crying, hurt so terribly that God just let them go to sleep.

If it was in the auto, Catherine thought, then he wouldn't be in the slop jar.

They couldn't be happy any more if He hadn't, his mother had said. They could never get well.

Hannah wondered whether they could comprehend it at all and whether she should try to tell them. She doubted it. Deeply uncertain, she tried again.

"He was driving home last night," she said, "about nine, and apparently something was already wrong with the steering mech—with the wheel you guide the machine with. But your father didn't know it. Because there wasn't any way he could know until something went wrong and then it was too late. But one of the wheels struck a loose stone in the road and the wheel turned aside very suddenly, and when . . ." She paused and went on more quietly and slowly: "You see, when your father tried to make the auto go where it should, stay on the road, he found he couldn't, he didn't have any control. Because something was wrong with the steering gear. So, instead of doing as he tried to make it, the auto twisted aside because of the loose stone and ran off the road into a deep ditch." She paused again. "Do you understand?"

They kept looking at her.

"Your father was thrown from the auto," she said. "Then the auto went on without him up the other side of the ditch. It went up an eight-foot embankment and then it fell down backward, turned over and landed just beside him.

"They're pretty sure he was dead even before he was thrown out. Because the only mark on his whole body," and now they began to hear in her voice a troubling intensity and resentment, "was right—here!" She pressed the front of her forefinger to the point of her chin, and looked at them almost as if she were accusing them.

They said nothing.

I suppose I've got to finish, Hannah thought; I've gone this far.

"They're pretty sure how it happened," she said. "The auto gave such a sudden terrible *jerk*"—she jerked so violently that both children jumped, and startled her; she demonstrated what she saw next more gently: "that your father was thrown forward and struck his chin, very hard, against the wheel, the steering wheel, and from that instant he never knew anything more."

She looked at Rufus, at Catherine, and again at Rufus. "Do you understand?" They looked at her.

After a while Catherine said, "He hurt his chin."

235

"Yes, Catherine. He did," she replied. "They believe he was *instantly killed,* with that one single blow, because it happened to strike just exactly where it did. Because if you're struck very hard in just that place, it jars your whole head, your brain so hard that—sometimes people die in that very instant." She drew a deep breath and let it out long and shaky. "Concussion of the brain, that is called," she said with most careful distinctness, and bowed her head for a moment; they saw her thumb make a small cross on her chest.

She looked up. "Now do you understand, children?" she asked earnestly. "I know it's very hard to understand. You please tell me if there's anything you want to know and I'll do my best to expl—tell you better."

Rufus and Catherine looked at each other and looked away. After a while Rufus said, "Did it hurt him bad?"

"He could never have felt it. That's the one great mercy" (or *is* it, she wondered); "the doctor is sure of that."

Catherine wondered whether she could ask one question. She thought she'd better not.

"What's an eightfoot embackmut?" asked Rufus.

"Em-bank-ment," she replied. "Just a bank. A steep little hill, eight feet high. Bout's high's the ceiling."

He and Catherine saw the auto climb it and fall backward rolling and come to rest beside their father. Umbackmut, Catherine thought; em-*bank*-ment, Rufus said to himself.

"What's instintly?"

"Instantly is—quick's that"; she snapped her fingers, more loudly than she had expected to; Catherine flinched and kept her eyes on the fingers. "Like snapping off an electric light." Rufus nodded. "So you can be very sure, both of you, he never felt a moment's pain. Not one moment."

"When's . . ." Catherine began.

"What's . . ." Rufus began at the same moment; they glared at each other.

"What is it, Catherine?"

"When's Daddy coming home?"

"Why *good golly,* Catherine," Rufus began. "Hold your tongue!" his Aunt Hannah said fiercely, and he listened, scared, and ashamed of himself.

"Catherine, he *can't* come home," she said very kindly. "That's just what all this means, child." She put her hand over Catherine's hand and Rufus could see that her chin was trembling. "He died, Catherine," she said. "That's what your mother means. God put him to sleep and took him, took his soul away with Him. So he can't come home ..." She stopped, and began again. "We'll see him once more," she said, "tomorrow or day after; that I promise you," she said, wishing she was sure of Mary's views about this. "But he'll be asleep then. And after that we won't see him any more in this world. Not until God takes us away too.

"Do you see, child?" Catherine was looking at her very seriously. "Of course you don't, God bless you"; she squeezed her hand. "Don't ever try too hard to understand, child. Just try to understand it's so. He'd come if he could but he simply can't because God wants him with Him. That's all." She kept her hand over Catherine's a little while more, while Rufus realized much more clearly than before that he really could not and would not come home again: because of God.

"He would if he could but he can't," Catherine finally said, remembering a joking phrase of her mother's.

Hannah, who knew the joking phrase too, was startled, but quickly realized that the child meant it in earnest. "That's it," she said gratefully.

But he'll come once more, anyway, Rufus realized, looking forward to it. Even if he *is* asleep.

"What was it you wanted to ask, Rufus?" he heard his aunt say.

He tried to remember and remembered. "What's kuh, kuhkush, kih ... ?"

"Con-*cus*-sion, Rufus. Concus-sion of the brain. That's the doctor's name for what happened. It means, it's as if the brain were hit very hard and suddenly, and joggled loose. The instant that happens, your father was—he . . ."

"Instantly killed."

She nodded.

"Then it was that, that put him to sleep."

"Hyess."

"*Not* God."

Catherine looked at him, bewildered.

Chapter 16

WHEN BREAKFAST WAS OVER he wandered listlessly into the sitting room and looked all around, but he did not see any place where he would like to sit down. He felt deeply idle and empty and at the same time gravely exhilarated, as if this were the morning of his birthday, except that this day seemed even more particularly his own day. There was nothing in the way it looked which was not ordinary, but it was filled with a noiseless and invisible kind of energy. He could see his mother's face while she told them about it and hear her voice, over and over, and silently, over and over, while he looked around the sitting room and through the window into the street, words repeated themselves. He's dead. He died last night while I was asleep and now it was already morning. He has already been dead since way last night and I didn't even know until I woke up. He has been dead all night while I was asleep and now it is morning and I am awake but he is still dead and he will stay right on being dead all afternoon and all night and all tomorrow while I am asleep again and wake up again and go to sleep again and he can't come back home again ever any more but I will see him once more before he is taken away. Dead now. He died last night while I was asleep and now it is already morning.

A boy went by with his books in a strap.

Two girls went by with their satchels.

He went to the hat rack and took his satchel and his hat and started back down the hall to the kitchen to get his lunch; then he remembered his new cap. But it was upstairs. It would be in Mama's and Daddy's room, he could remember when she took it off his head. He did not want to go in for it where she was lying down and now he realized, too, that he did not want to wear it. He would like to tell her good-bye before he went to school, but he did not want to go in and see her lying down and looking like that. He kept on towards the kitchen. He would tell Aunt Hannah good-bye instead.

She was at the sink washing dishes and Catherine sat on a kitchen chair watching her. He looked all around but he could not see any lunch. I guess she doesn't know about lunch, he reflected. She did not seem to realize that he was there so, after a moment, he said, "Good-bye."

"What-*is*-it?" she said and turned her lowered head, peering. "Why, Rufus!" she exclaimed, in such a tone that he wondered what he had done. "You're not going to *school*," she said, and now he realized that she was not mad at him.

"I can stay out of school?"

"Of course you can. You must. Today and tomorrow as well and—for a sufficient time. A few days. Now put up your things, and stay right in this house, child."

He looked at her and said to himself: but then they can't see me; but he knew there was no use begging her; already she was busy with the dishes again.

He went back along the hall towards the hat rack. In the first moment he had been only surprised and exhilarated not to have to go to school, and something of this sense of privilege remained, but almost immediately he was also disappointed. He could now see vividly how they would all look up when he came into the schoolroom and how the teacher would say something nice about

240

his father and about him, and he knew that on this day everybody would treat him well, and even look up to him, for something had happened to him today which had not happened to any other boy in school, any other boy in town. They might even give him part of their lunches.

He felt even more profoundly empty and idle than before.

He laid down his satchel on the seat of the hat rack, but he kept his hat on. She'll spank me, he thought. Even worse, he could foresee her particular, crackling kind of anger. I won't let her find out, he told himself. Taking great care to be silent, he let himself out the front door.

The air was cool and gray and here and there along the street, shapeless and watery sunlight strayed and vanished. Now that he was in this outdoor air he felt even more listless and powerful; he was alone, and the silent, invisible energy was everywhere. He stood on the porch and supposed that everyone he saw passing knew of an event so famous. A man was walking quickly up the street and as Rufus watched him, and waited for the man to meet his eyes, he felt a great quiet lifting within him of pride and of shyness, and he felt his face break into a smile, and then an uncontrollable grin, which he knew he must try to make sober again; but the man walked past without looking at him, and so did the next man who walked past in the other direction. Two schoolboys passed whose faces he knew, so he knew that they must know his, but they did not seem to see him. Arthur and Alvin Tripp came down their front steps and along the far sidewalk and now he was sure, and came down his own front steps and halfway out to the sidewalk, but then he stopped, for now, although both of them looked across into his eyes, and he into theirs, they did not cross the street to him or even say hello, but kept on their way, still looking into his eyes with a kind of shy curiosity, even when their heads were turned almost backwards on their necks, and he turned his own head slowly, watching them go by, but when he saw that they were not going to speak he took care not to speak either.

What's the matter with them, he wondered, and still watched them; and even now, far down the street, Arthur kept turning his head, and for several steps Alvin walked backwards.

What are they mad about?

Now they no longer looked around, and now he watched them vanish under the hill.

Maybe they don't know, he thought. Maybe the others don't know either.

He came out to the sidewalk.

Maybe everybody knew. Or maybe he knew something of great importance which nobody else knew. The alternatives were not at all distinct in his mind; he was puzzled, but no less proud and expectant than before. My daddy's dead, he said to himself slowly, and then, shyly, he said it aloud: "My daddy's dead." Nobody in sight seemed to have heard; he had said it to nobody in particular. "My daddy's dead," he said again, chiefly for his own benefit. It sounded powerful, solid, and entirely creditable, and he knew that if need be he would tell people. He watched a large, slow man come towards him and waited for the man to look at him and acknowledge the fact first, but when the man was just ahead of him, and still did not appear even to have seen him, he told him, "My daddy's dead," but the man did not seem to hear him, he just swung on by. He took care to tell the next man sooner and the man's face looked almost as if he were dodging a blow but he went on by, looking back a few steps later with a worried face; and after a few steps more he turned and came slowly back.

"What was that you said, sonny?" he asked; he was frowning slightly.

"My daddy's dead," Rufus said, expectantly.

"You mean that sure enough?" the man asked.

"He died last night when I was asleep and now he can't come home ever any more."

The man looked at him as if something hurt him.

"Where do you live, sonny?"

"Right here"; he showed with his eyes.

"Do your folks know you out here wandern round?"

He felt his stomach go empty. He looked frankly into his eyes and nodded quickly.

The man just looked at him and Rufus realized: He doesn't believe me. How do they always know?

"You better just go on back in the house, son," he said. "They won't like you being out here on the street." He kept looking at him, hard.

Rufus looked into his eyes with reproach and apprehension, and turned in at his walk. The man still stood there. Rufus went on slowly up his steps, and looked around. The man was on his way again but at the moment Rufus looked around, he did too, and now he stopped again.

He shook his head and said, in a friendly voice which made Rufus feel ashamed, "How would your daddy like it, you out here telling strangers how he's dead?"

Rufus opened the door, taking care not to make a sound, and stepped in and silently closed it, and hurried into the sitting room. Through the curtains he watched the man. He still stood there, lighting a cigarette, but now he started walking again. He looked back once and Rufus felt, with a quailing of shame and fear, he sees me; but the man immediately looked away again and Rufus watched him until he was out of sight.

How would your daddy like it?

He thought of the way they teased him and did things to him, and how mad his father got when he just came home. He thought how different it would be today if he only didn't have to stay home from school.

He let himself out again and stole back between the houses to the alley, and walked along the alley, listening to the cinders cracking under each step, until he came near the sidewalk. He was not in front of his own home now, or even on Highland Avenue; he was coming into the side street down from his home, and he felt that here nobody would identify him with his home and send him back to it. What he could see from the mouth of the alley was much less familiar to him, and he took the last few steps which brought him out onto the sidewalk with deliberation and shyness. He was doing something he had been told not to do.

He looked up the street and he could see the corner he knew so well, where he always met the others so unhappily, and, farther away, the corner around which his father always disappeared on the way to work, and first appeared on his way home from work. He felt it would be good luck that he would not be meeting them at that corner. Slowly, uneasily, he turned his head, and looked down the side street in the other direction; and there they were: three together, and two along the far side of the street, and one alone, farther off, and another alone, farther off, and, without importance to him, some girls here and there, as well. He knew the faces of all of these boys well, though he was not sure of any of their names. The moment he saw them all he was sure they saw him, and sure that they knew. He stood still and waited for them, looking from one to another of them, into their eyes, and step by step at their several distances, each of them at all times looking into his eyes and knowing, they came silently nearer. Waiting, in silence, during those many seconds before the first of them came really near him, he felt that it was so long to wait, and be watched so closely and silently, and to watch back, that he wanted to go back into the alley and not be seen by them or by anybody else, and yet at the same time he knew that they were all approaching him with the realization that something had happened to him that had not happened to any other boy in town, and that now at last they were bound to think well of him; and the nearer they came but were yet at a distance, the more the gray, sober air was charged with the great energy and with a sense of glory and of danger, and the deeper and more exciting the silence became, and the more tall, proud, shy and exposed he felt; so that as they came still nearer he once again felt his face break into a wide smile, with which he had nothing to do, and, feeling that there was something deeply wrong in such a smile, tried his best to quieten his face and told them, shyly and proudly, "My daddy's dead."

Of the first three who came up, two merely looked at him and the third said, "Huh! Betcha he ain't"; and Rufus, astounded that they did not know and that they should disbelieve him, said, "Why he is so!"

"Where's your satchel at?" said the boy who had spoken. "You're just making up a lie so you can lay out of school."

"I am not laying out," Rufus replied. "I was going to school and my Aunt Hannah told me I didn't have to go to school today or tomorrow or not till—not for a few days. She said I mustn't. So I am not laying out. I'm just staying out."

And another of the boys said, "That's right. If his daddy is dead he don't have to go back to school till after the funerl."

While Rufus had been speaking two other boys had crossed over to join them and now one of them said, "He don't have to. He can lay out cause his daddy got killed," and Rufus looked at the boy gratefully and the boy looked back at him, it seemed to Rufus, with deference.

But the first boy who had spoken said, resentfully, "How do you know?"

And the second boy, while his companion nodded, said, "Cause my daddy seen it in the paper. Can't your daddy read the paper?"

The paper, Rufus thought; it's even in the paper! And he looked wisely at the first boy. And the first boy, interested enough to ignore the remark against his father, said, "Well how did he get killed, then?" and Rufus, realizing with respect that it was even more creditable to get killed than just to die, took a deep breath and said, "Why, he was . . ."; but the boy whose father had seen it in the paper was already talking, so he listened, instead, feeling as if all this were being spoken for him, and on his behalf, and in his praise, and feeling it all the more as he looked from one silent boy to the next and saw that their eyes were constantly on him. And Rufus listened, too, with as much interest as they did, while the boy said with relish, "In his ole Tin Lizzie, that's how. He was driving along in his ole Tin Lizzie and it hit a rock and throwed him out in the ditch and run up a eight-foot bank and then fell back and turned over and over and landed right on top of him *whomph* and mashed every bone in his body, that's all. And somebody come and found him and he was dead already time they got there, that's how."

"He was instantly killed," Rufus began, and expected to go ahead and correct some of the details of the account, but nobody seemed to hear him, for two other boys had come up and just as he began to speak one of them said, "Your daddy got his name in the paper didn he, and you too," and he saw that now all the boys looked at him with new respect.

"He's dead," he told them. "He got killed."

"That's what my daddy says," one of them said, and the other said, "What you get for driving a auto when you're drunk, that's what my dad says," and the two of them looked gravely at the other boys, nodding, and at Rufus.

"What's drunk?" Rufus asked.

"What's drunk?" one of the boys mocked incredulously: "Drunk is fulla good ole whiskey"; and he began to stagger about in circles with his knees weak and his head lolling. "At's what drunk is."

"Then he wasn't," Rufus said.

"How do *you* know?"

"He wasn't drunk because that wasn't how he died. The wheel hit a rock and the other wheel, the one you steer with, just hit him on the chin, but it hit him so hard it killed him. He was instantly killed."

"What's instantly killed?" one of them asked.

"What do *you* care?" another said.

"Right off like that," an older boy explained, snapping his fingers. Another boy joined the group. Thinking of what instantly meant, and how his father's name was in the paper and his own too, and how he had got killed, not just died, he was not listening to them very clearly for a few moments, and then, all of a sudden, he began to realize that he was the center of everything and that they all knew it and that they waited to hear him tell the true account of it.

"I don't know nothing about no chin," the boy whose father saw it in the paper was saying. "Way I heard it he was a-drivin along in his ole Tin Lizzie and he hit a rock and ole Tin Lizzie run off the road and throwed him out and run up a eight-foot bank and turned over and over and fell back down on top of him *whomp*."

"How do *you* know?" an older boy was saying. "*You* wasn't there. Anyboy here knows it's *him*." And he pointed at Rufus and Rufus was startled from his revery.

"Why?" asked the boy who had just come up.

"Cause it's his daddy," one of them explained.

"It's my daddy," Rufus said.

"What happened?" asked still another boy, at the fringe of the group.

"My daddy got killed," Rufus said.

"His daddy got killed," several of the others explained.

"My daddy says he bets he was drunk."

"Good ole whiskey!"

"Shut up, what's *your* daddy know about it."

"Was he drunk?"

"No," Rufus said.

"No," two others said.

"Let *him* tell it."

"Yeah, *you* tell it."

"Anybody here ought to know, it's him."

"Come on and tell us."

"Good ole whiskey."

"Shut your mouth."

"Well come on and tell us, then."

They became silent and all of them looked at him. Rufus looked back into their eyes in the sudden deep stillness. A man walked by, stepping into the gutter to skirt them.

Rufus said, quietly, "He was coming home from Grampa's last night, Grampa Follet. He's very sick and Daddy had to go up way in the middle of the night to see him, and he was hurrying as fast as he could to get back home because he was so late. And there was a cotter pin worked loose."

"What's a cotter pin?"

"Shut up."

"A cotter pin is what holds things together underneath, that you steer with. It worked loose and fell out so that when one of the front wheels hit a loose rock it wrenched the wheel and he couldn't steer and the auto ran down off the road with an awful bump and they saw where the wheel you steer with hit him right on the chin and he was instantly killed. He was thrown all the way out of the auto and it ran up an eight-foot emb—emback-ment and then it rolled back down and it was upside down beside him when they found him. There was not a mark on his body. Only a little tiny blue mark right on the end of the chin and another on his lip."

In the silence he could see the auto upside down with its wheels in the air and his father lying beside it with the little blue marks on his chin and on his lip.

"Heck," one of them said, "how can *that* kill anybody?"

He felt a kind of sullen stirring among the others, and he felt that he was not believed, or that they did not think very well of his father for being killed so easily.

"It was just exactly the way it just happened to hit him, Uncle Andrew says. He says it was just a chance in a million. It gave him a concussh, con, concussh—it did something to his brain that killed him."

"Just a chance in a million," one of the older boys said gravely, and another gravely nodded.

"A million trillion," another said.

"Knocked him crazy as a loon," another cried, and with a waggling forefinger he made a rapid blubbery noise against his loose lower lip.

"Shut yer Goddamn mouth," an older boy said coldly. "Ain't you got no sense at all?"

"Way I heard it, ole Tin Lizzie just rolled right back on top of him *whomp*."

This account of it was false, Rufus was sure, but it seemed to him more exciting than his own, and more creditable to his father and to him, and nobody could question, scornfully, whether that could kill, as they could of just a blow on the chin; so he didn't try to contradict. He felt that he was lying, and in some way being disloyal as well, but he said only, "He was instantly killed. He didn't have to feel any pain."

"Never even knowed what hit him," a boy said quietly. "That's what my dad says."

"No," Rufus said. It had not occurred to him that way. "I guess he didn't." Never even knowed what hit him. Knew.

"Reckon that ole Tin Lizzie is done for now. Huh?"

He wondered if there was some meanness behind calling it an ole Tin Lizzie. "I guess so," he said.

"Good ole waggin, but she done broke down."

His father sang that.

"No more joy rides in that ole Tin Lizzie, huh Rufus?"

"I guess not," Rufus replied shyly.

He began to realize that for some moments now a bell, the school bell, had been weltering on the dark gray air; he realized it because at this moment the last of its reverberations were fading.

"Last bell," one of the boys said in sudden alarm.

"Come on, we're goana git hell," another said; and within another second Rufus was watching them all run dwindling away up the street, and around the corner into Highland Avenue, as fast as they could go, and all round him the morning was empty and still. He stood still and watched the corner for almost half a minute after the fattest of them, and then the smallest, had disappeared; then he walked slowly back along the alley, hearing once more the sober crumbling of the cinders under each step, and up through the narrow side yard between the houses, and up the steps of the front porch.

In the paper! He looked for it beside the door, but it was not there. He listened carefully, but he could not hear anything. He let himself quietly through the front door, at the moment his Aunt Hannah came from the sitting room into the front hall. She wore a cloth over her hair and in her hands she was carrying the smoking stand. She did not see him at first and he saw how fierce and lonely her face looked. He tried to make himself small but just then she wheeled on him, her lenses flashing, and exclaimed, "Rufus Follet, where on earth have you been!" His stomach quailed, for her voice was so angry it was as if it were crackling with sparks.

"Outdoors."

"Where, outdoors! I've been looking for you all over the place."

"Just out. Back in the alley."

"Did you hear me calling you?"

He shook his head.

"I shouted until my voice was hoarse."

He kept shaking his head. "Honest," he said.

"Now listen to me carefully. You mustn't go outdoors today. Stay right here inside this house, do you understand?"

He nodded. He felt suddenly that he had done an awful thing.

"I know it's hard to," she said more gently, "but you've got to. Help Catherine with her coloring. Read a book. You promise?"

"Yes'm."

"And don't do anything to disturb your mother."

"No'm."

She went on down the hall and he watched her. What was she doing with the pipes and the ash trays, he wondered. He considered sneaking behind her, for he knew that she could not see at all well, yet he would be sure to get caught, for her hearing was very sharp. All the same, he sneaked along to the back of the hall and watched her empty the ashes into the garbage pail and rap out the pipes against its rim. Then she stood with the pipes in her hand, looking around uncertainly; finally she put the pipes and the ash tray on the cupboard shelf, and set the smoking stand in the corner of the kitchen behind the stove. He went back along the hall on tiptoe and into the sitting room.

Catherine sat in the little chair by the side window with a picture book on her knees. Her crayons were all over the window sill and she was working intently with an orange crayon. She looked up when he came in and looked down again and kept on working.

He did not want to help her, he wanted to be by himself and see if he could find the paper with the names in it, but he felt that he ought to try to be good, for by now he felt a dark uneasiness about something, he was not quite sure what, that he had done. He walked over to her. "I'll help you," he said.

"No," Catherine said, without even looking up. It was the Mother Goose book and with her orange crayon she was scrawling all over the cow which jumped over the moon, inside and outside the lines of the cow.

"Aunt Hannah says to," he said, disgusted to see what she was doing to the cow.

"No," Catherine said, and again she did not look up or stop scrawling for a second.

"That ain't no color for a cow," he said. "Whoever saw an orange cow?" She made no reply, but he could see that her face was getting red. "Besides, you're not even coloring inside the cow," he said. "Just look at that. You're just running that crayon around all over the place and it isn't even the right color." She bore down even harder and harder with the crayon and pushed it in a wider and wider tangle of lines and all of a sudden it snapped and the long part rolled to the floor. "See now, you busted it," Rufus said.

"Leave me alone!" She tried to draw with the stub of the crayon but it was too short, and the paper got in the way. She looked along the window sill and selected a brown crayon.

"What you goana do with that brown one?" Rufus said. "You already got all that orange all over everything, what you goana do with that brown one?" Catherine took the brown crayon and made a brutal tangle of dark lines all over the orange lines. "Now all you did is just spoil it," Rufus said. "You don't know how to draw!"

"*Quit* it!" Catherine yelled, and all of a sudden she was crying. He heard his Aunt Hannah's sharp voice from the kitchen: "Rufus?"

He was furious with Catherine. "Crybaby," he whispered with cold hatred: "Tattletale!"

And there was Aunt Hannah at the door, just as mad as a hornet. "Now, what's the matter? What have you done to her?" She walked straight at him.

It wasn't fair. How did she know he was doing anything? With a feeling of real righteousness he talked back: "I didn't do one single thing to her. She was just messing everything up on her picture and I tried to help her like you told me to and all of a sudden she started to cry."

"What did he do, Catherine?"

"He wouldn't let me alone."

"Why good night, I never even touched you and you're a liar if you say I did!"

All of a sudden he felt himself gripped by the shoulders and shaken and he turned his rattling head from his sister to look into his Aunt Hannah's freezing glare.

"Now you just listen to me," she said. "Are you listening?" she sputtered. *"Are you listening?"* she said still more intensely.

"Yes," he managed to get out, though the word was all shaken up.

"I don't want to spank you on this day of all days, but if I hear you say one more rough thing like that to your sister I'll give you a spanking you'll remember to your dying day, do you hear me? *Do you hear me?"*

"Yes."

"And if you tease her or make her cry just one more time, I'll—I'll turn the whole matter over to your Uncle Andrew and we'll see what *he'll* do about it. Do you want me to call him? He's upstairs this minute! Shall I call him?" She stopped shaking him and looked at him. "Shall I?" He shook his head; he was terrified. "All right, but this is my last warning. Do you understand?"

"Yes'm."

"Now if you can't play with Catherine in peace like a decent boy just—stay by yourself. Look at some pictures. Read a book. But you be quiet. And good. Do you hear me?"

"Yes'm."

"Very well." She stood up and her joints snapped. "Come with me, Catherine," she said. "Let's bring your crayons." And she helped Catherine gather up the crayons and the stubs from the window sill and from the carpet. Catherine's face was still red but she was not crying any more. As she passed Rufus she gave him a glance filled with satisfaction, and he answered it with a glance of helpless malevolence.

He listened towards upstairs. If his Uncle Andrew had overheard this, there would really be trouble. But there was no evidence that he had. Rufus felt weak in the knees and in the stomach. He went over to the chair beside the fireplace and sat down.

It was mean to pester Catherine like that but he hadn't wanted to do anything for her anyway. And why did she have to holler like that and bring Aunt Hannah running? He remembered the way her face got red and he knew that he had really been mean to her and he was sorry. But what did she holler for, like a regular crybaby? He would be very careful today, but sooner or later he sure would get back on her. Darn crybaby. Tattletale.

The others really did pay him some attention, though. Anybody here ought to know, it's him. His daddy got killed. Yeah *you* tell it. Come on and tell us. Just a chance in a million. A million trillion. Never even knowed, knew, what hit him. Shut yer Goddamn mouth. Ain't you got no sense at all?

Instantly killed.

Concussion, that was it. Concussion of the brain.

Knocked him crazy as a loon, bibblibblebble.

Shut yer Goddamn mouth.

But there was something that made him feel wrong.

Ole Tin Lizzie.

What you get for driving a auto when you're drunk, that's what my dad says.

Good ole whiskey.

Something he did.

Ole Tin Lizzie just rolled back down on top of him *whomp*.

Didn't either.

He didn't say it didn't. Not clear enough.

Heck, how can that kill anybody?

Did, though. Just a chance in a million. Million trillion.

Instantly killed.

Worse than that, he did.

What.

How would your daddy like it?

He would like me to be with them without them teasing; looking up to me.

How would your daddy like it?

Like what?

Going out in the street like that when he is dead.

Out in the street like what?

Showing off to people because he is dead.

He wants me to get along with them.

So I tell them he is dead and they look up to me, they don't tease me.

Showing off because he's dead, that's all you can show off about. Any other thing they'd tease me and I wouldn't fight back.

How would your daddy like it?

But he likes me to get along with them. That's why I—went out—showed off.

He felt so uneasy, deep inside his stomach, that he could not think about it any more. He wished he hadn't done it. He wished he could go back and not do anything of the kind. He wished his father could know about it and tell him that yes he was bad but it was all right he didn't mean to be bad. He was glad his father didn't know because if his father knew he would think even worse of him than ever. But if his father's soul was around, always, watching over them, then he knew. And that was worst of anything because there was no way to hide from a soul, and no way to talk to it, either. He just knows, and it couldn't say anything to him, and he couldn't say anything to it. It couldn't whip him either, but it could sit and look at him and be ashamed of him.

"I didn't mean it," he said aloud. "I didn't mean to do bad."

I wanted to show you my cap, he added, silently.

He looked at his father's morsechair.

Not a mark on his body.

He still looked at the chair. With a sense of deep stealth and secrecy he finally went over and stood beside it. After a few moments, and after listening most intently, to be sure that nobody was near, he smelled of the chair, its deeply hollowed seat, the arms, the back. There was only a cold smell of tobacco and, high along the back, a faint smell of hair. He thought of the ash tray on its weighted strap on the arm; it was empty. He ran his finger inside it; there was only a dim smudge of ash. There was nothing like enough to keep in his pocket or wrap up in a paper. He looked at his finger for a moment and licked it; his tongue tasted of darkness.

Chapter 17

THEY WERE TOLD THEY COULD EAT, that morning, in their nightgowns and wrappers. Their mother still wasn't there, and Aunt Hannah talked even less than at any meal before. They too were very quiet. They felt that this was an even more special day than day before yesterday. All the noises of their eating and from the street were especially clear, but seemed to come from a distance. They looked steadily at their plates and ate very carefully.

First thing after breakfast Aunt Hannah said, "Now come with me, children," and they followed her into the bathroom. There she washed their faces and hands and arms, and behind the ears, and their necks, and up each nostril, carefully and gently with soap and warm water; she did not get soap in the eyes of either of them, or hurt their skins with the washcloth. Then she took them into the bedroom and opened the bureaus and took out everything bran clean, from the skin out, and told Rufus to get his clothes on and to ask for help if he wanted it, and started dressing Catherine. Rufus began to see the connection between all this and the bath, the night before. When he had on his underclothes she brought out new black stockings and his Sunday serge. While she was helping Catherine on with her stockings, which were also new but white, the phone rang and she said, "Now sit still and be good. I'll be straight back," and hustled from the room. They heard her say, rather loudly and distinctly, up the hall, "I'm getting it, Mary," then her feet, fast on the stairs. They sat very still, looking at the open door, and tried to hear. They found they could hear quite distinctly, for Hannah spoke to the telephone as she did to her deaf brother and sister-in-law. They heard: "Hello . . . Hello . . . Yes . . . *Father?*", and when they heard the word "Father" they looked at each other with curiosity and with an uneasy premonition. They heard "Yes . . . yes . . . yes . . . yes . . . yes . . . yes, Father . . . yes . . . yes, as well as could be expected . . . yes . . . yes . . . Thank you. I'll tell her . . . yes . . . yes . . . very well . . . yes . . . The *Highland* Avenue . . . yes . . . yes . . . *any* . . . yes . . . *any* car to the corner of Church and Gay, then transfer to the Highland—yes—very well . . . yes . . . Thank you . . . we'll be waiting . . . yes . . . no . . . yes, Father . . . yes F— . . . good b . . . yes, Father . . . Thank you . . . goo— . . . yes . . . Thank you . . . good-bye . . . good-bye."

They heard her let out a long, tired, angry breath and they could hear her joints snapping as she sprinted up the stairs. They were sitting exactly where she had left them. Rufus thought, Maybe she will say we were good children, but without a word she finished with Catherine's stockings. She gave Rufus a new white shirt from which he slowly and with fascination drew the pins, running them between his teeth as he watched Aunt Hannah help Catherine into her new dress, which was white, speckled with small dark blue flowers. Catherine stood holding the hem and looking at the skirt and at her white-stockinged feet, which she could see through the skirt. "And now your necktie," Aunt Hannah said. She took his dark blue tie and made expert motions beneath his chin while alternately he tried to watch her hands and looked into her intent eyes behind their heavy lenses. Her eyes looked stern and sad and exhausted.

Then she cleaned their nails and combed and brushed their

hair, and put a clean handkerchief in Rufus' breast pocket and blacked their shoes. "Now wait a moment," she said, leaving the room. They heard her rap softly on their mother's door.

"Mary?" she said.

"Yes," they heard dimly.

"The children are ready. Shall I bring them in?"

"Yes, do, Hannah; thank you."

"Come in now and see your mother," she told them from the door.

They followed her in.

"Oh, they look *very nice,*" she exclaimed, in a voice so odd that it seemed to the children that she must be sorry that they did. Yet by her face they could see that she was not sorry. "Hannah, thank you so much, I don't know what I'd have . . ."

But Hannah left the room and closed the door.

They stood and looked at her with curiosity. Her eyes seemed larger and brighter than usual; her hair was done up as carefully as if she were going to a party. She wore her wrapper and where it opened in front they could see that she had on something dull and black underneath. Her face was like folded gray cloths.

She watched them look at her; they did not move. Her face altered as if a very low light had gone on behind it.

"Come here, my darlings," she said, and smiled, and squatted with her hands out towards them.

Rufus came shyly; Catherine ran. She took one of them in each arm.

"There, my darlings," she said above them, "there, there, my dear ones. Mother's here. Mother's here. Mother has wanted to see you more, these last days; a *lot* more: she just—couldn't, Rufus and Catherine. Just couldn't do it." When she said "couldn't" she held them very tightly and they knew they were loved. "Little Catherine"—and she held Catherine's head still more tightly to her—"bless her soul! and Rufus"—she held him away and looked into his eyes—"you both know how much Mother loves you, with all her heart and soul, all her life—you know, don't you? Don't you?" Rufus, puzzled, but moved, nodded politely, and again she caught him to her. "Of course you do," she said, as if she were not speaking to them. "Of course you do.

"Now," she said, after a moment. She stood up and drew them by their hands to the bed. They sat down and she sat in a chair and looked at them for a few seconds without speaking.

"Now," she said again. "I want to tell you about Daddy, because this morning, soon now, we're all going down to Grampa's and Grandma's, and see him once more, and tell him good-bye." Catherine's face brightened; her mother shook her head and placed a quieting hand on Catherine's knees, saying, "No, Catherine, it won't be like you think, that's what I must tell you about him. So listen very carefully, you too, Rufus."

She waited until she was sure they were listening carefully.

"You both understand what has happened to Daddy, don't you. That something happened in the auto, and God took him from us, very quickly, without any pain, and took him away to heaven. You understand that, don't you?"

They nodded.

"And you understand, that when God takes you away to heaven you can never come back?"

"*Never* come back?" Catherine asked.

She stroked Catherine's hair away from her face. "No, Catherine, not ever, in any way we can see and talk to. Daddy's soul will always be thinking of us, just as we will always think of him, but we will never see him again, after today." Catherine looked at her very intently; her face began to redden. "You must learn to believe that and know it, darling Catherine. It's so."

She seemed to be about to cry; she swallowed; and Catherine seemed to accept it as true.

"We'll always remember him," she told both of them. "*Always.* And he'll be thinking of us. Every day. He's waiting for us in heaven. And someday, if we're good, when God comes for us, He'll take us to heaven too and we'll see Daddy there, and all be together again, forever and ever."

Amen, Rufus almost said; then realized that this was not a prayer.

"But when we see Daddy today, children, his soul won't be there. It'll just be Daddy's body. Very much as you've always seen him. But because his soul has been taken away, he will be lying down, and he will lie very still. It will be just as if he were asleep, so you must both be just as quiet as if he were asleep and you didn't want to wake him. Quieter."

"But I do," said Catherine.

"But Catherine, you can't, dear, you mustn't even think of trying. Because Daddy is dead now, and when you are dead that means you go to sleep and you never wake up—until God wakes you."

"Well when *will* He?"

"We don't know, Rufus, but probably a long, long time from now. Long after we are all dead."

Rufus wondered what was the good of that, then, but he was sure he should not ask.

"So I don't want you to wonder about it, children. Daddy may seem very queer to you, because he's so still, but that's—just simply the way he's got to look."

Suddenly she pressed her lips tightly together and they trembled violently. She clenched her cheekbone against her left shoulder, squeezing their hands with her trembling hands, and tears slipped from her tightly shut eyes. Rufus watched her with awe, Catherine with forlorn worry. She suddenly hissed out, "Just-a-minute," with her eyes still closed, startling and shocking Catherine, so that she looked as if she were ready to cry. But before Catherine could commit herself to crying, her hands relaxed, pressing them gently, and she raised her head and opened her clear eyes, saying, "Now Mother must get dressed, and I want you to take Catherine downstairs, Rufus, and both of you be very

quiet and good till I come down. And don't make any bother for
Aunt Hannah, because she's been wonderful to all of us and she's
worn out.

"You be good," she said, smiling and looking at them in turn.
"I'll be down in a little while."

"Come on, Catherine," Rufus said.

"I'm coming," Catherine replied, looking at him as if he had
spoken of her unjustly.

"Mama"; Rufus stopped near the door. Catherine hesitated,
bewildered.

"Yes, Rufus?"

"Are we orphans, now?"

"Orphans?"

"Like the Belgians," he informed her. "French. When you
haven't got any daddy or mamma because they're killed in the
war you're an orphan and other children send you things and
write you letters."

She must have been unfamiliar with the word, for she
seemed to have to think very hard before she answered. Then she
said, "Of *course* you're not orphans, Rufus, and I don't want you
going around saying that you are. Do you hear me? Because it
isn't so. Orphans haven't got *either* a father *or* a mother, you see,
and nobody to take care of them or love them. You see? That's
why other children send things. But you both have your mother.
So you aren't orphans. Do you see? Do you?" He nodded;
Catherine nodded because he did. "And Rufus." She looked at
him very searchingly; without quite knowing why, he felt he had
been discovered in a discreditable secret. "Don't be sorry you're
not an orphan. *You be thankful.* Orphans sound lucky to you
because they're far away and everyone talks about them now. But
they're very, very unhappy little children. Because *nobody* loves
them. Do you understand?"

He nodded, ashamed of himself and secretly disappointed.

"Now run along," she said. They left the room. Aunt Hannah met them on the stairs. "Go into the liv—sitting room for a while like good children," she said. "I'll be right down." And as they reached the bottom of the stairs they heard their mother's door open and close. They sat, looking at their father's chair, thinking.

Catherine felt more virtuous and less troubled than she had for some time, for she had watched Rufus being scolded, all to himself, and it more than wiped out her unhappiness at his telling her to come along when of course she was coming and he had no right even if she wasn't. But she couldn't see how anyone could look as if they were asleep and not wake up, and something else her mother had said—she tried hard to remember what it was— troubled her more deeply than that. And what was a norphan?

Rufus felt that his mother was seriously displeased with him. It was the wrong time to ask her. Maybe he ought not to have asked her at all. But he did want to know. He had not been sure whether or not he was an orphan, or the right kind of orphans. If he claimed he was an orphan in school and it turned out that he was not, people would all laugh at him. But if he really was an orphan he wanted to know, so he would be able to say he was, and get the benefit. What was the good of being an orphan if nobody else knew it? Well, so he was not an orphan. Yet his father was dead. Not his mother, too, though. Only his father. But one was dead. One and one makes two. One-half of two equals one. He was half an orphan, no matter what his mother said. And he had a sister who was half an orphan too. Half and half equals a whole. Together they made a whole orphan. He felt that it was not worth mentioning, that he was half an orphan, although he privately considered it a good deal better than nothing; and that also, he would not volunteer the fact that he and his sister together made a whole orphan. But if anyone teased either of them about not being an orphan at all, then he would certainly speak of that. He decided that Catherine should be warned of this, so that if they were teased, they could back each other up.

"Both of us together is a whole orphan," he said.

"Huh?"

"Don't say 'huh,' say, 'What is it, Rufus?'"

"I will not!"

"You will so. Mama says to."

"She does not."

"She does so. When I say 'huh' she says, 'Don't say "huh," say "What is it, Mother?"' When you say 'huh' she tells you the same thing. So don't say 'huh.' Say, 'What is it, Rufus?'"

"I won't say it to you."

"Yes, you will."

"No, I won't."

"Yes, you will, because Mama said for us to be good. If you don't I'll tell her on you."

"You tell her and I'll tell on you."

"Tell on me for what?"

"Listening at the door."

"No you won't."

"I will so."

"You will not."

"I will so."

He thought it over.

"All right, *don't* say it, and I *won't* tell on you if you won't tell on me."

"I will if you tell on me."

"I said I won't, didn't I? Not if you don't tell on me."

"I won't if you don't tell on me."

"All right."

They glared at each other.

They heard loud feet on the porch, and the doorbell rang. Upstairs they heard their mother cry "Oh, goodness!" They ran to the door. He blocked Catherine away from the knob and opened it.

A man stood there, almost as tall as Daddy. He had a black

glaring collar like Dr. Whittaker but wore a purple vest. He wore a long shallow hat and he had a long, sharp, bluish chin almost like a plow. He carried a small, shining black suitcase. He seemed to be as disconcerted and displeased as they were. He said, "Oh, good morning," in a voice that had echoes in it and, frowning, glanced once again at the number along the side of the door. "Of course," he said, with a smile they did not understand. "You're Rufus and Catherine. May I come in?" And without waiting for their assent or withdrawal (for they were blocking the door) he strode forward, parting them with firm hands and saying "Isn't Miss L . . ."

They heard Aunt Hannah's voice behind them on the stairs, and turned. "Father?" she said, peering against the door's light. "Come right in." And she came up as he quickly removed his oddly shaped hat, and they shook hands. "This is Father Jackson, Rufus and Catherine," she said. "He has come specially from Chattanooga. Father, this is Rufus, and this is Catherine."

"Yes, we've already introduced ourselves," said Father Jackson, as if he thought it was funny. That's a lie, Rufus reflected. Father Jackson left one hand at rest for a moment on Catherine, then removed it as if he had forgotten her. "And where is Mrs. Follet?" he asked, almost whispering "Mrs. Follet."

"If you'll just wait a moment, Father, she isn't quite ready."

"Of course." He leaned towards Aunt Hannah and said, in a grinding, scarcely audible voice, "Is she—chuff-chuff-chuff?"

"Oh yes," Hannah replied.

"But does she Whehf-wheff-whehf-whef-tized?"

"I'm afraid not, Father," said Hannah, gravely. "I wasn't quite sure enough myself, to tell her. I'm sorry to burden you with it but I felt I should leave that to you."

"You were right, Miss Lynch. Absolutely." He looked around, his head gliding, his hat in his hand. "Now little man," he said, "if you'll kindly relieve me of my hat."

"Rufus," said Hannah. "Take Father's hat to the hat rack."

Bewildered, he did so. The hat rack was in plain sight.

"Now Father, if you won't mind waiting just a moment," Hannah said, showing him to the sitting room. "Rufus: Catherine: sit here with Father. Excuse me," she added, and she hastened upstairs.

Father Jackson strode efficiently across the room, sat in their father's chair, crossed his knees narrowly, and looked, frowning, at the carefully polished toe of his right shoe. They watched him, and Rufus wondered whether to tell him whose chair it was. Father Jackson held his long, heavily veined right hand palm outward, at arm's length, and frowning, examined his nails. He certainly wouldn't have sat in it, Rufus felt, if he had known whose chair it was, so it would be mean not to tell him. But if he was told now, it would make him feel bad, Rufus thought. Catherine noticed, with interest, that outside the purple vest he wore a thin gold chain; on the chain was a small gold crucifix. Father Jackson changed knees and, frowning, examined the carefully polished toe of his left shoe. Better not tell him, Rufus thought; it would be mean. How do you get such a blue face, Catherine wondered; I wish my face was blue, not red. Father Jackson, frowning, looked all around the room and smiled, faintly, as his gaze came to rest on some point above and beyond the heads of the children. Both turned to see what he was smiling at, but there was nothing there except the picture of Jesus when Jesus was a little boy, staying up late in his nightgown and talking to all the wise men in the temple. "Oh," Rufus realized; "that's why."

When they turned Father Jackson was frowning again and looking at them just as he had looked at his nails. He quickly smiled, though not as nicely as he had smiled at Jesus, and changed his way of looking so that it did not seem that he was curious whether they were really clean. But he still looked as if he were displeased about something. They both looked back, wondering what he was displeased about. Was Catherine wetting her panties, Rufus wondered; he looked at her but she looked all right to him. What was Rufus doing that the man looked so unpleasant, Catherine wondered. She looked at him, but all he was doing was looking at the man. They both looked at him, wishing that if he was displeased with them he would tell them why instead of looking like that, and wishing that he would sit in some other chair. He looked at both of them, feeling that their rude staring was undermining his gaze and his silence, by which he had intended to impress them into a sufficiently solemn and receptive state for the things he intended to say to them; and wondering whether or not he should reprimand them. Surely, he decided, if they lack manners even at such a time as this, this is the time to speak of it.

"Children must not stare at their elders," he said. "That is ill-bred."

"Huh?" both of them asked. What's "stare," they wondered; "elders"; "ill-bred"?

"Say, 'Sir,' or 'I beg your pardon, Father.'"

"Sir?" Rufus said.

"You," Father Jackson said to Catherine.

"Sir?" Catherine said.

"You must not stare at people—look at them, as you are looking at me."

"Oh," Rufus said. Catherine's face turned red.

"Say, 'Excuse me, Father.'"

"Excuse me, Father."

"You," Father Jackson said to Catherine.

Catherine became still redder.

"Excuse me, Father," Rufus whispered.

"No prompting, please," Father Jackson broke in, in a voice pitched for a large class. "Come now, little girl, it is never too soon to learn to be little ladies and little gentlemen, is it?"

Catherine said nothing.

"Is it?" Father Jackson asked Rufus.

"I don't know," Rufus replied.

"I consider that a thoroughly uncivil answer to a civil question," said Father Jackson.

"Yes," Rufus said, beginning to turn cold in the pit of his stomach. What was "uncivil"?

"You agree," Father Jackson said. "Say, 'Yes, Father.'"

"Yes, Father," Rufus said.

"Then you are aware of your incivility. It is deliberate and calculated," Father Jackson said.

"No," Rufus said. He could not understand the words but clearly he was being accused.

Father Jackson leaned back in their father's chair and closed his eyes and folded his hands. After a moment he opened his eyes and said, "Little boy, little sister" (he nudged his long blue chin towards Catherine), "this is neither the time nor place for reprimands." His hands unfolded; he leaned forward, tapping his right kneecap with his right forefinger, and frowning fiercely, said in a voice which sounded very gentle but was not, "But I just want to tell . . ." They heard Hannah on the stairs. "Children," he said, rising, "this must wait another time." He pointed his jaw at Hannah, raising his eyebrows.

"Will you come up, Father?" she asked in a shut voice.

Without looking again at the children, he followed her upstairs.

They looked each other in the eyes; their mouths hung open; they listened. It was as they had begun to expect it would be: the steps of two along the upper hallway, the opening of their mother's door, their mother's strangely shrouded voice, the closing of the door: silence.

Taking great care not to creak, they stole up to the middle of the stairs. They could hear no words, only the tilt and shape of voices: their mother's, still so curiously shrouded, so submissive, so gentle; it seemed to ask questions and to accept answers. The man's voice was subdued and gentle but rang very strongly with the knowledge that it was right and that no other voice could be quite as right; it seemed to say unpleasant things as if it felt they were kind things to say, or again, as if it did not care whether or not they were kind because in any case they were right, it seemed to make statements, to give information, to counter questions with replies which were beyond argument or even discussion and to try to give comfort whether what it was saying could give comfort or not. Now and again their mother's way of questioning sounded to the children as if she wondered whether something could be fair, could possibly be true, could be so cruel but whenever such tones came into their mother's voice the man's voice became still more ringing and overbearing, or still more desirous to comfort, or both; and their mother's next voice was always very soft. Aunt Hannah's voice was almost as clear and light as always, but there was now in it also a kind of sweetness and of sorrow they had not heard in it before. Mainly she seemed only to agree with Father Jackson, to add her voice to his, though much more kindly, in this overpowering of their mother. But now and again it seemed to explain more fully, and more gently, something which he had just explained, and twice it questioned almost as their mother questioned, but with more spirit, with an edge almost of bitterness or temper. And on these two occasions Father Jackson's voice shifted and lost a bit of its vibrancy, and for a moment he talked as rapidly in a circle, seeming to assure them that of course he did not at all mean what they had thought he meant, but only, that (and then the voice would begin to gather assurance); they must realize (and now it had almost its old drive); in fact, of course—and now he was back again, and seemed to be saying precisely what he had said before, only with still more authority and still less possibility of disagreement. And then their Aunt Hannah murmured agreement in an oddly cool, remote tone, and their mother's voice of acceptance was scarcely audible at all.

Once in a while when these voices came to crises in their subdued turmoil Rufus and Catherine looked into each other's cold bright eyes which brightened and chilled the more with every intensification of the man's voice, and every softening and defeat of their mother's voice. But most of the time they only stared at the knob on their mother's door, shifting delicately on the stairs whenever they became cramped. They could not conceive of what was being done to their mother, but in his own way each was sure that it was something evil, to which she was submitting almost without a struggle, and by which she was deceived. Rufus repeatedly saw himself flinging open the door and striding in, a big stone in his hand, and saying, "You stop hurting my mother." Catherine knew only that a tall stranger in black, with a frightening jaw and a queer hat, a man whom she hated and feared, had broken into their house, had been welcomed first by Aunt Hannah and then by her mother herself, had sat in her father's chair as if he thought he belonged there, talked meanly to her in words she could not understand, and was now doing secret and cruel things to her mother while Aunt Hannah looked on. If Daddy was here he would kill him. She wished Daddy would hurry up and come and kill him and she wanted to see it. But Rufus realized that his Aunt Hannah and even his mother were on Father Jackson's side and against him, and that they would just put him out of the room and punish him terribly and go right on with whatever awful thing it was they were doing. And Catherine remembered, with a jolt, that Daddy would not come back because he was down at Grandma's and Grandpa's and now they would see him again and then they would never see him any more until heaven.

But suddenly there was a kind of creaking and soft thumping and the voices changed. Father Jackson's voice was even more strongly in charge, now, than before, although it did not seem that he was arguing, or informing, or trying to bring comfort, or even that he was speaking to either of the two women. Most of its theatrical resonance had left it, and all of its dominance. He seemed to be speaking as if to someone at least as much more assured and strong than he was, as he was more assured and strong than their mother was, and his voice had something of their mother's humbleness. Yet it was a very confident voice, as if it were sure that the person who was being addressed would approve what was said and what was asked, and would not rebuff him as he had rebuffed their mother. And in some way the voice was even more authoritative than before, as if Father Jackson were speaking not for himself but for, as well as to, the person he addressed, and were speaking with the power of that person as well as in manly humility before that person. Clearly, also, the voice loved its own sound, inseparably from its love of the sound and contour of the words it spoke, as naturally as a fine singer delights inseparably in his voice and in the melody he is singing. And clearly, although not one word was audible to the children, the voice was not mistaken in this love. Not a word was distinct from where they stood, but the shapes and rhythms and the inflections were as lovely and as bemusing as any songs they had ever heard. In general rhythm, Rufus began to realize, it was not unlike the prayers that Dr. Whittaker said; and he realized, then, that Father Jackson also was praying. But where Dr. Whittaker gave his words and phrases special emphasis and personal coloring, as though they were matters which required argument and persuasion, Father Jackson spoke almost wholly without emphasis and with only the subtlest coloring, as if the personal emotion, the coloring, were cast against the words from a distance, like echoes. He spoke as if all that he said were in every idea and in every syllable final, finished, perfected beyond disquisition long before he was born; and truth and eternity dwelt like clearest water in the rhythms of his language and in the contours of his voice; his voice accepted and bore this language like the bed of a brook. They looked at each other once more; Rufus could see that Catherine did not understand. "He's saying his prayers," he whispered.

She neither understood him nor believed him but she realized, with puzzlement, that now the man was being nice, though she did not even want him to be nice to her mother, she did not want him to be anything, to anybody, anywhere. But it was clear to both of them that things were better now than they had been before; they could hear it in his voice, which at once enchanted and obscurely disturbed them, and they could hear it in the voices of the two women, which now and again, when he seemed to pause for breath, chimed in with a short word or two, a few times with whole sentences. Both their voices were more tender, more alive, and more inhuman, than they had ever heard them before; and this remoteness from humanity troubled them. They realized that there was something to which their mother and their great-aunt were devoted, something which gave their voices peculiar vitality and charm, which was beyond and outside any love that was felt for them; and they felt that this meant even more to their mother and their great-aunt than they did, or than anyone else in the world did. They realized, fairly clearly, that the object of this devotion was not this man whom they mistrusted, but they felt that he was altogether too deeply involved in it. And they felt that although everything was better for their mother than it had been a few minutes before, it was far worse in one way. For before, she had at least been questioning, however gently. But now she was wholly defeated and entranced, and the transition to prayer was the moment and mark of her surrender. They stared so long and so gloomily at the doorknob, turning over such unhappy and uncertain intuitions in their souls, that the staring, round white knob became all that they saw in the universe except a subtly beating haze pervaded with magnificent quiet sound; so that when the doorbell rang they were so frightened that their hearts contracted.

Then, with almost equal terror, they realized that they would be caught on the stairs. They started down, in haste as desperate as their efforts to be silent. The door burst open above them. She can't see, they realized (for it was Hannah who came out), and in the same instant they realized: but she can hear better than anybody. A stair creaked loudly; terror struck them; against it, they continued. "Yes," Hannah called sharply; she was already on the stairs. The doorbell rang again. On the last stair, they were hideously noisy; they wanted only to disappear in time. They ducked through the sitting-room door and watched her pass; they were as insane with excitement as if they could still dare hope they had not been discovered, and solemnly paralyzed in the inevitability of dreadful reprimand and of physical pain.

Hannah didn't even glance back at them: she went straight to the door.

It was Mr. Starr. Usually he wore suits as brown and hairy as his mustache, but this morning he wore a dark blue suit and a black tie. In his hand he carried a black derby.

"Walter," Aunt Hannah said, "you know what all you're doing means to us."

"Aw now," Walter said.

"Come in," she said. "Mary'll be right down. Children, you know Mr. Starr . . ."

"Course we do," Mr. Starr said, smiling at them with his warm brown eyes through the lenses. He put the hand holding the derby on Rufus' shoulder and the other on Catherine's cheek. "You come on in and sit with me, will you, till your mother's ready."

He walked straight for their father's chair, veered unhappily, and sat on a chair next the wall.

"Well, so you're coming down and visit us," he said.

"Huh?"

"Coming down," Walter said. "Or ma—did your mama say anything about maybe you were coming down sometime, and pay us a visit?"

"Huh-uh."

"Oh, well, there's lots of time. Did you ever hear a gramophone?"

"She can't hardly hear when she does."

"Eigh?" He seemed extremely puzzled.

"Uncle Andrew says she's crazy even to try."

"Who?"

"Why, Granma." Mr. Starr had never before seemed stupid, but now Rufus began to think his memory was as bad as those of the boys at the corner. Could he be teasing? It would be very queer if Mr. Starr would tease. He decided he should trust him. "You know, when she phones, like you said."

Mr. Starr thought that over for a moment and then he seemed to understand. But almost the moment he understood he started to laugh, so he must have been teasing, after all. Rufus was deeply hurt. Then almost immediately he stopped laughing as if he were shocked at himself.

"Well now," he said. "I begin to see how we both got a bit in a muddle. You'd never heard of the thing I was talking about, and it sounds mighty like grandma phone, did you ever hear grandmaphone. Of course. Naturally. But what I was talking about was a nice box that music comes out of. Did you ever hear music come out of a box?"

"Huh-uh."

"Well down home, believe it or not, we got a box that music comes out of. Would you like to hear it sometime?"

"Uh-huh."

"Good. We'll see if that can't be arranged. Soon. Now would you like to know what they call this box?"

"Uh-huh."

"A gram-o-phone. See? It sounds very much like grandma phone, but it's just a little different. Gram-o-phone. Can you say it?"

"Gram-uh-phone."

"That's right. Can Baby Sister say it, I wonder?"

"Catherine? He means you."

"Gran-muh-phone."

"Gra*mm*-uh-phone."

"*Gramm*-muh-phone."

"That's fine. You're a mighty smart little girl to say a big word like that."

"I can say some ever so big words," Rufus said. "Want to hear? The Dominant Primordrial Beast."

"Well now, that's mighty smart. But of course I don't mean smarter than Sister. You're a lot bigger boy."

"Yes, but I could say that when I was four years old. She's almost four and I bet she can't say it. Can you, Catherine? Can you?"

"Well, now, some people learn a little quicker than others. It's nice to learn fast but it's nice to take your time, too." He walked over and picked Catherine up and sat down with her in his lap. He smelled almost as good as her father, although he was soft in front, and she looked happy. "Now what does that word 'primordrial' mean?"

"I dunno, but it's nice and scary."

"Is it scary? Yes? Yes, spose it does have a sort of a scary sound. Now you can say it, you ought to find out what it means, sometime."

"What *does* it mean?"

"Not sure myself, but then I don't say it. Don't have occasion." He opened out one arm and Rufus walked across to him without realizing he was doing so. The arm felt strong and kind around him. "You're a fine little boy," Mr. Starr said. "But it isn't nice of you to lord it over your sister."

"What's 'lord it'?"

"Brag about things you can do, that she can't do yet. That isn't nice."

"No, sir."

"So you watch, and don't do it."

"No siree."

"Because Catherine's a fine little girl, too."

"Yes, sir."

"Aren't you, Catherine?" He smiled at her and she blushed with delight. Rufus liked Catherine so well, all of a sudden, that he smiled at her, and when she smiled back they were both happy and suddenly he was very much ashamed to have treated her so.

"I want to tell you two something," they heard Mr. Starr's quieted voice. They looked up at him. "Not because you'll understand it now, but I have to, my heart's full, and it's you I want to tell. Maybe you'll remember it later on. It is about your daddy. Because you never got a real chance to know him. Can I tell you?"

They nodded.

"Some people have a hard, hard time. No money, no good schooling. Scarcely enough food. Nothing that you children have, but good people to love them. Your daddy started like that. He didn't have one thing. He had to work till it practicly killed him, for every little thing he ever got.

"Well, some of the greatest men started with nothing. Like Abraham Lincoln. You know who he was?"

"He was born in a log cabin," Rufus said.

"That's right, and he became the greatest man we've ever had."

He said nothing for a moment and they wondered what he was going to tell them about their father.

"Somehow I never got a chance to know Jay—your father— well as I wish. I don't think he ever knew how much I thought of him. Well I thought the world of him, Rufus and Catherine. My own wife and son couldn't mean more to me I think." He waited again. "I'm a pretty ordinary man myself," he went on. "Not a bad one. Just ordinary. But I always thought your father was a lot like Lincoln. I don't mean getting ahead in the world. I mean a man. Some people get where they hope to in this world. Most of us don't. But there never was a man up against harder odds than your father. And there was never a man who tried harder, or hoped for more. I don't mean getting ahead. I mean the right things. He wanted a good life, and good understanding, for himself, for everybody. There never was a braver man than your father, or a man that was kinder, or more generous. They don't make them. All I wanted to tell you is, your father was one of the finest men that ever lived."

He suddenly closed his eyes tightly behind his glasses, and swallowed; a long sobbing sigh fell from him. Deeply and solemnly touched, they moved closer to him, whether to comfort him or themselves they did not now. "There, there," he said, his eyes still closed. "There, there now. There, there."

Upstairs, they heard the door open.

Chapter 18

WHEN GRIEF AND SHOCK surpass endurance there occur phases of exhaustion, of anesthesia in which relatively little is left and one has the illusion of recognizing, and understanding, a good deal. Throughout these days Mary had, during these breathing spells, drawn a kind of solace from the recurrent thought: at least I am enduring it. I am aware of what has happened, I am meeting it face to face, I am living through it. There had been, even, a kind of pride, a desolate kind of pleasure, in the feeling: I am carrying a heavier weight than I could have dreamed it possible for a human being to carry, yet I am living through it. It had of course occurred to her that this happens to many people, that it is very common, and she humbled and comforted herself in this thought. She thought: this is simply what living is; I never realized before what it is. She thought: now I am more nearly a grown member of the human race; bearing children, which had seemed so much, was just so much apprenticeship. She thought that she had never before had a chance to realize the strength that human beings have, to endure; she loved and revered all those who had ever suffered, even those who had failed to endure. She thought that she had never before had a chance to realize the might, grimness and tenderness of God. She thought that now for the first time she began to know herself, and she gained extraordinary hope in this beginning of knowledge. She thought that she had grown up almost overnight. She thought that she had realized all that was in her soul to realize in the event, and when at length the time came to put on her veil, leave the bedroom she had shared with her husband, leave their home, and go down to see him for the first time since his death and to see the long day through, which would cover him out of sight for the duration of this world, she thought that she was firm and ready. She had refused to "try on" her veil; the mere thought of approving or disapproving it before a mirror was obscene; so now when she came to the mirror and drew it down across her face to go, she saw herself for the first time since her husband's death. Without either desiring to see her face, or caring how it looked, she saw that it had changed; through the deep, clear veil her gray eyes watched her gray eyes watch her through the deep, clear veil. I must have fever, she thought, startled by their brightness; and turned away. It was when she came to the door, to walk through it, to leave this room and to leave this shape of existence forever, that realization poured upon and overwhelmed her through which, in retrospect, she would one day know that all that had gone before, all that she had thought she experienced and knew—true, more or less, though it all was—was nothing to this. The realization came without shape of definability, save as it was focused in the pure physical act of leaving the room, but came with such force, such monstrous piercing weight, in all her heart and soul and mind and body but above all in the womb, where it arrived and dwelt like a cold and prodigious, spreading stone, that she groaned almost inaudibly, almost a mere silent breath, an *Ohhhhhhh,* and doubled deeply over, hands to her belly, and her knee joints melted.

Hannah, smaller than she, caught her, and rapped out, *"Close that door!"* It would be a long time before either of the women realized their resentment of the priest and their contempt for him, and their compassion, for staying in the room. Now they did not even know that he was there. Hannah helped her to the edge of the bed and sat beside her exclaiming over and over, in a heart-broken voice, "Mary, Mary, Mary, Mary. Oh Mary, Mary, Mary," resting one already translucent, spinster's hand lightly upon the back of her veiled head, and with the other, so clenching one of Mary's wrists that she left a bracelet of bruise.

Mary meanwhile rocked quietly backward and forward, and from side to side, groaning, quietly, from the depths of her body, not like a human creature but a fatally hurt animal; sounds low, almost crooned, not strident, but shapeless and orderless, the sisters, except in their quietude, to those transcendent, idiot, bellowing screams which deliver children. And as she rocked and groaned, the realization gradually lost its fullest, most impaling concentration: there took shape, from its utter darkness, like the slow emergence of the countryside into first daylight, all those separate realizations which could be resolved into images, emotions, thought, words, obligations: so that after not more than a couple of minutes, during which Hannah never ceased to say to her, "Mary, Mary," and Father Jackson, his eyes closed, prayed, she sat still for a moment, then got quietly onto her knees, was silent for not more than a moment more, made the sign of the Cross, stood up, and said, "I'm ready now."

But she swayed; Hannah said, "Rest, Mary. There's no hurry," and Father Jackson said, "Perhaps you should lie down a little while"; but she said, "No; thank you; I want to go now," and walked unsteadily to the door, and opened it, and walked through.

Father Jackson took her arm, in the top hallway. Although she tried not to, she leaned on him very heavily.

"Come, now," their mother whispered, and, taking them each by the hand, led them through the Green Room and into the living room.

There it was, against the fireplace, and there seemed to be scarcely anything else in the room except the sunny light on the floor.

It was very long and dark; smooth like a boat; with bright handles. Half the top was open. There was a strange, sweet smell, so faint that it could scarcely be realized.

Rufus had never known such stillness. Their little sounds, as they approached his father, vanished upon it like the infinitesimal whisperings of snow, falling on open water.

There was his head, his arms; suit: there he was.

Rufus had never seen him so indifferent; and the instant he saw him, he knew that he would never see him otherwise. He had his look of faint impatience, the chin strained a little upward, as if he were concealing his objection to a collar which was too tight and too formal. And in this slight urgency of the chin; in the small trendings of a frown which stayed in the skin; in the arch of the nose; and in the still, strong mouth, there was a look of pride. But most of all, there was indifference; and through this indifference which held him in every particle of his being—an indifference which would have rejected them; have sent them away, except that it was too indifferent even to care whether they went or stayed—in this self-completedness which nothing could touch, there was something else, some other feeling which he gave, which there was no identifying even by feeling, for Rufus had never experienced this feeling before; there was perfected beauty. The head, the hand, dwelt in completion, immutable, indestructible: motionless. They moved upon existence quietly as stones which withdraw through water for which there is no floor.

The arm was bent. Out of the dark suit, the starched cuff, sprang the hairy wrist.

The wrist was angled; the hand was arched; none of the fingers touched each other.

The hand was so composed that it seemed at once casual and majestic. It stood exactly above the center of his body.

The fingers looked unusually clean and dry, as if they had been scrubbed with great care.

The hand looked very strong, and the veins were strong in it.

The nostrils were very dark, yet he thought he could see in one of them, something which looked like cotton.

On the lower lip, a trifle to the left of its middle, there was a small blue line which ran also a little below the lip.

At the exact point of the chin, there was another small blue mark, as straight and neat as might be drawn with a pencil, and scarcely wider.

The lines which formed the wings of the nose and the mouth were almost gone.

The hair was most carefully brushed.

The eyes were casually and quietly closed, the eyelids were like silk on the balls, and when Rufus glanced quickly from the eyes to the mouth it seemed as if his father were almost about to smile. Yet the mouth carried no suggestion either of smiling or of gravity; only strength, silence, manhood, and indifferent contentment.

He saw him much more clearly than he had ever seen him before; yet his face looked unreal, as if he had just been shaved by a barber. The whole head was waxed, and the hand, too, was as if perfectly made of wax.

The head was lifted on a small white satin pillow.

There was the subtle, curious odor, like fresh hay, and like a hospital, but not quite like either, and so faint that it was scarcely possible to be sure that it existed.

Rufus saw these things within a few seconds, and became aware that his mother was picking Catherine up in order that she might see more clearly; he drew a little aside. Out of the end of his eye he was faintly aware of his sister's rosy face and he could hear her gentle breathing as he continued to stare at his father, at his stillness, and his power, and his beauty.

He could see the tiny dark point of every shaven hair of the beard.

He watched the way the flesh was chiseled in a widening trough from the root of the nose to the white edge of the lip.

He watched the still more delicate dent beneath the lower lip.

It became strange, and restive, that it was possible for anyone to lie so still for so long; yet he knew that his father would never move again; yet this knowledge made his motionlessness no less strange.

Within him, and outside him, everything except his father was dry, light, unreal, and touched with a kind of warmth and impulse and a kind of sweetness which felt like the beating of a heart. But borne within this strange and unreal sweetness, its center yet alien in nature from all the rest, and as nothing else was actual, his father lay graven, whose noble hand he longed, in shyness, to touch.

"Now, Rufus," his mother whispered; they knelt. He could just see over the edge of the coffin. He gazed at the perfect hand.

His mother's arm came round him; he felt her hand on the crest of his shoulder. He slid his arm around her and felt her hand become alive on his shoulder and felt his sister's arm. He touched her bare arm tenderly, and felt her hand grapple for and take his arm. He put his hand around her arm and felt how little it was. He could feel a vein beating against the bone, just below her armpit.

"Our Father," she said.

They joined her, Catherine waiting for those words of which she was sure, Rufus lowering his voice almost to silence while she hesitated, trying to give her the words distinctly. Their mother spoke very gently.

"Our Father, Who art in Heaven, hallowed be Thy name; Thy kingdom come, Thy—"

"Thy will be d . . ." Rufus went on, alone; then waited, disconcerted.

"Thy will be done," his mother said. "On earth," she continued, with some strange shading of the word which touched him with awe and sadness; "as it is in heaven."

"Give us this d . . ."

Rufus was more careful this time.

"Daily bread," Catherine said confidently.

"Give us this day our daily bread," and in those words still more, he felt that his mother meant something quite otherwise, "And forgive us our trespasses as we forgive those who trespass against us.

"And lead us not into temptation; but deliver us from evil," and here their mother left her hands where they dwelt with her children, but bowed her head:

"For Thine is the kingdom, and the power, and the glory," she said with almost vindictive certitude, "forever and ever. Amen."

She was silent for some moments, and still he stared at the hand.

"God, bless us and help us all," she said. "God, help us to understand Thee. God, help us to know Thy will. God, help us to put all our trust in Thee, whether we can understand or not.

"God, help these little children to remember their father in all his goodness and strength and kindness and dearness, and in all of his tremendous love for them. God, help them ever to be all that was good and fine and brave in him, all that he would most have loved to see them grow up to be, if Thou in Thy great wisdom had thought best to spare him. God, let us be able to feel, to know, he can still see us as we grow, as we live, that he is still with us; that he is not deprived of his children and all he had hoped for them and loved them for; nor they of him. Nor they of him.

"God, make us to know he is still with us, still loves us, cares what comes to us, what we do, what we are; *so much*. O, God . . ."

She spoke these words sharply, and said no more; and Rufus felt that she was looking at his father, but he did not move his eyes, and felt that he should not know what he was sure of. After a few moments he heard the motions of her lips as softly again as that falling silence in which the whole world snowed, and he turned his eyes from the hand and looked towards his father's face and, seeing the blue-dented chin thrust upward, and the way the flesh was sunken behind the bones of the jaw, first recognized in its specific weight the word, *dead*. He looked quickly away, and solemn wonder tolled in him like the shuddering of a prodigious bell, and he heard his mother's snowy lips with wonder and with a desire that she should never suffer sorrow, and gazed once again at the hand, whose casual majesty was unaltered. He wished more sharply even than before that he might touch it, but whereas before he had wondered whether he might, if he could find a way to be alone, with no one to see or ever know, now he was sure that he must not. He therefore watched it all the more studiously, trying to bring all of his touch into all that he could see; but he could not bring much. He realized that his mother's hand was without feeling or meaning on his shoulder. He felt how sweaty his hand, and his sister's arm, had become, and changed his hand, and clasped her gently but without sympathy, and felt her hand tighten, and felt gentle towards her because she was too little to understand. The hand became, for a few moments, a mere object, and he could just hear his mother's breath repeating, "Good-bye, Jay, good-bye. Goody-bye. Good-bye. Good-bye, my Jay, my husband. Oh, Good-bye. Good-bye."

Then he heard nothing and was aware of nothing except the hand, which was an object; and felt a strong downward clasping pressure upon his skull, and heard a quiet but rich voice.

His mother was not—yes, he could see her skirts, out behind to the side; and Catherine, and a great hand on her head too, and her silent and astounded face. And between them, a little behind them, black polished shoes and black, sharply pressed trouser legs, without cuffs.

"Hail Mary, full of grace," the voice said; and his mother joined; "the Lord is with thee; blessed art thou among women, and blessed is the fruit of thy womb, Jesus.

"Holy Mary, Mother of God, pray for us sinners, now, and in the hour of *our* death. Amen."

"Our Father, Who art in heaven," the voice said; and the

children joined; "hallowed be Thy name," but in their mother's uncertainty, they stopped, and the voice went on: "Thy kingdom come, Thy will be done," said the voice, with particular warmth, "on earth as it is in heaven. Give us this day our daily bread. And forgive us our trespasses, As we forgive those who trespass against us." Everything had been taken off the mantelpiece. "And lead us not into temptation, But deliver us from evil," and with this his hand left Rufus' head and he crossed himself, immediately restoring the hand, "for Thine is the kingdom, and the power, and the glory, for ever and ever. Amen."

He was silent for a moment. Twisting a little under the hard hand, Rufus glanced upward. The priest's jaw was hard, his face was earnest, his eyes were tightly shut.

"O Lord, cherish and protect these innocent, orphaned children," he said, his eyes shut. *Then we are!* Rufus thought, and knew that he was very bad. "Guard them in all temptations which life may bring. That when they come to understand this thing which in Thy inscrutable wisdom Thou hast brought to pass, they may know and reverence Thy will. God, we beseech Thee that they may ever be the children, the boy and girl, the man and woman, which this good man would have desired them to be. Let them never discredit his memory, O Lord. And Lord, by Thy mercy may they come quickly and soon to know the true and all-loving Father Whom they have in Thee. Let them seek Thee out the more, in their troubles and in their joys, as they would have sought their good earthly father, had he been spared them. Let them ever be, by Thy great mercy, true Christian Catholic children. Amen."

Some of the tiles of the hearth which peeped from beneath the coffin stand, those at the border, were a grayish blue. All the others were streaked and angry, reddish yellow.

The voice altered, and said delicately: "The Peace of God, which passeth all understanding, keep your hearts and minds in the knowledge and love of God, and of his Son Jesus Christ our

Lord": His hand again lifted from Rufus' head, and he drew a great cross above each of them as he said, "And the blessing of God Almighty, the Father, the Son, and the Holy Ghost, be amongst you, and remain with you always."

"Amen," their mother said.

The priest touched his shoulder, and Rufus stood up. Catherine stood up. Their father had not, of course not, Rufus thought, he had not moved, but he looked to have changed. Although he lay in such calm and beauty, and grandeur, it looked to Rufus as if he had been flung down and left on the street, and as if he were a very successfully disguised stranger. He felt a pang of distress and disbelief and was about to lean to look more closely, when he felt a light hand on his head, his mother's, he knew, and heard her say, "Now children"; and they were conveyed to the hall door.

The piano, he saw, was shut.

"Now Mother wants to stay just a minute or two," she told them. "She'll be with you directly. So you go straight into the East Room, with Aunt Hannah, and wait for me."

She touched their faces, and noiselessly closed the door.

Crossing to the East Room they became aware that they were not alone in the dark hall. Andrew stood by the hat rack, holding to the banister, and his rigid, weeping eyes, shining with fury, struck to the roots of their souls like ice, so that they hastened into the room where their great-aunt sat in an unmoving rocking chair with her hands in her lap, the sunless light glazing her lenses, frostlike upon her hair.

They heard feet on the front stairs, and knew it was their grandfather. They heard him turn to go down the hall and then they heard his subdued, surprised voice: "Andrew? Where's Poll?"

And their uncle's voice, cold, close to his ear: "In—there—with—Father—Jackson."

"Unh!" they heard their grandfather growl. Their Aunt Hannah hurried towards the door.

James Agee

"Praying."

"Unh!" he growled again.

Their Aunt Hannah quickly closed the door, and hurried back to her chair.

But much as she had hurried, all that she did after she got back to her chair was to sit with her hands in her lap and stare straight ahead of her through her heavy lenses, and all that they could do was to sit quietly too, and look at the clean lace curtains at the window, and at the magnolia tree and the locust tree in the yard, and at the wall of the next house, and at a heavy robin which fed along the lawn, until he flew away, and at the people who now and then moved past along the sunny sidewalk, and at the buggies and automobiles which now and then moved along the sunny street. They felt mysteriously immaculate, strange and careful in their clean clothes, and it seemed as if the house were in shadow and were walking on tiptoe in the middle of an easy, sunny world. When they tired of looking at these things, they looked at their Aunt Hannah, but she did not appear to realize that they were looking at her; and when there was no response from their Aunt Hannah they looked at each other. But it had never given them any pleasure or interest to look at each other and it gave them none today. Each could only see that the other was much too clean, and each realized, through that the more acutely, that he himself was much too clean, and that something was wrong which required of each of them such careful conduct, and particularly good manners, that there was really nothing imaginable that might be proper to do except to sit still. But though sitting so still, with nothing to fix their attention upon except each other, they saw each other perhaps more clearly than at any time before; and each felt uneasiness and shyness over what he saw. Rufus saw a much littler child than he was, with a puzzled, round, red face which looked angry, and he was somewhat sorry for her in the bewilderment and loneliness he felt she was lost in, but more, he was annoyed by this look of shut-in anger and this look of

288

incomprehension and he thought over and over: "Dead. He's dead. That's what he is; he's dead"; and the room where his father lay felt like a boundless hollowness in the house and in his own being, as if he stood in the dark near the edge of an abyss and could feel that droop of space in the darkness; and watching his sister's face he could see his father's almost as clearly, as he had just seen it, and said to himself, over and over: "Dead. Dead"; and looked with uneasiness and displeasure at his sister's face, which was so different, so flushed and busy, so angry, and so uncomprehending. And Catherine saw him stuck down there in the long box like a huge mute doll, who would not smile or stir, and smelled sweet and frightening, and because of whom she sat alone and stiffly and too clean, and nobody was kind or attentive, and everything went on tiptoe, and with her mother's willingness a man she feared and hated put his great hand on her head and spoke incomprehensibly. Something very wrong was being done, and nobody seemed to care or to tell her what or to help her or love her or protect her from it and there was her too-clean brother, who always thought he was so smart, looking at her with dislike and contempt.

So after gazing coldly at each other for a little while, they once more looked into the side yard and down into the street and tried to interest themselves in what they saw, and to forget the thing which so powerfully pervaded their thoughts, and to subdue their physical restiveness in order that they should not be disapproved; and tiring of these, would look over once more at their aunt, who was as aloof almost as their father; and uneased by that, would look once more into each other's eyes; and so again to the yard and the street, upon which the sunlight moved slowly. And there they saw an automobile draw up and Mr. Starr got quickly out of it and walked slowly up towards the house.

Chapter 19

As they came back with Mr. Starr, Rufus noticed that a man who went past along the sidewalk looked back at his grandfather's house, then quickly away, then back once more, and again quickly away.

He saw that there were several buggies and automobiles, idle and empty, along the opposite side of the street, but that the space in front of the house was empty. The house seemed at once especially bare, and changed, and silent, and its corners seemed particularly hard and distinct; and beside the front door there hung a great knotted bloom and streamer of black cloth. The front door was opened before it was touched and there stood their Uncle Andrew and their mother and behind them the dark hallway, and they were all but overwhelmed by a dizzying, sickening fragrance, and by a surging outward upon them likewise of multitudinous vitality. Almost immediately they were drawn within the darkness of the hallway and the fragrance became recognizable as the fragrance of flowers, and the vitality which poured upon them was that of the people with whom the house was crowded. Rufus experienced an intuition as of great force and possible danger on his right, and glancing quickly into the East Room, saw that every window shade was drawn except one and that against the cold light which came through that window the room was filled with dark figures which crouched disconsolately at the edge of chairs, heavy and primordial as bears in a pit; and even as he looked he heard the rising of a great, low groan, which was joined by a higher groan, which was surmounted by a low wailing and by a higher wailing, and he could see that a woman stood up suddenly and with a wailing and bellowing sob caught the hair at her temples and pulled, then flung her hands upward and outward: but upon this moment Andrew rushed and with desperate and brutal speed and silence, pulled the door shut, and Rufus was aware in the same instant that their own footstep and the wailing had caused a commotion on his left and, glancing as sharply into the sunlit room where his father lay, saw an incredibly dense crowd of soberly dressed people on weak, complaining chairs, catching his eye, looking past him, looking quickly away, trying to look as if they had not looked around.

"It's all right, Andrew," his mother whispered. "Open the door. Tell them we'll be in, in just a minute." And she drew the children more deeply into the hallway, where they could not be seen through either door, and whispered to Walter Starr, "Papa is in the Green Room, and Mama. Thank you, Walter."

"Don't you think of it," Walter said, as he passed her; and his hand hovered near her shoulder, and he went quietly through the door into the dining room.

"Now, children," their mother said, lowering her face above them. "We're all going in to see Daddy, just once more. But we won't be able to stay, we can just look for a moment. And then you'll see your Grandma Follet, just for a minute. And then Mr. Starr will take you down again to his house and Mother will see you again later this afternoon."

Andrew came toward her and nodded sharply.

"All right, Andrew," she said. "All right, children." Reaching suddenly behind the crest of her skull she lowered her veil and they saw her face and her eyes through its darkness. She took their hands. "Now come with Mother," she whispered.

There was Uncle Hubert in a dark suit; he was very clean

and pink and his face was full of little lines. He looked quickly at them and quickly away. There was old Miss Storrs and there were Miss Amy Field and Miss Nettie Field and Doctor Dekalb and Mrs. Dekalb and Uncle Gordon Dekalb and Aunt Celia Gunn and Mrs. Gunn and Dan Gunn and Aunt Sarah Eldridge and Aunt Ann Taylor, and ever so many others, as well, whom the children were not sure they had seen before, and all of them looked as if they were trying not to look and as if they shared a secret they were offended to have been asked to tell; and there was the most enormous heap of flowers of all kinds that the children had ever seen, tall and extravagantly fresh and red and yellow, tall and starchy white, dark roses and white roses, ferns, carnations, great leaves of varnished-looking palm, all wreathed and wired and running with ribbons of black and silver and bright gold and dark gold, and almost suffocating in their fragrance; and there, almost hidden among these flowers, was the coffin, and beside it, two last strangers who, now that they had entered the room, turned away and quickly took chairs; and now a stranger man in a long, dark coat stepped towards their mother with silent alacrity, his eyes shining like dark jelly, and with a courtly gesture ushered her forward and stood proudly and humbly to one side; and there was Daddy again.

He had not stirred one inch; yet he had changed. His face looked more remote than before and much more ordinary and it was as if he were tired, or bored. He did not look as big as he really was, and the fragrance of the flowers was so strong and the vitality of the mourners was so many-souled and so pervasive, and so permeated and compounded by propriety and restraint, and they felt so urgently the force of all the eyes upon them, that they saw their father almost as idly as if he had been a picture, or a substituted image, and felt little realization of his presence and little interest. And while they were still looking, bemused with this empty curiosity, they felt themselves drawn away, and walked with their mother past the closed piano into the Green

Room. And there were Grandpa and Grandma and Uncle Andrew and Aunt Amelia and Aunt Hannah; and Grandma got up quickly and took their mother in her arms and patted her several times emphatically across the shoulders, and Grandpa stood up, too; and while Grandma stooped and embraced and kissed each of the children, saying "Darlings, darlings," in a somewhat loud and ill-controlled voice, they could see their grandfather's graceful and cynical head as he embraced their mother, and realized that he was not quite as tall as she was; and their Aunt Amelia stood up shyly with her elbows out. As their mother led them from the room they looked back through the door and saw that the man in the long coat and another strange man had closed the coffin and were silently and quickly screwing it shut.

Walter Starr stood back in the middle of the hall, looking as if he did not know what to do. Their mother went straight up to him.

"Now we're all ready, Walter," she said. He nodded very shyly and stepped a little to one side as she spoke to the children.

"Now it's time to go," she told them. "Back to Mr. Starr's, as he told you this morning. And have a nice time and be very good and quiet and Mr. Starr will bring you back to Mother later this afternoon." She straightened Catherine's little collar, which was wilting. "Now good-bye," she said. "Mother will see you before long." She kissed them lightly.

Before long, now; before long.

They went so quietly past the living-room door and along the hushed porch and down the steps that Rufus felt that they were moving as stealthily as burglars.

When they had driven almost all the way to Mr. Starr's home Mr. Starr surprisingly turned a wrong corner, and then another, and then said to the children, "I think you'll want to see. Maybe not, but I think you'll be glad later on I took you back." And he drove somewhat more rapidly up the silent, empty, back street, then once again turned a corner, moved very slowly and quietly, and came to a stop.

They were in the side street, just across from Dr. Dekalb's house, and across the street corner and the wide lawn. They could see their grandfather's house and everything that went on, and they knew that they were not seen. Six men, their Uncle Andrew, their Uncle Ralph, their Uncle Hubert Kane, their Uncle George Bailey, and Mr. Drake, and a man whom they had never seen before, were carrying a long, gray, shining box by handles very carefully and slowly down the curved brick walk from the house to the street, and they realized that this was the box in which their father lay, and that it must be very heavy. The men were of different heights so that Uncle Andrew, who was tall, and Uncle George Bailey, who was even taller, had to squat slightly at the knees, whereas Uncle Hubert, who was shortest, was leaning outward and lifting upward. Just behind, seeming to walk even more slowly, came their grandfather, and a tall woman all veiled in black whom by her tallness and humbled grace they knew was their mother; and just behind her, with Aunt Jessie on one side and Father Jackson on the other, came a second woman, all veiled in black, who by her shortness and lameness they knew was their Grandmother Follet. And just behind them came Granma and Aunt Hannah, and Aunt Sally and Aunt Amelia, and Aunt Celia Gunn and Mrs. Gunn and Miss Bess Gunn, and old Mr. Kane, and Miss Amy Field and Miss Nettie Field, and Doctor Dekalb and Mrs. Dekalb and Uncle Gordon Dekalb, and the porch and the porch steps were still full of darkly dressed people whose faces and bearing they could unsurely recognize but whose names they did not know, and of people whom they could not be sure whether they had ever seen before, and more were still shuffling slowly out through the front door onto the porch. And up the hill alongside the house, behind it, stood a shining black automobile, and two, small, quick men dressed in black sped constantly between the house and the wagon, bringing from the house great armsful of bright flowers, and stowing them in the automobile. And down in front of the front steps the man in the long coat who had ushered them to the coffin now made an imperious gesture and, drawn by three shining black horses and one horse of a shining red-brown, a long, tall, narrow box of whorled and glittering black and of black glass was pulled forward a few feet, and then a foot more, so that its black and glittering rear end was just beyond the opening of the steps; and the men who carried their father's coffin now hesitated at the head of the steps, and the man in the long coat nodded courteously as he turned and opened the shining back doors of the tall, blind-looking wagon, so that they carefully and uneasily made their way down the narrow steps, squeezing gingerly together, and he stood aside from the open doors and seemed to speak and to instruct them with his hands; and while their mother and her father hesitated at the head of the steps and behind them, all the dark column of mourners hesitated likewise, the men who carried their heavy father lifted him as if he were hard to lift and they were careful but unwilling, and studiously, with reverent nudgings and hitchings, shoved the coffin so deeply into the dark wagon that only its hard end showed, and they could hear a streetcar coming. And the man in the long coat closed one of the doors, and they could see only a corner of the box, and then he closed the other door and they could not see it at all, and he tightened even the shining silver handle which held the doors locked, and one of the horses twitched his ears, and the streetcar, which had paused, was now louder. And the long, dark wagon was drawn forward a few paces, and paused again, and a closed and shining black buggy moved forward and took its place, and the streetcar moved past and they could see heads turning through its windows and a man took off his hat, and their mother and their grandfather came down the steps and their grandfather helped their mother to climb in, and their Grandmother Follet and their Aunt Jessie and Father Jackson came down the steps and their Grandfather and Father Jackson helped their Grandmother Follet to climb in, and they helped Aunt Jessie in, and the noise of the streetcar was fading, and Uncle Ralph stood aside so that their grandfather might get in, and then they both stood aside so that their Grandmother Lynch might get in, and after some hesitation, their grandmother was helped in and then Uncle Ralph stepped in after her, and the curtains of the windows were drawn and the long, dark wagon and the dark buggy moved forward, and a second buggy took its place, and a long line of buggies and automobiles, after a moment's hesitancy, advanced a few feet, and now a man who had stood in the empty sidewalk across from the house walked westward and crossed the street in front of the children, putting on his hat as he reached the farther curb, and they heard the last of the streetcar, but now they heard the hard chipping of two sparrows, worrying a bit of debris in the street, and Mr. Starr said, "Better go now," and they realized that he had never shut off his engine, for as soon as he said this he began to back the car, as silently as he could and with great care; and he twisted it backward around the corner, and they slowly descended the same quiet back street up which he had brought them.

When he had stopped the car in front of his home, he said, before he moved to get out, "Maybe you'd better not say anything about this." He still did not move to get out, so they too sat still. After a little he said, "No, you do as you think best." He did not look at them; he had not looked at them during all of this time. They watched the shadows work, and the leaves waving.

He got out of the car, and opened the door on their side, and held out his hands to Catherine.

"Up she goes," he said.

Chapter 20

THE HOUSE ECHOED, and there was still an extraordinary fragrance of carnations.

Their mother was in the East Room.

"My darlings," she said; she looked as if she had traveled a great distance, and now they knew that everything had changed. They put their heads against her, still knowing that nothing would ever be the same again, and she caught them so close they could smell her, and they loved her, but it made no difference.

She could not say anything, and neither could they; they began to realize that she was silently praying, and now instead of love for her they felt sadness, and politely waited for her to finish.

"Now we'll stay here at Granma's," she finally said. "Tonight, anyway." And again there was nothing further that she could say.

Her hands on them began to feel merely heavy. Rufus moved nearer, trying to recover the lost tenderness; at the same moment Catherine pulled away.

He understands, their mother thought; and tried not to feel hurt by Catherine's restiveness. Catherine, aware at this absolute moment that her brother was preferred, was hurt so bitterly that her mother felt it in her body, and lightened her hold, at just the moment when Catherine most desired to be taken close in to her kindness. By the way she held him Rufus realized, she thinks I'm better than I am; he felt as if he had been believed in a lie, but this time it was not a good feeling.

"God bless my children," she whispered. "God bless and keep us all."

"Amen," Rufus whispered courteously; he tried to lose his uneasiness by holding her still more closely, and felt her still more passionate hand; while Catherine, in an enchantment of pain and loneliness, stayed like a stone.

There they stayed quiet, the deceived mother, the false son, the fatally wounded daughter; it was thus that Andrew found them and, with a glimpse of the noble painting it could be, said to himself, crying within himself, "It beats the Holy Family."

"Come for a walk with me," Andrew said; from the front porch Catherine watched them until she could no longer see them. Then she pulled one of the chairs away from the wall and sat in it and rocked. She had a feeling that it would be all right to rock if she could rock without making any noise, and it interested her to try. But no matter how carefully and quietly she moved, the rockers gave out a cobbling noise on the boards of the porch, and the chair squeaked gently. She stopped rocking, less because she felt that the noise was wrong, than because she felt that she did not want to be heard. She sat with her arms and hands high and straight along the arms of the chair and looked through the railing at the lawn and down into the street. A robin hopped heavily along the grass. He gave her a short, hard look, then a second, short and hard as the jab of a needle, then paid her no further attention, but hopped, heavily, and jabbed and jabbed in the short grass with jabs which were much like his short, hard way of looking.

Down across the street she saw Dr. Dekalb come along the sidewalk towards home; he was still in his dark clothes. Remembering how her father always saw her from a distance and waved, she waited for the moment when he would look over and wave, but he did not wave, or even look over; he went straight into his house.

Deep in the side yard among her flowers she saw Mrs. Dekalb in a long, white dress and long, white gloves, wearing a paper bag on her head. She bent deeply above the flowers, rather than squatting, and whenever she moved to another place, she straightened, tall and very thin, and gathered her skirt in one hand and delicately lifted it, as Grandma did when she stepped up or down from a curb. Then she would bend deeply over again, as if she were leaning over a crib to say good night.

There were quite a few people along the sidewalks, and most of them were walking in one direction, away from downtown.

On the sage-orange tree beside the porch the leaves lay along the air as lazily as if they were almost asleep, and ever so quietly moved, and lay still again.

The robin had hold of a worm; he braced his heels, walked backward, and pulled hard. It stretched like a rubber band and snapped in two; Catherine felt the snapping in her stomach. He quickly gobbled what he had and, darting his beak even more quickly, took hold of the rest and pulled again. It stretched but did not break, and then all came loose from the ground; she could see it twisting as he flew away with it. He flung himself upward in a great curve among the branches of a tree in the side yard, and Catherine could just hear the thin hissing cries of the little robins.

Now Dr. Dekalb stood beside his wife and they were looking at each other and talking. She was taller than he was, but he was thicker through. He had taken off his coat, and pale blue suspenders crossed on his back. Above his white shirt his neck was dark red.

All the way down the block where the next street crossed she could see that there were still other people along the walks, looking tired yet walking fast, tiny at this distance, and nearly all of these people, too, were walking away from downtown.

Uncle Gordon Dekalb came towards his house. He was still wearing his dark suit and he carried his hat in one hand. His bottom was fat and he walked like a duck. Even from here Catherine could see how choked-up and thick he looked in the face and neck, Uncle Andrew said, as if his mouth was stuffed full of hot mashed potato. He looked up and across at the house and Catherine raised her hand, but he looked quickly away again, and cut across the lawn to join his father and mother. They all three talked.

A small, sudden noise frightened Catherine; then she realized it came from the living room. There was no more sound. She got from the chair in perfect silence and stole to the window in the angle of the porch. Grandma was sitting at the piano and she had opened it; Catherine could see the keys. She sat for a long while without lifting her hands from her lap. Then she stood up and shut the piano and went into the Green Room; she was wearing her apron. But before Catherine could move from the window she came in again (she can't see this far, Catherine quickly reassured herself), looked carefully about with her near-sighted, peering look, pursed her lips, and sat down again at the piano. Now she opened the keyboard once more and curved her hands powerfully above the keys and moved her fingers, but there was no sound. Grandma can't hear very well, Catherine remembered; talk very loud. So she can't hear very well when she plays music, either. She was bent way over, with her good ear close to the keys, the way she always was when she played, and her feet were working the pedals, yet she couldn't hear a sound.

But why can't *I* hear? Catherine suddenly thought. I always do. She watched and listened much more sharply: not one sound.

With sudden pleasure, Catherine thought of listening through a large black ear trumpet, then she realized that she was still hearing the shuffling street and the murmurous city, and knew why she could hear no music. Grandma was just making the notes go down without making any noise.

Then, close beside Catherine, her grandfather came through the door, and stopped abruptly. He was looking at Grandma. He couldn't hear very well either, but he could hear better than Grandma could; he always sat at this far end of the room when there was music. So he knew too. After he had stood a few moments he walked quickly down almost to where she sat with her back to him and both of his hands lifted above her as if he were going to touch her humped-over shoulders or her hair. Then after standing for a moment again, he turned away and walked even more quickly and quietly out by the way he had come in, and his face was so tucked down that Catherine was sure she had not been seen.

Now Grandma finished and left her hands quiet among the keys, moving them only to stroke the black keys and the white ones between. Then she took her hands away and folded them in her lap. Then she stood up, closed the piano, and went into the Green Room.

Dr. Dekalb and Mrs. Dekalb and Uncle Gordon were no longer in the garden.

Where's Daddy?

All of a sudden she felt that she could not bear to be alone. She went into the hall and into the East Room, but her mother was no longer in the East Room. She went down the hall towards the dining room and she could hear her grandmother busy in the pantry, but she knew that she did not want to see her or be found by her. She hurried on tiptoe across the corner of the dining room, hiding behind the table, and into the Green Room, but there was nobody there. She looked out and saw her grandfather standing in the middle of the garden, gazing down into the strong spikes of the century plant. She hurried through the dizzying fragrance of the living room and climbed the front stairs as quickly and quietly as she was able; Aunt Amelia's door was closed.

By now her face felt very hot and she was crying. She hurried along the hallway; shut. Aunt Hannah's door was shut. Behind it there was a coldly tender waning of a voice; Aunt Hannah's voice; her mother's. She set her ear close to the door and listened.

O GOD, the Creator and Preserver of all mankind, we humbly beseech thee for all sorts and conditions of men; that thou wouldest be pleased to make thy ways known unto them, thy saving health unto all nations. More especially we pray for thy holy Church universal; that it may be so guided and governed by thy good Spirit, that all who profess and call themselves Christians may be led into the way of truth, and hold the faith in unity of spirit, in the bond of peace, and in righteousness of life. Finally, we commend to thy fatherly goodness all those who are any ways afflicted, or distressed, in mind, body, or estate; that it may please thee to comfort and relieve them, according to their several necessities; giving them patience under their sufferings, and a happy issue out of all their afflictions. And this we beg for Jesus Christ's sake. Amen.

ALMIGHTY God, Father of all mercies, we, thine unworthy servants, do give thee most humble and hearty thanks for all thy goodness and loving-kindness to us, and to all men. We bless thee for our creation, preservation, and all the blessings of this life; but above all, for thine inestimable love in the redemption of the world by our Lord Jesus Christ; for the means of grace, and for the hope of glory. And, we beseech thee, give us that due sense of all thy mercies, that our hearts may be unfeignedly thankful; and that we show forth thy praise, not only with our lips, but in our lives, by giving up our selves to thy service, and by walking before thee in holiness and righteousness all our days; through Jesus Christ our Lord, to whom, with thee and the Holy Ghost, be all honour and glory, world without end. Amen.

Her mother's voice choked. Aunt Hannah's, with great quietness, spoke what she had been speaking from the beginning, and continued it and brought it to a close. Then, even more quietly, she said, "Mary, my dear, let's stop."

And after a moment Catherine could hear her mother's voice, shaken and almost squeaking, "No, no; no, no; I asked you to, Aunt Hannah. I—I . . ."

And again, Aunt Hannah's voice: "Let's just stop it."

And her mother's: "Without this I don't think I could bear it *at all*."

And Aunt Hannah's: "There, dear. God bless and keep you. There. There."

And her mother's: "Just a minute and I'll be all right."

And a silence.

And then Aunt Hannah's voice coldly tender:—— and her mother's:——

In intense quietness, Catherine stole through the open door opposite Aunt Hannah's door, and hid herself beneath her grandparents' bed. She was no longer crying. She only wanted never to be seen by anybody again. She lay on her side and stared down into the grim grain of the carpet. When Aunt Hannah's door opened she felt such terror that she gasped, and drew her knees up tight against her chest. When the voices began calling her, downstairs, she made herself even smaller, and when she heard their feet on the stairs and the rising concern in their voices she began to tremble all over. But by the time she heard them along the hallway she was out from under the bed and sitting on its edge, her back to them as they came in, her heart knocking her breath to pieces.

"Why *there* you *are,*" her mother cried, and turning, Catherine was frightened by the fright and the tears on her face. "Didn't you *hear* us?"

She shook her head, no.

"Why how could you *help* but—were you asleep?"

She nodded, yes.

"I thought she was with you, Amelia."

"I thought she was with you or Mama."

"Why, where on earth *were* you, darling? Heavens and earth, have you been all *alone*?"

Catherine nodded yes; her lower lip thrust out farther and farther and she felt her chin trembling and hated everybody.

"Why, bless your little heart, come to Mother"; her mother came toward her stooping with her arms stretched out and Catherine ran to her as fast as she could run, and plunged her head into her, and cried as if she were made only of tears; and it was only when her mother said, just as kindly, "Just look at your panties, why they're *sopping* wet," that she realized that indeed they were.

Andrew had never invited him to take a walk with him before, and he felt honored, and worked hard to keep up with him. He realized that now, maybe, he would hear about it, but he knew it would not be a good thing to ask. When they got well into the next block beyond his grandfather's, and the houses and trees were unfamiliar, he took Andrew's hand and Andrew took his primly, but did not press it or look down at him. Pretty soon maybe he'll tell me, Rufus thought. Or anyway say something. But his uncle did not say anything. Looking up at him, from a half step behind him, Rufus could see that he looked mad about something. He looked ahead so fixedly that Rufus suspected he was not really looking at anything, even when they stepped from the curb, and stepped up from the curb across from it, his eyes did not change. He was frowning, and the corners of his nose were curled as if he smelled something bad. Did I do something? Rufus wondered. No, he wouldn't ask me for a walk if I did. Yes, he would too if he was real mad and wanted to give me a talking-to and not raise a fuss about it there. But he won't say anything, so I guess he doesn't want to give me a talking-to. Maybe he's thinking. Maybe about Daddy. The funeral. (He saw the sunlight on the hearse as it began to move.) What all did they do out there?

They put him down in the ground and then they put all the flowers on top. Then they say their prayers and then they all come home again. In Greenwood Cemetery. He saw in his mind a clear image of Greenwood Cemetery; it was on a low hill and among many white stones there were many green trees through which the wind blew in the sunlight, and in the middle there was a heap of flowers and beneath the flowers, in his closed coffin, looking exactly as he had looked this morning, lay his father. Only it was dark, so he could not be seen. It would always be dark there. Dark as the inside of a cow.

The sun's agonna shine, and the wind's agonna blow.

The charcoal scraping of the needle against the record was in his ears and he saw the many sharp, grinning teeth in Buster Brown's dog.

"If anything ever makes me believe in God," his uncle said.

Rufus looked up at him quickly. He was still looking straight ahead, and he still looked angry but his voice was not angry. "Or life after death," his uncle said.

They were working and breathing rather hard, for they were walking westward up the steep hill towards Fort Sanders. The sky ahead of them was bright and they walked among the bright, moving shadows of trees.

"It'll be what happened this afternoon."

Rufus looked up at him carefully.

"There were a lot of clouds," his uncle said, and continued to look straight before him, "but they were blowing fast, so there was a lot of sunshine too. Right when they began to lower your father into the ground, into his grave, a cloud came over and there was a shadow just like iron, and a perfectly magnificent butterfly settled on the—coffin, just rested there, right over the breast, and stayed there, just barely making his wings breathe, like a heart."

Andrew stopped and for the first time looked at Rufus. His eyes were desperate. "He stayed there all the way down, Rufus," he said. "He never stirred, except just to move his wings that way, until it grated against the bottom like a—rowboat. And just when it did the sun came out just dazzling bright and he flew up out of that—hole in the ground, straight up into the sky, so high I couldn't even see him any more." He began to climb the hill again, and Rufus worked hard again to stay abreast of him. "Don't you think that's wonderful, Rufus?" he said, again looking straight and despairingly before him.

"Yes," Rufus said, now that his uncle really was asking him. "Yes," he was sure was not enough, but it was all he could say.

"If there are any such things as miracles," his uncle said, as if someone were arguing with him, "then *that's* surely miraculous."

Miraculous. Magnificent. He was sure he had better not ask what they were. He saw a giant butterfly clearly, and how he moved his wings so quietly and grandly, and the colors of the wings, and how he sprang straight up into the sky and how the colors all took fire in the sunshine, and he felt that he probably had a fair idea what "magnificent" meant. But "miraculous." He still saw the butterfly, which was resting there again, waving his great wings. Maybe "miraculous" was the way the colors were streaks and spots in patterns on the wings, or the bright flickering way they worked in the light when he flew fast, straight upwards. Miraculous. Magnificent.

He could see it very clearly, because his uncle saw it so clearly when he told about it, and what he saw made him feel that a special and good thing was happening. He felt that it was good for his father and that lying there in the darkness did not matter so much. He did not know what this good thing was, but because his uncle felt that it was good, and felt so strongly about it, it must be even more of a good thing than he himself could comprehend. His uncle even spoke of believing in God, or anyway, if anything could ever make him believe in God, and he had never before heard his uncle speak of God except as if he disliked Him, or anyway, disliked people who believed in Him. So it must be about as good a thing as a thing could be. And suddenly he began to realize that his uncle told it to him, out of everyone he might have told it to, and he breathed in a deep breath of pride and of love. He would not admit it to those who did believe in God, and he would not tell it to those who didn't, because he cared so much about it and they might swear at it, but he had to tell somebody, so he told it to him. And it made it much better than it had been, about his father, and about his not being let to be there at just that time he most needed to be there; it was all right now, almost. It was not all right about his father because his father could never come back again, but it was better than it had been, anyway, and it was all right about his not being let be there, because now it was almost as if he had been there and seen it with his own eyes, and seen the butterfly, which showed that even for his father, it was all right. It was all right and he felt as his uncle did. There was nobody else, not even his mother, not even his father if he could, that he even wanted to tell, or talk about it to. Not even his uncle, now that it was told.

"And *that* son of a bitch!" Andrew said.

He was not quite sure what it meant but he knew it was the worst thing you could call anybody; call anybody that, they had to fight, they had a right to kill you. He felt as if he had been hit in the stomach.

"That Jackson," Andrew said; and now he looked so really angry that Rufus realized that he had not been at all angry before. "*'Father'* Jackson," Andrew said, "as he insists on being called.

"Do you know what he did?"

He glared at him so, that Rufus was frightened. "What?" he asked.

"He said he couldn't read the complete, the complete burial service over your father because your father had never been baptized." He kept glaring at Rufus; he seemed to be waiting for him to answer. Rufus looked up at him, feeling scared and stupid. He was glad his uncle did not like Father Jackson, but that did not seem exactly the point, and he could not think of anything to say.

"He said he was deeply sorry," Andrew savagely caricatured the inflection, "but it was simply a rule of the Church.

"Some church," he snarled. "And they call themselves Christians. Bury a man who's a hundred times the man *he'll* ever be, in his stinking, swishing black petticoats, and a hundred times as good a man too, and 'No, there are certain requests and recommendations I cannot make Almighty God for the repose of this soul, for he never stuck his head under a holy-water tap.' Genuflecting, and ducking and bowing and scraping, and basting themselves with signs of the Cross, and all that disgusting hocus-pocus, and you come to one simple, single act of Christian charity and what happens? The rules of the Church forbid it. He's not a member of our little club.

"I tell you, Rufus, it's enough to make a man puke up his soul.

"That—that butterfly has got more of God in him than Jackson will ever see for the rest of eternity.

"Priggish, mealy-mouthed son of a bitch."

They were standing at the edge of Fort Sanders and looking out across the waste of briers and of embanked clay, and Rufus was trying to hold his feelings intact. Everything had seemed so nearly all right, up to a minute ago, and now it was changed and confused. It was still all right, everything which had been, still was, he did not see how it could stop being, yet it was hard to remember it clearly and to remember how he had felt and why it had seemed all right, for since then his uncle had said so much. He was glad he did not like Father Jackson and he wished his mother did not like him either, but that was not all. His uncle had talked about God, and Christians, and faith, with as much hatred as he had seemed, a minute before, to talk with reverence or even with love. But it was worse than that. It was when he was talking about everybody bowing and scraping and hocus-pocus and things like that, that Rufus began to realize that he was talking not just about Father Jackson but about all of them and that he hated all of them. He hates Mother, he said to himself. He really honestly does hate her. Aunt Hannah, too. He hates them. They don't hate him at all, they love him, but he hates them. But he doesn't hate them, really, he thought. He could remember how many ways he had shown how fond he was of both of them, all kinds of ways, and most of all by how easy he was with them when nothing was wrong and everybody was having a good time, and by how he had been with them in this time too. He doesn't hate them, he thought, he loves them, just as much as they love him. But he hates them, too. He talked about them as if he'd like to spit in their faces. When he's with them he's nice to them, he even likes them, loves them. When he's away from them and thinks about them saying their prayers and things, he hates them. When he's with them he just acts as if he likes them, but this is how he really feels, all the time. He told me about the butterfly and he wouldn't tell them because he hates them, but I don't hate them, I love them, and when he told me he told me a secret he wouldn't tell them as if I hated them too.

But they saw it too. They sure saw it too. So he didn't, he wouldn't tell them, there wouldn't be anything to tell. That's it. He told me because I wasn't there and he wanted to tell somebody and thought I would want to know and I do. But not if he hates them. And he does. He hates them just like opening a furnace door but he doesn't want them to know it. He doesn't want them to know it because he doesn't want to hurt their feelings. He doesn't want them to know it because he knows they love him and think he loves them. He doesn't want them to know it because he loves them. But how can he love them if he hates them so? How can he hate them if he loves them? Is he mad at them because they can say their prayers and he doesn't? He could if he wanted to, why doesn't he? Because he hates prayers. And them too for saying them.

He wished he could ask his uncle, "Why do you hate Mama?" but he was afraid to. While he thought he looked now across the devastated Fort, and again into his uncle's face, and wished that he could ask. But he did not ask, and his uncle did not speak except to say, after a few minutes, "It's time to go home," and all the way home they walked in silence.

READ MORE IN PENGUIN

In every corner of the world, on every subject under the sun, Penguin represents quality and variety – the very best in publishing today.

For complete information about books available from Penguin – including Puffins, Penguin Classics and Arkana – and how to order them, write to us at the appropriate address below. Please note that for copyright reasons the selection of books varies from country to country.

In the United Kingdom: Please write to *Dept. EP, Penguin Books Ltd, Bath Road, Harmondsworth, West Drayton, Middlesex UB7 0DA*

In the United States: Please write to *Consumer Services, Penguin Putnam Inc., 405 Murray Hill Parkway, East Rutherford, New Jersey 07073-2136.* VISA and MasterCard holders call 1-800-631-8571 to order Penguin titles

In Canada: Please write to *Penguin Books Canada Ltd, 10 Alcorn Avenue, Suite 300, Toronto, Ontario M4V 3B2*

In Australia: Please write to *Penguin Books Australia Ltd, 487 Maroondah Highway, Ringwood, Victoria 3134*

In New Zealand: Please write to *Penguin Books (NZ) Ltd, Private Bag 102902, North Shore Mail Centre, Auckland 10*

In India: Please write to *Penguin Books India Pvt Ltd, 11 Community Centre, Panchsheel Park, New Delhi 110017*

In the Netherlands: Please write to *Penguin Books Netherlands bv, Postbus 3507, NL-1001 AH Amsterdam*

In Germany: Please write to *Penguin Books Deutschland GmbH, Metzlerstrasse 26, 60594 Frankfurt am Main*

In Spain: Please write to *Penguin Books S. A., Bravo Murillo 19, 1°B, 28015 Madrid*

In Italy: Please write to *Penguin Italia s.r.l., Via Vittorio Emanuele 45/a, 20094 Corsico, Milano*

In France: Please write to *Penguin France, 12, Rue Prosper Ferradou, 31700 Blagnac*

In Japan: Please write to *Penguin Books Japan Ltd, Iidabashi KM-Bldg, 2-23-9 Koraku, Bunkyo-Ku, Tokyo 112-0004*

In South Africa: Please write to *Penguin Books South Africa (Pty) Ltd, P.O. Box 751093, Gardenview, 2047 Johannesburg*

Penguin Modern Classics

FORTY STORIES
DONALD BARTHELME

'[A] magical gift of deadpan incongruity' John Updike

In *Forty Stories*, Donald Barthelme invented a random universe in which time, reality, meaning and language are turned exuberantly upside-down. He describes a startling array of occurrences – a lumberjack falls in love with a tree nymph; the poet Goethe becomes a loveable buffoon, spouting such eccentric aphorisms as 'Music is the frozen tapioca in the ice chest of History'; St Anthony's reclusive behaviour causes consternation among his friends and neighbours; and a vast swarm of porcupines, about to descend upon a university to enrol, forces the Dean to turn wrangler to herd them away. Tangling with the ludicrous and challenging the familiar, these small masterpieces provide piercing and hilarious insights into human idiosyncrasies.

'Among the leading innovative writers of modern fiction' *The New York Times*

With an Introduction by Dave Eggers

Penguin Modern Classics

FALCONER
JOHN CHEEVER

'As dynamic and simmering as the atmosphere in prison before a riot'
Sunday Times

Ezekiel Farragut, a college professor and heroin addict hooked on methadone, is sent to Falconer Correctional Facility after murdering his brother. Enclosed in a filthy cell, witness to the day-to-day savagery of the guards and his fellow prisoners – murderers, conmen and thieves – Farragut believes he is one of the living dead.

But although he lives behind bars, no one can imprison his mind. As memories of his traumatic childhood and troubled marriage come flooding back, Farragut must struggle to survive and remain human amid the relentless brutality of Falconer.

'It is rough, it is elegant, it is pure. It is also indispensable if you earnestly desire to know what is happening to the human soul in the USA' Saul Bellow